As Hollypaw followed him back to the clearing, carrying her vole and the shrew, she kept casting sidelong glances at Brook. Curiosity bit at her, sharp as a fox's fangs. She wanted to visit the Tribe and see how cats lived when they knew right from the start what kind of life they would have and what their responsibilities would be.

But they're so far away! Hollypaw let out a sigh. *I don't suppose I'll ever travel as far as the mountains.*

WARRIORS

THE PROPHECIES BEGIN

Book One: Into the Wild

Book Two: Fire and Ice

Book Three: Forest of Secrets

Book Four: Rising Storm

Book Five: A Dangerous Path

Book Six: The Darkest Hour

THE NEW PROPHECY

Book One: Midnight

Book Two: Moonrise

Book Three: Dawn

Book Four: Starlight

Book Five: Twilight

Book Six: Sunset

POWER OF THREE

Book One: The Sight

Book Two: Dark River

Book Three: Outcast

Book Four: Eclipse

Book Five: Long Shadows

Book Six: Sunrise

OMEN OF THE STARS

Book One: The Fourth Apprentice

Book Two: Fading Echoes

Book Three: Night Whispers

Book Four: Sign of the Moon

Book Five: The Forgotten Warrior

Book Six: The Last Hope

DAWN OF THE CLANS

Book One: The Sun Trail

Book Two: Thunder Rising

Book Three: The First Battle

Book Four: The Blazing Star

Book Five: A Forest Divided

EXPLORE THE WARRIORS WORLD

Warriors Super Edition: Firestar's Quest

Warriors Super Edition: Bluestar's Prophecy

Warriors Super Edition: SkyClan's Destiny

Warriors Super Edition: Crookedstar's Promise

Warriors Super Edition: Yellowfang's Secret

Warriors Super Edition: Tallstar's Revenge

Warriors Super Edition: Bramblestar's Storm

Warriors Field Guide: Secrets of the Clans

Warriors: Cats of the Clans

Warriors: Code of the Clans

Warriors: Battles of the Clans

Warriors: Enter the Clans

Warriors: The Ultimate Guide

Warriors: The Untold Stories

Warriors: Tales from the Clans

MANGA

The Lost Warrior

Warrior's Refuge

Warrior's Return

The Rise of Scourge

Tigerstar and Sasha #1: Into the Woods

Tigerstar and Sasha #2: Escape from the Forest

Tigerstar and Sasha #3: Return to the Clans

Ravenpaw's Path #1: Shattered Peace

Ravenpaw's Path #2: A Clan in Need

Ravenpaw's Path #3: The Heart of a Warrior

SkyClan and the Stranger #1: The Rescue

SkyClan and the Stranger #2: Beyond the Code

SkyClan and the Stranger #3: After the Flood

NOVELLAS

Hollyleaf's Story

Mistystar's Omen

Cloudstar's Journey

Tigerclaw's Fury

Leafpool's Wish

Dovewing's Silence

Mapleshade's Vengeance

Also by Erin Hunter

SEEKERS

Book One: The Quest Begins

Book Two: Great Bear Lake

Book Three: Smoke Mountain

Book Four: The Last Wilderness

Book Five: Fire in the Sky

Book Six: Spirits in the Stars

RETURN TO THE WILD

Book One: Island of Shadows

Book Two: The Melting Sea

Book Three: River of Lost Bears

Book Four: Forest of Wolves

Book Five: The Burning Horizon

MANGA

Toklo's Story

Kallik's Adventure

SURVIVORS

Book One: The Empty City

Book Two: A Hidden Enemy

Book Three: Darkness Falls

Book Four: The Broken Path

Book Five: The Endless Lake

Book Six: Storm of Dogs

Survivors: Tales from the Packs

NOVELLAS

Alpha's Tale

Sweet's Journey

Moon's Choice

POWER OF THREE

WARRIORS

OUTCAST

ERIN
HUNTER

HARPER
An Imprint of HarperCollinsPublishers

Special thanks to Cherith Baldry

 For information address HarperCollins Children's Books, a division of HarperCollins Publishers, 195 Broadway, New York, NY 10007.
www.harpercollinschildrens.com

Library of Congress Cataloging-in-Publication Data
Hunter, Erin.
Outcast / Erin Hunter – 1st ed.
p. cm. (Warriors, power of three ; bk. 3)
Summary: Firestar's grandchildren—Lionpaw, Hollypaw, and Jaypaw—progress in their training to become warrior cats and are drawn for different reasons to the mountains and the Tribe of Rushing Water.
ISBN 978-0-06-236710-5
[1. Cats—Fiction. 2. Brothers and sisters—Fiction. 3. Adventure and adventurers—Fiction. 4. Fantasy.] I. Title.
PZ7.H916625Ou 2008 2007049576
[Fic]—dc22 CIP
AC

Typography by Ellice M. Lee
19 20 CG/BRR 20 19 18 17
❖
Revised paperback edition, 2015

To Jessica

ALLEGIANCES

THUNDERCLAN

LEADER

FIRESTAR—ginger tom with a flame-colored pelt

DEPUTY

BRAMBLECLAW—dark brown tabby tom with amber eyes
APPRENTICE, BERRYPAW

MEDICINE CAT

LEAFPOOL—light brown tabby she-cat with amber eyes
APPRENTICE, JAYPAW

WARRIORS

(toms and she-cats without kits)

SQUIRRELFLIGHT—dark ginger she-cat with green eyes

DUSTPELT—dark brown tabby tom
APPRENTICE, HAZELPAW

SANDSTORM—pale ginger she-cat
APPRENTICE, HONEYPAW

CLOUDTAIL—long-haired white tom
APPRENTICE, CINDERPAW

BRACKENFUR—golden brown tabby tom
APPRENTICE, HOLLYPAW

SORRELTAIL—tortoiseshell-and-white she-cat with amber eyes

THORNCLAW—golden brown tabby tom
APPRENTICE, POPPYPAW

BRIGHTHEART—white she-cat with ginger patches

ASHFUR—pale gray (with darker flecks) tom, dark blue eyes
APPRENTICE, LIONPAW

SPIDERLEG—long-limbed black tom with brown underbelly and amber eyes
APPRENTICE, MOUSEPAW

BROOK WHERE SMALL FISH SWIM (BROOK)—brown tabby she-cat, formerly of the Tribe of Rushing Water

STORMFUR—dark gray tom with amber eyes, formerly of RiverClan

WHITEWING—white she-cat with green eyes

BIRCHFALL—light brown tabby tom

GRAYSTRIPE—long-haired gray tom

APPRENTICES

(more than six moons old, in training to become warriors)

BERRYPAW—cream-colored tom

HAZELPAW—small gray-and-white she-cat

MOUSEPAW—gray-and-white tom

CINDERPAW—gray tabby she-cat

HONEYPAW—light brown tabby she-cat

POPPYPAW—tortoiseshell she-cat

LIONPAW—golden tabby tom

HOLLYPAW—black she-cat

JAYPAW—gray tabby tom

QUEENS

(she-cats expecting or nursing kits)

FERNCLOUD—pale gray (with darker flecks) she-cat, green eyes, mother of Dustpelt's kits: Icekit (white she-cat) and Foxkit (reddish tabby tom)

DAISY—cream long-furred cat from the horseplace, mother of Spiderleg's kits: Rosekit (dark cream she-cat) and Toadkit (black-and-white tom)

MILLIE—striped gray tabby she-cat, former kittypet

ELDERS (former warriors and queens, now retired)

LONGTAIL—pale tabby tom with dark black stripes, retired early due to failing sight

MOUSEFUR—small dusky brown she-cat

SHADOWCLAN

LEADER **BLACKSTAR**—large white tom with huge jet-black paws

DEPUTY **RUSSETFUR**—dark ginger she-cat

MEDICINE CAT **LITTLECLOUD**—very small tabby tom

WARRIORS **OAKFUR**—small brown tom

ROWANCLAW—ginger tom

SMOKEFOOT—black tom
APPRENTICE, OWLPAW

IVYTAIL—black, white, and tortoiseshell she-cat

TOADFOOT—dark brown tom

QUEENS **TAWNYPELT**—tortoiseshell she-cat with green eyes

SNOWBIRD—pure white she-cat

ELDERS **CEDARHEART**—dark gray tom

TALLPOPPY—long-legged light brown tabby she-cat

WINDCLAN

LEADER — **ONESTAR**—brown tabby tom

DEPUTY — **ASHFOOT**—gray she-cat

MEDICINE CAT — **BARKFACE**—short-tailed brown tom
APPRENTICE, KESTRELPAW

WARRIORS — **TORNEAR**—tabby tom

CROWFEATHER—dark gray tom
APPRENTICE, HEATHERPAW (light brown tabby, blue eyes)

OWLWHISKER—light brown tabby tom

WHITETAIL—small white she-cat
APPRENTICE, BREEZEPAW (black, amber eyes)

NIGHTCLOUD—black she-cat

WEASELFUR—ginger tom with white paws

HARESPRING—brown-and-white tom

QUEENS — **GORSETAIL**—very pale gray-and-white cat with blue eyes, mother of Thistlekit, Sedgekit, and Swallowkit

ELDERS — **MORNINGFLOWER**—very old tortoiseshell queen

WEBFOOT—dark gray tabby tom

RIVERCLAN

LEADER — **LEOPARDSTAR**—unusually spotted golden tabby she-cat

DEPUTY — **MISTYFOOT**—gray she-cat with blue eyes

MEDICINE CAT — **MOTHWING**—dappled golden she-cat
APPRENTICE, WILLOWPAW

WARRIORS — **BLACKCLAW**—smoky-black tom

VOLETOOTH—small brown tabby tom
APPRENTICE, MINNOWPAW

REEDWHISKER—black tom

MOSSPELT—tortoiseshell she-cat with blue eyes
APPRENTICE, PEBBLEPAW

BEECHFUR—light brown tom

RIPPLETAIL—dark gray tabby tom

DAWNFLOWER—pale gray she-cat

DAPPLENOSE—mottled gray she-cat

POUNCETAIL—ginger-and-white tom

QUEENS — **GRAYMIST**—pale gray tabby, mother of Sneezekit and Mallowkit

ICEWING—white cat with green eyes, mother of Beetlekit, Pricklekit, Petalkit, and Grasskit

ELDERS — **SWALLOWTAIL**—dark tabby she-cat

STONESTREAM—gray tom

THE TRIBE OF RUSHING WATER

TRIBE-HEALER — **TELLER OF THE POINTED STONES (STONETELLER)**—brown tabby tom with blue eyes

PREY-HUNTERS
(toms and she-cats responsible for providing food)

GRAY SKY BEFORE DAWN (GRAY)—pale gray tabby tom

WING SHADOW OVER WATER (WING)—gray-and-white she-cat

STORM CLOUDS AT DUSK (STORM)—dark gray tom

CAVE-GUARDS
(toms and she-cats responsible for guarding the cave)

TALON OF SWOOPING EAGLE (TALON)—dark brown tabby tom

JAGGED ROCK WHERE HERON SITS (JAG)—dark gray tom

BIRD THAT RIDES THE WIND (BIRD)—gray-brown she-cat

CRAG WHERE EAGLES NEST (CRAG)—dark gray tom (Brook's brother)

SHEER PATH BESIDE WATERFALL (SHEER)—dark brown tabby tom

NIGHT OF NO STARS (NIGHT)—black she-cat

MOSS THAT GROWS BY RIVER (MOSS)—light brown she-cat

KIT-MOTHERS
(she-cats expecting or nursing kits)

FLIGHT OF STARTLED HERON (FLIGHT)—brown tabby she-cat (has three very young kits)

SWOOP OF CHESTNUT HAWK (SWOOP)—dark ginger she-cat (has two older kits)

TO-BES (tribe apprentices)

SCREECH OF ANGRY OWL (SCREECH)—black tom (prey-hunter)

SPLASH WHEN FISH LEAPS (SPLASH)—light brown tabby she-cat (prey-hunter)

PEBBLE THAT ROLLS DOWN MOUNTAIN (PEBBLE)—gray she-cat (cave-guard)

ELDERS (former prey-hunters and cave-guards, now retired)

CLOUD WITH STORM IN BELLY (CLOUD)—white she-cat

RAIN THAT RATTLES ON STONES (RAIN)—speckled brown tom

CATS OUTSIDE CLANS

STRIPES—large silver tabby tom with dark stripes and amber eyes

FLICK—skinny light brown tom with large pointed ears

FLORA—dark-brown-and-white she-cat with green eyes

TWIST—young tortoiseshell she-cat with white stripes on her face

PURDY—elderly, plump tabby loner with a gray muzzle

POWER OF THREE

WARRIORS

OUTCAST

CAT VIEW

TWOLEG NEST
GREENLEAF
TWOLEGPLACE
TWOLEG PATH
TWOLEG PATH
CLEARING
SHADOWCLAN
CAMP
HALFBRIDGE
SMALL
THUNDERPATH
GREENLEAF
TWOLEGPLACE
HALFBRIDGE
ISLAND
STREAM
RIVERCLAN
CAMP
HORSEPLACE

MOONPOOL

ABANDONED
TWOLEG NEST

OLD THUNDERPATH

THUNDERCLAN
CAMP

ANCIENT OAK

LAKE

WINDCLAN
CAMP

BROKEN
HALFBRIDGE

TWOLEGPLACE

THUNDERPATH

KEY
To The
CLANS

THUNDERCLAN

RIVERCLAN

SHADOWCLAN

WINDCLAN

STARCLAN

NORTH

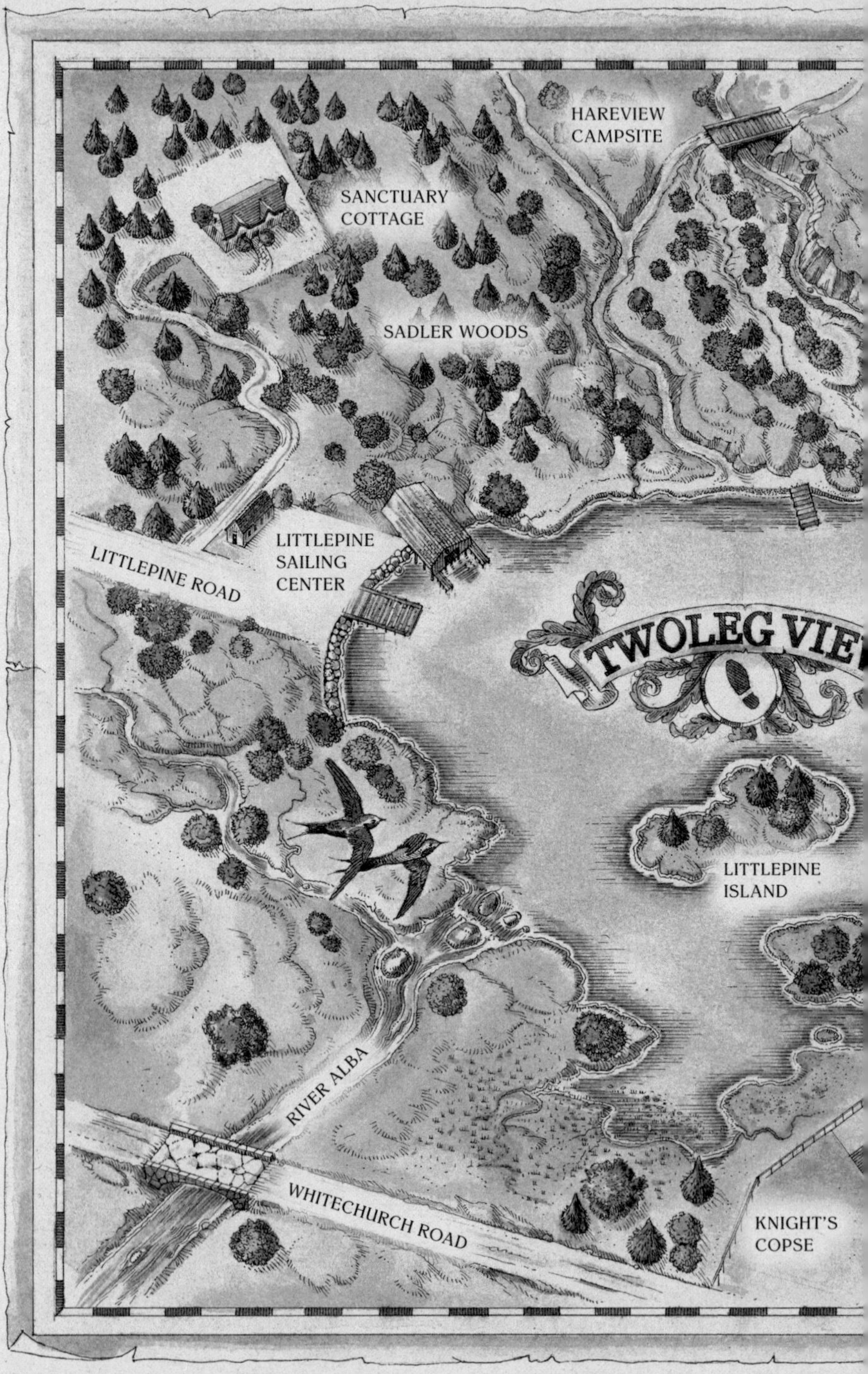

HAREVIEW
CAMPSITE

SANCTUARY
COTTAGE

SADLER WOODS

LITTLEPINE
SAILING
CENTER

LITTLEPINE ROAD

TWOLEG VIE

LITTLEPINE
ISLAND

RIVER ALBA

WHITECHURCH ROAD

KNIGHT'S
COPSE

ABANDONED
WORKMAN'S
HOUSE
QUARRY ROAD (disused)
CRYSTAL
POOL
QUARRY
HARE HILL
WOODS
SANCTUARY
LAKE
HARE HILL
HARE HILL
RIDING STABLES
HARE HILL ROAD
KEY
To The
TERRAIN
DECIDUOUS WOODLAND
PINE FOREST
MARSH
LAKE
FOOTPATHS
NORTH

Prologue

"Prey-stealers! This is our territory." A gray tomcat spat out the words. His neck fur bristled and his lips were drawn back in a snarl. His gaze raked over the group of cats who crouched below him on the steep path. Their claws were unsheathed and their eyes were bright and hungry. One of them had a limp rabbit dangling from her jaws. "*Our* territory and *our* prey."

A silver tabby tom gave him an insolent stare. "If it's your territory, why are there no border markings? The prey here belongs to every cat."

"That's not true and you know it." A black she-cat stood close to the gray tom's shoulder, her tail lashing. "Get out now!" From the side of her mouth she added in a low mutter, "Crag, we can't fight them. Remember what happened last time."

"I know, Night," the gray tom replied. "But what else can we do?"

On Crag's other side a huge brown tabby tom thrust his way forward, letting out a hiss of fury. "Take one more paw step and we'll rip your fur off," he growled.

Crag touched him on the shoulder with the tip of his tail.

"Steady, Talon," he warned. "Let's get out of this without ripping fur if we can."

More cats appeared around a curve in the path, filling the narrow space behind the silver tabby.

"Sheer." Crag summoned a small tabby tom with a flick of his ears. "Get back to the cave, quickly. Tell them the invaders are back."

"But—" Sheer was obviously reluctant to leave his friends when they were already outnumbered.

"Now!" Crag snapped.

Sheer turned and fled up the path.

The sun was going down. Rocks cast long shadows over the rough ground, stained red as blood. The faint sound of tumbling water broke the silence, and from the sky came the harsh cry of a hawk.

"This is as far as you go," Crag meowed. "Turn back and find somewhere else to hunt."

"Who's going to make us?" the silver tabby sneered.

"Try staying here, and you'll see," Talon hissed.

Crag's patrol pressed up beside him, blocking the path. But the intruders began fanning out, scrambling onto the boulders on either side. Crag crouched, tensing his muscles. He would fight if he had to, in spite of what had happened last time.

"Stop!"

A brown tabby tom shouldered his way through Crag's patrol to stand in front of the invaders. Though his muzzle was gray with age, his muscles were still wiry and powerful and he held his head high.

"I am Stoneteller, Tribe-Healer of the Tribe of Rushing Water," he announced, his voice echoing hoarsely off the rocks. "This is our territory, and you are not welcome here."

"Territory only belongs to cats who can defend it," the silver tabby retorted.

"Remember how we drove you out, before the time of frozen water?" Stoneteller growled. "We will do the same again, unless you leave now."

The silver tabby narrowed his eyes. "Drove us out? That's not how I remember it."

"We *chose* to leave," a brown-and-white she-cat added from where she crouched on top of a boulder. "We found a better place to spend leaf-bare, with more prey."

"And now we *choose* to come back." The tabby tom lashed his tail. "A few scrawny, flea-ridden excuses for cats aren't going to stop us." He flexed his claws, scraping the stones.

"The Tribe of Rushing Water has always made its home in these mountains," Stoneteller meowed. "We—"

His words were lost in a yowl of fury as the brown-and-white she-cat launched herself from the boulder and fastened her claws in Night's shoulder. The tabby tom let out a fearsome screech and hurled himself at Crag. As Crag rolled over and over, clawing at his attacker, the air filled with the shrieks of battling cats.

Far above, the Tribe of Endless Hunting looked on helplessly.

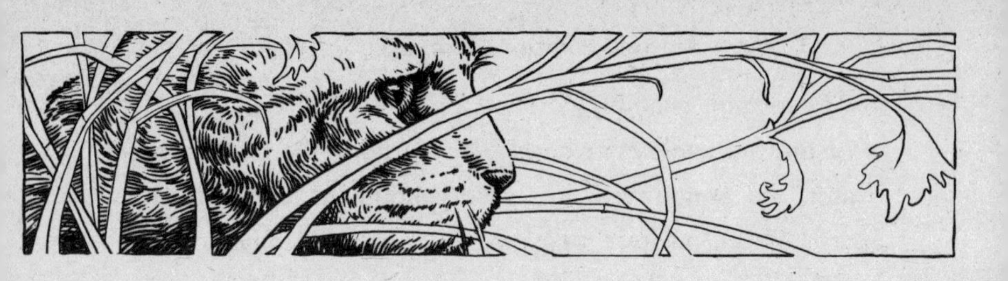

CHAPTER 1

Jaypaw stretched, feeling the sun beat down on his fur. A warm breeze whispered around him, full of the scents of green, growing things. Somewhere above his head a bird was trilling, and he could hear the muffled slap of lake water on the shore.

"Jaypaw!"

Light paw steps ruffled the sound of the waves. Jaypaw pictured his mentor, Leafpool, splashing through the shallow water at the edge of the lake.

"Jaypaw!" she repeated, her voice sounding closer. "Come join me. The cool water feels wonderful."

"No, thanks," Jaypaw muttered.

For him, water was more than the gentle lapping of the lake against his paws. Instead, the sound of the waves brought back memories of cold water surging around him, the weight of soaked fur dragging him down, water filling his mouth and nose and choking the life out of him. He had drowned once in his dreams, lost in the underground tunnels with the ancient warrior Fallen Leaves, and had almost drowned for real when he and his Clanmates rescued the missing WindClan kits.

I've had enough water to last for the rest of my life.

"Okay." Leafpool's paw steps retreated, faster now as if she was bounding through the shallows, carefree as a kit.

Jaypaw padded on along the shoreline. He was supposed to be looking for mallow, but when he tasted the breeze he couldn't pick up any of the familiar pungent scent. As soon as the sound of Leafpool's paw steps faded, he veered away from the water and scrambled up the bank. He had something more important than herbs to find. He prowled forward, nose close to the ground as he sniffed his way through clumps of grass and around shrubs until he came to the gnarled roots of a tree.

Here it is!

He dug his teeth into one end of the stick and pulled it out from behind the root that held it fast to the bank, away from the hungry waves. Crouching beside it, he ran his paw over the scratches, finding the group of five long and three short that stood for the five apprentices and three kits who had been trapped in the tunnels as the waters rose. All of them were scored through: Every cat had made it out alive. Jaypaw remembered making the scratches with Rock's scent wreathing around him; he had almost felt as though the hairless paw of the ancient spirit was guiding his claws.

But Jaypaw could also feel the single unscored scratch. Fallen Leaves, the ancient cat who had guided them, still walked the tunnels alone.

He closed his eyes and listened for the voices that used to whisper to him, but he could hear nothing except the wind in the trees and the ripple of the lake. "Fallen Leaves? Rock?"

he murmured. "Where are you? Why won't you talk to me anymore?"

There was no reply. Jaypaw dragged the stick farther into the open, rolling it down the bank until the lake water could wash over it. He sniffed along its length, but all echoes of the past had vanished.

Jaypaw swallowed hard, almost ready to start wailing like a kit that had lost its mother. He wanted to speak to Rock, to find out more about the cats who had lived around the lake so long ago. He wanted to know why Fallen Leaves had been left to walk the caves when all the other ancient cats, even the others who had died down there, had passed on somewhere else.

He was convinced these were the same cats he had felt around him at the Moonpool, whose paw prints dimpled the spiral path that led down to the water. They were far older than the Clans, older even than StarClan. What wisdom they would be able to share with him! They might even be able to explain the prophecy to him, the mysterious words he had heard in Firestar's dream.

There will be three, kin of your kin, who will hold the power of the stars in their paws.

"Jaypaw, what do you think you're doing?"

Jaypaw started. He had been so intent on the stick and his thoughts of the ancient cats that he hadn't heard Leafpool approaching. Now he could scent her close to him and pick up the irritation that flowed off her.

"Sorry," he mumbled.

"We need more mallow, Jaypaw. Just because we aren't on

the brink of battle now doesn't mean that cats won't get sick or injured. Medicine cats have to be ready."

"I know, okay?" Jaypaw retorted. *And who stopped the battle?* he demanded silently. *WindClan and ThunderClan would have ripped each other apart if it wasn't for me and the others finding those lost kits.*

He didn't want to explain himself to his mentor. He could sense her looking on severely while he rolled the stick back up the bank and hid it again under the tree root. Then he padded away from her, along the top of the bank, jaws parted to pick up the scents of growing things.

Before he had covered many fox-lengths he paused, staring sightlessly out across the lake. Wind buffeted his fur, pressing it close to his body.

Where are you? His mind called out to those long-ago cats. *Speak to me, please!*

"Jaypaw! Hey, Jaypaw!"

That wasn't the voice he wanted to hear. Biting back a hiss of irritation, Jaypaw turned to face Hazelpaw; he could pick up her scent and hear her paw steps as she bounded up to him. *Blundering through the bracken like a fox in a fit!*

"Look what I've got!" Hazelpaw's voice sounded gleeful and also half stifled, as if she was speaking around a piece of prey gripped in her jaws.

Jaypaw didn't bother to point out that he couldn't *look* at anything. Besides, the strong scent of vole told him what Hazelpaw was carrying.

"This is my last hunting assessment." The apprentice's voice was clearer now; she must have put down her prey. "If we do well, Berrypaw, Mousepaw, and I will be made warriors today."

"Great." Jaypaw tried to sound enthusiastic, but he was still annoyed at her for distracting him from ancient cats.

"I'm sure Dustpelt will be pleased with me," Hazelpaw went on. "This vole is *huge*! It's enough to feed both of Daisy's new kits."

"Daisy's new kits can't eat vole yet," Jaypaw reminded her. *Is she completely mouse-brained?* "They were only born four sunrises ago."

"Well, it'll do for Daisy, then." Hazelpaw still sounded excited. "She'll need to eat well now that she's feeding kits. Have you visited them yet? They're the sweetest things I've ever seen! Daisy told me she's named them Rosekit and Toadkit."

"I know," Jaypaw mewed shortly.

"I can't wait until they're old enough to come out of the nursery and play," Hazelpaw went on. "Do you think Firestar might let me mentor one of them? I'll have warrior experience by the time they're ready."

"They're your half brother and sister," Jaypaw meowed discouragingly. "Firestar probably won't—"

"Hazelpaw!" A sharp voice interrupted, and Jaypaw heard the rustle of Hazelpaw's mentor, Dustpelt, pushing his way through bracken. Annoyance was rolling off him in waves. "Are you hunting or gossiping?" he demanded.

"Sorry. Have you seen my vole, Dustpelt? It's *enormous*!"

Jaypaw heard Dustpelt pad up and sniff the vole.

"Very good," the warrior mewed. "But that doesn't mean you can sit back and wash your tail. There's lots more prey in the forest. I'll take this back to camp, and you can carry on."

"Okay. See you later, Jaypaw!"

Jaypaw remembered to call out, "Good luck!" as Hazelpaw bounded away, but his mind was already drifting back to the ancient cats. Their silence troubled him. *Have I done something wrong? Are Rock and Fallen Leaves angry with me?* His mind gnawed at the problem while he found a clump of mallow and bit off the stems to carry back to camp.

"Well done, Jaypaw." Leafpool's voice came from behind him as he was finishing the task. "Let's go."

Jaypaw gathered up the bundle of stems in his jaws. It was a good excuse not to talk. As he padded back through the forest behind his mentor he was still absentminded, hardly noticing the scents of prey or the scuffling of small creatures in the undergrowth. He was far away, trying to walk in the paw steps of those ancient cats.

Then a bird let out a sudden alarm call. Jaypaw started at the fierce beating of wings right in front of his nose, dropping his mallow as he jumped back.

"Hey!" Berrypaw's indignant yowl came from a few tail-lengths away. "That was my thrush you just scared off. Couldn't you see I was stalking it?"

"No, I couldn't *see* that." Guilt and annoyance at his own clumsiness made Jaypaw savage. "I'm *blind,* in case you hadn't noticed."

"But you can do better than that," Leafpool meowed crossly.

"Keep your mind on what you're doing, Jaypaw. You've been scattier than a rabbit all morning."

"Well, I hope he hasn't messed up my assessment," Berrypaw muttered. "I'd have had that thrush if it wasn't for him."

"I know," Brambleclaw meowed.

Jaypaw picked up the ThunderClan deputy's scent a little farther away. Mousepaw and his mentor, Spiderleg, were nearby, too. *Oh, no! Has all of ThunderClan been watching?*

"There's no point in wailing over lost prey," Brambleclaw went on, padding closer. "And a warrior doesn't get worked up over one little setback. Come on, Berrypaw, see if you can find a mouse among the tree roots over there."

"Okay." Jaypaw could tell that Berrypaw was still angry, in spite of what his mentor had said. "Jaypaw, just keep out of my way, will you?"

"No problem," Jaypaw shot back at him.

"Yes, it's time we got back to the clearing." Leafpool gave Jaypaw a nudge with her shoulder. "This way."

I know where the camp is, thanks!

Jaypaw collected his herbs and padded behind his mentor through the thorn tunnel and into the stone hollow. Brushing past the screen of brambles in front of the medicine cats' den, he deposited his bundle in the cave at the back.

"I'm going to get some fresh-kill, okay?" he mewed.

"Just a moment, Jaypaw." Leafpool set her own herbs down and sat in front of him. Jaypaw could sense her impatience and frustration. "I don't know what's gotten into you lately," she began. "Ever since you and the others found the WindClan kits by the edge of the lake . . ."

There was a question in her voice, and Jaypaw could taste a powerful scent of curiosity coming from her. Leafpool clearly knew there was more to the story of the lost kits than he and his littermates were telling. But there was no way he would reveal that the kits had actually been wandering in the network of tunnels that lay beneath ThunderClan and WindClan territory. He knew that Lionpaw and Hollypaw, as well as the WindClan apprentices Heatherpaw and Breezepaw, would keep quiet too. No cat wanted to admit that Lionpaw and Heatherpaw had been playing in the tunnels for moons.

So they couldn't tell the story of how nearly they had drowned, along with the missing kits, as rain filled the tunnels and swelled the underground stream into a terrifying flood. Jaypaw still had nightmares about the surging, suffocating river.

"Jaypaw, are you all right?" Leafpool went on. Her irritation was fading, giving way to concern, a sticky flood that threatened to overwhelm Jaypaw just like the water in the tunnels. "You would tell me, wouldn't you, if anything was wrong?"

"Sure," he muttered, hoping his mentor wouldn't detect the lie. "Everything's fine."

Leafpool hesitated. Jaypaw felt his fur begin to prickle defensively. But the medicine cat only sighed and mewed, "Go and eat, then. Later, when it's a bit cooler, we'll go up to the old Twoleg nest and collect some catmint."

Before she had finished speaking, Jaypaw was on his paws and pushing his way out past the brambles. He padded over to the fresh-kill pile, sniffed out a plump mouse, and carried it back to a sunny spot outside his den to eat it. Sunhigh was just past, and the stone hollow was filled with warmth. His belly comfortably full, Jaypaw lay on his side and cleaned his whiskers with one paw.

Cinderpaw and Hollypaw had just pushed their way in through the thorn tunnel. Even at a distance Jaypaw could pick up the mossy scent of the training hollow clinging to their fur.

"I'm sorry I beat you every time," Hollypaw meowed. "Are you sure you're okay?"

"I'm fine," Cinderpaw insisted. "I *wouldn't* be okay if you let me win by not fighting your best."

Her voice sounded brave, but Jaypaw could tell from her paw steps that Cinderpaw's injured leg was troubling her. There was nothing more the medicine cats could do; only time could strengthen the leg. Or was Cinderpaw destined never to be a warrior, like Cinderpelt before her?

Jaypaw was distracted from Cinderpaw's problem by the sound of shrill squeals coming from the nursery. He winced. Daisy's kits were only four sunrises old, but they had huge voices. Their father, Spiderleg, had insisted on taking Mousepaw out for his assessment, even though Dustpelt had offered to take his place so he could spend more time in the nursery. Jaypaw thought Spiderleg seemed awkward around his kits, as if he couldn't adjust to the idea of being a father.

In any case, Jaypaw thought, the nursery was pretty crowded. Icekit and Foxkit, Ferncloud's latest litter, were still there, though they were nearly old enough to become apprentices. And Millie, who was expecting Graystripe's kits, had just moved in. Jaypaw knew that Firestar was proud of how strong ThunderClan was becoming, though he sometimes worried about how they would all be fed.

More rustling came from the thorn tunnel and Lionpaw staggered into the camp with his mentor, Ashfur, just behind him.

"Two mice and a squirrel!" Ashfur meowed. "Well done, Lionpaw. That's the sort of hunting I expect from you."

In spite of the words of praise, Ashfur didn't sound enthusiastic. Jaypaw thought that his brother and Ashfur had never gotten on as well as mentor and apprentice should. There was something there that puzzled him, and something in Ashfur that he couldn't read.

But it was probably unimportant. Jaypaw dismissed the question from his mind as his brother flopped down beside him, a mouse in his jaws.

"I'm worn out!" Lionpaw announced. "I thought I'd have to chase that squirrel all the way to ShadowClan."

"Why bother?" Jaypaw asked. "It's not *your* assessment today."

"I know," Lionpaw mumbled around a mouthful of fresh-kill. "But that's not the point. A good warrior will always do as much as he can to feed the Clan."

And Lionpaw wanted to be the best warrior he could. Jaypaw knew that, and he knew how tense and determined his brother had been ever since they found the kits in the tunnels.

He knew the reason, too, even without reading Lionpaw's mind: His brother had decided to concentrate on his training to make up for meeting the WindClan apprentice Heatherpaw in secret.

Jaypaw's whiskers twitched in sympathy. As a medicine cat, he was allowed to have friends outside his Clan, though he couldn't imagine wanting to. How could anyone trust a cat from a different Clan?

The patter of a falling pebble alerted him that Firestar was bounding down from the Highledge. His voice came from close to the warriors' den.

"We need a border patrol. Which of you—"

Beside Jaypaw, Lionpaw leaped to his feet. "I'll go!"

For a moment Jaypaw wondered why Firestar was organizing a patrol, until he remembered that the Clan deputy, Brambleclaw, was out in the forest giving Berrypaw his assessment.

"Thanks, Lionpaw," Firestar meowed, "but I can see you've been working hard today."

Lionpaw sat down again; Jaypaw could tell he was disappointed.

"I'll go." Graystripe spoke as he pushed his way out of the warriors' den.

"So will I." Squirrelflight was just behind him.

"And I'll come with Honeypaw." Jaypaw heard Sandstorm padding up from the direction of the apprentices' den, with her apprentice at her side.

"Good," meowed Firestar. "I think you should take a look

at the border with WindClan. Everything's been quiet since the kits were found, but you never know."

"We'll make sure the scent marks are fresh," Graystripe promised. "And if we see—"

He broke off at the sound of excited meows and loud rustling from the thorn tunnel. Jaypaw sat up, jaws parted to distinguish the different scents of the newcomers. Berrypaw was first into the clearing, with Hazelpaw and Mousepaw bundling just behind him. They were followed by their mentors, Brambleclaw, Dustpelt, and Spiderleg.

"We did it!" Berrypaw's triumphant yowl echoed around the stone hollow. "We all passed our assessment, and now we'll be warriors!"

"Berrypaw." Brambleclaw sounded stern. "That's for Firestar to decide."

"Sorry." Jaypaw could feel Berrypaw's sudden dejection and pictured him with head and tail drooping. "But we will get to be warriors, won't we?"

"Maybe we should assess how well you can keep your mouth shut," Dustpelt snapped.

"It's okay." Firestar sounded amused. "If the mentors will come and speak to me, we'll arrange the warrior ceremony."

"What about the border patrol?" Graystripe asked.

"It can wait till dusk. We're not expecting trouble, after all."

All the apprentices were gathering in an excited cluster near their den. Lionpaw pelted across to join them. Jaypaw rose, stretched, and followed more slowly.

". . . and *two* voles," Berrypaw was meowing as Jaypaw came into earshot. "I'd have had a thrush as well if *he* hadn't frightened it away."

Jaypaw's neck fur bristled, but before he could speak Hollypaw jumped to his defense. "What does it matter? You passed the assessment."

Jaypaw's tail-tip twitched. *I can look after myself, thanks.*

"I got a humongous vole." Hazelpaw was too excited to notice the hostility between Berrypaw and Jaypaw. "And I brought down a blackbird just as it was flying away. Dustpelt said he'd never seen such a good leap."

"That's great!" mewed Honeypaw.

"I caught a squirrel," Mousepaw boasted. Jaypaw remembered how the apprentice had climbed the Sky Oak in pursuit of a squirrel, and then was too scared to climb down again. Cinderpaw had broken her leg going up to fetch him when a branch gave way and she fell. Jaypaw would have bet a moon of searching the elders' fur for ticks that the squirrel Mousepaw caught had been on the ground.

"I wish *we* were being assessed, don't you?" Hollypaw murmured to Lionpaw. "Sometimes I think we'll never be warriors."

"I know." Lionpaw sounded just as envious; then a jolt of determination shot through him. "We'll just have to work harder, that's all."

Jaypaw didn't join in the conversation. His paws were set on a different path. He wouldn't finish his medicine cat training for a long, long time, and when he received his proper name he would still be Leafpool's apprentice. He wouldn't be a full medicine cat until she died. Even though his fur prickled at the thought of his littermates moving on without him, he didn't want his mentor to die.

Besides, the prophecy said that he and the others would have the power of the stars in their paws as soon as they were born. It didn't say that they had to be warriors first.

Firestar's voice rang out from the Highledge. "Let all cats old enough to catch their own prey gather for a Clan meeting!"

The clearing flooded with different scents as the Clan began to emerge. Jaypaw could make out Mousefur and Longtail, the elders, as they left the shelter of their den under the hazel bush. Leafpool came out of the medicine cats' den and sat in front of the screen of brambles.

Then the other scents were overwhelmed by Daisy's, as she bounded over to the group of apprentices.

"Berrypaw, just look at you!" she exclaimed. "Your fur is sticking out all over the place. And Hazelpaw—have you collected every single burr between here and the lake?"

Jaypaw heard the sound of fierce licking.

"It's okay, I can do it," Berrypaw protested.

"Nonsense," Daisy scolded. "You can't go to your warrior ceremony looking like some scruffy band of rogue kits. Any cat would think I hadn't brought you up properly." She began licking Berrypaw again, then broke off to add, "Mousepaw, you're just as bad! Have you seen the state of your tail?"

"I hope Firestar has forgotten about *my* tail," Berrypaw

mewed anxiously. "He might use it to give me my warrior name."

Berrypaw's tail was just a short stump. When he was a kit he had snuck out of the camp to go hunting and caught his tail in a fox trap.

"What, Berrystumpytail?" Poppypaw suggested. "That would be a mouthful!"

"Oh, no!" Berrypaw wailed. "Firestar wouldn't, would he?"

"Don't be silly," Daisy mewed.

"I'm sure you don't have to worry." Brightheart's voice joined the conversation. Among all the different scents, Jaypaw hadn't noticed her approach. "When the dog pack attacked me, Bluestar gave me Lostface as my warrior name. But when Firestar became leader, he changed it. I'm sure he wouldn't give any cat a cruel name."

"I hope not!" Berrypaw still sounded doubtful.

Suddenly alarmed, Jaypaw thought over what Brightheart had said. "You don't think Leafpool might mention that I'm blind when she gives me my full medicine cat name?" he muttered into Hollypaw's ear.

"Like, Jayno-eyes? That's just as stupid as Berrystumpytail," his sister replied.

"*You* think it's stupid, but will Leafpool—"

"Be quiet, all of you," Graystripe interrupted. "The ceremony is about to start."

Lionpaw gave Jaypaw a nudge. "Come on. Let's get a good place at the front. I want to see everything that happens."

"Yes, it'll be our turn soon," Hollypaw meowed enthusiastically.

Jaypaw followed his littermates and the other apprentices to the front of the crowd that had gathered around Firestar. He could sense fizzing pride in the three who were to be made warriors. He pictured them sleek-furred and shiny after their mother's frantic licking. Daisy felt just as proud, though Jaypaw picked up anxiety, too, for the two tiny kits she had left in the nursery.

Then he located Ferncloud, sitting just outside the nursery with Icekit and Foxkit. The gentle queen would make sure no harm came to the two newborns while their mother watched her first litter become warriors.

"This is a good day for ThunderClan." The excited murmuring of the Clan cats died into silence as Firestar began to speak. "No Clan can survive without new warriors. Brambleclaw, is your apprentice Berrypaw ready for his warrior ceremony?"

"He has trained well," Brambleclaw replied.

Jaypaw could feel the excitement of the three apprentices building as Firestar addressed the other two mentors, Dustpelt and Spiderleg. Then he heard their paw steps as they padded forward to stand in front of Firestar.

"I, Firestar, leader of ThunderClan, call upon my warrior ancestors to look down on these three apprentices." The Clan leader's voice rang out above the rustle of trees at the top of the hollow. "They have trained hard to understand the ways of your noble code, and I commend them to you as warriors in their turn. Berrypaw, Hazelpaw, Mousepaw, do you promise to uphold the warrior code and to protect and defend this Clan, even at the cost of your lives?"

"I do!" the three young cats replied, Berrypaw loudest of all.

For a few heartbeats Jaypaw felt his fur prickle with envy. One day he would have his own naming ceremony as a medicine cat, but he would never stand before his Clan and make the promise to defend it with his life.

"Then by the powers of StarClan I give you your warrior names," Firestar went on. "Berrypaw, from this moment you will be known as Berrynose."

"Oh, thank you!" the new warrior exclaimed, interrupting his Clan leader.

A ripple of amusement passed through the Clan, though Jaypaw caught a hiss of annoyance from Berrynose's former mentor, Brambleclaw.

Firestar waited for the noise to die down before continuing. "StarClan honors your bravery and your enthusiasm, and we welcome you as a full warrior of ThunderClan."

There was a pause; Jaypaw knew that Firestar would rest his muzzle on the top of Berrynose's head, and Berrynose would lick his leader's shoulder. Then Firestar went on to give Hazelpaw the name of Hazeltail, and Mousepaw became Mousewhisker.

"ThunderClan is proud of you all," Firestar finished. "May you serve your Clan faithfully."

"Mousewhisker! Hazeltail! Berrynose!" The Clan welcomed the three new warriors with enthusiastic yowls.

Jaypaw sensed their pride in their new responsibilities, and a renewed confidence in every cat that the Clan was growing in strength and numbers, the hardships of the Great Journey now a fading memory.

But there was something more lingering in the hollow like mist—traditions that stretched back beyond ThunderClan to the ancient cats who had walked the forest long ago. If Fallen Leaves had made it alive out of the tunnels, would he have been greeted like this?

What happened to those cats? Jaypaw wondered. *Where did they go?*

CHAPTER 2

Lionpaw pushed his way through clumps of long grass wet with dew; he shivered as the moisture soaked his fur, and blinked sleep from his eyes. Clouds lay low over the forest, though a growing brightness above the trees showed where the sun was rising.

The dawn patrol was heading toward WindClan territory. Ashfur and Berrynose had drawn slightly ahead, discussing something in voices too low for Lionpaw to catch. After a few moments Berrynose glanced over his shoulder. "Don't lag behind, Lionpaw," he meowed loudly. "And watch out for fox traps."

"Watch out yourself," Lionpaw muttered. The cream-colored tom had been a warrior for three whole days, and already he was acting like a mentor. *But he needn't think I'm going to obey his orders!*

Lionpaw let himself drop even farther behind. His paws were tingling with memory as he rounded a bramble thicket and saw the entrance to the tunnels. It looked like a disused rabbit hole, half-hidden by bracken, but once it had led down to a cave with an underground river and then up again into WindClan territory. Pain stabbed Lionpaw's heart as he remembered how he used to plunge into the tunnels at night and meet Heatherpaw in the cave. He wished they could go back to the time when she had been Heatherstar, leader of DarkClan, and he was her loyal deputy.

He hesitated outside the entrance for a heartbeat, then couldn't resist squeezing through it and crawling along the tunnel until he came to the avalanche of mud left behind when the tunnels flooded. He opened his mouth, but all he could taste was wet soil and worms.

"Lionpaw! I know you're in there!" Berrynose called. "Come out *now*!"

For a moment Lionpaw felt like ignoring him, but he realized how stupid that would be. He didn't want to stay in this damp, stifling hole. Slowly he wriggled backward until he could stand up and shake the mud out of his fur.

Berrynose was standing in front of him, cream-colored fur bristling. Ashfur was a couple of tail-lengths away; his blue eyes were calm and unreadable.

"What do you think you're doing, exploring in a dangerous place like that?" Berrynose demanded. "What if the roof had fallen in? You'd expect us to dig you out, I suppose, like last time."

Lionpaw had almost suffocated when he fell into an old badger set during the daylight Gathering. But that was completely different. And anyway, Berrynose hadn't been the one to dig him out.

"Stop ordering me around," he snapped. "You're not my mentor."

"Then stop behaving like a stupid kit!"

Lionpaw dug his claws into the ground to stop himself from taking a swipe at the arrogant tom. "Don't call me a kit," he growled. "Your scent hasn't faded out of the apprentice den, and you're already—"

"That's enough," Ashfur interrupted. "Berrynose, I'll do the mentoring, thanks. But he's right, Lionpaw. There's no point in sticking your nose down every hole between here and WindClan. Unless there were any suspicious scents down there."

"No. But there might have been!" Lionpaw defended himself.

Ashfur made no comment, except for an impatient twitch of the tail. "Let's get moving."

Lionpaw gave Berrynose a final glare and padded after his mentor. He could still feel a tug of longing for Heatherpaw, drawing him down into the caves. But he knew he would never walk there again—and not just because mud had blocked the tunnels.

He wanted to be the greatest ThunderClan warrior ever. And he couldn't be that if his best friend was a cat from another Clan.

"Jump! High as you can—now!"

Lionpaw leaped into the air, twisting as he landed so that he was facing his opponent. He managed to land a blow on Poppypaw's haunches before she scrambled around to face him. Flashing a glance toward the edge of the clearing, he could just make out the shadow of a tabby-striped pelt and the gleam of amber eyes.

Thanks, Tigerstar!

Poppypaw sprang at him, and Lionpaw launched himself forward, slipping underneath her with his belly brushing the moss. Hooking her hind legs out from under her, he planted his forepaws on her belly as she rolled over.

"Well done, Lionpaw." Ashfur gave him a nod of approval, though there was no warmth in his blue eyes.

What am I doing wrong now? Lionpaw wondered. He had understood Ashfur's annoyance with him when he was spending every night in the caves with Heatherpaw. Then he'd been almost too tired to put one paw in front of another during the day. *But I'm training well now. I'm working really hard!*

"I've never seen that last move before." Thornclaw, Poppypaw's mentor, padded up to the two apprentices. "Where did you learn it?"

"Er . . . I just figured it out, I suppose," Lionpaw mumbled.

He had learned the move from Tigerstar, during a training bout with Hawkfrost. The two shadowy cats visited him so often, he felt as if he always had voices in his ears, telling him to jump higher, strike harder, twist out of the way. The constant practice had made his muscles harder and stronger. He knew without any cat telling him that his battle skills had improved faster than any other apprentice's. But it was difficult sometimes to explain where the skills came from.

"You can let me up now," Poppypaw mewed.

"Oh, sorry."

Lionpaw stepped away from her and she bounced to her paws, shaking scraps of moss from her fur. "Will you teach me how to do that?"

"Sure. When a cat leaps at you, you need to flatten yourself, but keep moving forward."

"Like this?" Poppypaw tried to imitate the move.

"Yes, but a bit faster."

While the young tortoiseshell she-cat practiced, Lionpaw glanced toward the edge of the clearing again. But the ghostly presence of Tigerstar was gone.

Lionpaw maneuvered a long tendril of bramble through the tunnel into the stone hollow, tugging hard as it snagged on the thorns. His paws were aching with tiredness. First the dawn patrol, then the training session, then, after a short break for a few mouthfuls of fresh-kill, Ashfur had set him to repairing the elders' den. And it was only just past sunhigh!

As he dragged the bramble across the clearing, something heavy landed on the other end of it, bringing him up short and making him stumble. Dropping his end, Lionpaw glanced back to see Foxkit. The reddish tabby tom had sunk his teeth into the other end of the tendril and was battering it with his paws. A low growl came from his throat.

"ShadowClan is invading!" Icekit squealed, dashing up beside her brother and leaping onto the bramble. "Get out of our camp!"

Whitewing halted on her way across the clearing, her neck fur beginning to bristle, then carried on with a flick of her tail.

Cloudtail thrust his head out of the warriors' den, blue eyes wide with alarm. When he spotted the two kits he twitched his ears in disgust and disappeared.

"Hey, you're disturbing every cat," Lionpaw meowed. "And I need this to patch the elders' den."

"Can we help?" Icekit asked.

"Yes, we'll be apprentices soon," Foxkit added, letting go of the bramble.

"Okay, but be careful you don't get thorns in your pads."

Lionpaw went on dragging the tendril across the clearing. The two kits tried to help him tug it along, but they mostly got under his paws and made the task harder.

When they drew closer to the elders' den, Foxkit and Icekit seemed to forget about helping. Instead they dashed across to Mousefur and Longtail, who were sunning themselves at the entrance to the den.

"Tell us a story!" Foxkit demanded. "Tell us about the Great Journey. Tell us how the Twolegs—"

"No, I want to hear about the old forest," Icekit interrupted.

Mousefur yawned. "You tell them something," she mewed to Longtail. "Then maybe they'll settle down and some cats can get a bit of sleep." She closed her eyes and wrapped her tail over her nose.

Longtail sighed, then settled into a comfortable crouch with his paws tucked under his chest. He turned his face toward the kits, even though he couldn't see them. "Okay, what do you want to hear about?"

"Tigerstar!" Foxkit's fur bristled with excitement.

"Yes, Tigerstar!" Icekit added. "Tell us how he tried to take over the forest."

Lionpaw saw Longtail's tail-tip flick as the blind cat hesitated. Curiosity clawed at him as he began weaving the length of bramble to block up a hole in the honeysuckle fronds that sheltered the den. He wanted to hear about Tigerstar as much as the kits did.

"Tigerstar was a great warrior," Longtail began at last. "He was the strongest cat in the forest and the best fighter. When I was a young cat, I thought he would be the next leader of ThunderClan. I wanted to be just like him," the pale tabby added awkwardly.

"But he was *evil*!" Foxkit burst out, round-eyed.

"We didn't know that back then," Longtail explained. "He killed Redtail, the ThunderClan deputy, but every cat believed that Redtail had died in battle. . . ."

Lionpaw's belly churned as he listened to the tale of blood and conspiracy. It was hard to keep his paws moving, fixing the bramble into place, and to pretend that this was just a story to him, no more than it was to the kits. This was the cat who padded beside him through the forest, teaching him how to be a warrior!

"It was Tigerstar's ambition that destroyed him," Longtail concluded. "If he'd been willing to wait for power to come to him, he would have been the greatest leader in the forest."

Lionpaw relaxed. There was no reason for him to avoid Tigerstar. The dark tabby couldn't be ambitious now. He was *dead*; there was nothing left to plan for.

And he had never suggested that Lionpaw should break the warrior code. He had been angry when he discovered the meetings with Heatherpaw in the cave. All he wanted was to make Lionpaw a really good warrior. Perhaps Tigerstar was sorry for what he had done and was trying to make up for it by helping ThunderClan.

Lionpaw left the kits pestering Longtail with questions and padded thoughtfully out of the camp to fetch more brambles.

CHAPTER 3

Hollypaw pushed through the brambles into the nursery and set down a blackbird in front of Daisy. Rosekit and Toadkit lay in the curve of their mother's belly, suckling with their tiny tails stretched out behind them.

"Thank you," Daisy mewed, reaching out one paw to drag the blackbird closer. "That feels like a good plump one."

"Can we have some?" Foxkit sat up from where he was wrestling with his sister. "I'm starving!"

"Certainly not," their mother, Ferncloud, replied. "You're old enough to fetch your own fresh-kill."

"Can we?" Icekit's head popped up out of the bracken. "I could eat a whole rabbit."

"All right," Ferncloud meowed. "Fetch some for Millie, too!" she called after them as the two kits shot out through the opening in the brambles.

Millie blinked sleepily from where she lay in a mossy nest. Her belly looked huge; Hollypaw guessed that it wouldn't be long before her kits were born.

"Thank you," Millie purred to Ferncloud.

Ferncloud sighed. "It's time those two were apprenticed.

They need mentors to keep an eye on them."

Hollypaw silently agreed as she left the nursery and padded across to the fresh-kill pile to fetch prey for the elders. Foxkit and Icekit were already there, play fighting over a chaffinch.

"What about some prey for Millie?" Hollypaw reminded them.

"Oh, sorry." Foxkit scrambled up, grabbed a couple of mice by their tails, and scampered off across the clearing with the prey swinging from his jaws.

Icekit let out a little purr of triumph and settled down to eat the chaffinch.

Hollypaw began nosing through the fresh-kill pile to find something for the elders. The scents of the nursery still clung to her fur. She felt as if the whole camp was full of kits and mothers expecting kits.

Will the Clan expect me to have kits? she wondered. She knew that kits were the future of the Clan, but when she thought about becoming a mother herself, she felt as if she were carrying the weight of the whole forest on her shoulders.

She was beginning to drag a rabbit out of the pile when Honeypaw came bounding up to her. "Who's that for?" Honeypaw asked.

"The elders."

"I just took them a squirrel," Honeypaw told her. "If they're okay in the nursery, then we're done."

Hollypaw let the rabbit drop back onto the pile. "There's not much fresh-kill left," she meowed. "I'm going to ask Brackenfur if we can go hunting."

Though there had been a heavy shower at dawn, the clouds had cleared away and the sun was shining. Every leaf and blade of grass sparkled. A stiff breeze carried prey-scent from the forest; Hollypaw's paws itched with longing to get out of the camp.

"There's a hunting patrol just coming back," Honeypaw pointed out, flicking her tail toward the camp entrance.

Graystripe emerged, carrying a squirrel and two mice in his jaws, followed by Brightheart with a couple of voles and Berrynose with a rabbit.

"Oh, look!" Honeypaw's eyes stretched wide. "Berrynose has caught a *huge* rabbit. He's amazing!"

"Berrynose?" Hollypaw couldn't stop her voice from squeaking in surprise. Ever since he had become a warrior five days earlier, the cream-colored tom had been the bossiest cat in the Clan.

Honeypaw blinked in embarrassment and scuffled at the sandy floor of the clearing with her forepaws. "I really like him," she confessed. "But I don't suppose he'll look at me, not now that he's a warrior."

Hollypaw privately thought Berrynose's nose was so high in the air he wouldn't be able to look at any cat. And if he knew that Honeypaw liked him, he would become even more unbearable.

"You're good enough for—" she began, only to break off as Honeypaw dashed away to meet Berrynose in the middle of the clearing.

Hollypaw sighed. They were only apprentices; surely it was

too early to think about taking a mate? She wanted to prove herself as a warrior first, to show courage in defending her Clan and skill in hunting to feed her Clanmates. She wanted to take responsibility for how her Clan was run, to make ThunderClan great for season after season. . . .

Hollypaw stood rigid, paws frozen to the ground. *Yes!* she thought. *I'd much rather be Clan leader than a nursing queen.*

For a heartbeat the strength of her ambition frightened her. Then she calmed down. There was nothing wrong with wanting to be Clan leader, if it meant she would serve her Clan with every muscle in her body and every hair on her pelt. Turning away from the fresh-kill pile, fed up with the sight of Honeypaw hanging adoringly around Berrynose, she saw her mother, Squirrelflight, emerging from the warriors' den.

Hollypaw bounded over to her. "Squirrelflight, can I ask you something?"

Her mother's ears twitched. "Sure."

"You had kits," Hollypaw meowed, "but you manage to be a warrior as well. How do you do it?"

Squirrelflight narrowed her eyes, and for a moment Hollypaw thought she saw something flash in their green depths, some emotion she couldn't understand. But her mother's voice was even as she asked, "Why do you want to know that?"

"I was just wondering. . . ." Hollypaw felt awkward. "I just feel like every cat expects she-cats to have kits, and I'm not sure I want that. I want to be a warrior."

To her annoyance, Squirrelflight's tail curled up in amusement. "Don't try to plan so far ahead!" her mother meowed.

"StarClan already has your path marked out, and there'll be twists and turns in it that you can't possibly expect."

"But—"

"Look around you," Squirrelflight went on. "Plenty of she-cats have kits and then return to the warriors' den."

But do they become Clan leader?

"Don't worry about it," Squirrelflight finished, resting her tail-tip on her daughter's shoulder. "Just concentrate on your training."

That doesn't help, Hollypaw thought frustratedly. *That doesn't help me at all.*

Hollypaw returned from hunting to find the Clan beginning to gather in the middle of the clearing. Firestar was standing on the Highledge, his flame-colored pelt blazing in a ray of sunlight.

Hollypaw carried her prey across to the fresh-kill pile. "What's going on?" she asked Cloudtail, who was sharing a thrush with his mate, Brightheart.

"Icekit and Foxkit are going to be apprenticed," Brightheart replied.

"And about time, too," Cloudtail muttered. "They frightened my fur off the other day, yowling that ShadowClan was attacking us."

His mate gave him a gentle prod with one forepaw. "Kits are kits, Cloudtail. You know they'll be good warriors one day."

His only reply was a snort.

Hollypaw looked around for the other apprentices. Honeypaw was sitting close to Berrynose, who was ignoring her and talking to Birchfall instead. Jaypaw appeared from behind the bramble screen at the entrance to the medicine cats' den, and a heartbeat later Leafpool joined him. Hollypaw took a paw step toward them, but she felt awkward about joining them in case they were discussing medicine cat business.

Poppypaw and Cinderpaw were sitting near Sandstorm and Graystripe, and as Hollypaw glanced around she spotted Lionpaw emerging from the apprentices' den to find a place next to them. Hollypaw bounded across.

Ferncloud emerged from the nursery with Foxkit and Icekit. Dustpelt followed; the brown tabby warrior looked ready to burst with pride.

The kits' eyes were bright with excitement, and their glossy pelts shone in the sunlight. Both of them were trying hard to be dignified, but halfway across the clearing Icekit gave a little bounce; her father caught up to her and flicked her over the ear with his tail. After that she managed to walk calmly until she and her brother reached the front.

Firestar bounded down the tumbled rocks from the Highledge and called both kits to stand in front of him. "Squirrelflight," he began, "your time for an apprentice is long overdue. You will be mentor to Foxpaw."

Squirrelflight stepped out of the crowd, her head and tail held high. As she padded toward Firestar, Foxkit ran up to meet her.

"Squirrelflight, the whole Clan knows your courage and

loyalty," Firestar continued. "Do your best to pass these qualities on to Foxpaw."

Foxpaw reached up to touch noses with Squirrelflight, and the two cats withdrew to the side of the hollow.

Squirrelflight's a mentor now, Hollypaw told herself. *And she had kits. It* is *possible to do both.*

Firestar's gaze rested on a young white she-cat. "Whitewing, you too are ready for your first apprentice. You will be mentor to Icepaw."

Eyes glowing with happiness, Whitewing padded over to her apprentice. They touched noses and followed the other new apprentice and his mentor to the side of the clearing. The rest of the Clan began to crowd around, congratulating them and calling the apprentices by their new names.

Hollypaw noticed that Berrynose and Birchfall stayed where they were.

"Huh!" Birchfall exclaimed, loud enough for the cats around him to hear. "I don't know why Firestar picked Whitewing. I'd be just as good as her at mentoring."

"Firestar picks the best cat for the job," Sandstorm told him as she walked past. "Whitewing is older than you. And don't forget she could have been made a warrior much sooner, but she asked to put it off so *you* wouldn't be the only apprentice."

Birchfall muttered something Hollypaw didn't catch.

"You'll have an apprentice soon," Sandstorm assured him. "For once the Clan has plenty of kits."

Birchfall didn't dare complain any more, but he still looked discontented. Berrynose whispered something in his ear, and the two young toms moved away with their heads close together.

Hollypaw sighed. She didn't know what had gotten into Birchfall lately. He used to be good fun; he had been made a warrior so recently that he still remembered what it was like to be an apprentice. *Now he's being as much of a pain in the tail as Berrynose,* she thought.

By the time Hollypaw got close enough to congratulate the apprentices, the cats were drifting away to get on with their duties. Hollypaw felt a touch on her shoulder and turned to see her mentor, Brackenfur.

"Firestar wants us to do the evening patrol with him," the golden tabby tom mewed. "Are you ready?"

"Sure."

Hollypaw's heart began to race and she felt every hair on her pelt rise with excitement. Apprentices didn't often go on patrol with the Clan leader. This was her chance to show Firestar what she had learned! Twisting her neck, she gave her shoulders a few swift licks. She would have liked to give herself a thorough grooming, but there wasn't enough time. As Firestar padded over to join her and Brackenfur, she just hoped her fur wasn't sticking up and she hadn't collected any burrs in her pelt.

"Let's go," the Clan leader meowed. "We need to renew the scent markers along the ShadowClan border."

The sun was going down as Hollypaw followed the two toms through the thorn tunnel and into the forest. Scarlet light washed over the ground, barred with the long shadows of trees. Only the wind rustling in the branches broke the silence, along with the faint scuffling of prey in the undergrowth.

Hollypaw ignored the enticing prey-scents; this wasn't a hunting patrol. She concentrated on looking and listening, and when she tasted the air it was to make sure that there were no unusual scents—especially not the scent of ShadowClan warriors on ThunderClan territory.

Firestar halted. "Listen!"

Hollypaw froze, ears straining. Her neck fur bristled when she heard, faint in the distance, the yowls and shrieks of fighting cats.

"That way!" Firestar mewed, sweeping his tail around to point. "Come on!"

He bounded off through the ferns with Brackenfur hard on his paws. Hollypaw raced after them. Grass brushed her belly fur and brambles clawed at her pelt as she sped past. The noise of squalling and spitting grew louder.

For a heartbeat she lost sight of her leader as the cats rounded a hazel thicket. She heard Firestar yowl, "Stop!" Bursting into the open, she halted at the top of a bank. Below, in a hollow lined with bracken, five cats writhed viciously. Powerful scents of ShadowClan and ThunderClan flooded over her. Horrified, Hollypaw spotted Berrynose's cream-colored pelt and Birchfall's tabby one. The two ThunderClan warriors were clearly outmatched by the three hefty ShadowClan cats.

Hollypaw sprang forward, eager to help her Clanmates,

only to find Firestar's tail barring her way.

"No," he mewed. "That's ShadowClan territory."

Hollypaw dug her claws into the ground as she stared down at her Clanmates. What were Berrynose and Birchfall doing in another Clan's territory? Opening her jaws to draw in air, she picked out both ThunderClan and ShadowClan scent markings, faint and mingled together. She realized she was standing right on the border.

Raising his voice again, Firestar repeated, "Stop!"

To Hollypaw's relief, the cats sprang apart. She recognized Russetfur, the ShadowClan deputy, with warriors Oakfur and Rowanclaw, who gave Birchfall a last cuff around the ear before facing Firestar.

"What's going on here?" Firestar demanded.

"I could ask you the same thing," Russetfur retorted. "Why are your warriors trespassing on our territory?"

"We *know* why," Oakfur added, with a lash of his tail. "ThunderClan never cared about boundaries."

"That's not—" Hollypaw began to protest, but Brackenfur slapped his tail across her mouth to keep her quiet.

Firestar's gaze raked over Berrynose and Birchfall. Though his voice was quiet, it was cold as the lake in leaf-bare, and Hollypaw realized that he was furious. "Well?" he asked.

Berrynose scrambled to his paws and gave his pelt a shake. He was bleeding from one ear, and several clumps of his fur had been clawed out. "We didn't know it was ShadowClan territory," he defended himself. "You should tell these warriors to renew their scent markers."

"I don't tell warriors of another Clan to do *anything*," Firestar responded, while Russetfur bristled with rage. "Berrynose, Birchfall, if you had checked carefully, you would have noticed the scent markers up here."

Berrynose looked furious; he couldn't excuse himself by contradicting his Clan leader.

"We're sorry, Firestar," Birchfall meowed, hanging his head.

"The markers are faint," Firestar acknowledged. He glanced at the other cats. "Ours and ShadowClan's."

"We're the evening patrol," Oakfur put in. "We're here to renew the scent markers."

"And then we found ThunderClan warriors on this side of the border," Rowanclaw added. "They were stealing prey."

"Is that true?" Firestar demanded.

Birchfall nodded; Hollypaw was glad to see he looked thoroughly ashamed of himself.

But Berrynose didn't seem to realize how much trouble he was in. "I was stalking a mouse," he explained, "until *they* came along and frightened it off."

"A good thing they did," Firestar commented. "Russetfur, I'm very sorry this has happened. They are inexperienced warriors, and I'm sure they'll be more careful from now on."

"I hope you'll punish them," Rowanclaw mewed sharply.

"Of course I will," Firestar replied.

"I'm glad to hear it."

Hollypaw jumped as another voice joined the conversation. A few fox-lengths deeper into ShadowClan territory, fronds of bracken parted to let Blackstar push his way into the open. The powerful white tom stalked past the trespassing warriors and up the bank to confront Firestar. His neck fur bristled and one of his huge black forepaws tore at the grass.

"Greetings, Blackstar." Firestar dipped his head. "I'll make sure my warriors understand they must never cross your border again."

"It was a mistake!" Berrynose protested.

A low growl came from deep in Blackstar's throat. Hollypaw half expected him to attack Firestar.

But when he spoke, he sounded tired and despondent rather than hostile. "We never should have come here, Firestar. StarClan was wrong to bring us, when it's so hard to tell where one territory ends and the next begins. It was a lot simpler back in the forest."

Firestar's eyes clouded. "But the forest is *gone,* Blackstar," he meowed softly, and suddenly they were like two old friends sharing memories rather than leaders of rival Clans. "I miss it as much as any cat, but we have to make our life here now. Besides, StarClan brought cats to the old forest, just as they brought us to the lake."

"No, they didn't!" Blackstar's neck fur, which had begun to lie flat, bristled up again. Hollypaw wondered what was making him so edgy; it seemed like something more than finding another Clan's cats on his territory. "All the cats of StarClan once lived in the forest, so there must have been a group of ancient cats living there before they divided up into Clans."

Ancient cats! Hollypaw's paws began to tingle. Where had

those cats come from, to settle in the forest? And what about the cats who settled here by the lake? Cats whose paw prints had left marks at the Moonpool and who had something to do with the underground tunnels where they found the Wind-Clan kits. She knew that Jaypaw hadn't told them everything when they escaped from the flooding river. She shivered, suddenly aware of seasons beyond seasons leading up to this moment, raining down like leaves in leaf-fall and stretching back into an unfathomable darkness.

"Are you okay?" Brackenfur murmured into her ear. "This is going to end without any more clawed fur, don't worry."

Hollypaw straightened up. "I'm fine!"

Blackstar stepped back with a curt nod to Firestar. "Take your warriors away," he growled. "And don't think they'll get off so lightly if we catch them on our territory again."

"Believe me, they're not getting off lightly." Firestar's voice was grim. He beckoned with his tail for Birchfall and Berry-nose to climb the slope. Berrynose stalked across the border, his eyes narrowed in fury, but Birchfall paused and dipped his head respectfully to Blackstar.

"We're very sorry," he meowed. "I promise we won't do it again."

"See that you don't," the ShadowClan leader retorted. He turned to his own warriors. "Carry on with your patrol," he snapped, before vanishing back into the bracken.

While the ShadowClan cats renewed their scent markers, Firestar led the two young warriors a couple of tail-lengths from the border.

"Go back to camp. Wait for me underneath the Highledge."

"Yes, Firestar," Birchfall mewed.

He and Berrynose disappeared around the hazel thicket. Berrynose cast an angry glance back at his Clan leader, but Firestar had turned away and didn't see.

"Let's finish this patrol," Firestar meowed. "And make sure the scent markers are clear this time."

Hollypaw followed as he led the way into the bracken along the top of the hollow. She thought of the strange, almost nostalgic mood between the two leaders when they had talked about the forest. Blackstar felt they didn't belong here because it wasn't where their ancestors had lived. But some cats had lived here, a long time ago—so where were they now?

Chapter 4

Hollypaw slipped out under the brambles that sheltered the apprentice den. Gray clouds moved sluggishly across the sky and she could scent rain on the breeze. Shivering, she sat down, licking one paw and rubbing it over her face.

The dawn patrol was just leaving; Dustpelt was in the lead, with Mousewhisker, Sandstorm, and Honeypaw. Ferncloud popped her head out of the nursery, sniffed the air, and disappeared inside again. A heartbeat later, Birchfall and Berrynose appeared from the elders' den, each carrying a huge wad of moss.

Hollypaw's tail curled up in amusement. *Good! Firestar put them back on apprentice duties.* She watched them cross the camp and vanish into the thorn tunnel. "Make sure you squeeze all the water out of the fresh moss!" she called mischievously. "Mousefur will claw you if her pelt gets damp!" Berrynose lashed his tail as he entered the tunnel, but neither of them stopped to reply.

A thin drizzle set in as the rest of the camp began to stir. Lionpaw scrabbled out of the apprentice den behind Hollypaw, still looking half asleep, and blundered across the camp to the dirtplace tunnel. Brackenfur and Stormfur emerged from the warriors' den and headed for the fresh-kill pile.

Hollypaw jumped up and bounded over to her mentor. "Are we going hunting?"

Brackenfur shook his head. "All the prey will be in their holes. Maybe later."

But Hollypaw's paws were itching to be doing something. She didn't want to spend the morning hanging around the camp. "Can I go out by myself, then?" she asked.

"If you want," her mentor replied. "Stay away from the borders, though. We don't want any more trouble like yesterday."

"I'll be careful," Hollypaw promised.

"And be back by sunhigh," her mentor added. "We'll have a training session."

"Sure." Hollypaw dashed off.

As she prowled away from the stone hollow, senses straining for any sign of prey, the rain grew steadily heavier, pattering on the leaves, filling every dip in the ground with water. Each branch and tussock of grass was loaded with droplets that soaked Hollypaw's fur as she brushed past. She started to think that Brackenfur had been right, and she wouldn't catch anything, but for once that didn't bother her too much. She wanted to be out of the camp, and she wanted to think.

Everything seemed to be getting much more complicated. She needed to concentrate on her training, but her mind was continually tugging her one way or the other—to the future and wondering if she could ever be Clan leader, or to the past and the traces of those ancient cats. She saw herself standing on the Highledge, calling a summons to her Clan. . . .

Hollypaw realized she had stopped concentrating on prey. She was just standing in the forest, getting wetter and wetter. Flicking drops from her ears, she dived into a hole in a sandy bank and crouched there, watching the hissing screen of rain a mouse-length from her nose. Her tongue rasped over her fur in an effort to dry herself off and get warm. She froze when she heard a scuffling from farther down the hole where she was sheltering. Something big—at least as big as she was—was coming up the tunnel behind her. *Stupid!* she scolded herself. She had been so wet, she hadn't bothered to check if she had the burrow to herself.

She tensed her muscles and took a gulp of air, expecting to taste fox or even worse, badger. Instead, the scent of cat flooded into her jaws. And it was a familiar scent, too. Limp with relief, Hollypaw twisted around in the entrance to the hole.

"Jaypaw! What are you doing down there?"

Her brother squeezed into the sheltered space beside her. His pelt smelled of earth and stale fox. "Nothing," he mumbled. "Sheltering."

"No, you're not!" Hollypaw was annoyed that he was so obviously lying. "Your fur is dry. You must have been here since before the rain started." When Jaypaw didn't reply, she added, "You've been trying to get down into the tunnels again, haven't you?"

Jaypaw's paws scuffled the sandy earth. "What if I have?"

"It's dangerous!" Hollypaw protested. "Think what

happened to Lionpaw when the roof of that badger set fell in. And remember what it was like in the cave. We nearly drowned. And—"

"I know all that," Jaypaw interrupted.

"You're not acting as if you do. It's raining hard now. The tunnels will flood again. And you just stroll down there as if you were strolling into camp! Honestly, Jaypaw, I don't know how you can be so mouse-brained."

"You don't have to go on," her brother grumbled. "Anyway, I couldn't get in. This is just an old foxhole. It doesn't lead anywhere."

"But you tried." Why couldn't Jaypaw see the trouble he was getting into? "I don't see what's so special about the caves. There's nothing down there."

"Yes, there is!" He crouched in front of her; his blue eyes gazed up at her so intensely that Hollypaw could hardly believe he was blind. He hesitated, twitching his ears, then went on. "The ancient cats spoke to me. When I go to the Moonpool my paws slip into their paw prints. And I used to hear their voices on the wind. But since we rescued the kits, I haven't heard them. That's why I *have* to get back into the tunnels."

Hollypaw stretched her neck forward and gave Jaypaw a sympathetic lick on his ear. She couldn't bear to hear the sorrow in his voice; he sounded as if he had lost something precious.

Jaypaw jerked his head away. "You don't understand."

"Explain it to me, then."

Jaypaw hesitated. His forepaws traced spirals in the earth. "There were other cats in the caves," he mewed at last.

Hollypaw was puzzled. "What do you mean?"

"Spirits of the ancient cats who lived here seasons ago. One of them is called Fallen Leaves. He went down there in the ceremony to make him a warrior, and he never came out. He showed me where to find the lost kits."

Every hair on Hollypaw's pelt rose. The ordeal in the caves had been bad enough without the thought of invisible cats watching them.

"The other cat is called Rock," Jaypaw went on. "He's old—I mean, *really* old. He was in the cave. He showed me that we would escape, and he helped me think of the way to do it."

Hollypaw took a deep breath. Perhaps there was nothing to be afraid of. If Jaypaw was right, then neither they nor the kits would be alive if it weren't for the help of the ancient cats.

"Why do you want to go back now?" she asked.

"I want to know why they don't talk to me anymore," Jaypaw mewed miserably. "Besides, they lived here once, too. They might be able to tell us the best places to hunt or shelter."

"We can find those things for ourselves." Hollypaw looked out of the mouth of the burrow. The rain had stopped; above the trees ragged patches of blue were opening up as the last of the clouds scudded across the sky. Sunlight sparkled on raindrops, making the whole forest shimmer. "We should get back to camp," she added.

"But don't you understand?" Jaypaw's voice rose. "It's important, I know it is."

For a moment Hollypaw was tempted to agree with him. When Blackstar had mentioned the ancient cats, she too had felt their fascination. She would like to know more about them—but not enough to risk her life or Jaypaw's.

"You're important too," she mewed. "Your Clan needs you, Jaypaw. You shouldn't put yourself in danger when there's no need."

"All right," Jaypaw muttered. He had a mutinous look on his face. Hollypaw stifled a sigh; she knew that look well. Jaypaw might agree with her now, but he would go on doing exactly what he wanted. She gave him a nudge. "Let's go."

Jaypaw rose to his paws and shook loose earth off his pelt. Hollypaw led the way into the open, setting down her paws carefully to avoid the worst of the wet grass.

"Hollypaw?"

She halted and glanced over her shoulder. "What?"

"You won't tell any cat what I just told you?"

Hollypaw wasn't sure how to reply. She wanted to go straight to Firestar or Leafpool and tell them about his crazy obsession with cats that died out long ago. If any cat could stop Jaypaw from risking his life, it would be his Clan leader or his mentor. But Jaypaw was her brother, and she would always be loyal to him first.

"No, I won't." She sighed. "I promise."

"Mouse dung!" Hollypaw let out a cry of frustration as she leaped for the mouse, only to see it dart away from her claws and slip into safety down a hole. That was the second piece of prey she'd lost; she was starting to feel as if her paws didn't belong to her anymore.

"Hollypaw, you've got to put your paws down *lightly*." Brackenfur never lost his temper with her, but even he was sounding impatient. "Remember that a mouse will feel your paw steps before it hears you or scents you."

"Yes, I know," Hollypaw mewed. *That's the first thing an apprentice learns about hunting.* "I'm sorry."

Brackenfur, Brook, and Stormfur had taken all the apprentices into the forest for a hunting session. Hollypaw wasn't sure which of them had suggested making it into a competition. Lionpaw was winning, with one of the biggest squirrels Hollypaw had ever seen, but all the others had amassed a good pile of fresh-kill. All she had managed to catch was one miserable shrew.

"Is there anything bothering you?" Brackenfur asked. "You're just not concentrating today."

"No," Hollypaw lied. "I'm fine."

I would be, she told herself, *if I wasn't worrying about wanting to be Clan leader. Just because that's what Tigerstar wanted doesn't mean it's wrong, does it? I know I'm his kin, but I'd never do what he did to gain power. And what about Jaypaw? If he gets himself killed looking for those ancient cats, it'll be my fault!*

Brook touched her nose sympathetically to Hollypaw's ear. "I had a lot of trouble when I first came here," she admitted. "I was used to hunting on bare mountain slopes, and I couldn't get the hang of how to hunt in the forest. One thing Stormfur taught me is that sometimes it helps to slide your paws forward while you're stalking. That way a mouse can't feel your paw steps. Like this," she added, rubbing her paws softly over the moss.

"I never thought of that," Hollypaw meowed. "I'll give it a try."

"It's important to stay away from long grasses and fern, too," Brook went on. "If you brush against them, the moving shadow will scare off the prey."

Hollypaw nodded; she had known that, but with everything else on her mind she had forgotten.

"You'll soon get the hang of it again," the tabby she-cat assured her. "You'd be a great hunter in the mountains, because you have strong back legs for leaping."

"You need to leap when you're hunting?" Cinderpaw asked, padding up to listen.

"Yes. Here in ThunderClan, you mostly catch birds on the ground. But in the Tribe, we jump up to catch them when they're taking off or landing." A hint of pride tinged Brook's voice. "We catch hawks like that, and sometimes even eagles."

"How big are the eagles?" Lionpaw joined them. "Do they ever carry cats away?"

"Most of them aren't strong enough to take a full-grown cat." Brook sat down with her tail wrapped over her paws, while the rest of the apprentices clustered around to listen. "They might be able to take kits or to-bes, but kits stay in the cave with their mothers, where it's safe. And all the hunting patrols have at least one cave-guard with them."

"What's a to-be?" Poppypaw demanded.

"And what's a cave-guard?" Honeypaw added.

"You're to-bes," Brook explained, sweeping her tail around to indicate all the apprentices. "Young cats who are learning the skills you need to be warriors. Cave-guards are, well, cats who guard the cave. They're strong and trained to fight off hawks and eagles. Stormfur was a cave-guard when he lived with the Tribe, and I was a prey-hunter."

Hollypaw was puzzled. "Do you mean that cats have separate duties? You don't hunt *and* fight, like Clan cats?"

"No," Brook replied. "When kits are born, our leader chooses what they'll be. The biggest and strongest become cave-guards, and the fast, nimble ones become prey-hunters."

"So you can't choose for yourself? I wouldn't like that," Lionpaw mewed.

"It feels different when you grow up with it," Brook assured him.

Lionpaw didn't look convinced, but before he could say any more, Poppypaw broke in. "Tell us about your leader, and your medicine cat. Does StarClan choose them?"

Brook shook her head. "The Tribe of Rushing Water doesn't know StarClan," she explained. She waited until the shocked gasps had died down. "The Tribe of Endless Hunting walks our skies. We don't have a leader *and* a medicine cat. In the Tribe, one cat is both. He's called the Healer, and his name is Teller of the Pointed Stones."

"Or Stoneteller," Stormfur put in, padding up to sit beside his mate.

"What a weird name!" Poppypaw exclaimed.

Her sister Honeypaw gave her a nudge. "Don't be so rude! Tribe names are different from ours, that's all."

"Stoneteller has his den just off the main cave behind the waterfall," Stormfur explained. "It's full of pointed stones, rising up from the cave floor and hanging from the roof. There's a hole in the roof, and when it rains the floor is covered with pools of water. Stoneteller looks at the reflections in the water and reads signs there."

"And he's a medicine cat as well?" Hollypaw meowed. *That's a lot of power for one cat!* "Does he have a deputy?"

"No, but eventually he'll have a to-be—an apprentice," Brook told her. "The Tribe of Endless Hunting will send him a sign so that he can choose a tiny kit who will become Stoneteller after him."

Hollypaw felt a pang of envy. How much simpler it would be to have your life planned out! She wouldn't have made her earlier mistake of choosing to be a medicine cat when she was really best suited to be a warrior. Sometimes her head had ached with the effort of learning all the different herbs. Training to be a warrior was tough as well, but it didn't feel like such an impossible task. There were fighting moves and hunting moves and all the details of the warrior code that had to be memorized. And if she wanted to be Clan leader she would have to learn the intricate relations between Clan and Clan, how to be diplomatic with her own warriors and the cats of other Clans, and how to react in a crisis.

She remembered watching Firestar on the border the day before. She had been impressed by how calm the ThunderClan leader had stayed, even when his own warriors were clearly at fault. That was the kind of leader Hollypaw wanted to be, one who relied on the warrior code to keep the peace instead of dragging her Clan into an unnecessary battle. A leader who wasn't selfish or greedy, who put the good of her own Clan above everything, but still remembered the rights of the other Clans in the forest.

"I think there's a mouse under the roots over there." Stormfur broke into her thoughts, pointing with his ears to the bottom of a nearby beech tree. "Why don't you see if you can catch it?"

"Okay."

The other apprentices scattered, keeping well away from the beech tree to give Hollypaw the best chance. Whiskers quivering, she tasted the air. *Vole, not mouse,* she decided. A heartbeat later she spotted it, a plump creature scuffling among the debris under the tree. She began to creep forward, sliding her paws over the moss in the way Brook had shown her. The vole seemed not to notice her at first, but as she dropped into a crouch, ready to pounce, it froze for a heartbeat, then darted away.

Hollypaw let out a yowl. Her first pounce brought her to the spot where the vole had been; instantly she leaped again and trapped it between her front paws just before it slipped into the safety of a crack between two rocks. She killed it with one blow of her paw.

"Well done!" Brackenfur meowed.

A warm feeling of triumph flooded Hollypaw from ears to

tail-tip. She picked up her prey and turned back to her mentor.

"See what I said about your strong back legs?" Brook reminded her, touching Hollypaw's shoulder with the tip of her tail. "That was a great leap!"

"I think that's enough for one day," Brackenfur added. "Let's carry the prey back to camp. The Clan will eat well tonight."

As Hollypaw followed him back to the clearing, carrying her vole and the shrew, she kept casting sidelong glances at Brook. She must love Stormfur a lot to give up everything she knew and come with him to a strange place and a strange way of life.

Curiosity bit at her, sharp as a fox's fangs. She wanted to visit the Tribe and see how cats lived when they knew right from the start what kind of life they would have and what their responsibilities would be.

But they're so far away! Hollypaw let out a sigh. *I don't suppose I'll ever travel as far as the mountains.*

Chapter 5

Cool night air whispered through Jaypaw's fur. Up above, he knew the half moon would be floating in a clear sky. His mentor, Leafpool, padded beside him, following the stream that divided WindClan's territory from ThunderClan's.

Jaypaw's belly was churning with anticipation. Would Rock speak to him at the Moonpool? The thought that he might encounter only the cats of StarClan made his tail twitch with impatience. StarClan wasn't important, after all. They were only Clan cats who had moved on to a different place. The prophecy had said he would have the power of the stars in his paws. That must mean that he would be more powerful than StarClan, so why should he waste time walking with them in his dreams?

He needed to go further back, to find the ancient cats who had once gathered at the Moonpool. They must be the truly powerful cats, who would help him find his destiny.

It's Lionpaw's and Hollypaw's destiny, too. Jaypaw did his best to ignore the small voice niggling at the back of his mind. His brother and sister would have to find their own source of power. He had been chosen to be a medicine cat, so this must be the right way for him alone.

"Leafpool, wait for us!"

The distant call came from WindClan territory. Leafpool halted, and Jaypaw waited by her side. Tasting the air, he picked up the scents of three cats: Barkface and Kestrelpaw, and Willowpaw, who must have met up with the WindClan cats on her way from RiverClan.

"Where's Mothwing?" Leafpool asked anxiously as the other medicine cats caught up. "She's not ill, is she?"

"No, she's fine," Willowpaw replied. "But Beechfur has an infected bee sting, so Mothwing thought she'd better stay in camp and look after him."

Huh! Jaypaw thought. *And hedgehogs fly!* He could guess why Mothwing wasn't with her apprentice. The infected warrior was just an excuse. Mothwing didn't have any connection with StarClan. She must have decided that she could get a good night's sleep in her own den instead of trekking all the way up to the Moonpool to have it there.

"Hello, Jaypaw," Willowpaw mewed. Her voice was cool and polite.

"Hi, Willowpaw." *Okay, I know you don't like me. I'm not all that besotted with you, either.*

"Hi, Jaypaw." Kestrelpaw sounded more friendly. "How's the prey running in ThunderClan?"

"Fine, thanks," Jaypaw replied.

Before he had to think of anything else to say, he caught the strong ShadowClan scent of another cat bounding up behind them.

"I thought I'd missed you," Littlecloud panted.

"We would have waited for you," Leafpool mewed.

The cats set off for the Moonpool. Jaypaw felt Kestrelpaw padding along at his side. "Hey, Jaypaw," he began, "what's it like, being blind?"

Well, you can't see, mouse-brain! Jaypaw felt his neck fur bristling at the stupid question. "Everything's dark. But I can hear and scent okay, so that's how I find my way around."

"That's really tough."

The other apprentice's sympathy made Jaypaw flex his claws. From the sound of his voice and the whisper of his paws on the moorland turf, he had a pretty good idea where Kestrelpaw's ear was. *How would you like it slashed, huh?*

"I manage," he retorted.

Quickening his pace, he caught up to Littlecloud; his paws itched to run on ahead but that would draw too much attention to the fact that he walked here in his dreams—when he could see. He couldn't wait to get to the Moonpool.

But after he had paced down the spiral track, feeling his paws slip into the paw prints of those long-ago cats, after he had touched his nose to the water and settled himself comfortably, Jaypaw found it hard to sleep. All around the pool he could hear the other cats' breathing sink into the rhythmic patterns of dream-sleep, while he stayed obstinately awake.

"Come *on,*" he muttered. "What's the matter with you?" For once he didn't want to enter the others' dreams. He wanted a dream of his own: to wake underneath the hill, in the tunnels where he had met Rock and Fallen Leaves. If he didn't manage it now, it would be a whole moon before he had another chance to visit the Moonpool.

He closed his eyes, willing sleep to come, but he could still feel the damp rock under his paws and hear the sound of the waterfall and the breathing of the cats around him. Stretching his jaws in a yawn, he opened his eyes again. His fur prickled with excitement as he realized that he could see.

Instantly his ears twitched in frustration. He wasn't in the underground cave. Instead, he had never left the Moonpool. He could see the curled-up bodies of his companions and reflected starlight glimmering in the water.

"Now what?" he demanded.

A quiet voice spoke behind him. "You wanted to speak with me?"

Jaypaw spun around, almost tripping over his own paws. Rock stood in front of him. His long, twisted claws scraped on the bare rock. Here in the open, out of the shadows of his cave, his bare skin looked raw and painful, and his bulging eyes glowed silver in his disfigured face. With an unexpected quiver of fear, Jaypaw wondered if Rock could see him or if he only sensed his presence.

"Why did you stop talking to me?" Jaypaw asked. "I tried and tried, but you wouldn't answer."

Rock dismissed the question with a flick of his ratlike tail. "I'm here now," he rasped. "Say what you have to say."

"Are you part of StarClan?"

Rock blinked. "No. I share tongues with the ones who came before."

"You mean the cats like Fallen Leaves, who went into the

tunnels to prove themselves?"

"No." Rock's voice grated like shifting stones. "More ancient even than those."

"Then where did they come from?" Jaypaw meowed, exasperated. "Is there a set of ancestors who are older than all the others? Did we all come from them—Fallen Leaves's cats, and the Tribe cats, and the Clans?"

Rock turned his silver gaze on Jaypaw. "There will always be stories older than any cat remembers," he rumbled.

That's not an answer! "Then where did *you* come from?"

The old cat stood silent for many heartbeats, staring out across the Moonpool as if he could look back across the abyss of time that separated Jaypaw from those ancient cats.

"You will find your answers in the mountains," he murmured at last. "Though they may not be the ones you most want to hear."

"What do you mean? Tell me now!" Jaypaw insisted.

But Rock was beginning to fade. The patches of reflected moonlight on his skin, the silver gleam of his bulging eyes, thinned out like mist until Jaypaw could see nothing but the shimmer of starlight on rock and water. He shivered in a sudden cold breeze.

"Come back!" he yowled.

There was no reply. The starshine faded, and scents of tree and bracken filled his mouth. He was standing in a dusky forest, in the midst of fern and grasses. Moonlight dappled the ground as it shone through gaps in the branches above his head. The air was warm, full of the tempting scents of prey.

Just ahead of him, Leafpool was following a narrow path that wound between clumps of bracken. She paused and glanced back over her shoulder. "I wondered if you'd join me," she mewed.

Jaypaw was about to reply when the bushes just ahead of Leafpool rustled and a group of StarClan cats burst out into the open. Jaypaw spotted prey scurrying away from their claws.

A blue-furred she-cat halted briefly to mew, "Greetings, Leafpool." Leafpool dipped her head, but the she-cat bounded onward before she could speak. Another cat, a powerful white tom, gave Jaypaw a friendly flick over the ear with his tail as he sped past.

Most of the StarClan warriors were intent on their prey. Their eyes were bright with delight in the hunt; their pelts gleamed and their muscles rippled in the moonlight. Jaypaw watched as each cat pounced on its prey and turned to race away with the limp body dangling from its jaws. He supposed they were taking it to some starry fresh-kill pile.

Leafpool padded up to him and touched her nose to his shoulder. "You see the silver tabby over there?" She pointed with her tail to where a beautiful she-cat was leaping to catch a plump vole. "That's Feathertail. She was Stormfur's sister. She died in the mountains."

Jaypaw gazed curiously at the cat, wondering if she knew anything about the mountain cats' ancestors.

"Can we talk to her?"

"She might not wait for us," Leafpool replied. "She'll want

to take her prey back to the StarClan camp."

"I want to ask her—" Jaypaw broke off as Feathertail bounded away. But she didn't follow the other StarClan cats; she headed in a different direction, where the trees and bushes were thicker. "Where is she going?"

"I don't know." Leafpool looked troubled. "Feathertail, wait!"

She set off after the silver tabby, and Jaypaw raced along at her side. They plunged through dense undergrowth and came out into a clearing. A stream ran through it, and on the other side the trees gave way to rocky slopes covered in stunted bushes.

"Feathertail!" Leafpool called again.

The she-cat paused on the bank of the stream and looked over her shoulder at them.

"Where are you going?" Leafpool panted, dashing up to her.

Feathertail set down her vole. "This fresh-kill is not for StarClan," she explained. "I bear a responsibility to other cats, ones who still need the help of the Clans, even though many moons have passed."

Other cats?

Leafpool touched her nose to Feathertail's ear. "Are you talking about the Tribe of Rushing Water? Haven't you done enough for them? You gave your life to save them from Sharptooth!"

"A shared past counts for a lot," Feathertail replied, her blue eyes glowing with emotion. "Even if it was brief."

She pressed her muzzle against Leafpool's, then picked up her prey, leaped lightly across the stream, and was swallowed up in the shadows under the bushes.

Mouse dung! Jaypaw thought. *I never got to ask her anything.*

Letting out a faint sigh, Leafpool headed back into the trees. As Jaypaw followed her, he picked up a silver glimmer in the corner of his eye. Glancing around, he spotted Rock, crouched under a bush. The ancient cat's sightless eyes gazed straight at him; then he heaved himself to his paws and padded off in the direction Feathertail had taken.

Jaypaw shivered. Somehow, StarClan, the ancient cats, and the Tribe of Rushing Water all seemed to be merging to shape the destiny of the cats by the lake. It made sense to Jaypaw. To have the power of the stars in his paws, he would need to have power over all the ancestors, past and present. Shadows pressed around him as he plunged into the undergrowth again. The lush forest scents faded away, and he felt rock beneath his paws. He could hear the gentle splash of the waterfall and knew he was crouching once again beside the Moonpool. He opened his eyes on darkness.

Around him he could hear the other cats waking from their dreams. They said little, and Leafpool didn't speak to him at all as they climbed the spiral path and set off across the moorland, back toward the lake. Jaypaw could feel her anxiety like a swarm of stinging insects.

He waited impatiently for the other cats to say their goodbyes and head off toward their own territories. As soon as he and Leafpool were alone, he demanded, "What do you think your dream meant? Are you going to tell Firestar?"

Leafpool hesitated, and when she spoke her voice was troubled. "It sounds as if the Tribe of Rushing Water is in some sort of trouble," she replied. "I'm not sure whether I should tell Firestar. Whatever's happening, it doesn't seem as if ThunderClan cats will be affected."

Jaypaw twitched his tail in frustration. How could he discover his destiny if his mentor was going to pretend she never had the dream? "What about Stormfur and Brook? If there's something wrong in the mountains, they should be told."

"I don't know." Her mew was soft and uncertain. "You could be right. Yes, perhaps I should tell Firestar. But ThunderClan isn't involved, so I don't think he'll do anything."

ThunderClan might be more involved than Leafpool realized, Jaypaw thought, as he followed his mentor along the border stream toward the camp.

At least I'm *involved!*

He bared his teeth as if he were about to snap up a juicy piece of prey. There was only one way to discover the truth about his power. Somehow, he would have to find a way to go to the mountains.

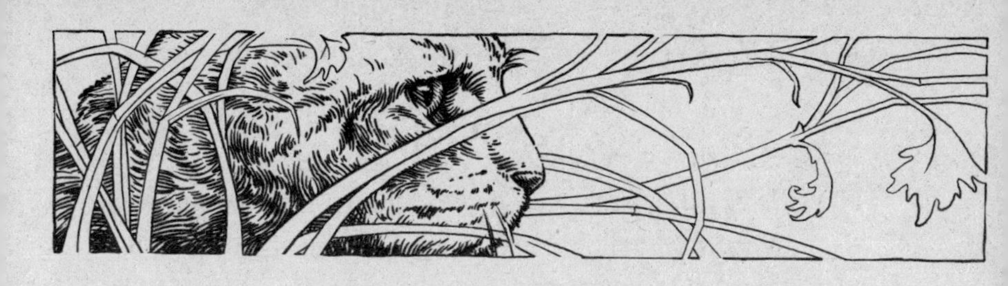

Chapter 6

Poppypaw dived forward; Lionpaw could see she was trying to use the move he had taught her in their earlier training session, the one Tigerstar had shown him. But when she tried to hook out Honeypaw's legs from under her, Honeypaw was too fast. Leaping backward, she met Poppypaw head-on and delivered two blows to her nose before darting away.

"You'll need to be quicker than that," Berrynose meowed.

Lionpaw bristled. Firestar had released the two young warriors from their apprentice duties, but didn't Berrynose have anything better to do than interfere in the training session? He was sprawled on a rock at the edge of the clearing, making loud comments on the apprentices' performance.

"That was very good," he remarked condescendingly to Honeypaw. "Your moves are coming along nicely."

"Thanks, Berrynose!" Honeypaw blinked adoringly at the cream-colored warrior.

Lionpaw stifled a twinge of jealousy. Not long ago, Honeypaw had seemed to like him best. It was hard to lose her admiration so soon after he had been forced to give up his friendship with Heatherpaw.

"Your turn, Lionpaw!" Berrynose broke into his thoughts. "Let's see what you can do."

Who made you my mentor? Lionpaw glanced around the clearing for Ashfur, who should have been in charge of the training session, but he was several fox-lengths away, demonstrating a move to Hollypaw.

"Come on, you lazy lump," Berrynose urged him. "You'll never get to be a warrior sitting on your tail all day."

No? Lionpaw gritted his teeth. *If I looked at you, I'd think that's all warriors do!*

"Come on, Cinderpaw," he meowed, beckoning with his tail to the gray apprentice who sat at the side of the clearing. "Let's practice."

Cinderpaw bounced up to him, her fur bristling with eagerness and her tail fluffed out. She was moving confidently, Lionpaw thought, as if the leg she had injured felt fine. As she approached, she aimed a blow at his ear with sheathed claws. He dodged to one side and tried to unbalance her by butting his head into her shoulder, but Cinderpaw stayed on her feet and wrapped her forepaws around his neck, thrusting him to the ground. Lionpaw battered at her belly with his hind paws. After a few heartbeats Cinderpaw let go and sprang away from him, waiting for him to get up again.

"That was great!" he panted. He knew he would have won eventually.

Cinderpaw was glowing with pride that she was getting her fighting skill back again. "Let's try again!"

"You know, Lionpaw, you got that move all wrong,"

Berrynose interrupted. "You should never have let her knock you over. If that had been a real fight, she could have bitten your throat out."

Lionpaw spun around to face him; hot fury flooded through him from ears to tail-tip. "I suppose you found that out when you were fighting ShadowClan," he taunted.

Berrynose sprang off the rock, his ears flattened and his neck fur standing on end. "Don't talk to a warrior like that!" he spat.

"Then stop being such a know-it-all!" Lionpaw retorted. "You're not my mentor, so stay out of my fur."

For two mousetails he would have hurled himself at Berrynose and raked his claws across the cream warrior's muzzle. But he knew he would be in big trouble if he attacked a Clanmate for real, not as part of a training bout. Turning his back on Berrynose, he stormed off to the side of the clearing, where he stood with his flanks heaving, trying to control the waves of rage that surged through him.

"Just wait till I'm a warrior," he vowed under his breath. "Then I'll show you who's best at fighting."

"Take it easy, Lionpaw." The calm voice felt like a draft of cool water. At first Lionpaw thought it must be Tigerstar, and he looked around for the shadowy tabby figure. Instead, he spotted Stormfur sunning himself in a quiet patch of sunlight at the foot of an oak tree.

Awkwardly Lionpaw dipped his head to him. "Sorry," he mewed. "But I can't stand it when Berrynose acts like he's Clan leader."

Stormfur let out a sympathetic murmur.

"I know I shouldn't let him get to me, but I can't help it," Lionpaw confessed. "Sometimes it's the other apprentices too. Well, not Hollypaw, but the rest of them. I feel like I have to be the best all the time."

Part of him was horrified that he'd blurted all that out to a senior warrior. There was no reason for Stormfur to care about his problems.

"Why?" the gray-furred tom asked.

"I don't know why!" Lionpaw hesitated, thoughts battering his mind like a storm, then added, "I suppose I *do* know, really. It's because I'm Firestar's kin. There's never been a leader like him, and every cat will expect me to be just as good because I'm related to him."

"And Tigerstar?" Stormfur prompted.

Lionpaw dug his claws into the ground. How could Stormfur possibly know about his meetings with Tigerstar and Hawkfrost? "T-Tigerstar?" he gulped.

Stormfur blinked at him. "I know what problems your father had. Brambleclaw was always afraid the Clan would never trust him, because they hated Tigerstar so much."

Lionpaw had never thought of that before. It was hard to imagine his father as a young cat, uncertain of his place in the Clan.

"What was my father like?" he asked, padding up to Stormfur and sitting beside him in the comforting splash of sunlight. The fur on his shoulders began to lie flat again; he had almost forgotten the quarrel with Berrynose. "What was it like when you went on the quest together?"

"Terrifying." Memory glowed in Stormfur's amber eyes, fear and courage, humor and friendship, all at once. "I don't know what was harder—traveling through unfamiliar, dangerous territory, or trying to get along with cats from other Clans. We all came back changed." He paused to rasp his tongue over his shoulder, and then went on. "At first we seemed to argue all the time. But it was usually your father who had the best ideas, and pretty soon we realized that he was the natural leader among us."

"Tell me what happened," Lionpaw prompted.

"Four cats, one in each Clan, had a dream telling them to go to the sun-drown-place," Stormfur began. "They were supposed to listen to what midnight told them. None of us realized that Midnight was a badger."

Lionpaw nodded; he and his littermates had never met the badger who helped the Clans find their new home, but his mother had told them stories about her.

"It must have been really hard," Lionpaw mewed, trying to imagine getting along with cats from other Clans. Okay, he'd been friendly with Heatherpaw, but suppose he'd had to cooperate with Breezepaw or warriors from ShadowClan?

"It wasn't all bad," Stormfur replied. His tail curled in amusement. "There was the time your mother got stuck in a Twoleg fence. She was spitting with fury, and she couldn't move!"

Lionpaw let out a little *mrrow* of laughter, imagining Squirrelflight stuck and furious. "Did my father rescue her?"

Stormfur shook his head. "No. Brambleclaw was thinking about digging up the fence post, and I thought we might bite through the shiny fence stuff. Meanwhile Tawnypelt and Feathertail smoothed down your mother's fur with some dock leaves and got her out that way."

"I wish I'd been there," Lionpaw mewed.

"I wouldn't have missed it. Even though we were scared a lot of the time, or tired, or hungry, we all knew we were doing our best to help our Clans."

"And you became really good friends with my father."

Stormfur twitched his whiskers. "We weren't all that friendly to begin with. I was jealous of Brambleclaw."

"Why?" Lionpaw asked, surprised.

"Because I liked your mother too much. But a blind rabbit could have seen that Brambleclaw was the cat she liked best, even though they spent most of their time arguing."

"You liked Squirrelflight?" Lionpaw blinked in astonishment. Suppose Stormfur had been his father instead of Brambleclaw? *I would have been a different cat. . . .*

"I'd never met a cat like her," Stormfur admitted. "So bright and brave and determined, even though she was only an apprentice then. But then we stayed with the Tribe in the mountains, and when I met Brook I knew that she was the right cat for me."

His amber eyes clouded and he fell silent. Lionpaw couldn't understand why he should look like that, when he'd been talking about finding Brook. "What's the matter?"

Stormfur let out a long sigh. "My sister, Feathertail, was

with us on the journey," he explained. "She was a beautiful, warm-hearted cat. She died in the mountains."

Lionpaw dared to reach out with his tail and rest it on the gray warrior's shoulder. "What happened?"

"The Tribe was being hunted by a mountain lion. There was a prophecy that a silver cat would come to save them. At first they thought it was me, but it was Feathertail. She died saving them." His voice shook. "I had to leave her there, buried in the mountains."

"I'm so sorry," Lionpaw mewed, trying to imagine what he would feel like if Hollypaw died.

Stormfur licked his chest fur a few times and jerked his head as if he was shaking off a fly. "Moons pass, and you have to carry on."

"I hope you didn't mind my asking."

"Of course not." Stormfur sounded more like himself again. "You can ask me anything you like. If I can help at all, I'll be glad to."

"Thanks." Lionpaw felt as warm and comforted as if he'd just eaten a plump piece of fresh-kill. "It's easier talking to you than to a ThunderClan cat—oh, sorry." He broke off, scuffling his paws with embarrassment. "I didn't mean—"

"That's okay," Stormfur meowed. "I know what you meant. It's true that I'm only a visitor here, however loyal I feel toward Firestar and your father and the other ThunderClan cats."

"Where do you feel most at home?" Lionpaw mewed curiously. "In RiverClan, or with the Tribe of Rushing Water, or in ThunderClan?"

Stormfur didn't reply at once. His eyes grew thoughtful; he licked one paw and drew it over his ear a few times. "I'm a RiverClan cat at heart," he replied at last. "That's where I grew up and where I became a warrior. But that was back in the forest, and no cat has a home there now. Right now I feel loyal to ThunderClan, because you welcomed me and Brook. And it's good to live in the same Clan as Graystripe and get to know him better."

"Will you stay here forever?"

"I don't know. This isn't Brook's home, and if she doesn't want to stay, I won't force her."

"Why don't you go back to the mountains, then?"

A somber look crept into Stormfur's eyes. "It's not that easy."

"You could go for a visit," Lionpaw suggested.

"No, it's too far," Stormfur mewed briskly. He rose to his paws and gave his fur a shake. "Come on, it's time we were going back to camp."

Glancing over his shoulder, Lionpaw saw that the training session was over. Ashfur and the other apprentices were heading toward the stone hollow. There was no sign of Berrynose.

"You go ahead," he meowed to Stormfur. "I'll be back in a while."

"Okay." Stormfur bounded off to catch up with Ashfur and the others.

"Thanks, Stormfur!" Lionpaw called after him.

Stormfur waved his tail in reply as he vanished into the bushes.

Lionpaw turned and padded into the trees in the opposite direction from the camp. He paused to make sure that Stormfur really had gone, then picked up the pace until he was racing toward the WindClan border. Panting, he halted at the edge of the stream, looking across the open moorland. The sun was going down, washing the surface of the lake with scarlet and throwing his long shadow to one side. Lionpaw enjoyed the warmth of its rays and the gentle breeze that ruffled his fur.

But the landscape ahead of him looked bleak and unwelcoming. There was no cover, no soft moss, no undergrowth where prey could hide. Lionpaw knew he could never live in WindClan. He would miss the trees: He could hear them now, just behind him, the faint creak of branches and the rustle of their leaves in the wind. He could never have given that up, however much he loved Heatherpaw.

And she could never have lived in ThunderClan, he realized. She felt trapped under the trees; she loved the open moorland, the tough, springy grass and the wild dash across the slopes in pursuit of rabbits. Stormfur must really have loved Brook, to give up his home and stay with her in the mountains.

Lionpaw raised his head and gazed into the distance. He could just make out a dark, misty band on the horizon, where the mountains lay. Brook had pointed it out to him once, on a border patrol; he wondered if she felt her paws tugging her toward it.

What do the mountains look like? he wondered. All his life he had heard about the Great Journey and the territories the

Clans had crossed to find their new home by the lake.

Lionpaw felt his paws itching to explore. He longed to discover what lay beyond ThunderClan's borders, beyond all the Clans' borders. The world was so wide, and he had seen so little of it. There was so much out there, beyond the reach of the warrior code, beyond the knowledge even of the medicine cats and elders.

It was hard to wrench his paws away from the border and start padding back toward the camp. *It's as though the mountains are calling me. . . .*

But how could he ever answer the call? . . .

Chapter 7

"I've got a plan," Hollypaw announced. She and Cinderpaw had cleared the old bedding out of the elders' den and were clawing fresh moss from around the roots of an oak tree. Shreds of mist drifted among the trees, while overhead the sun was struggling to break through a covering of cloud.

Cinderpaw stopped with her claws deep in the soft green covering. "What plan?"

"It's about becoming a warrior." Hollypaw left the ball of moss she was gathering and padded over to sit on a twisted root beside her friend. "It's so confusing, learning about fighting and hunting and all the stuff about the warrior code. I can't think of everything at once, so I'm going to concentrate on one thing at a time."

Cinderpaw blinked. "I don't get it."

Hollypaw sighed; it seemed straightforward enough to her. "I'm going to start with hunting. If a Clan isn't well fed, it can't defend its borders and fight battles. I'll practice and practice until I'm really good at it. Then I'll go on to something else."

Her friend started clawing up the moss again. "I think that

sounds mouse-brained," she mewed. "I mean, you can't stop doing everything else, can you? Are you going to leave me to finish the bedding while you go off looking for prey?"

Hollypaw swiped out a paw, claws sheathed, just missing Cinderpaw's ear. "No, of course I'm not. I know I'll have to do duties and training sessions and all that. But I'm going to *concentrate* on hunting."

Cinderpaw let out a faint snort of amusement. "I'd like to hear what Brackenfur has to say if he thinks you're not *concentrating* on fighting."

Exasperated, Hollypaw snagged up a bit of moss and tossed it at her friend. She expected Cinderpaw to toss some back at her, but instead the young she-cat stopped what she was doing and looked up at her, blue eyes serious.

"Honestly, Hollypaw, I don't think this is a good idea. Being a warrior means you have to do everything together. You can't put stuff in order. I know I'm not explaining it very well, but—"

"No, you're not," Hollypaw snapped, then stopped herself. Cinderpaw was her best friend, and she didn't want to quarrel with her. "Sorry, Cinderpaw," she went on. "I just think this will be a way that will work for me. You don't have to join in if you don't want to."

Cinderpaw reached up to touch Hollypaw's nose with her ear. "It's okay. And you know I'll help if I can."

By the time Hollypaw and Cinderpaw had finished refreshing the elders' bedding, Thornclaw and Brackenfur were gathering the apprentices together in the middle of the clearing.

"Are we hunting?" Hollypaw asked eagerly.

It was Thornclaw who replied. "No, Cloudtail and I are taking our apprentices to the mossy clearing for some advanced battle training. You and Lionpaw can come along and watch."

"And join in if you want to," Brackenfur added.

Cinderpaw gave an excited little bounce. "Let's go!"

Her mentor, Cloudtail, padded up behind her and flicked her on the shoulder with his tail. "You be careful of that leg. If I'm asking too much of you, I want to know."

Cinderpaw's excitement faded. "My leg's fine, Cloudtail. It won't hold me back from being a warrior, will it?"

"I hope not. We'll have to see," was Cloudtail's discouraging response.

Hollypaw pressed her muzzle against Cinderpaw's. "Don't worry. You *will* be a warrior. I just know it."

Ashfur came padding over with Lionpaw from the apprentices' den. "Are we all ready?" the gray warrior asked. "Where's Honeypaw?"

"Sandstorm took her on a hunting patrol," Brackenfur replied. "She'll join us later."

The clouds had cleared away and the sun was burning up the mist. In the shadow of the trees the grass was still laden with dew. Hollypaw brushed past a clump of fern and flicked her ears as droplets fell on her head. The undergrowth was full of exciting scents and sounds; she longed to put her plan into practice on a hunting patrol, instead of going to a training session when she would have to spend most of her time watching.

With four apprentices and their mentors, the clearing was crowded. Hollypaw sat in a sunny spot at one side with Brackenfur. Lionpaw and Ashfur were a couple of tail-lengths away. Hollypaw tried to hide a yawn as Cloudtail and Thornclaw demonstrated a move to the two older apprentices: Cloudtail leaped into the air with a twist so that he came down on Thornclaw's shoulders.

"Now you try," he invited Cinderpaw.

Cinderpaw crouched to face her mentor and launched herself into the air. She got the twist right, but she hadn't leaped high enough, so instead of landing on Cloudtail's shoulders she blundered clumsily into his side, and he pinned her down with one paw on her chest.

"Not bad for a first try," he commented, letting her get up, "but you need more strength in that leap. Is your leg bothering you?"

Cinderpaw blinked. "No, it's fine. I'll get it right next time."

"And don't forget," Thornclaw added, "in a real fight your enemy won't stand still and wait for you to land on him. You've got to anticipate his next move."

"Let me have a try," Poppypaw meowed.

As the training session went on, Hollypaw noticed that Lionpaw was fidgeting. "*I* can do that," he told Ashfur. "Can I try it?"

Ashfur hesitated. "It's advanced stuff," he pointed out. "There's no point in trying before you're ready."

"I *am* ready," Lionpaw insisted, his fur starting to fluff up.

Ashfur shrugged. "Don't say I didn't warn you."

Hollypaw watched nervously as Lionpaw and his mentor moved out into the clearing, well away from the other practice session.

"Go on, then, show me," Ashfur mewed.

Lionpaw leaped into the air, sunlight turning his golden pelt to flame. With all four paws off the ground he twisted and came down perfectly balanced on Ashfur's shoulders. Ashfur let out a grunt of surprise, while Hollypaw stared in astonishment. How had Lionpaw learned how to do that move so perfectly?

"See?" Lionpaw challenged his mentor as he leaped to the ground. "*Now* will you be a bit tougher on me?"

"You want tough?" There was the hint of a growl in Ashfur's voice, and his blue eyes gleamed. "Be careful what you wish for, Lionpaw."

Hollypaw felt the fur on her shoulder begin to rise. Was Ashfur joking?

"I can cope with anything," Lionpaw insisted.

Ashfur leaped on Lionpaw, landing a hard blow on his ear. Lionpaw rolled to one side, raking his hind paws down Ashfur's flank. A heartbeat later he was back on his paws, leaping into the air and landing on his mentor's shoulders in the move Cloudtail had just demonstrated. Ashfur reared up on his hind paws, shaking off Lionpaw; Hollypaw winced at the thud as her brother hit the ground. Instantly his mentor jumped on top of him and the two cats wrestled together in a screeching tangle of fur, rolling closer to the other apprentices.

Poppypaw had to dodge to one side to avoid them. Thornclaw curled his tail around her shoulders and drew her to the side of the clearing. Cloudtail and Cinderpaw joined them, their training session forgotten as they stared at the furious battle.

Ashfur was fighting as if Lionpaw was a warrior—but so was Lionpaw! Hollypaw watched in amazement as he bit down on Ashfur's tail, then jerked it hard so that Ashfur was unbalanced and fell on his side. She'd seen Berrynose and his littermates practicing that move just before they were made warriors; she hadn't expected to learn it for at least another moon.

Hollypaw stiffened as she saw flecks of scarlet on Ashfur's gray pelt. Lionpaw would get into big trouble for fighting with claws unsheathed! Then she noticed that her brother was bleeding, too. Ashfur's blue eyes were blazing with fury, as if he'd forgotten this wasn't a real battle.

"They're hurting each other!" She turned to Brackenfur. "Can't you make them stop?"

Before Brackenfur could do anything, Ashfur launched himself on top of Lionpaw and held him down with both forepaws on his chest. "Was that tough enough for you?" he panted.

But Lionpaw wouldn't give in. He went on battering at

Ashfur's belly with his hind paws, twisting from side to side in an effort to throw off the heavier cat. Ashfur raised his paw, aiming a blow at Lionpaw's ear.

"That's enough." Brackenfur bounded forward, his voice sharp with shock. "Ashfur, let him up. Lionpaw, sheathe your claws. This bout is over."

Ashfur turned his head to glare at Brackenfur. The blaze in his blue eyes faded and he stepped back. Lionpaw scrambled to his paws, while Brackenfur thrust himself between them in case the fight broke out all over again. Lionpaw's chest heaved as he fought for breath. The fur on one shoulder was torn and blood was welling out of the scratches; Hollypaw could see the marks of Ashfur's claws down his side.

But Ashfur was bleeding too, from one ear and a hind leg. After a heartbeat to catch his breath, he meowed loudly, "Well done, Lionpaw. You fought like a warrior." Looking around, he added, "I hope the rest of you were watching. You should all be trying to be as good as Lionpaw."

Cinderpaw and Poppypaw exchanged glances; they both looked too shocked to say anything. Even Hollypaw couldn't bring herself to congratulate her brother. The way the practice session had turned savage had disturbed her.

"Come on." Ashfur beckoned to Lionpaw with his tail. "That was so good, you don't have to do any more training. We'll go back to camp, and you can have first pick of the fresh-kill pile."

"Thanks, Ashfur!" Lionpaw was recovering now, his breathing easier and his fur beginning to lie flat again.

"I'll tell Firestar, too," his mentor added. "ThunderClan will have a warrior to be proud of when you finish your apprenticeship."

Lionpaw's amber eyes glowed. He padded off beside Ashfur with his head and tail held high. No cat spoke until they had disappeared into the undergrowth, heading for the camp.

Then Cloudtail puffed out his breath as if he'd been holding it. "Right. Let's see what the rest of you can do."

"Are you going to fight us like that?" Poppypaw asked nervously.

It was Brackenfur who replied. "Certainly not." His fur was still ruffled, Hollypaw could tell, either by the ferocity of the fight or by how well her brother had fought. "We'll just go on practicing the techniques. And we'll *all* keep our claws sheathed."

Hollypaw joined in, but she found it hard to concentrate. She could still see in her mind the blaze of rage in Ashfur's eyes, as if he'd forgotten he was fighting his own apprentice.

When the training session was over, Hollypaw ran back to camp ahead of the other apprentices. She wanted to make sure her brother was okay.

She found Lionpaw asleep in their den, half buried in a nest of moss and bracken. He was breathing deeply and didn't stir when Hollypaw padded up and sniffed the wound on his shoulder. The bleeding had stopped; dried blood was crusted around the scratches and the fur was torn loose and bloodstained. Obviously he hadn't been to Leafpool to have the wound checked out.

"Mouse-brain," Hollypaw murmured affectionately.

Lionpaw still didn't stir as she rasped her tongue over his shoulder until the wound was clean. It wasn't surprising that he was exhausted. Hollypaw touched her nose gently to his ear and left him to sleep. Pushing her way out through the brambles, she spotted her father by the fresh-kill pile.

"Hi," Brambleclaw meowed. "I'm getting a hunting patrol together. Do you want to come?"

Earlier that morning Hollypaw would have jumped at the chance, but now she had more important things on her mind. "There's something I have to tell you," she began, launching into the story of Lionpaw's fight with Ashfur. "I don't think Ashfur should have pushed Lionpaw that hard," she finished. "I thought they were going to tear each other apart!"

Brambleclaw let out a soothing purr. "You don't need to worry. I met Ashfur in the forest, and he told me all about it. He's really pleased with Lionpaw." His eyes narrowed, half in amusement, half embarrassment. "He told me Lionpaw's going to make a warrior like his father. I assume that was a compliment."

Hollypaw raked her claws in the ground in frustration. "But you didn't see it," she protested. "It was really scary."

Brambleclaw's tail-tip flicked. "Fighting *is* scary," he pointed out. "If we have to fight another Clan, they won't sheathe their claws."

"But we're not fighting another Clan *now*."

"Sooner or later there will be a battle, and we have to be

ready for it. One day Lionpaw will need all his skills. I'm proud of him. I'm proud of all my kits: Lionpaw is a brilliant fighter, Leafpool tells me Jaypaw knows all the herbs already . . ."

"And what about me?" Hollypaw asked, trying to push down a pang of jealousy. *Aren't I special too?*

Brambleclaw leaned over to give her ear a comforting lick. "You're my little thinker," he purred. "I rely on you to make the best decisions—and to keep your brothers in line!"

Hollypaw brightened. That was a skill she would need if she was ever to be Clan leader.

"Good," Brambleclaw mewed. "Now, what about this hunting patrol?"

"But *why* can't Berrynose come?" Honeypaw complained.

"Because he's the most annoying furball in the forest," Hollypaw muttered through gritted teeth, though not loud enough for her friend to hear her.

Sandstorm and Honeypaw had joined Brambleclaw and Hollypaw on the hunting patrol. Honeypaw hadn't arrived at the training session until it was almost over, and she had kept trying to tell every cat how much better Berrynose could perform the fighting techniques. Now Hollypaw was finding it hard to sense prey, because her fellow apprentice was still meowing on about the cream-colored warrior.

"Berrynose was on the dawn patrol," Sandstorm explained, with more patience than Hollypaw could have mustered. "He deserves a rest."

"But we'd catch much more if he was with us," Honeypaw insisted. "He's a *brilliant* hunter."

"Well, we'll just have to do the best we can without him," Sandstorm mewed.

Hollypaw thought that Honeypaw must have missed the sarcastic edge to the ginger she-cat's tone. She just kept on babbling about Berrynose until Hollypaw wanted to wrap her tail around her friend's muzzle to keep it shut. Exasperated, she ran ahead a little way, trying to get out of range of Honeypaw's voice.

Sunhigh was just past. Golden rays warmed Hollypaw's fur, while her paws padded through cool, lush grass. The trees were thick with birdsong and the air was laden with fresh green scents. She bounded forward until the sound of the patrol had faded behind her. At the top of a rise, she halted. Ahead of her, trees grew closer together, the spaces between them choked by bracken and briar, and for a few heartbeats she wasn't sure where she was. She was a long way past the entrance to the tunnels, and she couldn't spot any other familiar landmarks. Then she picked up the faint sound of running water and realized that she stood at the very edge of ThunderClan's hunting territory, not far from the WindClan border.

Everything around her was peaceful, but something made Hollypaw's fur prickle with apprehension. Her paws were tugging her to run back and find the rest of the patrol. *You're not a kit!* she scolded herself. *This is ThunderClan territory. There's nothing to be afraid of.*

She would go back, she decided, but she would catch a piece of prey first, just to prove to herself that she wasn't a coward who ran away from nothing. She raised her head and opened her jaws to draw in a long breath.

Cat scent! Hollypaw tasted it carefully, wondering if WindClan was trespassing on ThunderClan territory again. But it wasn't WindClan scent. It wasn't any cat scent Hollypaw had encountered before. Had a group of rogues invaded the territory?

"Are you okay?"

Hollypaw let out a long breath of relief at the sound of her father's voice. She turned to see Brambleclaw padding up to her, his powerful shoulders brushing through the bracken. Sandstorm and Honeypaw followed a little way behind.

"I'm fine," Hollypaw replied, trying to hide how the strange scent had spooked her. "I can scent cats, but it's not any scent I know."

Brambleclaw tasted the air, then glanced sharply at Sandstorm, who was doing the same. The ginger she-cat took a pace toward him and murmured something in his ear; Brambleclaw nodded. His amber eyes looked troubled.

"Run back to camp, as fast as you can," he meowed to both apprentices. "Tell Firestar to send more warriors."

"But not Stormfur or Brook," Sandstorm added.

Hollypaw couldn't understand the urgency in the warriors' voices. The tension in their fur crackled like greenleaf lightning.

"What is it?" Honeypaw asked. "What's the matter?"

"We can't leave you here if there's danger," Hollypaw protested.

"Just do as you're told!" Sandstorm snapped.

"There's no danger," Brambleclaw added quietly. "But we need more warriors. Go *now*."

Hollypaw and Honeypaw exchanged one scared glance and pelted back through the forest toward the camp. Fear made Hollypaw's fur stand on end, and her heart thudded with more than the speed of her running.

"Firestar!" she yowled as she thrust her way through the thorn tunnel. "Firestar, come quickly!"

As Hollypaw skidded to a stop beneath the Highledge, she spotted Mousefur jerk awake from her place outside the elders' den and leap to her paws, tail lashing. Cloudtail erupted from the warriors' den, his fur bristling and his claws scraping the ground. Behind him, Brightheart and Sorreltail popped their heads through the branches, eyes wide with alarm. Daisy swept her tail protectively around her two tiny kits, who were playing in a patch of sunlight near the nursery, and herded them back inside.

Firestar emerged from his den on the Highledge. "What's going on?" he demanded.

"Strange cats . . ." Hollypaw gasped, still trying to catch her breath.

"Near the WindClan border," Honeypaw added.

"Brambleclaw said—" Hollypaw whirled around as yowling broke out behind her. More cats were tumbling through the thorn tunnel into the camp: Graystripe was in the lead, with

Birchfall and Whitewing just behind.

But that wasn't what made Hollypaw arch her back while every hair on her pelt rose and tingled. With the three ThunderClan cats were two others that she didn't recognize: a massive dark brown tabby tom and a pure black she-cat, who was smaller and skinnier than the cats of ThunderClan. Graystripe and the two younger warriors stood close around them, not allowing them any farther into the camp. As the she-cat opened her jaws to speak, Graystripe silenced her with a threatening hiss.

Hollypaw flexed her claws and let her tail-tip flick to and fro. The scent coming from the two strange cats was the same one she had picked up near the WindClan border. The scent of intruders!

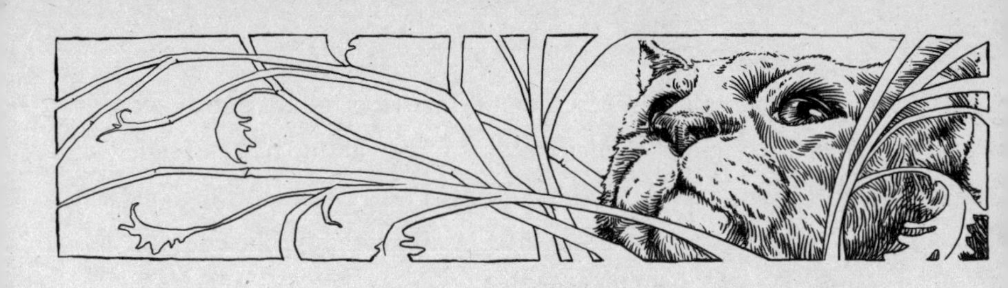

CHAPTER 8

Jaypaw stiffened at the sound of screeching from the entrance to the camp. He paused with one paw raised, a stem of watermint still snagged in his claws. "What's that?" he meowed.

Leafpool didn't reply. Thornclaw had come to see her, complaining about bellyache, and Jaypaw guessed she wouldn't notice a whole herd of badgers trampling through the stone hollow until she had finished treating her patient.

"Jaypaw, where's that watermint?" she called.

"Here." Jaypaw grabbed up more of the stems and thrust them at his mentor as he darted past the bramble screen and into the main clearing. He could hear the rustling of leaves as warriors came out of their den and the swift pattering of paws as apprentices bounded up to see what was going on. Whispers of alarm came from every corner of the clearing, and from beneath the Highledge, Jaypaw detected powerful fear-scent from Hollypaw and Honeypaw.

Graystripe was speaking, his voice raised in a fierce growl. "Not another paw step, until you tell us what you're doing on our territory."

Jaypaw's fur began to bristle as he picked up the scent of

two strange cats. It seemed as if Graystripe and his patrol had caught a couple of rogues trespassing on ThunderClan territory. Jaypaw tasted the air carefully. The scent was strong, but with a bitter tinge that seemed familiar, though he couldn't remember where he had smelled it before.

Concentrating fiercely, Jaypaw tried to pull the newcomers' feelings into himself as if he was drawing in their scent. He could sense fear, suspicion, and an overwhelming desperation. It had been difficult for them to come here, yet they'd had no choice.

They need something from ThunderClan!

Before any cat spoke, there was the sound of more cats approaching through the tunnel. It was Stormfur and Brook, with fresh-kill in their jaws.

"Talon! Night!" Brook exclaimed, dropping the vole. "What are you doing here?"

Cloudtail spoke first, his voice sharp with suspicion. "You mean you *know* these cats?"

"Firestar, these are the cats we scented near the WindClan border," Hollypaw broke in, before either of the strangers could reply. "Brambleclaw sent us to warn you about intruders."

"They're not intruders." Leafpool spoke calmly as she emerged from her den, her pelt brushing Jaypaw's. "They come from the Tribe of Rushing Water."

Firestar bounded down the rocks that led to his den. "Of course! It's Talon of Swooping Eagle, isn't it, and Night of No Stars?"

"That's right," a quiet, accented voice replied.

Jaypaw sensed the tension in the clearing begin to relax. He could make out a few murmurs of recognition coming from the older ThunderClan cats, the ones who had made the Great Journey and stayed with the Tribe of Rushing Water in the mountains.

"I knew I'd seen that black she-cat somewhere before," Dustpelt muttered.

"I wonder what they want?" Sorreltail asked; she sounded puzzled rather than hostile.

"I suppose we'll soon find out," Brackenfur replied. "It must be important, for them to come all this way."

"Stormfur, Brook." Firestar spoke again. "Bring your prey over to the fresh-kill pile. You must want to catch up with old friends."

"It doesn't look much like it," Hollypaw whispered into Jaypaw's ear; she had bounded up to him while he was concentrating on the voices. "Brook seems really upset, and Stormfur looks as if he's got a bit of crow-food under his nose."

"He just gave Brook a nudge," Lionpaw added, padding up in his turn. "She doesn't want to go near them."

Jaypaw could tell from his littermate's paw steps that he was still stiff from his wounds from the fight with Ashfur. Yet he sensed pride coming from Lionpaw, too, as if he knew he had fought well.

"They're touching noses now," Hollypaw reported softly. "But they still look as if—"

Jaypaw didn't hear the rest of what she said. Suddenly the ground lurched beneath his paws and he felt blood pounding in his ears. The stench of blood was in his nose. Scarlet light washed over him and he realized that he could see.

On every side he was jostled by fighting cats. He could hear their screeching and the slash of claws through fur. Blood spattered against his pelt, hot and sticky. Underpaw the ground was hard stone; Jaypaw's claws scrabbled on it as he tried to keep his balance. His paws were splayed across a tilted boulder, sliding slowly downward. He scrambled across a narrow crevice, barely saving himself from being trapped, then caught a glimpse of a sheer drop beneath him and nothing ahead but the open sky, stained bloodred as the sun went down.

Dizzy from the height and the fierceness of the battle, Jaypaw felt as though his paws were frozen to the rock. Where was he? This was no dream, and yet the clearing by the lake had vanished as if it had never been. He bit back a yowl of terror as the scene flickered; darkness returned, but not the unbroken night of his blindness. He was in a cave, where the noise of falling water echoed from the rocks. Moonlight shone through a glittering screen of water that covered the entrance.

Cats were sitting all around him, talking to one another in quiet, serious voices. Jaypaw could pick up their scents and recognized those that belonged to the intruders who had just arrived at the camp. They were sitting opposite him: a huge tabby tom and a smaller black she-cat. Movement at the far side of the cave caught his eye, and he spotted a muscular gray warrior rising to his paws. Scent told him that he was looking at Stormfur. *So the tabby she-cat with him must be Brook.*

Stormfur addressed a brown tabby cat who sat on a boulder at the head of a cave. "It's no use expecting these cats to leave," he meowed. "They want to settle here, and they don't care how much trouble they're giving us. We have to show them that they must respect our territory."

"And how do we do that?" another cat asked.

"Hang on, we don't *want* any other cats living near us." It was the tabby tom who spoke. "The mountains are ours."

"Not anymore, Talon," Stormfur mewed regretfully.

"We'll just have to get used to it," Brook added.

Stormfur dipped his head in agreement. "I suggest—" he began.

The brown tabby cat on the rock twitched his tail. "The Tribe of Endless Hunting has shown me nothing about this," he protested.

"Then perhaps the ancestors of these new cats walk in different skies." Stormfur's tone was respectful, but Jaypaw could sense his frustration, sharp as thorns. "The Tribe is used to driving off stray loners," the gray warrior continued, "but this is different. We have to find a different way of dealing with them."

Night, the black she-cat, leaned forward, stretching her neck to look at Stormfur. "What do you suggest?"

"Why ask him?" The question came from a skinny, speckled brown cat crouched near the rippling screen of water. His muzzle was white with age and he had lost an eye. "He's only just set paw in the mountains. What does he know about our ways?"

"That's just why we should listen," Talon snapped back at

him. "Stormfur lived where there are many other cats. He must know better than us how to deal with these strangers."

"That's right!" a cat called from the shadows.

More cats joined in, some protesting, some encouraging Stormfur, until the whole cave was filled with caterwauling. Stormfur mewed something softly to Brook, and she touched his shoulder with her nose.

Jaypaw flicked his ears. "Get on with it," he muttered. "Let him speak."

Eventually the brown cat on the rock raised his tail for silence. "We will hear what Stormfur has to say," he announced.

"Thank you, Stoneteller." Stormfur dipped his head. Turning to the rest of the Tribe, he hesitated for a heartbeat. "Where I lived in the forest," he began at last, "all four Clans knew that they had to stay out of one another's territory. Cats who trespassed would be driven out."

"And how do we do that?" the skinny elder demanded. "These intruders go where they like."

"We need a show of strength, Rain," Stormfur explained. His amber eyes glowed. "One battle should be all it takes. After that, these newcomers will either go away for good, or they'll stay well away from us."

To Jaypaw's surprise, Brook stepped forward to stand beside her mate. In the hollow by the lake, she was always quiet, but now her eyes shone and she held her tail high as she looked around at her Tribemates.

"Stormfur will teach us what to do," she meowed. "He knows battle moves these strangers can't even imagine."

"He'll likely get us all killed," the elder called Rain grumbled.

"The Tribe has lived in these mountains for seasons upon seasons," Brook insisted. "Are we going to leave, just like that?"

Several cries of "No!" came from around the cave. Almost every cat in the Tribe had risen to its paws, its pelt bristling and its teeth bared. Only a few, like the speckled brown elder, stayed where they were, glaring at their Tribemates. Amid the uproar, Stoneteller sat unmoving on his rock. Jaypaw could not read his expression or sense anything of what he felt.

Suddenly Jaypaw realized the moonlight was fading. The enthusiastic yowls of the Tribe changed to screeches of terror and fury. Icy wind ruffled his fur and he was knocked off his paws as another cat charged past him. The air was filled with the reek of blood.

Blinking, Jaypaw found himself out on the bare mountainside again. The faint light of dawn drizzled into the sky; clouds hung low over the peaks. He lay on his side on the very edge of a stream, his tail dangling in the gushing water. With a hiss of annoyance he scrambled to his paws, shaking off the icy droplets and struggling to keep his balance on the slick, wet rock.

Around him the narrow valley heaved with the bodies of fighting cats. Close by he spotted Talon, rolling over and over in the grip of a powerful silver tom, battering at the intruder's belly with his hind paws. For a heartbeat the intruder's throat was exposed, but Talon was too slow to sink his teeth in.

An apprentice could do better than that! Jaypaw thought.

A few fox-lengths farther down the valley, Stormfur jumped onto a boulder. "Leap onto their shoulders!" he yowled. "Don't let them pin you down!"

He flung himself back into the battle, raking his claws across the pelt of a tabby she-cat, then whirling to confront a muscular black tom who was shaking a small Tribe cat in his jaws as if she were a piece of prey.

Brook was close by, with Night a paw step behind her, stalking around the side of a boulder to creep up on a couple of the attackers as they would have crept up on their prey. Jaypaw gritted his teeth. The slender she-cats had never been trained to fight. They sprang bravely at their enemies, but the two invaders were almost twice their size and fought back with slashing claws.

Jaypaw was jostled aside by another pair of fighting cats, snagging his pelt on a thorny bush that grew in the crevice between two rocks. One cat fell on top of him; pushing vainly at the weight of fur and muscle, his jaws flooding with the stench of blood, Jaypaw thought at first that it was dead. Then it jerked convulsively, pulled itself to its paws, and dragged itself into the shadows behind a boulder.

Jaypaw staggered to his paws, ripping his fur as he tore himself free of the bush. Another Tribe cat fled past him, a powerful gray-black tom, his fur ripped and one shoulder soaked in blood. A black-and-white cat caught up with him, crashing into his side and flinging him to the ground.

"Slit its belly open!" Jaypaw hissed.

The Tribe cat didn't hear him. He fought with courage,

refusing to give up even when the invader slashed open a wound down the length of his flank, but he had none of the skills that would let him throw off his attacker. The invading tom bit down hard on his throat, then sprang away, leaving the limp body of the Tribe cat half in and half out of the water. His gray fur darkened as blood soaked into it.

Jaypaw caught sight of Stormfur again, at the center of a group of Tribe cats, including Talon. The gray warrior was yowling encouragement, trying to force a way through the crowd of intruders and drive them back, but the attackers flowed over them like floodwater.

"Knock them off balance!" Stormfur yowled. "Don't let them—" Whatever orders he was trying to give were lost as two of the attackers leaped at him from opposite sides; Stormfur vanished in a whirl of teeth and claws.

One by one the Tribe cats broke away, fleeing upstream toward the steeper slopes. One of them halted beside the body of the gray tom and let out a wail of grief and despair, before pelting onward and disappearing into the shadows.

"That's right, run!" The silver tabby tom bounded to the top of a boulder, jeering at the Tribe cats as they fled. "Run and don't come back!"

"Rabbits!" a brown-and-white she-cat added, leaping up to the silver tom's side. "This is our place now!"

"No—stop!" Stormfur screeched, shaking off his attackers with a spatter of blood. "We can still drive them back!"

No cat listened to him except for Brook, standing at his shoulder and begging her Tribemates to come back. Then she glanced over her shoulder and her neck fur bristled as she saw a fresh wave of intruders hurtling up the slope.

"Stormfur! It's no use!" Brook wailed. "We can't fight them all."

"You go." Stormfur's voice was a hoarse growl; he touched his mate's shoulder with his tail-tip.

"Not without you." Brook's eyes were wide with fear, but she dug her claws into the thin soil.

Stormfur let out a hiss of frustration. "Go!" He gave Brook a hefty shove with one shoulder. "Go on—I'm coming." Letting out one last snarl at the invaders, who were now barely a tail-length away, he raced upstream behind Brook.

The attackers didn't bother to chase them. They just stood watching, their eyes gleaming with triumph, until the last Tribe cat had disappeared.

Jaypaw staggered, and when his vision cleared he found himself in the Tribe's cave again. His pelt was still sticky with blood, but the noise of the battle had faded away. Silver light trembled on the cave walls as the moon shone through the falling water. The rushing of the river was the only sound.

Stoneteller was sitting on his rock, his fur ruffled and one ear dark with crusted blood. The rest of the Tribe was huddled around him. Jaypaw couldn't see one of them who didn't bear wounds from the battle. In the center of the cave several limp bodies were lying; Stormfur was stooping over one of them, and Jaypaw recognized the dark gray tom whose death he had witnessed.

"Jag," Stormfur murmured. "You were a good friend. May

you walk the mountains forever with the Tribe of Endless Hunting." He bent his head and touched his nose to the matted gray fur. Quietly Brook padded up beside him.

"Come and rest," she mewed.

But before the gray warrior could move, Stoneteller's voice rang out from the other end of the cave. "Stormfur!"

The gray tom looked up.

"Stormfur, what have you to say?"

Stormfur's eyes clouded. "What do you want me to say? The Tribe fought as well as it could have done. I couldn't hope to stand beside braver warriors. We must make another plan, so that—"

"No." Stoneteller's voice was cold. "No more plans. Not from you. We took your advice, and we were defeated. Many good cats are dead." His tail flicked once toward the bodies lying on the cave floor.

"I told you what would happen." Rain was crouched at the foot of Stoneteller's rock. "But would any cat listen?"

"I'm sorry—" Stormfur tried again.

"There is no place here for the ways of the Clans," Stoneteller interrupted. "There is no place for Clan cats in the mountains. You will bring only more death and bad luck if you stay here. You must go and never return."

"What?" Stormfur stared at him in disbelief. "You're blaming *me* for this, when I—"

"Enough!" Stoneteller snarled. "Go now."

Brook stepped forward. "Stoneteller, this isn't right. Stormfur did his best to help us. He took the same risks as every cat.

He could be lying there now, with Jag and the others."

"If we hadn't listened to him, those cats would still be alive." Stoneteller's gaze was colder than ice.

"He's right, Brook." Talon, standing beside Stoneteller's boulder, flicked his ears uneasily. "Clan ways aren't for us."

Brook's eyes widened; Jaypaw could feel the distress flooding through her as if it was his own. "But, Talon, you're my brother." Her voice quivered. "Can't you understand?"

Talon scraped at the cave floor with his forepaws. "It's what's best for the Tribe."

"Night?" Brook turned to appeal to the black she-cat. "We've been friends since before we were to-bes. We've hunted together. We fought together. Can't you see that the Tribe needs Stormfur?"

Night's green eyes narrowed. "I can see that *you* need Stormfur."

Brook's ears flattened and her jaws parted in the beginning of a snarl. "Are you saying I'm no longer loyal to my Tribe?"

Night turned her head away without answering.

"Enough of this," Stoneteller meowed. "Stormfur, you are no longer welcome among the Tribe. You must leave at once."

Brook's tail fluffed up. "If he goes, I go!" she hissed.

"Brook, be careful," Stormfur murmured.

The gentle prey-hunter's eyes were blazing. "Do you think I could stay here, after this?"

"Stormfur is right when he says you should think about what you say." Stoneteller rose to his paws, towering over the other cats from the top of his boulder. "Do you truly want to abandon your fate to this cat and his Clan? Can you trust him?"

"With my life," Brook mewed.

Stoneteller's contempt was obvious in the flick of his tail. "You have no more sense than a kit, after what this *Clan* cat has done to our Tribe."

Stormfur arched his back and hissed. "You seem to have forgotten that my sister *died* for the Tribe. If it weren't for Clan cats, every last one of you would have been eaten by Sharptooth."

Jaypaw noticed that some of the Tribe cats—Talon included—looked uneasy, but none of them spoke.

"Come on, Brook." Stormfur urged his mate toward the cave opening where the glittering water fell. "We'll go and find the Clans."

"Brook, if you leave now, you leave forever," Stoneteller warned.

Brook didn't even look at him as she and Stormfur padded away.

"Very well," Stoneteller called after them. "I shall tell the Tribe of Endless Hunting that you are both dead to the cats you leave behind."

CHAPTER 9

"Jaypaw! Hey, Jaypaw!" Jaypaw felt a sharp nudge in his side; Hollypaw's scent drifted over him, tinged with exasperation.

He lurched on his paws, confused at the sudden return to blindness and the scents and sounds of the stone hollow. Every hair on his pelt still quivered with the feelings of grief and anger and betrayal he had felt in the cave.

Brook! he thought. *I was feeling what she felt! And it wasn't a dream; I've been awake all the time. Could I have found a way into her memories?*

He drew in his breath sharply, full of excitement at the thought of a new and different power, but there was no time to explore it now.

"Jaypaw, I don't know how you can daydream at a time like this," Lionpaw mewed. "We need to listen to find out why these strange cats have come here."

Jaypaw realized that while he felt as if he had spent several days with the Tribe, here in the clearing only a few heartbeats had passed. The newcomers were still crouched beside the fresh-kill pile, along with Stormfur, Brook, and Firestar.

"I think I know why," he murmured. "And I don't think Stormfur and Brook will be too pleased to see them."

"What do you mean?" Hollypaw asked curiously. "Why wouldn't they want to see their Tribemates?"

Before Jaypaw could explain—telling the story of his experience would have taken until moonhigh—he heard the harsh voice of Talon.

"Firestar, we have come to ask Stormfur and Brook to return to the mountains. The Tribe of Rushing Water needs them."

Jaypaw felt his pelt prickling with excitement. The Tribe's rejection of Brook and Stormfur still rang in his ears. But from the ThunderClan cats he picked up nothing but a cautious interest.

"What?" Stormfur's voice was a low snarl of outrage. "How *dare* you come here and ask that? As far as the Tribe is concerned, Brook and I are dead!"

Jaypaw heard gasps of astonishment from the ThunderClan cats. "Told you," he muttered to his littermates with a shrug.

"Stormfur, I think you'd better explain." Firestar's voice was calm, but Jaypaw could tell he was concerned for the two cats who had come to make their lives with ThunderClan.

Stormfur began to tell the story of the invading cats, but Jaypaw didn't bother to listen. He had lived through it all, and he was far more interested in finding out how he had done it. *I must have been inside Brook's memories.* He tried do it again, but the tabby she-cat was concentrating on what her mate was saying and on the reactions of the other cats. Her memories were a blank.

Stormfur stopped at the sound of cats pushing their way through the thorn tunnel.

"Firestar!" Brambleclaw called out. "We scented intruders!"

"The intruders are here," Firestar replied.

Jaypaw realized that Sandstorm and Squirrelflight were with Brambleclaw.

"Talon! Night!" Squirrelflight meowed. "I thought I recognized Tribe scent."

"It's strange to think that our mother and father spent so much time with the Tribe," Lionpaw murmured.

"Well, we're not the only ones who can have adventures," Hollypaw purred.

"It's great to see you both again," Squirrelflight went on. "Why are you here?" She paused, then added, "And why is every cat looking as if the sky has fallen in?"

"I think you'd better hear what Stormfur has to tell us," Firestar mewed.

The gray warrior began to speak again. Having seen him in Brook's memories, Jaypaw could picture him now, strong and sleek-furred with anger smoldering in his amber eyes.

"Not long after the Clans left on the Great Journey," Stormfur meowed, "another group of strange cats came to the mountains."

"We thought at first they were only passing through," Brook explained. "We would have welcomed them as guests for a while . . ."

"But they made it clear they wanted to settle," Stormfur

went on. "They took prey from the Tribe, even hunting close to the cave behind the waterfall."

"Flea-bitten thieves," Talon growled.

"We'd never had to share our territory before," Brook meowed. "We drove out loners now and then, but we didn't know what to do about such a large group of cats."

Stormfur took up the story again. "I thought we needed a show of strength to defend our territory. And I led the Tribe cats into battle to make sure the strangers would know not to bother us or steal our prey."

"They tore us to pieces," Night mewed angrily.

"Tribe cats aren't trained to fight like Clan warriors," Stormfur explained. "We lost the battle and several cats died." He hesitated, and when he spoke again his voice was filled with sorrow. "Jag was one of them."

"Jag dead?" Squirrelflight exclaimed. "Oh, no—he helped us when we were stuck in the snow on the Great Journey."

"We'll all miss him," Brambleclaw added. "Every cat who knew him."

"Stoneteller blamed me for the deaths." Stormfur's voice sounded bitter as deathberries. "He banished me from the Tribe. Brook insisted on coming with me."

"What else could I do?" Brook murmured, as if her words were meant for Stormfur alone. Jaypaw remembered seeing them together in the cave, their pelts brushing as they defied the leader of the Tribe.

"And what else could Stoneteller do?" Talon countered. "Cats were dead; something had to be done."

"He told us we were dead!" Brook's voice, so gentle a heartbeat ago, became a furious hiss.

"I can't believe those Tribe cats dared to come here," Hollypaw whispered into Jaypaw's ear. "Not after what they did!"

"I'm so sorry, Stormfur." Brambleclaw's meow rumbled deep in his chest. "You should have told us before."

"What good would it have done?" Stormfur demanded. "You made us welcome. We're ThunderClan cats now."

Jaypaw picked up a murmur from Brook, too low for him to make out what she said. *She's not a ThunderClan cat*, he thought. *She's a Tribe cat and always will be. She's never felt at home here.*

Reaching out to her, he couldn't enter her memory again, but he sensed that her mind was full of rock and wind, of cascading water and screeching birds high in the air, the shadow of their wings big enough to cover a whole patrol.

His attention snapped back to the clearing as Talon began to speak. "We have come to ask for your help."

A swift intake of breath came from Stormfur, but he didn't interrupt.

"Stoneteller was wrong." Talon sounded awkward. "The other cats are stealing all our prey, and the Tribe is dying of hunger."

"And how is that my problem?" Stormfur asked icily.

"I understand how you feel," Talon meowed. "I was banished once, when I failed to kill Sharptooth, and I *know*. But—"

"It was only because of Stormfur and the other Clan cats that you were able to come back to the Tribe," Brook reminded him.

"That's true. But I was able to forgive the Tribe when I knew I could do something to help them. Besides, Brook, you're my sister, and I miss you. I want you to come home. You may live under the shadow of trees here, with grass under your paws, but you still belong to the Tribe."

Jaypaw heard a long sigh from Brook. "I will come back with you. I cannot let my Tribemates suffer, not if there is something I can do for them. Stormfur . . ." There was a catch in her voice. "You do not have to come. You are not a Tribe cat."

"Where you go, so do I," Stormfur told her. "That's what you said when Stoneteller banished me. Do you think I would do any less for you? I will never forgive Stoneteller for killing me in the eyes of the Tribe, but that is no reason to let your kin suffer."

"I'll go too." Jaypaw's ears pricked up in astonishment at the sound of Brambleclaw's voice. "My paw steps have been entwined with the Tribe's before. I will honor our friendship."

Jaypaw sensed Stormfur's surprise. "You don't have to do this," the gray warrior meowed.

"Yes, I do. What the Tribe needs now are strong, fit warriors. How can they defend themselves when they're weakened by hunger and constant fighting?"

"I'm coming too!" Squirrelflight sounded as if her mind was made up. "You didn't manage to leave me behind last time, and I wasn't even a warrior then."

"Firestar?" Brambleclaw asked. "What do you think? May we go?"

Jaypaw's belly tightened as he waited for Firestar's answer. He hadn't had the chance to work out what this might mean for him, yet he knew it was really important for ThunderClan warriors to go to the mountains. But Brambleclaw was Clan deputy; would Firestar let him leave the Clan?

"Yes, you may," Firestar meowed. "The Tribe gave the Clans food and shelter on the Great Journey. It is our turn to help them. It's for Stormfur and Brook, too," he added. "You've been loyal ThunderClan cats. We owe you for your help after the badgers attacked."

"Thank you." Talon's voice was husky with relief. "All the Tribe of Rushing Water thanks you for this."

Jaypaw was aware of excitement and shared purpose surging from the warriors. His paws itched to share it. But even if ThunderClan warriors were traveling to the mountains, would they ever let an apprentice join them?

Chapter 10

Every hair on Lionpaw's pelt prickled with excitement. The moment he'd longed for had come—the chance to go to the mountains! Four ThunderClan cats wouldn't be enough to deal with the invaders, not if they were as strong as Stormfur and Talon said. Surely StarClan had arranged this, so that he could go visit the Tribe and find out about them, and show them how real warriors lived.

His claws scratched the earth floor of the hollow as the walls loomed overhead, closing him in. He had never felt so confined before. The weight of stone seemed to press on his fur. He wanted to race up the nearest cliff and run through the forest, across the hills, all the way to the mountains, with the wind in his fur.

"Calm down," Jaypaw mewed. "They're hardly going to take apprentices along!"

Lionpaw rolled his eyes. "Jaypaw, I wish you wouldn't keep reading my mind."

"You mean *you* want to go to the mountains?" Hollypaw asked.

"They'll need more cats," Lionpaw pointed out, ready to

defend himself. "Four's not enough. But Jaypaw's probably right," he added, his excitement fading as he realized that what the Tribe needed was help from experienced warriors. "They won't take apprentices."

"Hollypaw wants to go, and so do I," Jaypaw announced unexpectedly. "Brambleclaw and Squirrelflight are going, so why shouldn't we see if we can go too? Even if they say no, they can't claw us just for asking."

"You really want to go?" Lionpaw meowed to Hollypaw.

She bounced to her paws, her tail fluffed out and her whiskers quivering. "I want to find out how the Tribe cats live. I've never met cats who are different from us. We could learn a lot."

Jaypaw murmured agreement, though he said nothing about his own reasons for wanting to go. But that was Jaypaw, Lionpaw reflected; he always buried his thoughts deeper than hidden prey.

"I want to know what else there is besides the forest, too," he confessed. "I know this is ThunderClan's home, but there are loads of other territories out there. What are they like?"

"Well, then, we should—" Hollypaw began, breaking off as Firestar rose to his paws.

"We need to discuss this," he meowed, "but my den is too small for all the cats who are going. Let's go into the forest." Glancing at the other cats who stood listening, he added, "Graystripe, Sandstorm, Leafpool, you come too."

Lionpaw watched as the cats headed toward the thorn tunnel. The rest of the Clan seemed reluctant to go back to their dens or return to their duties. They huddled together, their eyes doubtful.

"There's no way we should risk our own warriors to help the Tribe," Spiderleg complained, loud enough for the departing cats to hear him. "Haven't we got enough problems of our own?"

Firestar's ears flicked as if he had heard what the young warrior said, but he didn't stop to reply before vanishing down the tunnel.

"Things are pretty peaceful right now," Whitewing pointed out.

"Whitewing's right." Ashfur rose from where he was sitting between Cloudtail and Brightheart. "We can easily spare a few warriors. Brambleclaw's doing the right thing by helping the Tribe. Remember what they did for us when we made the Great Journey? We would have died in the snow if they hadn't found us."

"Well, *I* think that's all nonsense!" Mousefur stalked up to Ashfur, her skinny brown tail lashing. "If the Tribe cats can't defend their own borders, that's their problem, not ours."

Longtail padded up beside her and touched her shoulder briefly with his tail-tip. "I'd love to go back to the mountains." His voice was wistful. "I know I couldn't see where the Tribe lived, but I could feel the wide open spaces and the wind in my fur, and all the scents the wind carried from far away."

"I'd like to go back, too!" Birchfall's eyes glowed with memories. "The Great Journey was fun! I had three good friends in ShadowClan: Toadkit, Applekit, and Marshkit. I wonder how they are now."

"Who cares?" Berrynose flicked his tail; Lionpaw thought he could see jealousy in the cream warrior's eyes. "Shadow-Clan cats can't be your friends anymore. Have you forgotten how you nearly got your fur clawed off on the border?"

And whose fault was that? Lionpaw asked silently, while Birchfall looked downcast, his tail drooping.

"Anyway," Berrynose went on, "I don't see what's so great about the mountains. It sounds bare and cold up there, with no prey."

"You know nothing about it," Dustpelt rasped, narrowing his eyes. "You weren't there."

As Berrynose rudely turned his back on the senior warrior, Lionpaw beckoned with his tail for his littermates to follow him out of earshot of the group.

"That does it!" he exclaimed. "If Birchfall could travel through the mountains and survive when he was just a kit, why shouldn't apprentices go? You'd be okay too," he added to Jaypaw. "Longtail coped, after all."

He saw Jaypaw's neck fur begin to fluff up, but Lionpaw was too excited to fret about offending his brother. If Jaypaw wanted to be prickly every time some cat mentioned his blindness, that was his problem.

"We've got to find Firestar and ask him right now," he meowed. "Before Brambleclaw and the others leave." He glanced around to see if any cat was paying attention to them. By now the group of cats was beginning to break up. Cloudtail called Sorreltail and Dustpelt to go out on a hunting patrol, while the elders returned to their den. Two or three of the other warriors padded over to the fresh-kill pile and picked out prey. Outside the nursery, Daisy and Millie stretched out in the sunshine and began sharing tongues, with Daisy's kits skipping around them.

"Quick, while our mentors aren't looking!" Hollypaw urged, angling her ears to where Ashfur and Brackenfur were talking together in the middle of the clearing.

Lionpaw dived after her as she bounded across the clearing and thrust her way through the thorn tunnel. When all three apprentices were out in the forest, she turned to Jaypaw.

"Come on, you're best at scenting. Which way did Firestar go?"

The scent trail left by the Clan leader and the other cats had begun to fade, but Lionpaw could still distinguish it among the competing scents of the forest, especially the unfamiliar scent of the Tribe cats.

"You know," he mewed to Hollypaw as they followed Jaypaw through the trees, "I've just realized that Brook smells like a ThunderClan cat now. Do you think she'll be able to settle in when she goes back to her Tribemates?"

Hollypaw flashed him a brief glance. "That's for Stoneteller to say. He seems to speak for the Tribe."

"Stoneteller speaks too much, by the sound of it," Jaypaw mewed. "I'm glad Firestar isn't like that."

He led the way through the forest until Lionpaw could hear the ripple of waves on the lakeshore. The scent of cats was very strong here. Jaypaw crept quietly up to the top of a gentle rise and parted a clump of bracken carefully with one paw. Without speaking, he signaled with his tail for his brother and sister to join him.

Beyond the bracken, the ground fell away into a sunlit clearing with a soft covering of moss and leaf-mold. On the opposite side the lake was just visible between the trees. A breeze rustled through the leaves, blowing toward the three apprentices, so the group of warriors would be unlikely to pick up their scents.

Firestar was sitting in the middle of the clearing with his paws tucked under him. "Squirrelflight, you'll need to find a temporary mentor for Foxpaw," he was saying.

Squirrelflight dipped her head in agreement. "I'd like to ask Sorreltail, if that's okay with you. She's never had an apprentice, so it would be good experience for her as well."

"Sorreltail would be *great*," Leafpool added warmly.

"Fine, I'll have a word with her when we get back to camp." Firestar turned to Brambleclaw. "I'm not sure that four extra cats are going to be enough to help the Tribe. But I daren't weaken ThunderClan by sending more warriors with you."

Hollypaw nudged Lionpaw. "Maybe that's a chance for us," she whispered.

"I thought of that," Brambleclaw replied to Firestar. "I'd like to take cats from all four Clans with us. The ones who went with us on the first journey to find Midnight at the sun-drown-place."

Lionpaw pushed Jaypaw and beckoned Hollypaw with a

flick of his ears to creep along the top of the rise as far as a holly bush, where they could hide and still see and hear everything that was going on. Firestar began to speak again as they settled among the debris under the branches, their pelts brushing.

"That makes sense," Firestar meowed in reply to Brambleclaw. "The cats who've known the Tribe longest should be the ones most willing to go."

"It would be good to see Crowfeather and Tawnypelt again," Talon murmured.

"This isn't part of the warrior code," Firestar went on. "I can't ask any cat to go unless he or she already wants to—and of course I can't speak for cats in other Clans. But I believe that helping the Tribe is the right thing to do."

Lionpaw was puzzled. "If it's the right thing, why isn't it in the warrior code?"

"It *is* in the code," Hollypaw insisted. "The warrior code says that we're allowed to help other Clans in trouble. Firestar's obviously thinking of the Tribe as another Clan."

"That's decided, then," Firestar meowed. "Squirrelflight, you'll go to WindClan to ask Crowfeather, and Brambleclaw can go to ShadowClan to ask Tawnypelt."

"There's no need to go to RiverClan." Lionpaw's pelt prickled with sympathy at the sorrow in Stormfur's eyes. "Feathertail was the chosen cat, and she died in the mountains. I went with her, so I shall stand for RiverClan now."

The cats in the clearing were silent for a moment. Squirrelflight rested her tail comfortingly on Stormfur's shoulder.

"The Tribe will always honor Feathertail's memory," Night mewed softly.

Jaypaw twitched.

"This is a good plan." Talon broke the silence at last. "Stoneteller knows the five of you better than any other Clan cats, so he's more likely to trust you."

"What?" Brook's ears flattened, and she turned her head to stare at her brother. "Stoneteller did send you to fetch us, didn't he?"

Night and Talon looked at their paws; Talon's tail flicked uncomfortably. "Not exactly," he mumbled, then added, "but I'm sure he'll be glad when he knows you've come to help."

"Great." Stormfur's voice was bitter. "I get to be told I'm dead all over again."

Brook pressed her muzzle to her mate's. "Please, Stormfur, we have to do this. Stoneteller won't be the Healer forever, but the Tribe deserves to last beyond his lifespan."

"From what Talon and Night say, we don't have much time," Firestar meowed. "Brambleclaw, you can leave for Shadow-Clan right away."

"And you three can come out now." Squirrelflight rose to her paws and stared straight at the holly bush.

"Fox dung," Hollypaw muttered. "We'll end up searching the elders for ticks instead of going to the mountains."

"Come on," Squirrelflight repeated. "If you don't want to be seen, Lionpaw, don't leave your tail sticking out."

His fur hot with embarrassment, Lionpaw emerged from the bush and padded down the slope toward his mother.

"Mouse-brain!" Hollypaw hissed as she followed him with Jaypaw.

"You shouldn't have been spying," Squirrelflight mewed severely when the three apprentices were standing in front of her. "Cats who listen uninvited might hear things they don't want to."

"But we had to listen!" Lionpaw burst out. "We want to go with you!"

Squirrelflight's green eyes stretched wide in astonishment, while Brambleclaw's neck fur was fluffing up ominously. But to Lionpaw's relief Firestar blinked in amusement.

"Don't be angry with them," he told Squirrelflight. "They remind me of a certain ginger apprentice who also insisted on going on a journey when she hadn't been invited."

Squirrelflight huffed, making her whiskers flutter, and gave a single lash of her tail.

"Why do you want to go?" Firestar prompted.

Lionpaw was opening his jaws to reply when Hollypaw gave him a nudge. "We want to help the Tribe cats, too," she announced. "Lionpaw and I are good fighters, and Jaypaw . . . well, Jaypaw can help heal cats who are injured."

"Thanks a bunch," Jaypaw muttered.

"Jaypaw can do more than that," Leafpool meowed calmly. Jaypaw jumped as if he was surprised to find the medicine cat on his side.

"For what it's worth," Leafpool went on, "I think they should be allowed to go. When we lived in the forest, all the apprentices made the journey to Mothermouth, to visit the

Moonstone, before they became warriors. We seem to have left that tradition behind, but I think there's value in apprentices making a long journey, to see what lies beyond their territories."

Warmth spread through Lionpaw from whiskers to tail-tip as he heard Leafpool putting words to the longing in his own mind. "*Please* can we go?" he begged.

"I agree with Leafpool," Sandstorm mewed. "There's nothing to be lost in meeting other cats and seeing how they live." Her gaze held Firestar's for a moment as if she and the Clan leader were sharing memories.

"Brambleclaw, what do you think?" Firestar asked. "They'll be an extra responsibility, and it could be very tough for them. A long, hard journey, and fighting at the end of it."

"I'm sure my kits can manage it." There was a glow of approval in Brambleclaw's amber eyes as his gaze swept over the three apprentices. "I'd be proud to take them to meet the Tribe of Rushing Water."

"Even if we're not sure of our reception?" Stormfur reminded him softly.

No cat answered him. Instead, Brambleclaw rose to his paws. "Are you ready?" he asked Lionpaw.

"For what?" Lionpaw meowed, his paws tingling with a mixture of excitement and nervousness.

"We must go to ShadowClan and see if Tawnypelt will come with us," his father replied.

"Great!" Lionpaw couldn't stop himself from bouncing eagerly, then froze, cross that he was behaving like a stupid kit. "I'm looking forward to seeing Tawnypelt's kits. They're my kin," he added, trying to sound more dignified.

Squirrelflight glanced briefly at Leafpool. "Hollypaw, you can come with me to WindClan to find out if Crowfeather will come with us," she meowed.

"What about me?" Jaypaw asked.

"Come back to the clearing with me," Leafpool told him. "We'll need to prepare traveling herbs."

"If the other cats agree to go," Firestar mewed, "bring them back to the hollow. You can leave in the morning."

"Fine. Let's go, Hollypaw." Squirrelflight waved her tail and set off through the trees toward the WindClan border. Hollypaw darted after her, almost stumbling over her paws in her haste.

"All set, Lionpaw?" Brambleclaw asked.

Lionpaw nodded; his chest felt tight at the thought of crossing the border into another Clan's territory.

"Good luck, all of you!" Firestar called.

Lionpaw waited until Hollypaw's black pelt had vanished among the rustling bracken. Then he turned and plunged into the undergrowth, following his father.

Chapter 11

Wind whipped through Lionpaw's pelt as he raced toward the ShadowClan border. He couldn't think of anywhere he would rather be than running beside his father, with an important mission ahead and the chance to prove himself. He was proud of how he kept up with Brambleclaw; he wasn't as big, but his legs were nearly as long.

"Watch out," Brambleclaw warned. "Fallen tree ahead."

Lionpaw had already spotted it, a beech with smooth gray bark, brought down in the storms of the previous leaf-bare. A few dead leaves still clung to its branches, rustling in the breeze. Brambleclaw skirted the roots, but Lionpaw sprang upward, scrabbling with his hind paws to drag himself on top of the trunk, and pushed his way through the branches until he could leap down on the other side.

He wanted to show Brambleclaw just how fast and powerful he could be, so when a small stream crossed their path he gathered his muscles for an enormous leap and launched himself across the water. His paws stretched for a smooth flat stone on the opposite side, but just before he landed a blackbird erupted from a hazel bush just ahead, giving a raucous alarm call.

Startled, Lionpaw landed awkwardly; his hind paws slipped and cold water surged over his haunches and his tail. "Mouse dung!" he spat, his claws scoring the stone as he dragged himself out.

Brambleclaw was waiting for him on the bank, amusement glimmering in his amber eyes. "Steady on," he purred. "You're not a RiverClan cat, and we haven't time for fishing."

"Sorry," Lionpaw muttered. Glittering drops of water spun away from his pelt as he tried to shake himself dry.

As they drew closer to ShadowClan territory, Brambleclaw's pace slowed, until he came to a halt on the border not far from the dead tree.

"What are we waiting for?" Lionpaw mewed.

"A ShadowClan patrol," his father replied. "They'll escort us to their camp."

"But you *know* where the camp is," Lionpaw protested, flexing his claws in frustration. "It's not as if we're attacking them! Why can't we just go?"

"Because Blackstar won't see it like that." Brambleclaw looked down at him, serious now. "We're coming to take one of his warriors away on a long, dangerous journey, to help a completely different group of cats. He won't like it, and I can't say I blame him. Besides, the warrior code forbids us to trespass on another Clan's territory, whether we're friendly or not. We'll wait." He sat down just on the ThunderClan side of the border and wrapped his tail over his paws. "If you want something to do, you can groom that wet fur. I don't want ShadowClan thinking that ThunderClan apprentices can't look after themselves."

Lionpaw's pelt had begun to dry, the hairs clumping together in untidy tufts. He sat down and gave himself a thorough washing, stretching his neck over his back to reach every last scrap of fur. When he had finished there were still no ShadowClan warriors in sight.

"Don't they ever patrol their borders?" he grumbled, batting at a beetle that was climbing a grass stem near his nose.

Brambleclaw had settled into a crouch, his paws tucked comfortably under him and his eyes slitted, enjoying the sun. "They'll be along soon. You can hunt if you want, but make sure you stay on *this* side of the border."

Lionpaw sprang up, but before he could pinpoint any prey he heard the sound of pelts swishing through the bracken a few fox-lengths away. A ShadowClan patrol appeared from the arching fronds and stalked toward the border. Lionpaw recognized Russetfur, the ShadowClan deputy, but the other two—a young dark brown tom and a tortoiseshell she-cat—were strangers to him.

As soon as he spotted Brambleclaw and Lionpaw waiting by the border, the young tom exclaimed, "Intruders! I *knew* I'd scented them." He bounded forward, his fur bristling.

"Toadfoot, wait!" Russetfur overtook her Clanmate and padded up to Brambleclaw. "What do you want?"

"Greetings." Brambleclaw dipped his head, ignoring the deputy's hostile tone. "We're not intruding, Russetfur, just waiting for an escort to your camp. We need to speak to Blackstar."

Russetfur's whiskers twitched suspiciously. "What's so important that it can't wait until the Gathering?"

"A decision that Blackstar must make now."

The ShadowClan deputy lashed her tail; Lionpaw guessed she was furious that Brambleclaw wouldn't tell her what his business was. Reluctantly she stepped back, jerking her head to invite Brambleclaw and Lionpaw across the border.

"Ivytail, run back to the camp and warn Blackstar," she ordered. "Toadfoot, keep an eye out behind. We need to be sure that there aren't any more ThunderClan warriors lurking about."

She turned and stalked off, with Brambleclaw padding quietly at her shoulder, while Toadfoot drew close to Lionpaw, fixing him with a fierce glare. "Don't even *think* about unsheathing your claws," he hissed.

"Don't worry, I won't," Lionpaw retorted. He remembered Birchfall, back in camp, talking about his friendship with ShadowClan kits during the Great Journey. Toadkit was one of the names he mentioned; this young warrior must be the same cat.

"Do you remember Birchkit?" he asked, trying to be more friendly. "He's Birchfall now."

"So?" Toadfoot sounded just as hostile.

"He was telling us about you earlier today. He said what good friends he was with you and your littermates."

For a heartbeat he thought he saw a shadow of sadness in Toadfoot's eyes, but it was gone before he could be sure.

"That was on the Great Journey," Toadfoot meowed.

"Things were different then. I'm a ShadowClan warrior now."

Lionpaw stifled a sigh. Why couldn't you be a loyal warrior and still have friends in other Clans? He wondered if things had been better on the Great Journey, when there were no borders, so you didn't have to be enemies with other cats just because of where they lived.

But he couldn't go on thinking about that now, not when Russetfur was leading them deeper into ShadowClan territory. Lionpaw's whiskers twitched as they skirted the empty stretch of grass where Twolegs came in greenleaf. He had seen the flat green pelts they put there when he was on border patrols, but he had never set paw anywhere near them. He tasted Twoleg scent as Russetfur led them past, creeping close to the ground in the shadow of the ferns, but there was no noise of Twoleg yowling or any sign of the Twolegs themselves.

As they left the clearing behind, Lionpaw was surprised to find that the woodland on the other side looked just like ThunderClan territory. But gradually the familiar oaks and beeches gave way to tall, dark pines, with spiky shadows trapped in their branches. Birdsong echoed strangely from the narrow, leafless trunks. The undergrowth of fern and bramble thinned out until the cats were padding across ground that was bare except for a thick covering of brown pine needles.

Suppressing a shiver, Lionpaw hurried so he could catch up to Brambleclaw and walk at his side. His father flashed him a sympathetic glance and brushed his tail comfortingly across his shoulder.

At last Lionpaw began to pick up the mingled scents of many cats, coming from just ahead. Russetfur led them up a short slope and through a barrier of bushes that grew along the top.

"Wait here," she ordered.

She headed down a shallower slope into a wide hollow, while Toadfoot stayed to guard the two ThunderClan cats, glaring through narrowed eyes from a couple of tail-lengths away.

"Is this the ShadowClan camp?" Lionpaw whispered to Brambleclaw. "It looks so open."

"We're lucky to have the hollow to shelter us," Brambleclaw replied.

When he looked closer, Lionpaw began to see that this was a Clan camp very like his own, even though it looked so different. Russetfur had vanished into a gap behind a huge boulder, which he guessed was the Clan leader's den. Not far away from it was a straggly bramble thicket that was probably the apprentices' den; there was a dead log just outside it, thickly scored with scratch marks, which would be the place where the apprentices sharpened their claws.

He started at a yowl from a yew bush on the slope just below him. "This moss is dripping wet! I'll *scratch* that apprentice when I catch him!"

"The elders' den," Lionpaw muttered to his father. "I guess they're just the same everywhere."

He was distracted from his study of the camp by the reappearance of Russetfur. Blackstar followed her out of the gap behind the boulder and leaped onto a tree stump in the middle of the hollow. Russetfur gestured to Toadfoot with her tail, and the brown tom escorted Brambleclaw and Lionpaw down the slope until they stood in front of the ShadowClan leader. Lionpaw felt curious stares from the ShadowClan warriors scorch his pelt and heard the cats muttering to one another. They didn't sound friendly.

He had seen Blackstar before at Gatherings, but he had never been so close to him. Swallowing nervously, he realized that the white tom was a very powerful warrior. One swat from those huge black paws could shred a cat's ear. He wondered what Brambleclaw would do if Blackstar attacked him. Was he strong and skillful enough to fight him off and escape from the rival Clan's territory?

But for the moment Blackstar seemed calm, if not exactly welcoming. "Brambleclaw," he meowed. "What are you doing in our territory?"

"I've come to speak to my sister, Tawnypelt."

"What if she doesn't want to speak to you?" Russetfur's tone was sharp.

Blackstar raised his tail, warning his deputy to be quiet. "What do you want with her?"

Lionpaw's belly churned as Brambleclaw told the ShadowClan cats about the appearance of Talon and Night and the trouble that had come upon the Tribe of Rushing Water. "Firestar has agreed to let me and Squirrelflight go back to the mountains to help the Tribe cats," he finished. "We thought we should invite Tawnypelt and Crowfeather to come too. They know the Tribe well from the first journey we made together."

"*What!*" Russetfur exclaimed, before Blackstar could respond. "You dare to come here and expect to take one of our warriors away? Of course Tawnypelt's not going. She has kits, for StarClan's sake!"

Once again Blackstar gestured with his tail. "You'll make these ThunderClan cats think we don't want to cooperate," he told her. "Suppose we ask Tawnypelt what she wants to do? It's her decision."

Lionpaw flashed a glance at his father, but Brambleclaw avoided his gaze. It was clear that Blackstar expected Tawnypelt would decide to stay with her Clanmates and her kits.

Blackstar leaped down from the stump and led the way across the camp to a bramble thicket on the far side. "This is our nursery," he meowed. "Go in and see her."

Brambleclaw nodded in thanks and lowered his head to creep through the narrow entrance. Lionpaw followed; to his relief Blackstar remained outside.

ShadowClan's nursery was bigger than the one in the stone hollow, but it had the same cozy covering of moss on the floor and the same warm, milky smell. As Lionpaw's eyes adjusted to the dim light, he made out the glimmering shape of a white queen with a huge swollen belly, curled in a mossy nest. Her ears pricked anxiously as the two ThunderClan cats entered.

"Brambleclaw!" The exclamation came from farther inside the nursery. Lionpaw spotted Tawnypelt, her head raised and her eyes narrowed. "What are you doing here?"

"We came to see you," Brambleclaw replied. "I've got something to ask you."

Before he could say any more, Tawnypelt's kits scrambled out of their nest and bounced over to Brambleclaw and Lionpaw.

"Who are you?" The biggest kit, a tiger-striped tom, stretched up until his whiskers tickled Lionpaw's nose.

Lionpaw edged back, stifling a sneeze. "My name's Lionpaw. I'm an apprentice from—"

His father gave him a warning nudge. "We're ThunderClan cats," he replied.

"Oh, that's why you smell all yucky!" A tiny tom with dark ginger fur wrinkled his nose.

Not half as yucky as you do.

The third kit, a gray she-cat, bounded up to Lionpaw and flung herself at him; he was so surprised that he lost his balance and landed on his side in the moss.

"We're the best fighters!" the gray kit yowled. "Come on, let's defend the camp!"

Instantly the other two kits bundled on top of Lionpaw. For a heartbeat he wondered if ShadowClan was so hostile that even the kits tried to drive out intruders; then he realized that it was only a game. The kits' claws were sheathed, and their eyes gleamed with mischief, not anger. He fought back, pushing the kits off him and managing to get to his paws again, spitting out moss.

"That's no way to welcome a visitor," Tawnypelt scolded them. "Brambleclaw, these are my kits—the striped one is Tigerkit, the ginger is Flamekit, and the one who's asking for a cuff around the ear is Dawnkit." She glared at the she-cat, who was creeping up on Lionpaw's tail as if it were a piece of prey.

Tigerkit! Lionpaw stiffened. Did Tawnypelt hope that her son would become as great a warrior as Tigerstar? Would this kit receive the same training from their ancestor as Lionpaw did?

"Kits!" Tawnypelt warned her litter to behave. "Come over here, Brambleclaw, and tell me what all this is about."

Absorbed in trying to keep his tail out of reach of Dawnkit, who clearly hadn't listened to her mother's warning, Lionpaw didn't hear his father's explanation. But he stopped, fur tingling with excitement, when he heard Tawnypelt mew, "I will come."

The tortoiseshell she-cat's eyes were shining as she clambered out of her nest. All three kits gave up chasing Lionpaw and stared at their mother.

"What do you mean?" Tigerkit asked.

"You're not going to leave us?" Dawnkit wailed.

"I have to go with Brambleclaw for a while," Tawnypelt told them. "You remember the stories I've told you, about the cats who live in the mountains behind a wall of tumbling water? Well, those cats need my help, so I have to go."

"Then can we come with you?" Flamekit asked. "*Please.*"

"We'd be really helpful," Tigerkit added.

"No, you're too young." Tawnypelt padded over to the three kits and touched her nose to each one in turn. "Be good, and eat your fresh-kill, and expect me back when the moon has been the same shape twice."

"I'll keep an eye on them," the white she-cat promised from the shadows.

"Thanks, Snowbird. There, you see," Tawnypelt added to her kits, "Snowbird will take care of you, and she'll tell me if you've been naughty."

"We won't," Tigerkit promised.

"Even if we never get to have any fun," Dawnkit muttered.

Tawnypelt gave her daughter a gentle flick over the ear with her tail. "Good-bye then," she purred.

"Good-bye," the kits chorused, their eyes wide.

Tawnypelt led the way out of the nursery, with Brambleclaw hard on her paws. Lionpaw paused to look back at the kits. *Good-bye, kin,* he whispered to himself as he followed his father into the clearing.

Outside the nursery, Blackstar and Tawnypelt were confronting each other.

"What do you mean, you want to go?" the Clan leader demanded.

"You said it was her decision," Brambleclaw reminded him.

Blackstar lashed his tail but said nothing.

"We might have known," Russetfur spat. "It just goes to show that she's not a loyal ShadowClan cat."

Tawnypelt arched her back. "Don't you dare call me disloyal!"

"Tawnypelt." The warrior called Rowanclaw padded up beside Tawnypelt and pressed his ginger muzzle against her shoulder. She leaned against him, her fur beginning to lie flat again. Lionpaw remembered that Rowanclaw was her mate, the father of her kits.

"It's nonsense to say that Tawnypelt isn't loyal," he meowed to Russetfur. "I haven't forgotten all the Tribe cats did for us, even if you have. They deserve our help." He bent his head to give Tawnypelt a gentle lick between the ears. "I'm proud of you for going," he mewed. "And don't worry about the kits. I'll look after them."

Tawnypelt let out a soft purr. "Thanks, Rowanclaw." Turning to Brambleclaw, she meowed more briskly, "Shall we go?"

Lionpaw thought his father looked stunned, as if he hadn't expected to get her agreement so easily.

"There's no time to lose," Tawnypelt pointed out. "Not when we still have to make the long journey to the mountains."

"True," Brambleclaw murmured. "Thank you, Blackstar," he added to the ShadowClan leader. "I'm sure StarClan will approve of what you have done today."

Blackstar nodded, looking awkward; Lionpaw knew very well he hadn't intended things to turn out like this. Russetfur just let out an annoyed hiss and turned away, lashing her tail.

Excitement flooded through him once more as he raced back through the forest with Brambleclaw and Tawnypelt. He felt sure that Squirrelflight and Hollypaw must have had the same success in WindClan. Cats from all Clans were uniting to help the Tribe! This was even better than just going to visit the mountains. Maybe he would be part of another incredible story, and one day the Clans would tell it to their kits, just as they told the story of the Great Journey.

Chapter 12

Hollypaw stood on the bank of the stream that formed the border with WindClan, not far from the stepping-stones. Wind from the moor slicked her fur to her sides, bringing the scent of cats and rabbits and the tough moorland grass.

Beside her, Squirrelflight waited, the tip of her tail twitching. Hollypaw could understand why her mother was uneasy. The WindClan border was still a sensitive area, after all the trouble when the WindClan kits went missing.

Her thoughts fled back to the tunnels and the surging underground river. She and the other apprentices had barely made it out alive with the kits. Hollypaw hoped that the tunnels would stay hidden for a long time, so there would be no more chance of misunderstandings.

"They're coming." Squirrelflight was tasting the air.

A couple of heartbeats later a WindClan patrol appeared over the brow of the hill and headed toward them: Tornear, Whitetail, and Breezepaw. Hollypaw's belly began to churn as the apprentice charged toward her, streaking past his Clanmates. His pelt bristled; he was obviously ready for a border skirmish, but his stride faltered when he recognized Hollypaw.

"Oh, it's you," he muttered, coming to a halt on the opposite bank of the stream.

"That's right." Hollypaw couldn't forget what a pain he'd been in the tunnels, complaining and arguing the whole time. "I just can't keep away."

She flinched as Squirrelflight flicked her ear with her tail.

"Breezepaw!" Whitetail called, as she and Tornear caught up to the apprentice. "Come away from there."

Breezepaw bared his teeth in the beginning of a snarl, then lowered his head and padded away, muttering something under his breath.

"Why are you here?" Tornear asked; his voice was cool but not hostile.

"We need to speak to Crowfeather," Squirrelflight explained.

Both Tornear and Whitetail bristled, their neck fur fluffing up as they exchanged suspicious glances.

"It's about the journey we made to the sun-drown-place," Squirrelflight added quickly.

"That was a long time ago," Tornear growled.

"Crowfeather's memory isn't that bad," Squirrelflight retorted tartly. "He'll hardly have forgotten about it."

Hollypaw couldn't understand why the WindClan cats had switched from reserve to hostility, or why her mother was being so sharp in return. Why should the WindClan cats be so tense when Crowfeather was mentioned?

"I can't just go and fetch Crowfeather," Whitetail meowed. "You'll have to talk to Onestar first."

"That's fine. I understand." Squirrelflight bounded lightly across the stepping-stones and into WindClan territory, giving Tornear a glare as she passed him. Hollypaw crossed more carefully, the swift-flowing stream bubbling past a mouse tail away from her paws.

As she followed her mother and the WindClan warriors up the hill, Breezepaw hung back until he was padding beside her. "What are you doing here?" he muttered into her ear. "Have you come to spy on our camp?"

"Don't be ridiculous," Hollypaw replied. "What would we want with your stupid camp? We need to speak to Crowfeather, that's all."

"What about?" Breezepaw demanded.

"That's none of your business, mouse-brain!"

Breezepaw's eyes narrowed in anger. "But he's my father," he began. "He—"

"Breezepaw." Tornear glanced over his shoulder and flicked his tail to beckon the apprentice. "Come here and walk beside me."

Breezepaw let out a hiss of annoyance, but he quickened his pace and caught up to the senior warriors.

"How's your training going, Breezepaw?" Squirrelflight asked.

"Not well." Whitetail didn't wait for her apprentice to reply. "He led out a patrol of apprentices to see if the dogs had come back to the far corner of our territory. Without asking permission, of course, and without even a single warrior for backup."

"We were only trying to—"

"To get yourselves killed," Tornear interrupted.

Hollypaw had heard the stories of how dogs had killed Swiftpaw back in the forest, and she'd seen the terrible injuries they had given Brightheart. Breezepaw must be even more stupid than she thought if he imagined that a few apprentices could take on a pack of dogs and survive.

"And then there was the fight you provoked with the RiverClan patrol," Tornear continued, his voice sharp with annoyance. "They were *not* trespassing, they were *not* stealing prey, and Onestar didn't appreciate having to apologize to Mistyfoot for the trouble *you* caused." He let out a long sigh and added to Squirrelflight, "Breezepaw has many lessons to learn before he becomes a warrior."

Breezepaw glared at the senior warriors as they turned away and muttered something Hollypaw didn't catch.

Whitetail and Tornear led the way up a long slope to a barrier of gorse bushes. Hollypaw followed as they pushed their way through, feeling the thorns snag on her pelt. On the other side she found herself looking out over the WindClan camp.

A steep slope led down into a natural dip, dotted with gorse and bramble. Blinking, Hollypaw tried to guess the layout. The camp was more exposed than she was used to, though toward the bottom of the dip there were hollows where cats could shelter. She tasted the air, trying to work out from the scents where each group of cats lived. A pungent smell of mouse bile was coming from a deep hole that looked like an abandoned badger set. *That must be the elders' den. They're always needing mouse bile to get rid of their ticks.* From a crack in a huge boulder she picked up the aromatic scent of herbs and realized that must be Barkface's den. And warm, milky scents came from a gorse thicket; that would be the nursery.

"Go and take some fresh-kill to the elders," Whitetail ordered Breezepaw, interrupting Hollypaw's thoughts. Waving her tail to Squirrelflight she added, "Follow me. We'll see if Onestar is in his den."

Hollypaw bounded down the slope behind her mother, while Whitetail raced ahead. But before the ThunderClan cats reached the bottom of the hollow, Crowfeather appeared from the bushes at the other side, a rabbit dangling from his jaws. He spotted the visitors, froze for a heartbeat, then ran lightly down to deposit his prey on the fresh-kill pile.

As Squirrelflight padded up to him he turned to face her, his gray-black fur bristling. "What are you doing here?" he demanded. "Is something wrong?"

"No," Squirrelflight replied, while Hollypaw wondered what was bothering Crowfeather. Did he have ants in his pelt? "At least, yes, but not with the Clans."

Squirrelflight seemed to have gotten herself into a tangle, so Hollypaw stepped forward. "The Tribe of Rushing Water needs our help," she explained. "The cats who went to the sun-drown-place must go to the mountains."

Crowfeather looked surprised, and Hollypaw thought maybe she had been too outspoken. "And they want apprentices to come too, do they?" he growled.

Squirrelflight gave his shoulder an affectionate flick with her tail. "Crowfeather, neither of us can complain about apprentices making the journey." When Crowfeather didn't respond, she went on. "Talon and Night—do you remember them?—came to our camp to fetch Stormfur and Brook. The Tribe is being threatened by a group of invading cats who are trying to take over its hunting grounds. We—I mean Brambleclaw and I—thought we would go and help too."

Crowfeather paused before replying; Hollypaw couldn't read anything from his expression. "What's it got to do with us?" he asked eventually.

"They helped us on the Great Journey," Squirrelflight mewed.

"And Feathertail *died* for them!" Crowfeather spat, his blue eyes blazing. "We owe them nothing."

Feathertail had been a RiverClan cat, Stormfur's sister, who had died on the first journey. None of the other cats seemed to think her death was a reason not to help the Tribe now. Why should Crowfeather take it so personally? Feathertail hadn't even been his Clanmate.

"Feathertail was willing to help the Tribe before," Squirrelflight replied calmly. "She would help them again. It wasn't the Tribe's fault she died. You can blame Sharptooth for that."

A shiver ran through Hollypaw and she dug her claws hard into the tough moorland grass. Squirrelflight was talking so matter-of-factly about stories Hollypaw had heard since she was in the nursery! It was as if her mother and father belonged in a legend. Crowfeather, too, though it was hard for Hollypaw to reconcile the brave warrior, StarClan's chosen, with the suspicious, bad-tempered, skinny cat who stood in front of her. *No wonder Breezepaw is so grumpy. He got it from his father!*

"Squirrelflight, greetings."

Hollypaw whirled to see Whitetail returning with Onestar and Ashfoot, the WindClan deputy. It was Onestar who had spoken; he padded up to Squirrelflight with his head and tail held high.

"Greetings, Onestar." Squirrelflight dipped her head.

"You're welcome to our camp." The WindClan leader sounded friendly, though there was surprise in his amber eyes. "What can we do for you?"

Squirrelflight launched into a more detailed explanation of how the Tribe cats had come to ThunderClan looking for help. Crowfeather listened with the same disgruntled expression, while other WindClan cats gathered around. Hollypaw spotted Heatherpaw, and gave her a nod; Breezepaw had reappeared too, standing beside his fellow apprentice.

"So Brambleclaw and I thought that all the cats who went on the first journey should go now and help the Tribe," Squirrelflight finished. "Brambleclaw has gone to ShadowClan to speak to Tawnypelt, and I came here to tell Crowfeather."

Onestar narrowed his eyes. "He would be away for a long time, perhaps a moon or more."

"And I have an apprentice," Crowfeather reminded him.

"True. All the same, I think you should go," Onestar meowed. "The Tribe of Rushing Water gave us food and shelter on the Great Journey. Without their help, many cats would have died, and we might never have found this home by the lake. Besides," he went on, ignoring Crowfeather as he tried to interrupt, "the mountain cats were kind to Tallstar when he was on his last life. We would honor him by helping them now."

Crowfeather looked taken aback. "But what about Heatherpaw's training?"

"Whitetail can take over as her mentor," Onestar decided. "She will be without an apprentice, since I think it would be a good idea if Breezepaw went along with you."

Oh, no! Hollypaw thought. *You might be fed up with him, but we don't want him either, thanks.*

"What?" Breezepaw exclaimed. His eyes stretched wide with dismay.

"You're so lucky!" Heatherpaw put in, with a sigh of envy. "I'd give my tail to go."

"Well, I don't want to!"

"Don't worry, you'll be coming back," Hollypaw snapped.

"How do you know that?" Breezepaw's ears flattened and his tail drooped. "I think my Clanmates just want to get rid of me."

He sounded so miserable that Hollypaw felt a rush of pity for him, but it lasted no more than a couple of heartbeats. Breezepaw had broken the warrior code twice in the last moon; it was time he was taken down a tree branch or two.

Crowfeather padded forward a couple of paces to stand beside Squirrelflight. "It is my choice if I go," he meowed, with a glance at Onestar. Hollypaw wondered if he was defying his leader, but Onestar didn't rise to the challenge. "And I—I will go. I would like to stand again in the place where Feathertail lies."

"What about Breezepaw?" Squirrelflight asked.

Crowfeather sighed. "Yes, I suppose he must come too, if Onestar orders it."

Breezepaw shot his father a sulky look and started tearing up the grass with his claws. Hollypaw thought of her own mother and father; she was glad that they supported her when she wanted to try new things. It didn't look as if Crowfeather and Breezepaw got along at all. *And I can understand that, sort of,* she thought, *now that I've seen Crowfeather a few times. He's just . . . weird.*

"Do you want Crowfeather and Breezepaw to come with you now?" Onestar asked.

"Yes, please," Squirrelflight replied. "We thought we would all stay in the ThunderClan camp tonight and set off in the morning. Leafpool is preparing traveling herbs."

"I want to say good-bye to my friends first," Breezepaw objected.

"There isn't time!" Crowfeather snapped.

"I'll say good-bye for you." Heatherpaw darted forward and touched her nose to Breezepaw's shoulder. "And don't worry. You'll have some amazing stories to tell us when you come back."

Breezepaw didn't look as if the idea cheered him up.

A black she-cat emerged from the group of WindClan cats; Hollypaw recognized Crowfeather's mate, Nightcloud. She brushed her pelt against Crowfeather's. "Take care," she meowed.

Crowfeather gave her ear a quick lick, but Hollypaw noticed that his eyes were gazing into the distance.

Squirrelflight dipped her head to Onestar and thanked him. Then Crowfeather led the way up the slope and out of the WindClan camp. As they trekked across the moor he still looked sour, and Breezepaw sulked all the way, refusing to talk to Hollypaw even when she tried to be friendly.

I don't think this journey is going to be much fun after all, Hollypaw thought gloomily.

Chapter 13

Jaypaw shivered in the dawn chill. The sharp scent of the traveling herbs wreathed around him, almost masking the scent of Leafpool as she worked beside him in the medicine cat's den. Stifling a yawn, he thought back to his dreams of the night before, full of strange scents, jagged rocks, and unfamiliar cats, and the screech of warriors meeting in battle. He had lost count of the number of times he had jerked awake, his heart pounding until he realized that he was curled up in his own nest of ferns. Nothing in the dreams made any sense to him, and he flicked his tail impatiently. *What's the point of dreaming if I don't learn anything?*

Soft sounds filtered through the bramble screen as the cats in the clearing began to wake up. Jaypaw couldn't remember the hollow ever being so full, with the WindClan and ShadowClan cats as well as the visitors from the Tribe. It was just as well the night had been warm enough for some of them to sleep in the open; the WindClan cats especially were used to that. Jaypaw's claws slid out as he remembered his dismay when he discovered that Breezepaw had come along with his father.

I can't stand *that arrogant, mange-ridden excuse for a cat!*

He would never forget how useless Breezepaw had been when they were trapped underground. It was no wonder that the tunnels had been sealed up, so Jaypaw couldn't reach Rock and Fallen Leaves anymore. What could you expect when Breezepaw hadn't shown any sense or respect?

"Jaypaw, what are you daydreaming about?" Leafpool's voice broke into Jaypaw's thoughts. "You can start taking these herbs out to the cats who are leaving."

"Don't you want to do that?" Jaypaw was surprised; the Tribe cats would probably want a medicine cat to explain to them what they were eating.

"No." Leafpool sounded agitated. "I've got to check these herbs one more time."

Rubbish! Jaypaw thought. *It doesn't take all this fuss to make up a few traveling herbs.* But he just picked up the first portion of herbs and padded out into the clearing.

The scent of the herbs in his jaws made it harder to locate the cats, but after a couple of heartbeats he pinpointed a group of them just outside the warriors' den: Crowfeather, Breezepaw, Squirrelflight, and Tawnypelt.

Jaypaw padded up to them and dropped the herbs at Crowfeather's paws. "Traveling herbs," he mewed.

"Thank you." There was a tension about Crowfeather that Jaypaw didn't understand; it felt like more than the natural anticipation of the journey. *Who knows what goes on in the minds of those weird WindClan cats?*

Returning to his den, he was tempted by the thought of

sneaking something disgusting into Breezepaw's traveling herbs. A few yarrow leaves, maybe. The first part of their journey would be around the lake on WindClan territory; if Breezepaw started being sick, they would have to leave him behind.

Or maybe he'd just delay the rest of us. Jaypaw considered the punishment he'd receive if any cat found out what he'd done. He'd be made to stay at home, for sure. The risk wasn't worth it.

He went on dividing up the herbs. Soon the Tribe cats appeared with Stormfur and Brook and joined the others by the warriors' den.

"What's this?" Talon queried when Jaypaw put down his share of the herbs.

"Traveling herbs," Jaypaw replied. "They'll make you stronger, and you won't feel so hungry."

"Are you sure?" Jaypaw pictured the cave-guard prodding the herbs suspiciously with one paw. "I've never heard of anything like that."

"Stoneteller never heard of them, either," Night agreed. Jaypaw heard her sniffing at the little pile of leaves.

"For StarClan's sake!" he snapped. "Just eat them. We're not trying to poison you."

"They're okay," Stormfur meowed. Jaypaw felt the gray warrior's tail flick lightly across his muzzle. "They'll make the journey a lot easier."

"If you're sure . . ." Talon's voice was still dubious, but he licked up the herbs. "They taste bitter," he complained.

Stifling a sigh, Jaypaw carried on until he'd taken herbs to every cat except his father.

"Where's Brambleclaw?" he asked Squirrelflight, mumbling around his mouthful of leaves.

"I think he went to talk to Firestar," Squirrelflight replied. "I'll take those up to him, if you like."

"No, I'll do it." Jaypaw's fur bristled as he bounded across the camp. *I can climb up to the Highledge without falling!* He scrambled up the tumbled stones, making sure that his pelt brushed the cliff wall at every paw step. As he reached the Highledge, he heard Firestar's voice from inside the den.

"You'll be away for at least a moon, Brambleclaw. We need to decide who should be deputy while you're gone."

Jaypaw halted outside the den, drawing close against the rock wall so that the cats inside wouldn't see him.

"Graystripe is the obvious cat to choose," Brambleclaw answered. "He knows the deputy's duties, after all."

Jaypaw's whiskers twitched in dismay. His father had only become Clan deputy because every cat thought that Graystripe was dead. After the gray warrior's unexpected return, some cats had thought that Brambleclaw would step down. Graystripe hadn't wanted that; he said he didn't have enough experience of the Clan's new home, and he was tired after his journey. But none of that was true anymore. If Graystripe took over as deputy now, what would happen when Brambleclaw came home? Jaypaw gritted his teeth. Couldn't his father see that he might be giving up his position in the Clan?

"Fine, if you're happy with that." Firestar sounded relieved. "I'll tell him."

There was movement inside the den as if the cats were rising to their paws. Quickly Jaypaw found a loose pebble and flicked it with his paw so they would think he had just arrived. Stepping into the mouth of the den he meowed, "Firestar?"

"Come in," his leader responded.

"Are those my traveling herbs?" Brambleclaw asked. "Thanks, Jaypaw. Is every cat ready?"

"Nearly," Jaypaw replied. "I'd better find Leafpool and see if she wants me to do anything else."

He withdrew from the den with a quick dip of his head. As he hurried down the rocks again he tried to scent Lionpaw and Hollypaw. He wanted to tell them about Graystripe taking over as deputy while they could still talk in private. But as he reached the floor of the clearing, his littermates passed him with fresh-kill in their jaws, heading for the elders' den. Hollypaw called out, "Hi, Jaypaw," as they went by but they were too busy to stop.

Frustrated, Jaypaw went back to his own den. Leafpool was still there, fiddling with some leaves, though all the traveling herbs had been distributed now, except for Jaypaw's own.

"What are you doing?" he asked. "Do you want me to take some herbs with me?"

"What?" Leafpool sounded surprised, as if she hadn't realized he had come back. "Oh, no—there's no point in doing that. They'd be a nuisance to carry every day, and you don't know what you'll need."

"But I have no idea which herbs grow in the mountains," Jaypaw objected.

Leafpool scraped the ground with one paw; she was trying to hide it, but Jaypaw could feel she was on edge for some reason. "You won't *be* in the mountains for most of the way," she told him. "And when you get to the Tribe, Stoneteller will be able to show you the mountain herbs. You'll learn a lot from him."

I hope so, and not just about herbs.

"Come on, Jaypaw, don't just stand there. Eat your own herbs." Jaypaw felt his mentor's paw brush his as she pushed the remaining herbs toward him. "Brambleclaw will want to leave soon."

Jaypaw licked up the mouthful of herbs. "Yuck," he muttered.

"You'll be glad of them once you get going," Leafpool mewed sharply. "You're lucky to be going on this journey at all."

Lucky because I'm blind and shouldn't be allowed to go? Jaypaw thought mutinously. He said nothing, trying to swallow the last of the bitter leaves.

"You'll find the mountains fascinating," Leafpool went on, sounding more like her normal self. "You should take the chance to learn all you can about them."

That's just what I mean to do, Jaypaw told himself, though he suspected he meant something different from what his mentor was suggesting. Oh, he would learn about new herbs and new ways of living, but what he really wanted to know was how the Tribe came to settle in the mountains, and how they were connected to Rock and the ancient cats who had left their paw prints around the Moonpool. But he knew better than to say any of that to Leafpool.

"Jaypaw?" Brambleclaw's voice came from the clearing. "Are you ready?"

"Coming!" Jaypaw called back. He whisked around the bramble screen, then turned back to ask Leafpool, "Aren't you coming to say good-bye?"

Leafpool let out a long sigh. Tension was crackling off her like a storm in greenleaf. "I—I've said it already," she murmured.

"Okay. Good-bye then." Jaypaw knew he should leave, but something held his paws back. He found Leafpool incredibly annoying when she fussed, but he couldn't ignore her feelings of misery, even if he didn't understand them. He darted across to her and buried his nose in the fur on her shoulder. "Good-bye. I'll have lots to tell you when I get back."

"Good-bye, Jaypaw." Leafpool's voice quivered. He felt her tongue rasp over his ear. "Take care."

"Jaypaw!" Brambleclaw's voice came again from the clearing.

"Gotta go," Jaypaw meowed, dashing out past the brambles with a sigh of relief to be away from Leafpool's strange intensity. As he emerged he smelled Squirrelflight's scent and felt her pelt brush his as she slipped into the medicine cat's den to talk to her sister.

I hope she knows what's going on, because I sure don't, Jaypaw thought.

The cats who were leaving had gathered together in the

middle of the stone hollow. Jaypaw found Hollypaw and Lionpaw and bounded over to stand beside them.

"What kept you?" Hollypaw asked. "We're all waiting."

"I'm here now," Jaypaw retorted. "And I've got stuff to tell you two."

The chilly air of dawn had vanished as the sun rose. Jaypaw could feel the beams slicing down through the trees, falling across his pelt. It was a perfect morning to travel: cool and clear, with warm sunshine later on.

He heard rustling from the warriors' den as several of his Clanmates emerged to see the travelers off. There was a rapid patter of paws from the apprentices' den, and Jaypaw heard Icepaw mew, "It's not fair! I want to go too."

"Maybe your turn will come another time," Whitewing told her kindly.

The sound of a huge yawn came close to Jaypaw's ear, and Cloudtail's scent wafted over him. "Why don't you get moving?" he mumbled. "Then every cat can get a bit more sleep."

"No chance." Dustpelt spoke sharply nearby. "You're coming with me and Sandstorm on the dawn patrol."

"Mouse dung!" Cloudtail muttered.

Jaypaw picked up Firestar's scent and heard his paw steps as he padded across to join the traveling cats. Graystripe was just behind him; Jaypaw could picture the gray warrior standing at his leader's shoulder with a glow in his amber eyes.

As if he's deputy already!

"Farewell, all of you," Firestar meowed. "May StarClan light your path—and may you all come home safe."

A sudden tension sprang up between the departing cats, as if Clan warriors and Tribe cats were facing one another, gathering their courage for the first paw steps of their journey. Squirrelflight had returned, slipping up to Brambleclaw's side.

"Ready?" Brambleclaw asked.

"Yes, ready," Stormfur replied.

Jaypaw stood still and let all the scents and sounds of the stone hollow—the herbs from the den he had just left, the milky scents of the nursery and the dusty smell of the ground, the voices of his Clanmates and the rustle of wind in the trees—soak into his pelt.

What if I never come back? StarClan would have warned me, wouldn't they? Isn't that something they do, tell cats when they're going to die?

"Jaypaw!" Hollypaw's voice sounded from the thorn tunnel. "Wake up! Every cat is leaving."

Jaypaw jumped. Dashing across the clearing, he followed his sister into the tunnel and out into the forest.

Chapter 14

Jaypaw could feel dappled sunlight and shade on his pelt as he padded beneath the trees. Lionpaw flanked him on one side, while Hollypaw bounded ahead for a few paw steps, then returned to join her littermates. The air was full of birdsong and the rustling of leaves, and the scents of prey were sharp in the undergrowth.

The three apprentices brought up the rear of the group of traveling cats. Brambleclaw had taken the lead, with Stormfur and Brook, closely followed by Talon and Night. Just ahead of Jaypaw he could scent Squirrelflight and Tawnypelt.

". . . and Tigerkit has already learned the hunter's crouch," Tawnypelt was meowing. "But I think Dawnkit will be the best fighter, if only she listens to what her mentor tells her once she's apprenticed. Right now she doesn't listen to *any* cat."

"All kits can be deaf when they choose," Squirrelflight told her. "They'll grow into fine warriors, you'll see."

Kits! Jaypaw thought. *Boring!*

He angled his ears, trying to pick up more interesting snippets of conversation, but all he could hear was Crowfeather telling Breezepaw about the best way to catch prey in the mountains. The two WindClan cats were padding side by side a few tail-lengths from the rest; Jaypaw could feel Breezepaw's resentment at being forced to come on the journey. *I don't think he and his father even* like *each other,* Jaypaw decided.

"Hey, look!" Lionpaw exclaimed. "Bet you I can catch that butterfly!"

"Bet you can't," Hollypaw returned.

"Just watch!" Lionpaw took off in an enormous leap, then crashed back to the forest floor.

"Missed it!" Hollypaw let out a *mrrow* of laughter. "Told you!"

Jaypaw heard heavier paw steps in the bracken and his mother's scent drifted over him.

"Just *what* do you three think you're doing?" she scolded them. "Are you kits, let out of camp for the first time? This is a serious journey, and you need to save your strength. You'll need it later."

"Sorry," Lionpaw muttered.

Jaypaw drew his lips back in the beginning of a snarl as he imagined Breezepaw's smug expression; he knew the WindClan apprentice was listening.

If he says one word, I'll claw his ear off!

But Breezepaw had the sense to keep his jaws shut.

Soon Jaypaw began to pick up the clean scent of water. Stronger sunlight on his pelt told him they had left the shelter of the trees. He realized they had emerged beside the lake, and for a moment his paws itched to search for the stick with the marks Rock had made. But he couldn't carry the stick all the way to the mountains.

I'll have to leave it behind. But I'm not leaving you *behind, Rock. When I get to the mountains, I know I'll find you there.*

"We're near the WindClan border," Hollypaw whispered into his ear. "We have to cross the stream."

For a couple of heartbeats Jaypaw froze, remembering the smothering water in the tunnels. He *hated* getting his paws wet!

Lionpaw butted him gently in the shoulder. "It'll be okay. The water's really shallow."

Jaypaw bit back an indignant retort, though it was really himself he was angry with. Would he always have to fight this terror of drowning?

He could hear splashing as the other cats crossed the stream. Hollypaw guided him to the bank with her tail across his shoulders. Jaypaw tensed when he felt the current swirling around his paws. The stream bed shelved down until the water brushed his belly fur. He could feel Hollypaw and Lionpaw close on either side; Lionpaw murmured, "This way a bit; there's a deeper place just there." Then the stream grew shallower again, and Jaypaw could scramble up the bank on the other side. He halted a tail-length away and shook himself to hide his tremors of relief.

"Hey, do you mind?" Breezepaw's unfriendly voice came from just behind him. "You're making my fur wet!"

"Sor-ree," Jaypaw muttered.

The cats continued along the lakeshore, across WindClan territory and past the horseplace. Jaypaw could just pick up the scent of the horseplace cats beneath the overwhelming scent of horse, but neither Smoky nor Floss appeared to greet them. He pricked his ears at distant barking and decided that the dog who lived near the horseplace was too far away to be a nuisance.

Once past the horseplace, Brambleclaw led the way uphill. Jaypaw's paws tingled as he realized he was setting them down on unfamiliar ground. This was the real beginning of the adventure! The scents of home were fading behind him, and a stiff breeze brought new scents to him, wild and strange. His paws faltered briefly. *Stupid cat!* he berated himself. *This is what you wanted, isn't it?* He felt his littermates' pelts touching his on either side, and sensed that they too were daunted by the unknown path where they had set their paws.

The ground underfoot was growing wetter and more uneven. Jaypaw brushed past a clump of reeds and heard a splash accompanied by a strong scent of frog. A moment later, one of his paws slipped on a tussock of wet grass and water surged over his hindquarters.

"Fox dung!" he spat, clawing with his forepaws to heave himself out again.

"Are you okay?" Lionpaw asked.

"Fine." Jaypaw spoke through gritted teeth.

Just beyond his brother, he heard Talon murmur to Night, "This is crazy. Taking a blind to-be all the way to the mountains!"

"I know," Night replied. "He'll never keep up."

A sharp retort bubbled up inside Jaypaw, but before he

could speak he felt his mother's tail laid firmly over his mouth. "Jaypaw will manage just fine," she meowed. "He's as good at tackling new territory as any cat. Have *you* never put a paw in the wrong place, Talon?" she added.

When the big Tribe tabby didn't reply, she moved her tail from Jaypaw's mouth to his shoulder. "Come this way. It's drier over here."

Jaypaw followed her, thankful to feel more solid ground beneath his paws. He was surprised that Breezepaw hadn't made some sarcastic comment about his misstep. But Breezepaw was a Clan cat; maybe he felt a kind of loyalty to support any Clan cat against the Tribe.

Not that he stood up for me, Jaypaw thought sourly. *That would be too much to expect.*

Wind buffeted Jaypaw in the face, telling him they had reached the top of the ridge. There were so many new scents that he couldn't begin to sort them all out.

"This is awesome!" Hollypaw gasped. "I can see the whole of the lake and all the territories from here." She bounced up to Jaypaw and gave him a nudge with her head. "Down there is a stream with trees growing around it, where RiverClan has its camp. And beyond that is dark pine forest—that's ShadowClan's territory. I can even see the Gathering island, and the tree-bridge . . . It looks so tiny from up here!"

"Over this way are the woods where we live." Lionpaw joined Jaypaw on his other side. "I bet we could see the hollow if we were here in leaf-bare. And then there's open moorland where WindClan live. We can see *everything*!"

"WindClan looks at this all the time." Breezepaw had padded up behind them. "Our territory has loads of great views."

Annoying furball, Jaypaw thought.

"Do you remember the first time we stood here?" Jaypaw scented Brambleclaw a little way away, with Squirrelflight, Crowfeather, and Tawnypelt.

"I'll never forget it," Squirrelflight replied. "It was night, and all the cats of StarClan were reflected in the lake."

"I can't believe how brave you were," Night put in. "You traveled so far to find a new home, without even knowing where you were going."

"StarClan helped us," Squirrelflight murmured.

"And the Tribe of Endless Hunting would do the same for you," Tawnypelt pointed out, "if the Tribe of Rushing Water ever had to leave the mountains."

"Leave?" Night sounded alarmed. "We could never leave and nor could the spirits of our ancestors. We belong too much to the mountains."

Jaypaw wasn't sure she was right. If the Clan cats failed to drive out the intruders, the Tribe, and the spirits of its ancestors, might have to face a journey of their own.

CHAPTER 15

Lionpaw stood beside his sister, gazing down at the lake and the familiar Clan territories. A ripple of excitement pulsed through him as he turned his back on his home and saw for the first time a wide stretch of unknown country.

"What are we waiting for?" he complained to Hollypaw. "Why can't we keep going?"

"Didn't you hear Brambleclaw?" his sister meowed. "He told us all to rest, and he said we could hunt if we want to eat."

Lionpaw had been so focused on their journey that he hadn't noticed his father giving the order. His forepaws tore up the short grass of the ridge. "I don't want to sit around. We've hardly started."

"It's the traveling herbs giving you all that energy," Hollypaw mewed practically. "The mountains won't go away." She turned with a flick of her tail and began to stalk toward a gorse bush, her ears and whiskers alert for signs of prey.

Lionpaw's paws were sore from the stiff climb up the ridge, but he had never felt so alive, so eager to keep traveling. In front of him, dark forest covered the downward slope, and beyond it Lionpaw could see flat green stretches like the grass at the horseplace. It was sliced through by Thunderpaths and dotted with Twoleg nests—some of them close together, whole clusters of red stone dens.

Lionpaw bounded over the short, springy grass to a rocky outcrop, the highest part of the ridge. At the top of the rocks, wind flattened his fur along his sides. He felt as powerful as a warrior of LionClan! If he stretched out a paw, he could blot out whole Twoleg nests. The biggest Thunderpath looked as thin as a strand of bramble or a twig that he could snap with his teeth.

I could run farther than a hare! I could fight the fiercest fox that ever lived. Spotting the dark gray stain that hovered on the horizon, he added, *I could climb the highest mountain faster than an eagle could fly.*

He wondered if the other cats felt like this. When he looked down at his traveling companions dozing peacefully below him, he suspected that they didn't.

Lionpaw strained his ears to pick up Tigerstar's voice in the sighing of the wind and looked for the dark tabby shape in the shadows cast by rocks and bushes. This was exactly how Tigerstar had told him he should feel, as if his enemies were no bigger than beetles. But there was no trace of the former warrior. All these turbulent feelings seemed to come from inside Lionpaw himself.

"Lionpaw! We're waiting for you."

His father's voice made him jump. The other cats had finished resting and were getting to their paws.

"Coming!" he called.

He leaped down from the outcrop and joined his littermates as the cats began to make their way into the trees. His father and mother took the lead with Tawnypelt and Crowfeather.

"Remember how we felt when we first climbed up here?" Tawnypelt meowed.

"I remember how sore my paws were," Squirrelflight replied with a twitch of her tail.

Brambleclaw skirted a huge clump of bracken. "Tallpoppy's kit fell over here. Ferncloud picked her up and carried her. We all helped one another then."

"But it can't be like that anymore." Lionpaw thought Crowfeather sounded wistful, the familiar edge missing from his voice. "It's natural for Clans to be rivals."

Lionpaw thought sadly about Heatherpaw; he guessed that all four of the senior warriors missed the friendships they had forged on their journeys. He was relieved that they seemed to know the way. Now that he couldn't see his home anymore he was daunted by the vast stretches of unknown territory. His pelt grew hot with embarrassment when he remembered his dreams of power on the hilltop, and he was thankful that no other cat knew what he'd been thinking.

Unless Jaypaw knows. Lionpaw's pelt grew hotter still at the idea that his brother might have been eavesdropping on his thoughts.

"Come on, pick up your paws," Brambleclaw called back. "I want to be out of these trees by nightfall."

Lionpaw stifled a sigh. His paws were dragging already and his belly was yowling with hunger. The energy from the traveling herbs seemed to have worn off. He wished he'd taken the chance to rest and eat after all.

"Here." Squirrelflight's voice was muffled; Lionpaw glanced back to see her padding up to him with a mouse hanging from her jaws. "Eat as quickly as you can," she added, dropping her prey at his paws.

"Thank you!" Lionpaw touched his nose gratefully to his mother's shoulder.

"I was tired of listening to your belly growling," Squirrelflight mewed, her tail curling up in amusement. "I reckon they could hear it back in ThunderClan."

She ran ahead to join Brambleclaw, while Lionpaw crouched over the mouse and devoured it in a few famished bites.

By the time he had finished his companions were out of sight, but he could hear their voices ahead and followed their scent trail until he caught up. Strength had flooded back into his paws. Passing the rest of the group, he bounded up to his father.

"What do you know about these invading cats?" Brambleclaw was asking Talon. "How many are there?"

"Too many," Talon replied.

Brambleclaw twitched his ears. Lionpaw guessed that he didn't find the Tribe cat's answer much use in planning what they would do when they reached the mountains.

"Well, what have you done so far?" Brambleclaw went on.

"Have you worked out their ways of hunting and fighting? And what about regular patrols—"

"We're not Clan cats, you know." Talon's neck fur bristled. "We need help, but that doesn't mean we want to be treated like a bunch of to-bes."

"Calm down, Talon." Night touched her Tribemate's shoulder with the tip of her tail. "Brambleclaw's only trying to work out the best way of helping us."

For a heartbeat Lionpaw thought that the tabby cave-guard would snap at her too, but then his fur lay flat again and he gave Brambleclaw an awkward nod as if he was trying to apologize.

"We've never needed to set boundaries before," he explained. "We just chose some rocks around our cave and set guards to keep watch for the intruders. Stoneteller said . . ."

Growing bored with this talk of strategy, Lionpaw let his father and the others go ahead and waited for his littermates to catch up.

"The Tribe cats seem really tense," he meowed as he fell in beside Hollypaw. "I thought Talon was going to claw Brambleclaw's ear off."

Hollypaw blinked thoughtfully. "I think it's because they never told Stoneteller what they planned to do. He might be angry when a bunch of Clan cats turn up in his territory."

"Angry?" Lionpaw's pelt grew hot with outrage. "He should be grateful to us!"

His sister let out a snort. "Maybe his pride would be hurt. Leaders ought to be able to deal with problems without asking for help from outside. How do you think Firestar would feel if we were having trouble and you went to ask for help from WindClan?"

"He would probably line his nest with my pelt," Lionpaw admitted.

"So what would *you* do if you were Stoneteller?" Jaypaw's voice was curious as he flicked his sister's shoulder with his tail-tip.

Hollypaw paused for a few heartbeats before she replied. "I'd set up border patrols—"

"But they don't have borders," Lionpaw reminded her.

"Then I'd mark some." Hollypaw's ears twitched. "I'd make sure they were patrolled regularly, and I'd teach all my cats to fight. That would keep the intruders out."

Jaypaw shook his head. "You're thinking like a Clan cat. The Tribe's ways are different. I'm not sure we should try to change them."

"We should if they're being driven out of their territory and starved to death," Lionpaw argued. "What the Tribe needs is the warrior code, and we're going to teach it to them!"

The setting sun cast long shadows in front of them as they came to the edge of the trees. Lionpaw fluffed out his pelt against the breeze that whispered through the undergrowth. Ahead he could see a stretch of dusty grass sloping down into a narrow valley. More trees stretched up the far side, and beyond them hung the gray smudge of the mountains. Over to one side Lionpaw spotted the reddish stone of Twoleg nests, just visible through the trees.

"We'll stop here for the night," Brambleclaw announced. "It's sheltered, and there'll be plenty of prey."

Before he had finished speaking, Crowfeather broke away from the group, streaking across the open ground with his belly fur brushing the grass. Breezepaw raced after him. Lionpaw didn't spot the rabbit they were chasing until it broke for cover. The two WindClan cats separated, and as the rabbit dodged away from Crowfeather, it practically threw itself under Breezepaw's paws. The WindClan apprentice dispatched it with a swift bite to the neck.

"Great catch!" Lionpaw meowed as he came back dragging his prey.

Breezepaw ignored him, but Crowfeather gave him a nod as the two WindClan cats settled down to share their prey.

Lionpaw turned back into the woodland to find some prey of his own. Tasting the air, he found a mouse scrabbling among the debris at the edge of a bramble thicket. He leaped with paws outstretched, but as he sank his claws into the little creature he felt a tendril of bramble wrap itself around his shoulders. He pulled away, leaving a tuft of orange fur behind. His pelt prickled with embarrassment at the clumsy kill, and as he padded back to the edge of the trees with his prey he hoped that Breezepaw hadn't been watching.

Hollypaw and Jaypaw were already crouching in the shelter of a clump of bracken with their fresh-kill; Hollypaw was devouring a plump vole, while Jaypaw gulped down a sparrow.

"I wish we could stay here a bit longer," Hollypaw mumbled with her mouth full. "This place is crawling with prey!"

"Well, we can't," Jaypaw mewed unsympathetically. "And I don't think some of us would be happy if we did."

He flicked his tail toward Talon and Night, who had finished eating and were trying to settle down for the night between two gnarled tree roots. They were turning around uneasily, as if they couldn't get comfortable.

Night stiffened as the hoot of an owl sounded from somewhere close by. "What was that?"

"Only an owl." Brook padded up to her Tribemate and touched her nose to the black she-cat's shoulder. "It's okay. Squirrelflight is going to keep watch, then Stormfur."

"Well, I don't like it," Talon grumbled, whipping his head around at the sound of a creaking tree. "I'd rather be out in the open, where I can see if something is sneaking up on me."

"We will be soon," Brook promised. "And that noise was only a branch." She let out a soft *mrrow*, a mixture of sympathy and amusement. "Trees don't sneak up on you."

Lionpaw stretched his jaws in a huge yawn before curling up nose to tail with his littermates in a nest of long grass. He was warm and comfortable, and his belly was full. His eyes closed and the crisp mountain voices of the Tribe cats began to blur together with the hooting of the owls, like rain falling into a pool.

Then his ears pricked as he heard the complaining tones of Breezepaw, coming from a dip in the ground just beyond the outlying branches of the trees. "I don't see why we have to come at all. What can *we* do to help these weird cats—and why does it matter anyway? What has the Tribe ever done for us?"

"Feathertail gave her life saving them from Sharptooth. If they were worthy of our help then, they deserve it now. Otherwise she died for nothing," Crowfeather murmured.

Lionpaw raised his head to see the skinny WindClan cat sitting with his back to the trees, his shape outlined against the darkening sky. Breezepaw was a sprawled heap in the grass.

"Well, from the sounds of it we've helped them enough," Breezepaw objected.

Crowfeather sighed; Lionpaw thought he had never heard a cat sound so bone-weary. "You'll never understand loyalty," the gray-black tom meowed.

Lionpaw was puzzled. Feathertail had been a RiverClan cat, so why should Crowfeather be especially loyal to her?

He wrapped his tail over his nose. There were so many memories clinging to these warriors, so much that he found hard to understand. He pressed up against his littermates and the forest sounds around him faded as he slipped into sleep.

A paw prodding his shoulder woke Lionpaw. He jumped up at once, claws flexing as he scrambled out of his grassy nest.

Brambleclaw was standing over him. His tail flicked across Lionpaw's mouth to warn him to stay quiet. Beside him, Jaypaw and Hollypaw were crouching down with their fur bristling. Hollypaw's tail-tip twitched as she gazed out from the shelter of the trees, and Jaypaw's ears were pricked.

"There's another cat close by," Brambleclaw murmured.

Lionpaw tasted the air. At first he couldn't pick up anything beyond the mingled scents of the other Clan cats. Talon was on his paws, braced for a fight, and Squirrelflight bounded across to stand by Brambleclaw's side. The forest and the hillside beyond seemed peaceful. Early morning sunlight sliced through the trees, turning Lionpaw's pelt to flame. Dew glittered on the grass and on cobwebs strung across the nearby bramble thicket.

Lionpaw had begun to relax when a breeze sprang up, bringing a new scent with it. "That's a kittypet!" he exclaimed. "I'm not afraid of kittypets!"

"Shh!" Brambleclaw hissed. "We might have strayed into a kittypet's territory, and we don't want to fight unless we have to."

"We don't have to fight kittypets," Hollypaw mewed scornfully. "I bet if we show it our teeth it'll go wailing back to its Twolegs."

"And maybe it won't." Squirrelflight's voice was low but stern. "I've known kittypets who could fight, and one bad wound out here would be a problem for all of us. Now do as Brambleclaw says and be quiet."

Lionpaw stiffened as he heard a rustling in the undergrowth. The fronds of a nearby clump of bracken waved wildly and parted. A plump tabby tom stepped through them into the open. His fur was rumpled and covered with burrs, and his muzzle was gray with age. He halted just beyond the bracken and stared at the journeying cats.

Brambleclaw was staring back, his amber eyes wide with shock. Beside him, Squirrelflight bounced on her paws and let out a little cry of welcome.

"Purdy!"

CHAPTER 16

Hollypaw turned to stare at her mother. "You *know* this kittypet?"

Squirrelflight's eyes were bright. "We met him on our first journey," she explained. "He helped us find the way to the sun-drown-place."

Tawnypelt sprang up from where she had been sleeping in the shelter of the bramble thicket. "Hey, Purdy!" she called, bounding across the grass to touch noses with the old tabby. "How's the prey running?"

Stormfur padded up after her. "Greetings, Purdy. I'm glad that StarClan has joined our paths again."

"A friend o' mine told me there were strange cats in the woods, an' I reckoned they might be you," the old tom meowed. "But where's the rest of you? Where's that scrawny young apprentice who was always arguin'?"

"Here." Crowfeather stalked up to stand with the others.

"Are you going to let him talk to you like that?" Breezepaw demanded, gazing at the tabby tom with undisguised hostility. "I could rip his fur off with one paw."

Crowfeather's eyes narrowed. "You don't understand, Breezepaw. Purdy was part of our journey. That's important."

Breezepaw gave a disdainful sniff.

"Crowfeather's a warrior now," Brambleclaw mewed hurriedly. Hollypaw guessed he was trying to distract Purdy from Breezepaw's rudeness.

"So am I," Squirrelflight added. "My warrior name is Squirrelflight."

"Well I never!" Purdy's amber eyes gleamed. "But there were six of you," he added, glancing from side to side. "Where's the silver cat—Feathersomethin'?"

"She died," Crowfeather rasped, before any other cat could speak.

"I'm sorry to hear it." Purdy's tail drooped, but after a couple of heartbeats his eyes grew bright again. "I never thought I'd see Clan cats again, an' now here you all are."

"We're not all Clan cats," Stormfur pointed out. He waved his tail, beckoning Brook and the other Tribe cats to come closer. "This is Brook, and this is Night and Talon. They all come from the mountains."

"Wha'?" Purdy's neck fur bristled. "So there really are cats livin' in the mountains?" He inspected the three Tribe cats with narrowed eyes. "I thought you were just a tale queens told their kits to stop 'em from strayin'."

"No, we're real, all right," Talon mewed.

"So I see." Purdy gave his chest fur a couple of licks, casting sidelong glances at the mountain cats as if he expected them to leap on him with claws out and teeth bared.

"And these are my kits." Squirrelflight swept her tail around Hollypaw, Lionpaw, and Jaypaw, urging them closer to the old tabby. "Mine and Brambleclaw's."

"Kits!" Purdy's whiskers quivered in surprise. "And you hardly more'n kits yourselves. Come here, young 'uns, and let me look at you."

"This is my son, Breezepaw," Crowfeather added, shoving Breezepaw up with the others.

The three littermates padded up to Purdy. As Hollypaw dipped her head politely she caught a whiff of his sour breath and had to make an effort not to flinch away.

"He's way old!" Breezepaw muttered into her ear. "Older than any of our elders. Why isn't he dead yet?"

"Shut up, stupid furball," Hollypaw whispered. "Kittypets get looked after by their Twolegs. They don't have to catch their own food."

Purdy said nothing, but he flicked up one ragged ear, and Hollypaw knew he had heard Breezepaw's comment.

"I bet this old mange-pelt couldn't catch a mouse if he tried from now to leaf-bare," Breezepaw scoffed.

Purdy looked at him. "You're right, I don't catch prey no more. I get my food from Upwalkers. But I reckon just this once I might try eatin' ill-mannered kits."

"I'm not a—" Breezepaw began indignantly, only to clamp his jaws shut as his father lashed out a paw at his ear—a hard blow, though with his claws sheathed.

"Don't listen to Breezepaw," Jaypaw mewed to the old tom. "Every cat knows he's mouse-brained."

A purr rumbled in Purdy's chest. "Don't worry, young 'un. I've met more nuisancy young cats than you've had rabbits."

He lowered his head to inspect the three littermates. Close up, he looked as if he hadn't groomed his pelt in seasons. Hollypaw spotted a tick on the side of his neck and a few fleas hopping among the matted fur and tangled burrs.

Yuck, fleas! I don't want any of them hopping onto me, thanks.

In a Clan, apprentices would groom the elders' fur and get rid of ticks and fleas. Maybe Purdy wasn't as well looked after as Clan cats after all.

"So what are you doin' here?" Purdy asked, when he had given Hollypaw and her littermates a good sniff. "Not off to the sun-drown-place again?"

"Not this time," Brambleclaw replied. "We're going to the mountains. The Tribe cats need our help."

Purdy's eyes stretched wide with alarm. "That's no place for cats!" he protested. "Are you tellin' me you haven't found a better place than that to live?"

"We've found a *great* place," Squirrelflight assured him.

"It's beside a lake," Tawnypelt added. "There's enough territory for all four Clans and not much trouble from Twolegs."

"Then why don't you stay there?" Purdy asked.

"We'll be going back, but right now the Tribe cats need us," Brambleclaw meowed.

Hollypaw missed Purdy's reply as Lionpaw hissed into her ear, "Why don't we get going? This kittypet is holding us all up."

"I guess he's an old friend," Hollypaw meowed, though privately she agreed with Lionpaw. Cats in the mountains could be dying while the rescue party stood here meowing about old times.

To her relief, Brambleclaw dipped his head to the old cat. "We'd better be going. It's been great seeing you again, Purdy."

"No need to say good-bye just yet," Purdy meowed. "I reckon I'll come with you."

Hollypaw saw her own dismay reflected in the faces of the Tribe cats. Night muttered something urgently into Talon's ear.

"Brambleclaw—" Talon began.

"I don't think that's a good idea," Brambleclaw told Purdy; Hollypaw couldn't understand the regret in her father's amber eyes. "It's a tough journey, and there'll be fighting at the end of it."

Purdy fluffed out his pelt. "You sayin' I can't fight? Too old and fat, is that it?" Before any of the other cats could reply, he broke into a rusty *mrrow* of laughter. "Mebbe you're right, but I can come with you as far as the woods." He waved his tail at the trees on the opposite side of the valley. "I know a thing or two that might help you."

"Mouse dung!" Breezepaw muttered, loud enough for Purdy to hear him. "Now we're stuck with the stupid mange-pelt."

Purdy just flicked his tail and turned his back on the Wind-Clan apprentice, padding beside Brambleclaw to the edge of the trees and down the hillside. Squirrelflight bounded forward to join them on Purdy's other side.

Hollypaw didn't like Breezepaw's rudeness, but she found herself agreeing with him. This old cat was bound to slow them down, when every moment counted.

"Brambleclaw and the others have been here before," she

murmured to Lionpaw. "What can Purdy tell them that they don't already know?"

Lionpaw shrugged. "Like Breezepaw says, we're stuck with him."

As they headed into the valley, Hollypaw could hear Purdy rambling on about the Twolegplace that she could see in the distance.

"Remember those rats?" he asked.

"Will I ever forget?" Tawnypelt growled. "I thought I'd die of that bite." She swiped her tongue around her jaws and added with satisfaction, "The rat that gave it to me didn't have long to regret it."

A purr rumbled deep inside Purdy's chest. "Well, they're not there no more. Upwalkers came and put up a nest there and cleared out all the rats."

"Good!" Tawnypelt's tail lashed.

"And that open space where the monsters were sleepin' . . ."

Hollypaw stopped listening. They weren't going anywhere near the Twolegplace, so why did Purdy need to tell them about it? Her paws itched to race down into the valley, but she was forced to match her pace with Purdy's slow amble.

"Why is Brambleclaw doing this?" she muttered. "The Tribe of Rushing Water could be wiped out while we're hanging around here."

"The Tribe cats feel the same," Jaypaw mewed. "Talon's boiling under his fur."

Hollypaw didn't need her brother's perceptiveness to tell her that. Brook just looked unhappy, but Night and Talon were whispering fiercely together, their neck fur bristling. If Brambleclaw didn't pick up the pace soon, there would be a quarrel.

The sun rose above the trees and Hollypaw was grateful for the cool grass brushing against her flanks. Bees buzzed among the clover while birds swooped and cried in the clear blue sky. A little way ahead, a cluster of grayish-white animals cropped the grass.

"Look—sheep." Breezepaw pointed to them with a flick of his tail. "That means there must be a Twoleg farm near here."

"We know," Hollypaw retorted. She wasn't going to be friendly with Breezepaw, even if she did agree with him about Purdy. "We've seen sheep before, thanks."

"In WindClan—" Breezepaw began in superior tones.

"There's something else," Lionpaw interrupted. "Another animal scent, but I've never smelled it before."

Hollypaw halted to taste the air. Lionpaw was right; apart from the cats around her, the sheep, and a distant trace of dog, she picked up something different. She couldn't see anything, but her paws prickled with apprehension.

Brambleclaw led the way around the flank of a hill, and the valley opened up below them. At the bottom of the slope was a cluster of Twoleg nests, surrounded by a fence. The strange scent grew stronger; Hollypaw felt her pelt begin to bristle as she spotted where it was coming from. Between the nests and the journeying cats was a group of big black-and-white animals. They had feet like pointed stones and long tails that swished through the air with a reedy hiss.

"What are those?" Lionpaw asked, and for once Breezepaw had no reply.

"They're huge," Hollypaw meowed, trying not to sound as nervous as she felt. "And they're looking at us. Do you think they're going to attack?"

She was poised to flee when she heard Purdy's rusty laughter. "Don't you worry none," he rasped. "They're only cows."

"It's okay." Squirrelflight glanced over her shoulder. "We've seen cows before. They won't do you any harm so long as you stay away from their huge feet."

Even so, Hollypaw was relieved that Brambleclaw circled around to stay well away from the cows as they padded downhill, and happier still when the unfamiliar creatures were left behind.

"I can smell mice," Lionpaw announced as they drew near the Twoleg nests. He raced to catch up to Brambleclaw and ask, "Can we stop and hunt? I'm starving."

Hollypaw's jaws flooded as she picked up the tempting scent. It seemed to be coming from the two biggest nests, set a little way away from the others. She scampered forward to join her littermate. "Please, Brambleclaw. I'm hungry, too."

Brambleclaw hesitated, and it was Purdy who replied. "You don't want nothin' to do wi' that place, young 'uns. It's dangerous. Can't you smell dogs as well as mice?"

Brambleclaw nodded. "I can. Thanks, Purdy. We'll carry on until we find somewhere a bit safer."

Lionpaw let out a hiss of annoyance. "I'm not scared of dogs," he muttered.

"Neither am I," Breezepaw agreed. "We see them all the

time on WindClan territory. They're not dangerous if you know how to deal with them."

"The Twolegs probably keep the stupid things shut up anyway," added Lionpaw. "Purdy's just making a fuss about nothing."

"Yeah," meowed Breezepaw. "He's only a kittypet, so he's bound to be scared."

Toms! Hollypaw thought, shaking her head as she listened to her brother and the WindClan apprentice, on the same side for once. They went on muttering together as Brambleclaw led them into the shadow of a hedge.

Hollypaw kept her ears pricked for the sound of prey. She thought she spotted movement in the thickest part of the hedge, but when she turned to look more closely a hawthorn branch snagged her fur and the small creature, whatever it was, vanished. Spitting crossly, she stopped to give her shoulder a quick groom, and spotted Lionpaw and Breezepaw, their bellies flat to the ground, creeping away in the direction of the farm.

"Hey!" she called. "Where do you think you're going?"

Lionpaw signaled to her with his tail. "Quiet, for StarClan's sake!"

Hollypaw cast a glance at the others; they had drawn ahead by a few fox-lengths, and no cat had heard anything. Jaypaw was walking between Stormfur and Brook and hadn't noticed the others leave.

Hollypaw darted over to her brother and Breezepaw. "Where are you going?"

"Keep your fur on," Lionpaw hissed. "We're just going back

to the farm. Every cat's going so slowly that we can catch a few mice and be back before they miss us."

"Come on," Breezepaw urged, nudging Lionpaw's shoulder. "I can taste those mice now."

"Are you mouse-brained?" Hollypaw demanded. "What if you get left behind? We ought to stay together."

"We won't get left behind," Lionpaw mewed.

"That cat's only a kittypet *and* an elder," Breezepaw put in. "He's probably never caught a mouse in his life. Why should he tell us what to do?"

"*Brambleclaw* told us what to do," Hollypaw pointed out. "He'll have your tails for fresh-kill if he catches you."

"We'll make sure he doesn't catch us." Lionpaw's amber eyes glowed with a strange light. A shiver ran through Hollypaw from her ears to her tail-tip. She didn't want to let her brother go off in this mood, especially with Breezepaw, who'd already shown he couldn't be trusted in a crisis. But she knew that she couldn't stop him, unless she told the senior warriors what he was planning.

"Okay," she meowed. "I'm coming with you."

Breezepaw glared at her. "No cat invited you."

"Let her come." Lionpaw rested the tip of his tail on Hollypaw's shoulder. "Three will be better than two when we're searching for prey. And Hollypaw is one of the best hunters in the Clan. She's nearly as good as Sandstorm!"

"Okay, then," Breezepaw meowed ungraciously.

Hollypaw cast another glance up the line of the hedge. The other cats had disappeared, though their scent told her they weren't far away.

"Come on," Lionpaw whispered.

He spun around and raced across a stretch of open ground toward the Twoleg fence. Hollypaw and Breezepaw followed, the grass brushing their belly fur and their tails streaming out. Hollypaw pricked her ears for yowls of anger behind them, but all was quiet.

The fence was made of the same shiny stuff as the fence around the horseplace. Lionpaw flattened himself to the ground and wriggled underneath the lowest strand, springing to his paws as soon as he reached the other side.

"Hurry up!" he urged.

Hollypaw wriggled underneath, feeling the shiny fence-stuff scrape against her back, and remembering her mother's story of getting stuck on a fence like this during her first journey. Her paws tingled with the fear that she would get stuck too.

Then she was safely through, and Breezepaw was scrabbling under the fence after her. Lionpaw was already racing down a narrow gap between the Twoleg nests. Water flooded Hollypaw's mouth again at the overwhelming scent of mice. Following her brother, she halted briefly at the edge of another open space, this one covered with stone.

Opposite where the three apprentices were standing was one of the big Twoleg nests. Across the entrance was a wooden barrier that stood slightly ajar; inside, the nest was dark. Lionpaw glanced around. Although Hollypaw could scent both dogs and Twolegs, there was no sign of either.

"Get on with it!" Breezepaw muttered.

Lionpaw signaled with his tail, and the three young cats

bounded across the open space and slipped through the gap into the nest.

Once inside, Hollypaw stood still, panting from exertion and fear, until her eyes got used to the dim light. The walls of the nest were made of rough stone. Light angled in from the entrance and from a few narrow gaps high in the walls. Dust motes danced golden in the greenish rays, but the rest of the nest lay in shadow. The scent of mouse was stronger still, but Hollypaw was too edgy to hunt. She turned and looked back the way they had come.

Behind her she heard the scamper of paws, and a thin shriek that cut off abruptly.

"First kill!" Breezepaw declared with glee. Hollypaw glanced back to see him crouched over the body of a plump mouse.

Lionpaw had dropped into the hunter's crouch, his haunches waggling from side to side and his eyes fixed on something in the shadows. Hollypaw bit back a gasp as she made out the shape of an enormous rat. It was nearly as big as Lionpaw.

Lionpaw pounced; there was a brief flurry of movement and a squeal from the rat that broke off a heartbeat later as Lionpaw bit down hard on its neck. He stood over his prey, his eyes glowing with pride.

"Brilliant catch!" Hollypaw exclaimed.

"Not bad," Breezepaw mumbled around a mouthful of mouse.

Lionpaw started dragging his prey by its tail into the center of the nest. "Come and share," he invited Hollypaw. "I can't possibly eat all this by myself."

"Thanks, I—" Hollypaw broke off at the sound of movement from outside and a sudden sharp scent.

For a couple of heartbeats she stared, frozen, at the gap leading out into the open. She couldn't see anything, but she heard snuffling at the bottom of the wooden barrier, the thud of heavy paws, and a low-pitched growling.

Breezepaw's eyes stretched wide. "Dogs!"

Chapter 17

"We've got to get out!" The WindClan apprentice abandoned the remains of his mouse and bounded toward the entrance, only to skid to a halt a couple of fox-lengths away. Three skinny black-and-white shapes had appeared in the gap, their jaws hanging open and their eyes shining as they surveyed the cats.

"One each." Lionpaw's voice was dry with fear. "Great."

Hollypaw looked around. There were no other entrances to the nest and no gaps in the stone walls, except for those where the light came in, too high for a cat to leap.

The dogs began to creep forward, their heads lowered and their legs bent, ready to sprint after the cats. *Now I know what prey feels like,* Hollypaw thought. She and the two toms backed away nervously.

"Try to dodge around them," Lionpaw mewed quietly. "If we can get out, we can outrun them."

The first dog leaped forward. Hollypaw spun around and fled, imagining she could feel its breath hot on her hind paws. Her muscles flexed as she tried to make her legs move faster, but she was tired from journeying, and her paws slipped on the dusty stone floor. Ahead of her, at the far end of the nest, was an enormous pile of dried grass. Despairingly Hollypaw wondered if they could hide in it, but she knew the dogs would be able to plunge into it and drag them out. Beyond it was the bare wall.

Why did we let ourselves get trapped? I can't believe we were so stupid! "StarClan, help us!" she panted, but at the same time she hoped the starry warriors weren't watching and didn't know how disobedient they'd been.

"Up here!"

The yowl came from above her. Glancing up, she spotted a cat's head and shoulders in one of the narrow slits high in the wall. Her jaws gaped in astonishment. It was Purdy!

"Climb the hay!" the old cat urged. "D'you want to stay and be eaten?"

Lionpaw flung himself at the pile of dried grass and began to claw his way up it. Hollypaw plunged after him, just as she heard the snap of teeth a mouse-length from her hind paws. Behind her she heard a shriek. Glancing back she saw Breezepaw trying to climb, only to be dragged back by a dog with its teeth fastened in his tail.

Hollypaw tensed. She would have to go back and help. She didn't like Breezepaw, but he was a Clan cat, and she couldn't abandon him to be torn apart. But before she could scramble down Breezepaw gave a panic-stricken heave, tore his tail free, and struggled upward, away from the gaping jaws.

The dogs tried to follow him, but they were too heavy for the piled grass to bear their weight. They floundered around in it, snuffling and slavering over the trail of Breezepaw's blood.

Hollypaw fought her way up again, half buried in the grass. It caught in her pelt; seeds got into her nose and made her sneeze. Just ahead of her, Lionpaw reached the slit where Purdy waited. The old tabby grabbed him by the scruff and pulled him through, then dropped him somewhere out of Hollypaw's sight.

He reached for Hollypaw, grabbed her, and swung her off all four of her paws into the air. In a blur of fear she thought she would fall all the way to the ground. She tensed herself for the impact, only to drop, juddering, onto a sloping red roof a couple of tail-lengths below the slit in the wall. Caught off-balance, she felt herself slipping to the edge, until Lionpaw thrust himself in front of her and brought her to a halt.

"Thanks!" she gasped.

Looking back, she saw Purdy hauling Breezepaw through the gap.

"What about my tail?" the WindClan cat complained as Purdy dropped him to join the others. "It's bleeding!"

"Shut up and follow me," Purdy meowed, leaping down beside them with a thump. "Or you'll have more to worry about than your tail. This way," he added, creeping to the edge of the roof.

He jumped down onto the edge of a container filled with water, and from there to the ground, gesturing urgently for them to follow. Lionpaw went first, leaping down easily. Hol-lypaw followed him with more caution, imagining the cold shock of a plunge into the water. Breezepaw landed beside her and immediately flicked his tail forward to examine the ragged and bleeding end.

"Stop that," Purdy hissed. "We've got to run!"

A flurry of yelping sounded from inside the nest, followed by the thunder of paws breaking out into the open. Purdy took off, running as fast as any warrior, back the way the apprentices had come. The apprentices raced after him. Hollypaw's heart pounded even harder as they approached the fence; would they be able to squeeze through before the dogs caught them?

But Purdy led them to a different part of the fence and shoved Lionpaw roughly through a hole. Hollypaw scrambled through after him; it was easier and faster than squeezing underneath. Breezepaw followed, and last of all Purdy, who turned to face the dogs as they came bounding up, barking fit to wake StarClan.

"Get back to your Upwalkers," he taunted them. "Ask them to feed you. You won't get no cat today."

Hollypaw didn't think the dogs understood him. They flung themselves at the fence, but it didn't give way, and the hole was too small for them to get through. A moment later a Twoleg appeared around the corner of the nearest nest and yowled at them. The dogs' barking changed to whines and they slunk away, casting furious glances back at the cats.

"Right, let's go," Purdy meowed.

He led them back to the shelter of the hedge, where all three of them collapsed in the long grass. Hollypaw closed her eyes. When she opened them again Purdy had gone. Instead, Brambleclaw and Crowfeather were standing over her.

"Are the three of you completely mouse-brained?" Brambleclaw's voice was icy. "You were told there were dogs at the farm. Yet you still go putting yourselves in danger. And for what? A few mice!"

"Sorry," Hollypaw muttered, unable to meet her father's gaze.

"We weren't thinking," Lionpaw confessed.

"Obviously," Brambleclaw retorted.

"It's not all our fault, though." Breezepaw looked up from licking his tail. "If you hadn't let us get so hungry—"

"None of you has ever known what it means to be really hungry," Crowfeather spat.

"And I hope all three of you have thanked Purdy," Brambleclaw continued. "You're lucky he guessed where you'd gone. If he hadn't—"

"We could have found our own way up the hay," Breezepaw interrupted. "We don't owe anything to that crazy old cat."

Hollypaw gaped at him. Okay, maybe they could have found their own way out if they hadn't been so terrified, and if they had known which slit offered an easy way to the ground. But she was sure that if it hadn't been for Purdy, they would all three be lying dead in the Twoleg nest, torn apart by the dogs.

Crowfeather let out an irritable hiss and turned his back. Hollypaw felt an unexpected pang of sympathy for Breezepaw. She would rather be scolded by Brambleclaw than face

Crowfeather's coldness. Did he even *like* Breezepaw? She and her littermates couldn't stand the WindClan apprentice, but Crowfeather was his *father*, for StarClan's sake!

I'm glad he's not my *father*, she thought.

A rustling along the hedgerow made her jump, but it was only Jaypaw, padding up with a mouthful of herbs. "Chervil," he announced, dropping the leaves beside Breezepaw. "I'd rather use horsetail, but I can't find any. Chew it up and put the pulp on your tail," he told Breezepaw. He turned to Hollypaw and Lionpaw. "Are you hurt?"

"No, we're fine," Lionpaw assured him.

"I'd better check." Jaypaw nosed Lionpaw thoroughly from ears to tail-tip, then went on to Hollypaw.

"We're really okay," she meowed, realizing that her brother was quivering with tension. "I'm sorry we couldn't bring you back a mouse."

"You shouldn't be sorry for *that*." Hollypaw was shocked at the fear and anger in her brother's voice. "Be sorry you went off and did something so mouse-brained. You didn't think about me, did you? What would I do if I lost you?"

Hollypaw swallowed hard. She *hadn't* thought about Jaypaw, except to check that he didn't know they were leaving. She'd forgotten how much Jaypaw needed her and Lionpaw, and how much harder it would be for him to lead a normal life if they weren't there.

"We *are* sorry," she mewed, touching her nose to her brother's shoulder. "We—"

"'Sorry' catches no prey." Jaypaw pulled away from her,

gave a quick sniff at the pulped chervil on Breezepaw's tail, and stalked off down the line of the hedge. "They're fine, we can carry on." He tossed the words at Brambleclaw over his shoulder as he went.

"Come on," Brambleclaw meowed. "We've wasted enough time already."

He led the way back to the other cats, who were waiting in the shadow of the hedge. Purdy was curled up, apparently asleep. Squirrelflight and Tawnypelt were keeping watch, while Stormfur and Brook shared tongues and the two Tribe cats crouched close together, muttering.

"About time," Tawnypelt grunted, rising to her paws.

"Are you all okay?" Squirrelflight asked. Her voice was stern, but Hollypaw could sense her anxiety.

"We're fine," Lionpaw mewed quietly. "We won't do it again."

Brambleclaw's voice was grim. "You'd better not."

Stormfur prodded Purdy awake, and the journeying cats set off again. Hollypaw's pads stung from where they had scraped on the stone floor of the nest. Her fur felt hot and uncomfortable from the seeds and dried grasses still caught up in it. Soon they had to leave the shade of the hedge and trek across an open field. The sun beat down; thirst clawed at her throat and her belly was yowling with hunger. Her legs were trembling with exhaustion by the time they reached the forest on the other side of the valley.

Brambleclaw stopped under the trees. "We'll stay here for the night," he announced.

"But it's still daylight," Talon objected. "We can go farther before it's too dark to travel."

"I hope you're not stopping because of these apprentices," Crowfeather added, giving his son an unfriendly glare. "If they're tired, it's their own fault."

"No, I'm not." Brambleclaw spoke quietly. "Though none of us will get very far if they collapse. But if we rest here now we can get an early start tomorrow and reach the mountains before nightfall."

The warriors went off to hunt among the ferns and brambles at the edge of the wood. Lionpaw and Breezepaw flopped down side by side on the moss between some tree roots and fell instantly asleep.

Hollypaw would have liked to join them, but there was something else she had to do first. Tottering on exhausted legs, she forced herself farther into the wood until she spotted a mouse scuttling across the open space between two bushes. As she pounced, it darted under a heap of dead leaves; she scrambled after it and managed to trap it between her claws.

That was a really messy kill, she thought, though she was almost too tired to care.

Picking up the limp body, she padded back to the edge of the wood where Purdy was crouching, his paws tucked under him as he gazed with slitted eyes across the valley.

One amber eye opened wider as she approached. "What d'you want?" he asked. Hollypaw had expected him to be hostile, but his voice was gentle, even friendly.

"I brought you this." She dropped the mouse in front of

him. "Food, and something else." She scraped the grass with one forepaw, suddenly embarrassed. "I . . . er . . . I couldn't help noticing you've got lots of ticks," she stumbled. "I'll get them off, if you like."

Purdy raised one hind leg and scratched vigorously behind his ear. "I wouldn't say no."

Carefully Hollypaw extracted the mouse bile, trying not to gag at the dreadful smell. Fetching a scrap of moss to soak it up, she explained to Purdy, "This is what medicine cats do in the Clans. I was a medicine cat apprentice for a while, so I learned how."

"That's certainly some smell," Purdy meowed, turning his face away as Hollypaw began dabbing the bile on the ticks that swelled among his rumpled tabby fur. But he kept still and let out a sigh of relief as the creatures started to drop off.

"Don't your Twolegs take care of your ticks?" Hollypaw asked as she worked.

Purdy shook his head. "My Upwalker died. I've found a few others who feed me now an' then, but they don't mess with my pelt. It don't bother me none," he added unconvincingly.

Pity for him clawed Hollypaw's belly. *So he's not even a kittypet anymore! Just a loner who's getting old.* "There, I'm done," she told him.

A rumbling purr started up in Purdy's chest. "Thanks, that feels a whole lot better," he meowed. "So that's what you learn when you're a medicine cat, eh? At least the Clan cats get one thing right."

"We're all sorry about today," Hollypaw mewed quietly.

"We're really grateful for what you did, coming to rescue us like that."

"'T'weren't nothin'," the old cat responded. "Takin' on them dogs, it made me feel young again."

"I think there's a lot we could learn from you," Hollypaw told him.

The old cat just gave an amused snort and bent his head to devour the remains of the mouse. Hollypaw curled up beside him in the long grass, and the sound of his contented purr filled her ears as she slept.

Chapter 18

Jaypaw tried to sink his claws into the bare rock. The wind buffeted him, threatening to hurl him off the narrow ridge of stone where he clung, terrified. Above his head were the stars, cold and glittering; around his paws nothing but shadows, blotting out everything but a few tail-lengths of rock, sharp as a cat's spine.

Somewhere in front of him the shadows parted and a cat paced toward him. Jaypaw recognized the lumpy, hairless body and sightless eyes of Rock. The ancient cat drew closer, balancing as easily on the thin claw of stone as if the forest stretched all around him.

"I'm here, just like you said." Jaypaw tried not to let his voice quiver. "You told me to come to the mountains, remember?"

Rock shook his head. "There should be three of you."

"There *are* three of us," Jaypaw protested, glancing back over his shoulder to see if he could spot Lionpaw and Hollypaw. "I must have left them behind on the climb. They can't—"

His last word rose into a terrified yowl as his paws slipped on the rocky ridge. He clawed frantically, but he couldn't get a grip on the smooth stone. He felt himself plunging into the shadows, down and down . . .

"Wake up!" Jaypaw felt a paw jabbing him in the ribs. It was Lionpaw. "For StarClan's sake, you're thrashing around like a dying fish."

Relief flooded over him. He was safe in his makeshift nest at the edge of the forest, and Lionpaw was with him. Tasting the air, he picked up Hollypaw's scent nearby and relaxed even more, shaking off the last clinging cobwebs of the dream. He struggled to his paws and arched his back in a long stretch. The chill of dawn crept into his pelt, and he could hear the other cats stirring around him.

"Brambleclaw says we can hunt," Lionpaw mewed, "but we have to be quick. There's a long way to go if we're going to reach the mountains by nightfall."

Jaypaw was crouched on the dewy grass devouring a vole when he heard Tawnypelt's paw steps. "It's time to leave," she announced.

He gulped down the last couple of mouthfuls and padded over to join the other cats.

"Purdy, it's been great traveling with you again," Brambleclaw was meowing. "And we're especially grateful to you for rescuing those mouse-brained apprentices. But we can't ask you to go any farther from your home."

Calling out last good-byes to Purdy, the cats set off through the trees. Lionpaw and Hollypaw came to pad along beside Jaypaw, their pelts brushing his on either side. In contrast to the days before, they padded on in tense silence as the sun climbed above the trees.

Suddenly Hollypaw's tail on his shoulder brought Jaypaw to a halt. He could feel the sun warmer on his pelt and a whisper of breeze stirring his whiskers. They must have reached the other side of the forest.

"It's *amazing*!" Hollypaw whispered.

"What?" Irritation pricked at Jaypaw's pelt, annoyance that he couldn't see whatever it was Hollypaw was mewing about.

"The mountains." It was Lionpaw who replied, his voice awestruck. "They're *vast*!"

"It's this huge wall of stone," Hollypaw explained. "All gray and steep and bare, apart from a few cracks with grass growing in them. Jaypaw, I wish you could see. It goes up forever!"

"I can't even see the top," Lionpaw added. "It's hidden in the clouds."

"Home." Brook's whisper came from just in front of Jaypaw. He sensed her mingled longing and fear; the same tension came from the other Tribe cats. They must be scared of what lay ahead, facing intruders in the place they had always thought of as theirs and theirs alone.

"Tribe of Endless Hunting." The low murmur came from Night. "Watch over us and guide our paw steps."

Jaypaw shivered. *Can StarClan still see us here?* Even though he knew that one day he would have more power than StarClan, he felt exposed and vulnerable under an indifferent sky.

"We've made good time," Talon meowed. "We can climb up to our cave before dark."

"Are you sure?" Squirrelflight's voice was doubtful. "Remember the apprentices aren't experienced climbers. We don't want to be stuck out on the mountain overnight."

"Are we going to be held up by the apprentices *again*?" Talon retorted.

Jaypaw bristled at the anger in his tone, especially as he knew it was justified. What had Lionpaw and Hollypaw been thinking of, going into the barn like that and risking everything?

"The apprentices will be fine," Stormfur stated calmly. "We can help them. What do you think, Brambleclaw?"

There was a pause before Brambleclaw replied. "Okay, let's go."

Jaypaw bounded beside his littermates as they crossed an open space. Gradually the ground began to slope upward; the grass beneath his paws grew thinner, and there were patches of loose soil mixed with grit that caught between his claws. Soon the slope was so steep that his paws started to slip.

"Mouse dung!" he muttered, clawing for a grip.

"Here." Squirrelflight's scent wreathed around him and he felt her tail guiding him to one side. His paws met solid rock.

"There's a path we can follow," his mother mewed. "There's a drop on this side, so make sure your pelt keeps brushing the rock on the other."

Jaypaw padded behind Tawnypelt with Squirrelflight just behind him. He could scent his littermates a short way ahead. He began to feel more confident; this was a bit like climbing to the Highledge or making the journey to the Moonpool.

I can do those without any trouble. I'll be fine here.

But as the path twisted higher into the mountains his confidence began to ebb. He kept picturing the long drop his mother had warned him about, and knew that a single misstep would send him plummeting into the depths. Cold wind buffeted him, threatening to carry him off his paws. The rock was hard, and he couldn't see to avoid the sharp stones that cut his pads.

A harsh screech sounded from somewhere above. Startled, Jaypaw stumbled and only Squirrelflight's shoulder, pushing up against his side, kept him on his paws.

"What was that?" he gasped.

"An eagle," his mother replied. "They can be dangerous, but that one is far away. It won't bother us."

"I wish it would," Stormfur called from behind. "We'd all have a good meal then."

Squirrelflight gently nudged Jaypaw forward again, but before he'd gone more than a few paw steps, he heard Night's voice from somewhere above his head. "Wait! Stop, all of you!"

Jaypaw halted, his nose bumping Tawnypelt's tail. "What's going on?" he asked.

"There's a gap here," Brambleclaw called, his voice echoing from the rocks. "We'll have to jump."

Jaypaw's paws tingled with fear but he held his head high, refusing to show the Tribe cats he was scared. Squirrelflight pressed against his flank, and he was glad of her silent support.

"Come on, Lionpaw." Brambleclaw's voice came again,

warm and encouraging. "You've leaped the stream on the WindClan border, and this is no farther." There was a brief silence, then he meowed, "Well done! Breezepaw next."

Jaypaw flexed his claws, scraping them on the hard stone of the path as he waited for his turn. He hated this place and couldn't think why he had ever wanted to come. He had expected to discover the landscape of his dreams; instead, the wind wafted unfamiliar scents to him, and he had no sense of Rock's presence or any warrior ancestors. His helplessness made him angry, too.

His fear mounted as he heard Tawnypelt encouraging Hollypaw to make the leap. "Don't look down," the ShadowClan she-cat meowed. "Keep your eyes on Brambleclaw."

"I'll be okay." Hollypaw sounded tense.

A moment later Jaypaw heard a yowl of congratulations from Lionpaw and knew that his sister had made the leap safely. Tawnypelt's scent suddenly faded, telling him that she too had jumped across the gap. Now there was no cat between him and the yawning abyss that he could imagine in front of his paws. The fur on his shoulders began to bristle.

"Now listen." Squirrelflight was close beside him. "The gap is a couple of fox-lengths ahead and about three tail-lengths wide. You've jumped that far before. Take three paw steps for a run-up, then jump."

"I'm right here, Jaypaw," Brambleclaw called. "I'll grab you as soon as you're across."

"Okay," Jaypaw called back, proud that his voice didn't shake. All his muscles tensed. "I'm coming now."

Not giving himself a chance to hesitate, he launched himself forward, his paws skimming the rock before his hind legs thrust him into the air. His heart pounded in a moment's wild panic; then his paws hit rock with a thud. He staggered and felt Lionpaw's shoulder steadying him.

"Great leap!" his brother mewed. "Practice a bit more and you'll be a flying cat."

"No way," Jaypaw muttered. He stood still, forcing his breathing to steady and his pelt to lie flat again.

By the time the rest of the cats had leaped across the gap, he was ready to go on, even beginning to feel pleased with himself. That would show the Tribe cats whether a blind apprentice could make the journey!

Now he sensed that their path led between towering walls of stone. The air around them was still, though he could hear wind whining among the rocks above. Their voices echoed and the rattle of loose stones dislodged by their paw steps sounded unnaturally loud.

"Best keep quiet," Talon meowed. "We're getting closer, and there might be intruders around."

The path seemed to wind and curl back on itself. Once Jaypaw heard the gurgle of falling water and his paws splashed through a shallow stream. His belly rumbled as he picked up the scents of prey. They were faint and sparse, and he wondered why any cats would want to live in such an unfriendly place, much less fight over it.

He heard Breezepaw ask if they could stop and hunt, and Crowfeather snapped at him that there was no time. "You might want to spend the night out here, but I don't!"

"There'll be fresh-kill when we get to the cave," Brook mewed.

Jaypaw wondered if she was right. Wasn't part of the Tribe's problem that the intruders were taking all their prey? He tried to sense the passage of time. Was the sun going down, filling the cleft where they walked with shadows? Back in the forest, there was so much to tell him when sunset was approaching: changes in wind and scent, the fading of birdsong, the cool touch of grass blades as twilight covered them. Here there was nothing to guide him.

The rocky path began to slope upward and the breeze picked up again, as if they were climbing out of the valley. Suddenly Jaypaw heard a yowl from above his head.

"Lionpaw, come up here! I can see forever!" Hollypaw's voice was full of excitement.

Night gave a furious hiss. Talon growled, "I said *quiet*."

"Hollypaw, get down at once," Squirrelflight ordered.

The cats halted. A couple of heartbeats later came the patter of paws and Hollypaw's voice again. "Sorry, I forgot." But Jaypaw didn't think she was sorry; excitement was still rushing through her like a river in flood. "But it's *awesome*. You can see the whole world!"

"If you've warned the intruders—" Talon began and broke off.

Jaypaw was aware of something approaching. There was no sound, only a disturbance in the air that told him of swift movement. "Someone's coming," he whispered.

"It's them," Talon mewed tersely.

"Then we'd better get out of here," Brambleclaw began.

"Too late," Night interrupted him. "Keep together. Put the apprentices in the center."

Jaypaw was almost jostled off his paws as Crowfeather shoved him against the others.

"We can fight!" Lionpaw insisted.

"Yes, you don't have to protect us," Hollypaw added.

Breezepaw said nothing, only let out a defiant snarl.

None of the older cats paid them any attention. Jaypaw found himself crushed against Hollypaw on one side and Breezepaw on the other, with the experienced fighters in a circle around them. Hollypaw was muttering curses under her breath.

Now Jaypaw could hear the beat of paws on rock and pick up unfamiliar cat scent: three or four of them, he guessed. He heard aggressive hisses from the warriors around him.

Then a strange voice spoke. "What have we here?"

Chapter 19

Hollypaw slid out her claws, muscles tensed to spring into battle. If she hadn't yowled like that, they might have been able to sneak past the trespassers. At least there were only four strange cats confronting them. If it came to a fight, there was no way the newcomers would win. They might have had an easy time with the Tribe, but they would soon find out what it was like to mess with trained Clan warriors!

The cat who had spoken was a large tom; dark stripes rippled on his silver tabby fur and his insolent amber eyes traveled lazily from cat to cat. His three companions pressed up close behind him: a skinny light brown tom with large pointed ears that swiveled alertly back and forth, a dark-brown-and-white she-cat with green eyes, and a young tortoiseshell with white streaks like lightning on her face.

"I've seen *you* before," the silver tabby taunted Talon. "What are you doing, so far away from the waterfall? I didn't think you hunted in these parts anymore."

The skinny brown cat gave him a nudge in the shoulder. "Do you think they're *scared*, Stripes?"

Stripes blinked slowly. "Flick, you could be right. I reckon they've realized that the prey around here belongs to us." His tongue swiped across his jaws. "That was a great rabbit I had this morning. Good and fat, more than I could eat."

"You should show more respect for prey!" Crowfeather snapped.

Flick spat. "Who are you to tell us what to do?"

Crowfeather's lip curled to bare his teeth in a snarl. "Want to find out?"

Brambleclaw touched the WindClan warrior's shoulder with his tail-tip, a warning gesture. "We're not looking for a fight," he murmured.

Crowfeather cast him an angry glance but said no more, though his claws scraped the hard ground and his tail twitched.

"What are you going to do with them, Stripes?" the skinny cat asked.

Before the silver tabby could answer, Night took a pace forward. She was stiff-legged with fury, her pelt bristling. "You've no right to do anything with us!" she hissed. "You've no right to come here and steal our prey."

"Rights?" The brown-and-white she-cat spoke for the first time. "Who gave you the right in the first place?"

"Well said, Flora," the skinny cat snickered.

The brown-and-white cat's question cut across Hollypaw's fury. She had been ready to fight on behalf of the Tribe. This was their territory, watched over by their warrior ancestors! But Flora's question didn't have an answer. Maybe the Tribe cats *didn't* have the right to drive out the intruders.

"We're not looking for trouble," Brambleclaw mewed

quietly, resting his tail on Night's bristling shoulders. "We're just traveling to the waterfall. You should let us go in peace."

Stripes and Flick glanced at each other, then Stripes took a pace back, gesturing up the valley with his tail. "We're not trying to stop you."

Oh, no? Hollypaw thought. Their approach had been aggressive, bounding over the rocks with lashing tails and pelts fluffed out, until they realized that they had encountered too many cats to fight with any hope of winning. They could pretend all they liked, but she knew they would have attacked if they had met the Tribe cats on their own.

Brambleclaw dipped his head with cold politeness and led his group onward up the valley. The intruders watched them go, mockery in the eyes of the two toms. For a heartbeat Hollypaw met the gaze of the young tortoiseshell, who had waited a little way behind the others, watching but not speaking. If she had been a Clan cat, she would have been an apprentice. *She might have been my friend.*

Breezepaw was clearly seeing nothing but enemies. As he stalked past the intruders he lashed his tail, letting out a furious spit.

Instantly his father nudged his haunches, thrusting him ahead. "Are you mouse-brained? Do you *want* to cause a fight?"

"They're asking for it," Breezepaw mumbled.

Hollypaw noticed that Lionpaw still had his claws unsheathed, as if for a couple of mousetails he would have sprung at the newcomers, but he didn't make his hostility as obvious as Breezepaw.

All the way up the valley Hollypaw felt the eyes of the intruders boring into her back. She let out a sigh of relief when she rounded a jutting spur of rock and they were left behind. Around her she could feel the other cats beginning to relax, too.

"This is dreadful!" Brook exclaimed. "Do these cats think they can tell you where you can go? Are the Tribe cats prisoners in their own cave?"

"It's not quite as bad as that," Night replied.

"But they thought they could order us around! Can you still get out to hunt?"

Talon padded up to Brook's side. "It's true, the intruders are getting more and more confident. They come right up to the waterfall to take prey now."

"They know we can't stop them," Night added bitterly.

"What does Stoneteller think?" Brook asked.

Talon shrugged. "He says we shouldn't challenge them, for our own safety."

What good is that? Hollypaw wondered. *Stoneteller is the Tribe's leader. He should* do *something!*

Brook shook her head, dropping back a few paces so that she could brush pelts with Stormfur as they continued up the valley. The gray warrior had been silent through the encounter with the intruders. His eyes were full of sorrow; Hollypaw guessed he was remembering the battle he had led the Tribe into, and the cats who had lost their lives.

Scarlet streaked the sky as the sun went down. The jutting mountain peaks cast deep shadows; in the open the rocks looked as if they were bathed with blood. Hollypaw shivered, imagining she could hear the shrieks of cats dying in battle.

A ridge of broken rock blocked the entrance to the valley. Hollypaw reached the top after a hard scramble and stood looking out across a range of bare rock and plunging precipices, as far as she could see in all directions. A stiff breeze ruffled her fur, and she tried to dig her claws into the rock to keep her balance. She couldn't imagine where cats might live in this stony wilderness.

Talon padded toward one end of the ridge, overlooking a shelf of flat rock. "This way," he called.

The other cats began to follow him, except for Breezepaw, who bounded off to one side. "This way looks quicker!"

Hollypaw rolled her eyes. *You don't know where you're going, mouse-brain!*

Almost at once a terrified yowl burst from the WindClan apprentice. He was sliding forward, scrabbling frantically to stop himself. Hollypaw saw that a chasm split the top of the ridge, hidden from sight in the shadows.

She darted across to help Breezepaw, but Crowfeather raced past her. He fastened his teeth in Breezepaw's tail and dragged him backward until he could stand safely on the flat top of the ridge.

Breezepaw let out a screech of pain. "My sore tail!"

"Tough," Crowfeather snarled. "Next time, think before you start showing off, and do what the Tribe cats tell you."

Breezepaw glared at his father, then padded after the others with his head and tail drooping.

"Pity," Lionpaw commented as the WindClan apprentice caught up to him. "I was looking forward to seeing you bounce all the way to the bottom of the mountain."

"Shut up, stupid furball!"

"That's enough." Tawnypelt thrust her way between the two apprentices. "For StarClan's sake, stop bickering."

Lionpaw muttered, "Sorry," and gave his chest fur a couple of embarrassed licks, while Breezepaw just ignored her. They were all tired and hungry, Hollypaw thought, and more tempers were likely to snap if they didn't reach the Tribe's home soon.

Talon led the cats to the far end of the ridge where a narrow trail led downward, only wide enough for one cat to follow at a time. As Hollypaw waited for her turn she heard the beating of wings overhead. A black shadow passed over her. With a startled yowl she flattened herself against the rock. She saw her mother throw herself on top of Jaypaw.

Daring to lift her head, Hollypaw saw an enormous brown bird with its wings spread wide as it skimmed the ridge and headed for the rocks below. Cruel, hooked talons stretched to seize the body of a mouse that lay a few tail-lengths farther down. Hollypaw's belly rumbled. Though Clan cats didn't eat crow-food, she was so hungry that she wouldn't have said no to that mouse.

As the eagle's talons closed around the limp body, four cats erupted from the shadows among the rocks. Hollypaw's jaws gaped and her eyes stretched wide with amazement as they seized the huge bird. It let out a harsh screech and its wings beat frantically as it tried to take off. It managed to rise a tail-length above the ground, but the weight of cats dragging it down was too much. It flopped back onto the rock in a flurry of wings. The thin, gray-brown cats swarmed all over it. One of them pounced on its neck and bit down. There was a last spasm of struggling and then the eagle went limp.

"Great catch!" Talon yowled.

All four cats froze, looking upward. One of them called out, "Talon!" They sounded astonished, staring at one another and the group of cats on the ridge.

Stormfur came to stand beside Hollypaw. "Welcome to the Tribe of Rushing Water," he meowed.

Chapter 20

Lionpaw followed Talon as he picked his way down the trail to the rocks below. The cats who had killed the eagle were waiting for them, their eyes guarded and their tails twitching.

A pale gray tom stepped forward to touch noses with Talon. "It's good to see you again," he mewed. There was warmth in his voice. "And you, Night," he added, as the black she-cat padded up to join them.

"Thank you, Gray," Talon replied.

Lionpaw eyed the Tribe cats doubtfully. They were smaller and skinnier than most Clan cats, and their gray-brown pelts were smeared with mud so that they almost faded into the rocky background. Their eyes glowed strangely, reflecting the red light of the setting sun. As one of them turned to look at him, he took a step toward Squirrelflight. She bent her head and licked his ear, and for a heartbeat he felt ashamed.

I'm not a kit anymore.

Besides, he told himself, they were there to *help* these cats.

The cat Talon had called Gray was staring at the other cats who had descended the trail behind Night. "Stormfur!" he exclaimed, his eyes stretched wide. "Brook! What are you doing here? You're . . . you're supposed to be dead."

The Tribe cats edged closer together, their fur bristling. Lionpaw felt a flash of irritation. Just because Stoneteller had said Stormfur and Brook were dead to the Tribe didn't mean they were actually dead. Did these cats believe everything their leader told them?

Stormfur looked at Brook, and there was weariness in his expression. "No, we're not dead," he meowed, turning back to the Tribe cats. "We were outcasts for a while, that's all."

The cats stepped forward, stretching their necks to sniff at Stormfur's pelt. Their questions came slowly at first, then faster, like rain in greenleaf.

"Are you okay?"

"Where did you go?"

"Why have you come back?"

"Talon and Night came to fetch us." Brook spoke for the first time. "They said you needed us."

The Tribe cats exchanged uncertain glances. Lionpaw waited for them to say, *Yes, thank you, we hoped you'd come back to help.* But they didn't. Instead, they turned their attention to the Clan cats.

Gray stepped forward to give Brambleclaw a cautious sniff. "Hey, I've met you before. You're one of those cats who traveled through here a few seasons ago."

"That's right." Brambleclaw dipped his head. "And I remember you . . . you're Gray Sky Before Dawn, right?"

"Right!" Gray looked surprised that Brambleclaw had remembered his name. "Did . . . did you find the home you were looking for?"

"We did, thanks," Brambleclaw replied. "A good place, by a lake."

Gray put his head on one side. "Then why are you here now? And what have you done with all the others?"

"We came because—" Tawnypelt began to speak, then fell silent as Brook shot her a warning glance. Her tail-tip twitched irritably.

"They're just passing through," Brook explained.

Lionpaw bristled; Hollypaw leaned closer to him and murmured in his ear, "She doesn't want to offend the Tribe cats by telling them they need help from outsiders. It's enough of a shock that she and Stormfur have come back from the dead, by the look of it."

But they obviously need our help! These cats were so skinny he could count their ribs. They were no match for the trespassers. Lionpaw's fur felt hot with anger as he remembered the mocking looks of Stripes and Flick and the insolent way they'd spoken.

They think they can do what they want, and no cat will stop them!

By now the red sunset light was beginning to fade, leaving the mountains wrapped in twilight. Talon waved his tail as a signal for the journeying cats to move off again.

"See you later in the cave, Gray," he meowed. His tone was decisive, making it clear that he wasn't going to answer any more questions now.

The Tribe cats went back to their prey and began dragging it across the rocks. The eagle's feathers made a soft rustling sound on the stone. Lionpaw skirted the bird at a safe distance as he passed. Even though it was dead, he didn't like the look of the sharp, crooked talons or the bright beady eye that seemed to stare at him.

As he padded across the rocky plateau beside his littermates, Lionpaw heard a noise like thunder. He looked up, but the sky was clear, with stars beginning to shine above the peaks. The roaring noise grew louder and the air grew damp until beads of moisture hung on Lionpaw's fur.

They were close to the edge of the plateau. Hollypaw ran forward to peer over the edge. "Come and look at this!" she called.

Lionpaw bounded over to join her. He stopped with a jerk and looked back to check that Jaypaw wasn't too close to the edge. Just in front of his paws, the rocks fell away into a narrow, winding valley, leading steeply downward. A stream foamed along the bottom, throwing up spray where it dashed against rocks and swirling around the roots of straggling bushes that clung to the banks. The thundering noise came from farther down the valley, where the stream vanished over a lip of rock.

"That's the waterfall." Squirrelflight raised her voice and pointed with her tail. "We're almost there."

Still in the lead, Talon picked his way down the rocks to the stream. There was a tiny path, narrow as a bramble, clinging to the edge of the water. "Watch where you're putting your paws," he called.

"Do you remember when we first came here?" Squirrelflight asked Brambleclaw.

The tabby tom's whiskers twitched. "Will I ever forget it?"

"It was on the way back from the sun-drown-place," Squirrelflight explained to the apprentices. "It had been raining hard and a surge of floodwater swept us into the stream. We went right over the waterfall and ended up in the pool below."

"I thought I'd joined StarClan for sure," Stormfur added, pausing to gaze down at the stream before setting his paws cautiously on the rocky slope.

Squirrelflight began to follow Stormfur, then glanced back to add, "Let's see if we can all do it dry-pawed this time. Come, Jaypaw, hold my tail and follow exactly where I walk."

In single file and silence, the cats crept along the edge of the stream as far as the top of the waterfall. Even Breezepaw paid attention to the directions from the experienced Tribe cats at the front of the line.

When he reached the end of the valley, Lionpaw paused, looking down to where the pounding water hurtled into the pool. The air was misty with spray; the rocks were slick with it.

"How's Jaypaw going to get down?" he murmured to Hollypaw.

His sister shook her head worriedly. "He'll never make it."

Then Lionpaw heard a yowl of protest. Brambleclaw had picked up Jaypaw by the scruff and was edging downward with the young cat dangling from his jaws like a kit.

"I can do it by myself!" Jaypaw hissed, furious.

Squirrelflight, already safely down, watched with her tail-tip twitching. "Keep still, or I'll throw you in the pool," she warned him.

Lionpaw leaned close to whisper into Hollypaw's ear.

"Don't say a word about this to Jaypaw. He'd turn us into crow-food."

His sister gave him a quick nod before beginning to pick her own way down. Lionpaw followed her, last of all the cats except for Tawnypelt. His heart beat uncomfortably fast as he tried to find a firm paw hold on the wet stones. Once he slipped, his hind paws dangling helplessly over the thundering water, while he struggled to pull himself up. Tawnypelt fastened her teeth in his shoulder and dragged him back to safety.

"Thanks," he gasped.

Tawnypelt flicked her ears but said nothing.

Lionpaw had never been so thankful as when he leaped down the last tail-length and stood on level ground beside the pool. His legs were trembling and his pelt was sodden with spray, but inside he felt proud and strong. Nothing could stop the Clan cats, not even having to climb down a waterfall. They would soon sort out those wretched, crow-food-eating trespassers and show them who deserved to hunt in the mountains. No wonder the Tribe cats hadn't been able to cope; from what he'd seen they were too small and skinny to have real fighting strength. Talon and Night had done the right thing by asking the Clans for help. They were the Tribe of Rushing Water's only chance.

Several Tribe cats were lurking behind the rocks around the pool and peeping out nervously to watch the newcomers. Lionpaw tried to pretend he hadn't noticed them. He didn't like being studied as if he were an unusual bug, with suspicion as well as curiosity. These cats should be acting a lot more grateful that the Clan cats had come all this way to help!

Crowfeather had wandered away from the rest of the group and was sitting with his head bowed beside a heap of stones on the other side of the pool, underneath a twisted tree.

"What's Crowfeather doing?" Lionpaw asked.

"That's where Feathertail is buried," Tawnypelt explained.

Lionpaw stared at the small gray-black cat crouched beside the pile of stones. "Why is Crowfeather so upset? They weren't even in the same Clan. . . ."

"Crowfeather loved her." Tawnypelt's tone was gentle. "She died saving him from Sharptooth, and she saved the Tribe as well."

Understanding stirred in Lionpaw's mind like a mouse in a drift of leaves. Maybe losing Feathertail was what had made the WindClan cat so bad-tempered all the time. He noticed Breezepaw watching his father with a jealous glint in his narrowed eyes. For once Lionpaw felt a pang of sympathy for him. He wasn't sure how he'd feel if Brambleclaw got so upset over a cat that died ages ago, not when he had Squirrelflight now.

"Come on." Talon's voice interrupted his thoughts. "It's time to walk the Path of Rushing Water." He padded around the edge of the pool and leaped up the first few rocks.

Lionpaw's eyes stretched wide with astonishment when Talon vanished behind the sheet of tumbling water. "Where did he go?"

Tawnypelt touched her tail to his shoulder. "You'll see."

Lionpaw scrambled up the slippery rocks to join Hollypaw,

Jaypaw, and Squirrelflight at the point where Talon had disappeared. They were standing on a narrow ledge of rock that led behind the waterfall. A dark hole gaped menacingly at the far end. Lionpaw's fur prickled.

"Follow me," Squirrelflight mewed to Jaypaw. "And keep your pelt pressed up against the rock."

Jaypaw, still sulking about being carried down the waterfall, muttered something Lionpaw couldn't catch.

Squirrelflight went first, placing her paws precisely in a straight line, her fur brushing the rock wall. Jaypaw followed, and Lionpaw fell in behind him, ready to grab his brother if he slipped.

The water pounded past, filling his ears with thunder and loading his pelt with icy drops. Lionpaw was sure that it would snatch him up and toss him into the pool below. In the faint light of evening he could scarcely make out Jaypaw's gray fur against the wet rock. The moist air damped down the scents of his companions; he could have been alone, pacing into the darkness beneath the earth, never to return.

"This is it," he heard Jaypaw murmur. "This is where we're supposed to be."

Lionpaw wasn't sure what he meant—he'd never been more convinced that he belonged under trees with grass beneath his paws. Taking a deep breath, he stepped into the gaping hole and found himself at the entrance to a cave. Faint watery light filtered through the waterfall behind him, revealing steep rock walls that soared up on either side, vanishing into shadows.

Blinking, Lionpaw padded forward. As he left the narrow entrance behind, the thunder of the waterfall faded. Hollypaw and Jaypaw paced beside him, Hollypaw gazing around in astonishment, while Jaypaw quivered with tension.

Brambleclaw, Talon, and Squirrelflight were already standing farther into the cave. Around them were groups of the Tribe cats, wiry gray-brown shapes that crouched, staring, as if they hardly dared come forward to greet the newcomers. All of them looked thin and anxious.

Don't worry, Lionpaw thought. *Everything will be okay, now that we're here.*

Then a brown tabby tom appeared from the shadows at the back of the cave. He was stick-thin, as if his pelt were stretched over his bare bones, and his muzzle was grizzled with age. His blue eyes glowed in the faint light.

Brambleclaw dipped his head respectfully. "Greetings, Stoneteller."

Lionpaw's paws worked impatiently against the hard floor of the cave as he waited for the old cat to welcome them. They needed to start planning right away to get rid of the intruders.

Stoneteller halted, his blue gaze raking across the newcomers. The thin fur on his neck and shoulders began to bristle.

"How dare you come here?" he snarled.

CHAPTER 21

Lionpaw stared in disbelief. Stoneteller didn't want them here? Was he completely mouse-brained?

The Tribe's leader whipped around to face Talon and Night. "What have you done?" he spat.

Lionpaw saw Talon swallow. "We . . . we went to find the Clans," he stammered, one paw raking nervously at the cave floor. "We've brought help. . . ."

"We thought it was best," Night added.

"You thought wrong!" Stoneteller's voice was soft, vibrating with fury. "You abandoned your Tribemates when we needed you to hunt for food. You told the Clans of our weakness. And you have brought all these extra mouths to feed. How dare you set paw in our cave? None of you is welcome here."

Stormfur and Brook, who had followed Lionpaw and the other apprentices into the cave, padded forward until they stood in front of Stoneteller. The old cat's eyes narrowed. *"You are dead!"*

Stormfur didn't flinch. "No, we are not. And we are still loyal to the Tribe of Rushing Water, whatever you might think."

"We *have* to help you," Brook pleaded.

But Stoneteller's eyes were cold as the stone around him. "I banished you from the mountains with good reason. Do you think I did it lightly? No. But our ancestors willed it so."

"Then our ancestors were *wrong*." Brook's amber eyes glowed. "The Tribe is suffering even more than when we left. The trespassers are even more arrogant. We met a group of them on our way here. They behaved as if the mountains were their territory and they could drive us off if they wanted."

"We have come to help," Stormfur insisted. "You need us."

"Need you!" Stoneteller echoed scornfully. "What do you think you can do? Too many lives have been lost already, too much blood spilled—and that was your doing. You told us we needed a show of strength to defend our territory, but it didn't work."

"But there was no territory," Brambleclaw pointed out, taking a pace forward to stand beside Stormfur. "You need to mark your borders."

"We have never done that!" Stoneteller snapped. "That is not the way of the Tribe, and Stormfur knows it."

Stormfur bowed his head. Lionpaw exchanged a glance with Hollypaw, seeing his own anger reflected in his sister's eyes. How stupid could this old cat be, not only to banish Stormfur from the Tribe but then to refuse the help he offered when he came back?

"Stormfur did what he thought was best," Squirrelflight broke in, her green gaze sparkling with annoyance. "So did Talon and Night. There's nothing to be ashamed of in asking for help. Or would you rather let the Tribe die because you were too proud?"

Stoneteller took a pace toward the ginger she-cat, his neck fur bristling. Lionpaw tensed his muscles to spring if the Tribe's leader tried to attack his mother.

Then the old cat's tail drooped and the fur on his shoulders began to lie flat again. "The Tribe of Endless Hunting has sent me no signs about accepting help from the Clans." Turning to Brambleclaw, he added, "I mean no disrespect to you or your Clanmates. I know how much we owed you in the past, and I believe you mean well now."

Brambleclaw opened his jaws to speak, but Stoneteller raised his tail for silence. "You should not have come," he continued. "This is not your battle. You may stay here for tonight, but in the morning you will be escorted to the edge of the mountains, and you must not return."

"And how do you mean to stop us?" Breezepaw growled from just behind Lionpaw.

For once, Lionpaw agreed with the WindClan apprentice. The Tribe didn't have the strength to back up Stoneteller's orders. But he guessed that Brambleclaw wouldn't stay where the Clans weren't wanted.

"And what about us?" Brook demanded.

Stoneteller turned his blue gaze on her. "We cannot feed two more hungry bellies."

Is that it? Shock froze Lionpaw's paws in place and shivered through every hair on his pelt. *Do we just turn around and go home without lifting a claw to help?* He opened his jaws to protest, only to close them again when he caught Brambleclaw's warning glance.

"We're guests of the Tribe." Brambleclaw padded over and fixed all four apprentices with a stern gaze. "We mustn't cause trouble."

"Not even when that stupid—"

"No." Brambleclaw sighed. "I'm as disappointed as you are, but we mustn't make things worse. Do you all understand that?"

"If you say so . . ." Lionpaw mewed reluctantly. Hollypaw and Jaypaw nodded agreement, and even Breezepaw growled, "Suppose so."

A gray-brown Tribe she-cat trotted across the cave toward them. "Hi, Brambleclaw," she greeted him. "Remember me?"

Brambleclaw put his head on one side. "Bird That Rides the Wind. You were with Talon when we first met."

"That's right," Bird purred. "It's good to see you again. Stoneteller asked me to find you somewhere to sleep for the night. You and your warriors can come with me to the cave-guards' place"—she flicked her tail toward one side of the cave—"and your apprentices can sleep with our to-bes."

Lionpaw stiffened, wondering if Stoneteller wanted to split up the Clan cats so they could be attacked more easily. But Brambleclaw agreed calmly, and common sense told Lionpaw that the Clans would have done exactly the same if a large group of cats had arrived to stay in their camps.

As Bird led the apprentices farther into the cave, Lionpaw craned his neck to look around. By now night had fallen and the moon had risen, turning the waterfall to a sheet of tumbling silver and shedding a soft, wavering light throughout the cave. He could see scattered rocks around the edges of the cave, and here and there cracks in the walls that led up to narrow ledges. From the roof, high above his head, talons of stone pointed down to the cave floor.

His belly rumbled as the scent of fresh-kill tickled his nostrils. At one side of the cave, Gray and his hunting party had brought in their eagle and were tearing it apart. *I hope they give us some,* Lionpaw thought. His last meal had been in the forest, which seemed like seasons ago now. There wasn't much else on the fresh-kill pile: a couple of mice and a rabbit. *No wonder they're all so skinny!*

Bird took them to the back of the cave, where a pair of tunnels led off into darkness. A few tail-lengths away two young cats were wrestling while three or four others looked on.

"These are our to-bes," Bird announced.

The wrestling cats broke apart and sat up to stare at the newcomers. "Who are they?" a pale gray she-cat asked. "Are they prisoners?"

"No, Pebble, they're guests," Bird replied. "They'll be staying with us tonight. Look after them and find them somewhere to sleep."

"What, all four of them?" a black tom exclaimed. "There isn't room."

The gray she-cat gave him a hefty shove. "Don't be so rude!" To the Clan apprentices she added, "Don't pay any attention to Screech. He's beetle-brained."

"Beetle-brained yourself!" Screech muttered.

"You'll be fine for one night," Bird mewed briskly. With a friendly nod to the Clan cats she bounded back across the cave to where Brambleclaw and the others were waiting for her.

Lionpaw felt embarrassed as the to-bes crowded around him and the others, sniffing at them curiously. "I'm Lionpaw," he meowed, trying to sound confident. "This is my sister, Hollypaw, and my brother, Jaypaw, and that's Breezepaw."

The gray she-cat dipped her head and stretched out one paw. The gesture surprised Lionpaw, though he had to admit it looked polite. "I am Pebble That Rolls Down Mountain," she told them, "and this annoying furball is my brother, Screech of Angry Owl."

Screech curled his lip at his sister, before extending his paw in the same polite gesture. Lionpaw dipped his head in return, hoping the Tribe to-bes wouldn't think he and the others hadn't been mentored properly.

"I'm Splash When Fish Leaps," a small tabby she-cat added, bouncing up with her stubby tail sticking straight up. The other to-bes hung back, giving the newcomers doubtful looks.

"You've come a long way," Pebble commented. "I've never scented cats like you before."

Hollypaw began to tell the story of how Talon and Night had come to fetch them, but before she had reached the start of their journey she was interrupted by the prey-hunters, who padded over carrying pieces of the eagle in their jaws.

"There." Gray dropped his prey in front of the to-bes. "Plenty for all of you."

"Thanks." Screech swiped his tongue around his lips. "This'll be the first decent meal we've had in ages," he added quietly to the visitors.

"The intruders take all our prey," Pebble explained sadly. "They watched us to see how we hunt, and now they've learned to do it themselves. There aren't enough eagles to go around."

"Wait till I'm a prey-hunter," Screech boasted. "I'll soon find enough prey to feed all the Tribe."

"Yes, when eagles learn to talk!" his sister snapped.

Lionpaw was afraid they would all have to wait to eat until the brother and sister had finished arguing. "It seems really strange to us," he began, hoping to distract them. "We don't split up the duties like that. We all hunt *and* fight."

"It can't come naturally to you," Splash mewed. "Learning all that must be really tough."

"It is," Hollypaw agreed, to Lionpaw's surprise. "But it's fun, too."

"Stoneteller chooses what we'll be," Pebble told her. "Kits who look big and strong get to be cave-guards, and ones that look like they'll run fast and leap high become prey-hunters. I'm going to be a cave-guard."

Yes, fine, but when do we get to eat? Lionpaw's belly was yowling in protest. He knew all this stuff anyway, from what Brook had told them back in ThunderClan territory.

To his relief, Pebble and the other to-bes began dividing up the fresh-kill. The Tribe to-bes split into pairs; each cat took a bite out of its own piece of prey, then exchanged the food with its partner.

"Maybe we'd better do that," Hollypaw whispered. "Or they'll think we're really rude."

"Okay," Lionpaw mewed. "You share with Jaypaw, I'll have Breezepaw's piece."

"Do what?" Jaypaw asked irritably. "Prey's prey. Let's eat."

Hollypaw crouched close to Jaypaw's ear to explain to him what was happening, while Lionpaw tried not to make a face at the thought of eating prey that Breezepaw had bitten into.

"Why's she telling your brother what to do?" Pebble asked, raising her head from the fresh-kill she was devouring. "Why can't he just copy us?"

Lionpaw glanced uneasily at his brother, knowing how much Jaypaw hated it when cats talked about him as if he weren't there. "Well, because he's blind."

Pebble's eyes stretched wide. "Wow, that's really weird."

"How does he manage?" Screech asked curiously. "Do you have to lead him around by the tail?"

Lionpaw saw his brother's ears flatten. His jaws opened for a stinging retort, but Hollypaw slapped her tail across his muzzle. Jaypaw furiously spat out a mouthful of fur.

"He may be blind, but he's not deaf," Lionpaw meowed, feeling annoyed for his brother but not wanting to start a quarrel. "And he manages just fine. Haven't you ever seen a blind cat before?"

"No," Pebble replied, as if Lionpaw was foolish even to ask. "How can your Clan ever let him out on his own?"

Lionpaw saw what she meant and shuddered. A blind cat wouldn't last long in this rocky place. Even if it managed to avoid an eagle's talons, it would probably fall over a precipice.

"Jaypaw's training to be a medicine cat," Hollypaw put in, a touch of defensiveness in her tone.

Pebble looked even more astonished at that, and most of the other to-bes pricked up their ears to listen.

"That's impossible!" Splash exclaimed. "How could a blind cat lead your Clan?"

What? Lionpaw exchanged a glance with Hollypaw. "He won't be leader."

"But you . . . oh, I see!" The puzzled look in Pebble's eyes cleared. "In the Tribe Stoneteller is our Healer. And he picks out the cat who will be Healer after him. But I suppose you do things differently."

"We have a leader *and* a medicine cat," Breezepaw explained, in a superior tone.

"Weird . . ." murmured Screech.

Privately Lionpaw thought the Tribe's way was even more weird. How could Stoneteller make good decisions when he didn't have a medicine cat to advise him? It didn't look as if he even had a deputy. Maybe the Tribe could have come up with a solution to the problem of the intruders if every cat wasn't so convinced that they had to do exactly what Stoneteller told them.

"Hi. How are you getting on?"

Lionpaw jumped when he heard Squirrelflight's voice; she had padded up unseen behind him. "Fine, thanks." He tried to sound convincing.

"Great. But I think it's time you settled down to get a good night's sleep. It looks like we'll have a long journey tomorrow."

Lionpaw gulped his last bite of eagle and glanced up at his mother. She didn't look like her normal cheerful self; her tail trailed on the ground and her eyes were anxious. He guessed she felt they had made a huge mistake by coming so far, only to be turned away. Reaching up to brush his muzzle against hers, he wished he could comfort her and tell her that these stupid Tribe cats should be glad of their help, but it was impossible in front of all the to-bes.

"Okay," he meowed. "We'll see you in the morning."

Squirrelflight brushed his shoulder with her tail, bent over to give Hollypaw and Jaypaw a swift lick around the ear, and padded softly away. Lionpaw's gaze followed her as she headed across the cave to the other warriors, wishing he could be with them instead of a bunch of strange to-bes.

"Come on," Pebble mewed, flicking his ear with her tail. "I'll show you where to sleep."

She led the apprentices to a place where several shallow dips had been scooped out of the cave floor. They were warmly lined with moss and feathers.

"Choose any," Pebble invited them.

Lionpaw curled up in one of the larger hollows with Hollypaw and Jaypaw. At least the sleeping place was comfortable; for a moment he could almost believe they were back in the ThunderClan nursery. But in the nursery he had never had so many worries to keep him awake.

He lay with his eyes slitted, watching the constantly changing light flickering over the cave walls and listening to the endless rumble of the waterfall. So much for standing on the hill overlooking the lake and feeling as if he could do *anything*. Their journey had come to nothing; these strange, proud cats were turning them away without even giving them the chance to help.

Lionpaw let out a sigh. He had been desperate to make this journey for so long, to see the mountains for himself, and now that he was here, he just wanted to go home.

CHAPTER 22

Jaypaw heard his brother's sigh and felt disappointment rolling off him like the waves on the lakeshore. He had picked up the same feeling from Hollypaw before she fell asleep, but he couldn't share it. They had made it as far as the mountains, which was the main thing that mattered to him. His only worry was that he would be forced to go home before he had learned the secrets that awaited him here.

He lay quietly in the warm nest, trying to build up a picture of the cave. He could locate the waterfall from the sound it made and identify where the cats were from their scent. There was a difference between cave-guards and prey-hunters, he discovered, just as there was between Clan and Tribe.

Beneath their scents, he felt battered by the Tribe's emotions, their sense of fear and vulnerability in a situation they could not control. And in addition, a desperate weariness, as if they were ready to give up their claim to live in the mountains.

Where are their ancestors? Jaypaw wondered. *Why isn't the Tribe of Endless Hunting doing something to help?*

The image of Stoneteller rose in his mind, the grizzled tabby he had seen when he shared Brook's memory of the battle and Stormfur's banishment. The roaring of the waterfall grew louder, pulsing in his ears, until suddenly his eyes flicked open. He was standing on the exposed rocky outcrop where he had confronted Rock before. Stars glittered frostily above his head and an icy wind ruffled his fur. Stoneteller stood barely a tail-length away, with his back to him.

Jaypaw darted into the shadow of a rock and peered out. Along the spine of stone another cat was approaching, a slender tabby like most of the Tribe cats, but with the shimmer of stars in his fur. Jaypaw pressed himself farther into the shadows. This must be one of the Tribe's ancestors, from the Tribe of Endless Hunting. Curiously he wondered why Rock had brought him here in his earlier dream, if it was a place sacred to the Tribe.

Stoneteller waited until the ancestor stood a fox-length away from him, then dipped his head. "Greetings," he meowed. "What guidance have you come to give me?"

For a moment the ancestor did not reply. Jaypaw thought there was an air of defeat about him, as if even the Tribe of Endless Hunting was sick of the fighting and ready to give up.

"I have no guidance," the ancestor replied at last. "Never in the Tribe's history have we tried to fight an endless battle. Until now, the mountains have been protection enough." His sigh was like the whisper of wind over the rock. "We can see no end to it."

"There must be an end!" Stoneteller protested. "My Tribe is dying. There must be something we can do."

The ancestor shook his head. "Not this time," he mewed

sadly. "We thought this was a place of safety, but it is not." He turned and began to pace away, fading into the shadows.

"Wait!" Stoneteller took a step forward, lashing his tail, then halted, his head lowered in defeat. As if he was too exhausted to stay on his paws, he staggered to the shelter of a rocky overhang, flopped down, and closed his eyes.

Instantly Jaypaw sprang out of hiding and raced along the stony ridge, ignoring the precipices on either side. After a few pounding heartbeats, the shape of the ancestor reappeared from the shadows, still pacing slowly away.

"Wait for me!" Jaypaw called.

The ancestor halted and glanced back over his shoulder. When his gaze fell on Jaypaw his ears flicked up and his eyes widened in shock. "You have come," he whispered.

Jaypaw stared at him. What did he mean? How could a cat from the Tribe of Endless Hunting recognize a Clan cat who had never set paw in the mountains until now?

Before he could say anything, the cat spoke again. "Follow."

Jaypaw gulped. This wasn't what he had imagined. But he was here now—and there were so many questions he wanted answers to. His paws carried him on almost against his will, as the ancestor crossed the last few fox-lengths of the ridge and set paw on a trail that led down into thick shadow.

The narrow path, faint against the surface of the rocks, zigzagged across the face of a cliff. In the dim starshine Jaypaw couldn't see the bottom. *But at least I* can *see*. This couldn't be as bad as that awful journey yesterday, and it wouldn't end in the humiliation of being carried like a kit. He pressed himself close to the rock face and tried not to think of how far he might have to fall.

The ancestor padded on steadily, his pace never varying; now and again he glanced over his shoulder to make sure that Jaypaw was still following. Eventually he halted, beckoned Jaypaw with his tail, then leaped off the cliff and disappeared.

Jaypaw's claws scraped the stony surface of the ledge. Was he expected to launch himself into the shadows? If he didn't kill himself, it would still break his dream, and he couldn't bear to wake up until he'd had a chance to talk to the ancestor. But when he peered over the edge he saw the ground was only a couple of tail-lengths below. He jumped down easily and looked around.

The ancestor had brought him to the bottom of a stone hollow, a little like the ThunderClan camp, except that the sides were sheer and much, much taller. The only way up or down seemed to be by the trail that they had followed. In the center of the hollow, almost filling it, was a pool. Starlight shimmered on its surface. It reminded Jaypaw of the Moonpool, except it was much bigger, and instead of the constant plashing of the waterfall, the water was still and the hollow was utterly silent.

Jaypaw blinked. What he had thought was the reflection of starshine in the pool was a light that came from the ranks of starry cats sitting around it—or had they only just shown themselves? He shivered as he gazed around. He was used to StarClan now, but he had never imagined that one day he would confront ancestors who were not his own.

Some of the cat shapes were barely visible, as if the spirits were so old that they had almost faded away. Others shone more strongly, and some still bore the wounds of battle, seeping blood, as if they had only just come to join the Tribe of Endless Hunting.

Jaypaw stayed frozen in place as one of the ancient cats rose to its paws and came close enough to sniff him. Jaypaw could see the water of the pool through the outline of his fur. "We heard you would come," the ancestor murmured. His voice was muffled, as if he spoke through season upon season of dust. "But we did not expect you to come so soon."

Soon? Jaypaw could hardly imagine what "soon" meant to these old spirits. Surely they must have been waiting for a moon of lifetimes?

"Are you talking about the prophecy?" he asked.

"Yes." The old cat breathed out the word. "Three will come, kin of the cat with fire in his pelt, who hold the power of the stars in their paws."

Jaypaw's heart began to thud. *They knew! They knew, and so did StarClan! How long have they been waiting for us?*

"Where are the other two?" the ancient spirit asked.

"In the cave." Jaypaw wasn't going to admit that he hadn't told his littermates about the prophecy yet. "Where did the prophecy come from?" he whispered.

The ancient cat did not reply; instead, one of the brighter spirits spoke from farther around the pool. "Why did you bring him here?" she demanded, addressing the tabby cat who had led Jaypaw down the cliff. "He doesn't belong with us."

There was a murmur of agreement from some of the other cats. Their glowing eyes were hostile as their gaze raked across him. Jaypaw suppressed an impulse to make a dash for the trail that led back to the ridge.

I can walk where I like, he told himself, defiantly raising his head. *I wouldn't be here if I didn't belong. And maybe I can do more than Stoneteller to help the Tribe. . . .*

"You need to take a message to the Tribe of Rushing Water," he meowed. "Tell them that the Clan cats have come to help them with the trespassers."

The ancestral spirits glanced at one another, then shook their heads. The bright she-cat who had spoken before rose to her paws. "The Tribe does not need help."

"How can you say that?" Jaypaw gasped. "The Tribe is starving to death."

"There is nothing we can do." The ancestor who had led Jaypaw down from the ridge bowed his head in shame. "We have failed."

"The mountains are not safe anymore," another cat murmured. "We trusted them to protect us, and they have let us down."

For a moment Jaypaw could not speak through the wave of shame and betrayal that surged from the starry cats. He struggled to shake it off and clear his mind again.

"The Tribe doesn't have to give in so easily," he insisted. "They *must* fight to defend themselves."

Two of the cats who bore recent wounds rose from their places and padded around the pool until they stood in front of

Jaypaw. "We died in battle," the first of them mewed, glancing down at the deep slashes along his side. "No more blood must be spilled. The Tribe does not believe in fighting."

Jaypaw twitched his tail. "But the trespassers do. My Clanmates *will* help the Tribe cats, whether they want it or not."

The other wounded cat took a pace forward, his neck fur bristling. "The only way to do that is to make the Tribe more like a Clan. And that is not what they want. It is not the way of the Tribe to fight and kill other cats."

"Things change," Jaypaw pointed out with a flick of his ears.

"Not always for the better," the spirit cat retorted.

The words echoed in Jaypaw's ears. A mist seemed to be rising from the pool, swirling around him until he couldn't see the Tribe of Endless Hunting any longer. The mist gradually grew darker, until Jaypaw realized he was back in the cave, with Hollypaw nudging him awake.

"Come on," she urged him. "Stoneteller has called a meeting. All the cats are gathering in the middle of the cave."

Jaypaw scrambled groggily to his paws. The hollow in the mountains and the pool surrounded by shining cats seemed more real to him than this cave.

"Okay, keep your fur on," he grumbled. "I'm coming."

Tracking Hollypaw and Lionpaw by their scent, he followed them out of the sleeping hollow and across the floor of the cave. They joined the other Clan cats and found a place to sit beside them. Jaypaw shifted uncomfortably on the cold stone, the murmur of voices, Clan and Tribe, in his ears.

Suddenly the voices grew quiet. Jaypaw imagined the skinny old cat he had seen in his dreams appearing in front of the cats, perhaps leaping onto the boulder from where he had banished Stormfur. *So this is it,* he thought. *We're going to be made outcasts, too. I don't suppose they'll feed us before they throw us out, either.*

"Cats of the Tribe of Rushing Water," Stoneteller began. "Last night I read the signs in water and starlight, and the Tribe of Endless Hunting spoke to me. They do not want us to be driven out of our mountain home, so I have decided to let the Clan cats help us."

Jaypaw felt his mouth drop open. Stoneteller was lying! That wasn't what the Tribe of Endless Hunting had said at all. Stoneteller must have changed his own mind overnight, and decided to ignore his ancestors.

A babble of comment had broken out as soon as Stoneteller finished speaking. Jaypaw could hear some protests, but most cats sounded eager to hear what the Clan cats would suggest. Just as he suspected, the Tribe cats did whatever Stoneteller said. Yesterday he hadn't wanted the Clan cats to stay, so neither did his Tribe, and today he said they should accept their help. *Don't these cats ever think for themselves?*

"Silence!" Stoneteller raised his voice. "We will listen to what Brambleclaw has to say."

There was a brief pause; Jaypaw heard his father's paw steps as he emerged from the group of cats and went to stand beside Stoneteller.

"What should we do first?" the Tribe's Healer asked him.

"Assess the situation." Brambleclaw's tone was crisp and

positive; Jaypaw knew that his father would have worked out what he would say long before. "We need to know what the real threat is. Where are these trespassers taking prey? Where are they clashing with the Tribe? And we must discover where they've made their camp."

"We should work out how much territory the Tribe needs to survive, too," Tawnypelt called out from somewhere near Jaypaw.

"That's right," Stormfur put in, his voice deep but tense with excitement. "We can't sit here and wait to be attacked. We should establish borders and make sure they're properly defended."

An eager chorus broke out again, but a new voice cut across it. "Wait."

As the noise died down, Brambleclaw meowed, "Yes, Crag. What do you want to say?"

"We have known each other a long time, Brambleclaw," the new speaker began. "I was the first Tribe cat you met when you dragged yourselves out of the pool, all those moons ago. I'm a cave-guard, and I fought in the great battle beside Stormfur. No cat can say that I'm afraid to fight. But I'm telling you now that you're wrong."

"Why?" Even in the single word, Jaypaw could tell how much respect his father felt for this cat.

"Because you're trying to turn us into a Clan," Crag replied. "We're not. We are the Tribe."

"But this is the only way to survive!" Brambleclaw insisted. "You've never had to share your hunting grounds with other cats before. You can't live here like prisoners, afraid to venture out in search of food."

"That's right!" some cat called. "We need our own territory."

"We need to defend it!" another added.

"But think what we risk losing." Crag's strong meow rose above the voices of his Tribe. "All our traditions, everything that makes us who we are. Instead, we'll spend all our time running around trying to remember which rocks belong to us."

"What do you think?" Hollypaw whispered as the argument rumbled on above their heads.

"Brambleclaw's right," Lionpaw asserted without hesitation. "What choice do they have?"

"But then, Crag's right, too." Hollypaw sounded uncertain. "How would we like it if cats came into our territory and started telling us to do everything differently?"

"We're not starving to death," Lionpaw pointed out. "What's the matter, Hollypaw? On the way here you were planning how to organize the Tribe like a Clan."

"I know. But it's different when you see how they do things." Hollypaw's worry soaked into Jaypaw's fur like rain. "What about you, Jaypaw?" she prompted. "Do you think the Tribe should give up all its traditions because of these trespassing cats?"

Jaypaw shrugged. "It's not our decision. They're not our traditions."

He heard a hiss of annoyance from Hollypaw, as if she'd expected him to back her up. But the problem was more complicated than she or Lionpaw understood. Jaypaw was reluctant to talk about his dream. He had always relished the extra knowledge he gained through his connection with StarClan, but now he was thoroughly unnerved, knowing that the Tribe of Endless Hunting did not want the Tribe to become a Clan.

He remembered the feelings of shame he had picked up by the pool, the regret of the Tribe of Endless Hunting that they had failed their descendants, that they had not found a place of safety for the cats who looked to them for protection. He remembered their belief that the mountains had betrayed them.

Then something struck him. If the Tribe had tried to find a place of safety in the mountains, that meant they must have come from somewhere else—somewhere that was no longer safe.

So where did they come from? And what brought them here in the first place?

CHAPTER 23

Lionpaw watched as the Tribe cats broke up into small, quarrelsome groups.

They might as well save their breath, he thought. *Stoneteller has made up his mind, and now Brambleclaw's in charge.*

Even so, he was impressed by Crag's courage in speaking up and glad of the respect he could see between the cave-guard and his father. Crag was a strong, brave cat, and with the right training he would make a great warrior.

"At least we haven't come all this way for nothing," Breezepaw remarked, strolling over. "We'll soon lick this lot into shape. We might as well start calling them MountainClan right now."

"Say that in the hearing of a Tribe cat, and you'll be looking for your ears," Hollypaw hissed.

"Ignore him," Lionpaw told her. "If he wants to be stupid—"

He broke off as he saw Brambleclaw padding toward them. "I've got a job for you," the dark tabby meowed.

Lionpaw sprang to his paws, his tail straight up in the air. Action at last!

"Do you think you three could train the to-bes in some

fighting moves?" Brambleclaw asked.

Lionpaw started a little as he realized that "you three" included Breezepaw and not Jaypaw. The three apprentices glanced at one another, the argument with Breezepaw forgotten.

"Sure." Lionpaw nodded. "We'll be glad to help."

He touched his tail-tip to Jaypaw's shoulder in farewell as he followed his father across to the to-bes' part of the cave. Jaypaw didn't seem to notice; he was staring at the wall of the cave, lost in thought.

"Every cat, even the prey-hunters, will be trained in basic fighting," Brambleclaw explained. "But we'll give the cave-guards the responsibility of border patrols. They're the strongest cats, and they have some fighting techniques, though they still need battle training."

"There aren't any borders yet," Hollypaw pointed out.

Brambleclaw gave her a friendly flick on the ear with his tail. "There will be soon."

The to-bes were gathered in a tight cluster in their own part of the cave. They all turned to look at Brambleclaw and the apprentices as they approached.

"Greetings," Pebble meowed, dipping her head to Brambleclaw and extending a paw.

"Greetings," Brambleclaw replied. "I think you've met Lionpaw, Hollypaw, and Breezepaw. They're going to give you some training in fighting techniques."

To Lionpaw's dismay, none of the to-bes looked pleased at the prospect. They muttered together; Lionpaw caught the words ". . . only to-bes like us."

"Splash and I are prey-hunters." Screech spoke up boldly, flicking his tail at the light brown tabby she-cat beside him. "We don't do that stuff."

"The whole Tribe will be doing 'that stuff,'" Brambleclaw told him.

"It's for your own good," Lionpaw added.

Screech glared at him.

"Come on," Hollypaw mewed persuasively. "It'll be fun. And if the intruders attack you, you'll need to defend yourselves."

To Lionpaw's relief, he saw that Pebble and one or two others were looking interested. His paws tingled with anticipation. This would be good practice for when he was a mentor with an apprentice of his own.

Brambleclaw gave an approving nod. "I'll leave you to it, then. Tawnypelt, Crowfeather, and I are going to explore the territory and see if we can set the borders." He turned away, then glanced over his shoulder. "Lionpaw, would you like to come with us? Hollypaw and Breezepaw can handle the training for now."

For a heartbeat Lionpaw felt disappointed. Then he reminded himself that he had wanted to explore the world beyond the lake, and here was a chance to see more of it. "Okay," he mewed, waving his tail in farewell to the others and following Brambleclaw to the cavern entrance.

Tawnypelt and Crowfeather were waiting there, with Talon, Bird, and Gray.

"We'll come with you," Talon meowed. "You might need

backup if the trespassers are around."

"Thank you." Brambleclaw gestured with his tail to let the big cave-guard take the lead.

Lionpaw fell in behind his father to walk the Path of Rushing Water behind the waterfall. With sunlight dazzling through the sheet of foaming water, it didn't seem as frightening as in twilight the night before. When he emerged into the open he leaped down onto the ground beside the pool and shook drops of water from his pelt. The sky was blue, with a few white clouds scudding across it, driven by a stiff breeze. The sun was just grazing the topmost peaks, bathing the mountain slopes in light. High up, a single bird flew in lazy circles.

"Eagle," Bird murmured. "We'll need to keep an eye on it."

"This way," Talon mewed. He bounded over to the rocks opposite the pool and clawed his way up until he stood on a flat overhang of stone. Lionpaw and the other cats followed. Lionpaw stood panting on the edge and looked out across an empty forest of jutting rock. Only a few clumps of green foliage here and there interrupted the vast gray-brown landscape. There was no sign of movement.

"It's empty." He crouched to peer down at the rocks below the overhang. "It feels like there's no cat here but us."

"Don't you believe it," Talon growled, padding up behind him. "The trespassers aren't as good at hiding as we are, but they're getting better at it all the time."

"So you'll have to get better still," Brambleclaw mewed briskly. "Then you can fight back."

Talon gave a doubtful snort and began climbing a steep slope of scree that led to a ridge. When Lionpaw set paw on the shifting stones he thought he would never be able to climb it. For every paw step he took, he felt as if he was slipping back two. He watched the Tribe cats setting their paws sideways on the slope and gradually began to make better progress. At last he was able to haul himself up the last tail-length and stand on the top.

Wind buffeted his pelt and made his eyes water. Blinking, he made out an even wider landscape of jutting crags and narrow valleys, with streams that looked narrow as grass stems weaving their way among the rocks. Far away he could see a blur of green, and he realized that he was looking at the edge of the mountains, perhaps the forest they had crossed on their way.

"I feel like a bird!" he cried.

The words were hardly out of his mouth before he felt his paws slipping. For a heart-stopping moment he thought the wind would bowl him over to plummet down to the rocks below. The landscape whirled sickeningly around him. Then teeth fastened in his scruff and yanked him back to safety. He looked up to see Crowfeather.

"Thanks," he gasped.

"Just remember you're not a bird," the WindClan cat growled.

Lionpaw sat down for a few heartbeats until the dizziness passed and his heart stopped pounding. When he looked up, he saw Talon, Tawnypelt, and Brambleclaw standing a few paw steps away. The Tribe cat waved his tail to point at something below the ridge.

"That's where Stormfur led us into battle," he meowed.

More cautiously this time, Lionpaw padded up to the edge and peered over. The ground fell away into a steep valley, with jagged rocks on either side. At the bottom a narrow stream wound its way among boulders. He shivered, imagining that he could see the slopes running with the blood of cats and hear their screeches as they hurled themselves into the fight.

"We don't go that way anymore," Talon continued. "The intruders think it belongs to them now."

"Maybe we need to teach them they're wrong," Tawnypelt suggested with a lash of her tail.

Talon shook his head. "It's not worth it. We never found much prey there. If we go a bit farther along this ridge, we come to another valley with a stream. There's grass growing there and a few bushes, and you can generally pick up a mouse or two, or even a rabbit if you're lucky. We get moss for bedding from there, too."

Lionpaw looked in the direction he pointed. A few foxlengths farther along the ridge there was a twisted spike of stone like a lightning-blasted tree. "That would make a good border marker," he suggested to Brambleclaw.

Brambleclaw nodded. "Good thinking. And the valley with the stream should be part of the Tribe's territory."

The Tribe cats made no comment, though they exchanged doubtful glances. With a flash of sympathy Lionpaw guessed that they might feel they were losing their territory anyway, to the Clan cats who were telling them what to do.

"Can you take us there, Talon?" Brambleclaw asked.

"Sure." The big cave-guard set out along the ridge and Lionpaw followed with the other Clan cats, being very careful where he put his paws. The eagle, he was relieved to see, had disappeared.

The next valley, when they came to it, looked more inviting for hunting, with plenty of cover for prey. Talon would have turned down into it, but Brambleclaw urged them on, following the top of the ridge.

"We need to walk all the way around the border," he meowed, "or at least where we think the border might be."

"What?" Bird looked startled. "We can't possibly go all that way in a single day."

"It takes longer here, you know," Gray added. "It's not like traveling on flat ground."

"I know that," Brambleclaw responded, understanding in his amber eyes. "But time isn't on your side. The intruders aren't going to wait for you."

Talon let out a low growl. "You're right. Let's get going."

He led the group of cats along the top of the valley, taking in the spike of stone as a border marker. The ridge dipped at the point where it crossed the head of the valley, where the stream poured out from a cleft between two rocks.

"This is another good place for a marker," Brambleclaw explained. "Once the border is decided, you'll need to place scent markers every day, and it's best to choose places that are easy to remember."

Talon nodded, but Lionpaw thought he still didn't look

convinced that marking the territory was what the Tribe wanted to do.

From here their route lay across a plateau covered by loose, sharp stones, then over several steep ridges where there were no paths to guide them. The sun climbed high in the sky. Lionpaw's legs ached, and he lost count of the number of times he scraped his pads on rough stone. He left smudges of blood behind him as he walked. Even the Tribe cats began to look exhausted.

Brambleclaw halted abruptly as he rounded a huge boulder and Lionpaw almost crashed into him. The dark tabby's fur was bristling and Lionpaw picked up the scent of anger. Alert for danger, he stretched up to look over his father's shoulder.

He was overlooking a hollow with a pool at the bottom and a few straggly bushes. Three cats were just emerging from the shelter of the branches; the first one had a mouse dangling from his jaws. All three of them paused and looked up curiously.

"What's going on?" a black tom asked. "What do you want?"

"We could ask you the same question," Brambleclaw replied, taking a few paces forward to stand on the lip of the hollow.

Talon stalked up to stand beside him, and Tawnypelt joined him on the other side. Lionpaw noticed Bird and Gray taking up positions where they could spot any other intruders approaching, while Crowfeather skirted the top of the hollow until he could keep watch on the bushes from the other side.

The black tom who had spoken narrowed his eyes. "If you're looking for a fight, you can have one."

"We're not looking for a fight." Brambleclaw's voice was calm, though Lionpaw saw his neck fur still fluffed out and knew he was poised to launch himself into battle if he had to. "We're setting boundaries. This will be the Tribe's territory, but you and your friends can have the rest of the mountains. When we've finished, it will be clear which parts are which."

Lionpaw thought that sounded fair, but the trespassers obviously didn't agree. The third of the party, a pale gray she-cat, looked up at Brambleclaw with cold blue eyes. "Who are you to tell us where we can't go?" she asked scornfully. "We have a right to hunt where we like."

"This is our place," Talon growled.

"Then stop us," the she-cat challenged him. "You haven't managed it so far."

"And your borders won't stop us, either," the black tom added.

Talon's tail lashed and he crouched down, ready to spring. Across the hollow, Crowfeather let out an earsplitting yowl. The three intruders drew closer together, their claws out and their ears flattened.

"Stop!" Brambleclaw raised his tail. "There'll be no blood shed today. Go back to your leader, if you have one," he told the trespassing cats. "Tell all your cats that the borders will be in place from tomorrow and must not be crossed." He stepped back from the edge of the hollow and gestured to Talon with his tail. "Let them go."

The big cave-guard let out a snarl as the intruders stalked past him, but he didn't lift a paw to stop them. "Next time you won't be so lucky," he spat.

The only reply was an insolent tail wave from the gray she-cat as the intruders disappeared between two boulders. Tawnypelt bounded after them, halting at the spot where they had vanished.

"They've gone," she reported after a few heartbeats.

But they'll be back. Lionpaw didn't speak the thought aloud, but he guessed that every cat there shared it.

"What's the point of all this?" Gray asked despondently. "Those cats will never respect our borders."

"We might as well go back to the cave," Bird agreed.

"No, you mustn't give up," Brambleclaw urged them. "Once the borders are in place, you can keep reinforcing the scent markers until the trespassers finally get the message."

Lionpaw wasn't sure his father was right. Surely borders depended on agreement from both sides? And if one side didn't agree, the scent markers had to be backed up by teeth and claws. Were the Tribe cats capable of fighting to protect their territory?

Talon led the way around the hollow, enclosing it within the Tribe's territory, then headed between the boulders and through a narrow split in the rock wall, a twisting path just wide enough for one cat at a time. The fur on Talon's broad shoulders brushed the rock on either side.

They had traveled down this trail for several fox-lengths when they came to a place where it grew a little wider, with tumbled stones at the foot of the cliff face. A wild screech sounded from above their heads. A heartbeat later a body landed on top of Lionpaw, knocking him off his paws. He rolled onto his side to find he was facing a young tortoiseshell with lightning streaks on her face.

"I know you!" he gasped. "I saw you yesterday."

The tortoiseshell lashed out with one paw and batted him over the head. Lionpaw barely registered that she hadn't unsheathed her claws. After the exhausting, frustrating day, all he wanted was to stretch his muscles in a fight. He sprang up and hurled himself on top of the young cat.

As he battered her with his hind paws he caught a glimpse of Tawnypelt rolling over and over with a gray cat clinging to her fur. Another young cat was riding on Talon's shoulders, screeching and digging in his claws. More scuffling noises came from farther up the path; the air was filled with shrieks and caterwauls.

There was hardly enough room on the narrow trail to fight effectively. The tortoiseshell threw Lionpaw off, scrambled up onto a boulder, and spat defiance at him, her back arched and her tail fluffed out.

Spinning around, Lionpaw saw Brambleclaw with a huge paw planted on the neck of a young ginger tom, while just beyond him a pair of identical tabbies had Bird down on her side, raking their claws through her fur. With a yowl of rage,

Lionpaw leaped right over Brambleclaw and flung himself on the nearest tabby.

"Don't shed any more blood than you must!" Brambleclaw hissed at him.

Lionpaw was almost too furious to listen. But he kept his claws sheathed as he knocked one tabby aside and bared his teeth at the other while he helped Bird regain her paws.

Almost as soon as it had begun, the fight was over. The trespassing cats scattered, fleeing down the path in one direction or the other, or leaping back up the rocks and disappearing.

Brambleclaw padded up to Lionpaw and pushed his muzzle into the fur on his shoulder. "Well fought," he meowed. "Are you okay?"

Warmth spread through Lionpaw from ears to tail-tip at his father's praise. "I'm fine," he replied. "They weren't fighting hard."

"They looked like apprentices to me." Crowfeather padded up, spitting out a mouthful of gray fur.

"Maybe they were having a bit of fun," Brambleclaw suggested.

"Fun!" Crowfeather rolled his eyes.

"They were just trying to scare us." Tawnypelt leaped down from the boulder where she had sprung to chase off her attacker. "They weren't hunting or protecting their camp."

"You Clan cats fought well." Talon staggered back along the path. He hesitated and added almost to himself, "Won't these battles ever end?"

Gray and Bird were exchanging uneasy glances. Bird

murmured, "I don't think we'll ever have our home to ourselves again."

The Tribe cats had come off worst in the battle, Lionpaw realized. Gray's ear was bleeding, while Bird had scratches down one side and Talon had lost fur from his shoulders. They really needed to learn warrior fighting techniques.

But instead, they seemed to be giving up. What hope was there for the Clan cats to help them, if the Tribe cats wouldn't even help themselves?

CHAPTER 24

Hollypaw led the to-bes out of the cave in time to see Lionpaw and the rest of Brambleclaw's patrol disappear across the rocks. For a heartbeat she wished she could go with them. But she knew it was equally important to give the Tribe to-bes some practice in warrior fighting techniques.

"Sit there and watch," Breezepaw ordered when every cat had emerged from the cave and leaped down to the open space beside the pool. "Hollypaw and I will show you how to fight."

Hollypaw's pelt prickled. Even if they were acting as mentors, he didn't have to sound so bossy! "Why don't we let them show us what they know already?" she suggested. "We might be able to build on that."

"Well . . . okay." Breezepaw gave an ungracious shrug.

"Only the cave-guards learn this stuff," Pebble explained, stepping forward to face Hollypaw. "We're taught how to fight off eagles if they try to attack the prey-hunters."

Hollypaw sat down and wrapped her tail around her paws. "Fine. Show me what you do."

Pebble crouched down, then used her powerful hind legs

to thrust herself into the air. At the top of her leap she lashed out with both forepaws, then landed neatly and dropped right away into another crouch.

Hollypaw was impressed; the leap was beautifully timed to fight off a flying enemy. How could she adapt it to attack one on the ground?

"That was great," she meowed. "Can you all do it?"

A couple of the other to-bes stepped forward. "We can. We're going to be cave-guards like Pebble."

Three to-bes, including Screech and Splash, remained standing by the pool. All three of them were giving Hollypaw and Breezepaw hostile looks.

"I don't see why we have to do what you tell us," Screech muttered. "You're not warriors yet."

"We know more than you about fighting," Breezepaw shot back at him.

Hollypaw stifled a sigh. Breezepaw was right, but being so obnoxious about it was only going to ruffle Screech's fur. "We're doing it because Brambleclaw asked us to."

"So what?" Screech turned his back rudely, then glanced over his shoulder to add, "He's not *our* leader. We don't have to do what he says."

"Besides, we're prey-hunters." At least Splash was being more polite than her Tribemate. "We're trained to hunt."

"Okay, pretend Breezepaw over there is a rabbit."

"Hey!" Breezepaw protested.

Before he could say any more, Splash had dropped into something similar to the hunter's crouch and gave an enormous leap to land on top of him. The WindClan apprentice threw her off and scrambled to his paws, shaking his ruffled fur.

"Well done!" Hollypaw mewed. "That would be great in a battle, but you'd need to follow it up with some claw work, or sink your teeth into your opponent's throat."

Splash nodded; to Hollypaw's relief she was looking interested rather than hostile. "I'd do that to the rabbit," she pointed out, "but I thought I'd better not do it to him."

"I'd like to see you try," Breezepaw growled.

"Your leap would be good, too." Hollypaw turned back to the cave-guard group. "But instead of clawing at the top of the leap, land on your enemy's back, and then use your claws." That was quite an advanced move, and the trespassing cats might not be expecting it. "Now Breezepaw and I will show you some more basic skills," she added.

They ran through some of the techniques a new apprentice would learn: dashing past an enemy to rake its side with their claws, and rolling over to claw an opponent's belly with their hind paws.

"Now let's see you try," Breezepaw ordered. "In pairs, a cave-guard with a prey-hunter."

"And remember, claws sheathed for practice," Hollypaw added.

She and Breezepaw sat side by side to watch the to-bes. To her surprise, the prey-hunters were picking up the new techniques faster. They were more agile, and she guessed it helped that they didn't have to unlearn the moves the cave-guards already knew.

On the other side of the pool, Squirrelflight and Stormfur were training some of the older Tribe cats. Hollypaw heard one of them meow, "*Why* do we have to do this? We've stuck to our ways for season after season and we've been fine until now."

Hollypaw felt a stab of sympathy. She could understand why the Tribe cats wanted to continue in the ways of their ancestors, and she hated forcing them to change. *But they have to learn*, she told herself. *It's the only way they're going to survive.* She comforted herself with the thought that once the borders were properly established, less blood would be spilled. The trespassers would think twice before attacking cats who knew how to defend themselves.

When the practice was over, she let Breezepaw take the prey-hunters to learn one or two more advanced moves, while she worked with the cave-guards, trying to adapt some of their own techniques.

Sunhigh came and went. Hollypaw's belly was rumbling, but none of the to-bes suggested stopping to eat, and she guessed that they only had one meal a day. For a couple of heartbeats she longed to be back in ThunderClan, where she could take a piece of fresh-kill from the pile any time she liked, provided she had done all her apprentice duties.

Finally she signaled the to-bes to rest by the side of the pool. "That was great," she mewed. "I'm surprised Stoneteller hasn't been out to watch you. I think he'd be proud to see how much you've learned."

"Stoneteller hardly ever leaves the cave," Pebble told her.

Hollypaw's eyes stretched wide in shock. "Really?"

"He only comes out for ceremonies at the top of the waterfall, like when a to-be becomes a full Tribe cat," Splash meowed.

"And sometimes for emergencies," Pebble added.

"I suppose that's different in the Clans, too," Screech sneered. Eventually he'd started to work at the training, but Hollypaw could tell he didn't like it.

"Yes, a Clan leader hunts and patrols with his warriors," Breezepaw explained. "And fights if he has to."

"Doesn't that mean there's a danger he'll be killed?" Pebble asked, just as shocked as Hollypaw had been a moment before.

"Sort of." Hollypaw didn't want to get started on how a Clan leader had nine lives. She wasn't sure if the Tribe of Endless Hunting had given nine lives to Stoneteller, and the Tribe cats might feel resentful if not. Besides, the forest was a much safer place to live than the mountains; it was easier to shelter from hawks, and there weren't many places where a cat might fall to its death. She looked around at the cold gray rocks that surrounded her, and homesickness stabbed her again, sharp as a claw.

"I think we should keep going," she began, rising to her paws to begin another training session.

She broke off as something landed on her from behind, bowling her over until she finished up sprawling on the very edge of the pool, with her tail in the water. Breezepaw had pinned her down with both paws on her chest. His amber eyes shone gleefully.

"That's the best way to tackle an enemy!" he boasted. "When they're not expecting you."

He stepped back; Hollypaw heard *mrrows* of laughter from the to-bes as she scrambled to her paws.

"Stupid furball!" she meowed, flicking water from her tail into his face. But she couldn't really be angry. That was exactly the sort of thing she and Lionpaw might have done to each other, back in ThunderClan territory. "Breezepaw's right," she went on. "And hunting techniques are good for creeping up on an enemy who doesn't know you're there. Let's practice some."

But when the practice session started, Hollypaw felt too hollow with hunger to do it well. Her paws were clumsy; she couldn't set them down as lightly as she wanted. She was relieved when the scent of cats announced the return of Lionpaw with Brambleclaw and the rest of the border patrol.

Her brother was limping badly as he picked his way down the rocks toward the pool. Hollypaw quickly dismissed the to-bes; they were all getting too tired to go on much longer anyway. Breezepaw accompanied them back into the cave, telling them a story about battling a fox on WindClan territory.

Like there'll ever be foxes up here, Hollypaw thought. She padded up to Lionpaw and gave him her shoulder to lean on over the sharp stones to the pool. "Are you okay?" she asked.

"Fine." Lionpaw sighed wearily and crouched by the water to drink. Then he looked up, flicking droplets from his whiskers. "Today was hopeless. We couldn't get around the whole of the border. The route was just too difficult."

Hollypaw wished she could cheer him up with news of the to-be training, but she was still unhappy about teaching them Clan ways, and there were one or two like Screech who made it clear they didn't want to learn. She glanced at the warriors and Tribe cats, who were making their way slowly and dispiritedly along the path into the cave. For the first time she noticed that Jaypaw had emerged and was sitting on a rock by the waterfall with his paws tucked under him. When the full-grown cats had passed him, he leaped down and bounded across to his littermates.

"I'm sick of that cave," he announced as he came up. "I'm so bored I could claw my own fur off. I've been stuck in there all day, listening to she-cats moaning on about their sickly kits."

"Couldn't you help them?" Hollypaw asked.

"I'm not *their* medicine cat," he snapped. "Can you imagine what Stoneteller would say if I trod on his tail?"

"Well, you're *our* medicine cat." Hollypaw's frustrations were making her cross. "What about doing something for Lionpaw?"

"Why, what's the matter?" Jaypaw asked, giving Lionpaw a curious sniff.

Lionpaw was dipping his sore pads into the pool and then licking them. "I'm okay, honestly."

Hollypaw wasn't convinced. He sounded exhausted, and his pads were raw and bleeding. "His paws are sore. Can't you do anything?" she prompted Jaypaw.

Jaypaw twitched his ears irritably. "Where am I supposed to find herbs in this StarClan-forsaken place?" But he stood up, tasting the air, then padded over to the rock wall, where a few scrubby bushes and a narrow patch of grass were struggling to survive. A moment later he returned with a couple of dock leaves in his jaws. "Chew these up and rub the pulp into your pads," he told Lionpaw.

"Thanks." Lionpaw sighed with relief as the cooling juices soothed the pain.

Hollypaw heard the pad of paws on stone and looked up to see Squirrelflight walking toward them around the edge of the pool. "How did your training session go?" she asked.

"Okay, I think," Hollypaw replied. "Some of them learn really quickly. But I'm not sure . . ."

"What?"

"Whether we're doing the right thing. They've followed their traditions for so long. It feels wrong to be teaching them something different."

"It's the same with the border," Lionpaw meowed. "I don't think it's going to work, treating the mountains like Clan territory. The trespassers don't want borders, that's for sure, and I don't think the Tribe does, either. They want things the way they've always been."

"I don't know why you're getting your tails in a twist." Jaypaw still sounded sour. "The Tribe of Endless Hunting isn't helping the Tribe, and they don't want *our* help. So why should we try to make them do stuff they don't want?"

"Because they'll die without us," Squirrelflight snapped,

then touched Jaypaw's shoulder with her tail to show that she hadn't meant to be harsh. "I'm sorry, I'm just as frustrated as you. But I don't think we should give up yet. We *have* got valuable lessons to teach the Tribe, and sooner or later they'll realize it."

Hollypaw wasn't so sure. *There are too many battles going on around here*, she thought. *And not just the kind that spill blood.*

Chapter 25

Jaypaw lay in the moss-lined nest beside Lionpaw and Hollypaw, listening to the endless thunder of the waterfall. There seemed to be voices in it, too faint for him to catch, however hard he strained his ears. Nearby, he could hear the murmuring of tired cats as they settled down for the night.

Hollypaw and Lionpaw were sleeping like hedgehogs in leaf-bare, exhausted from working so hard. Curled up with his tail over his nose, Jaypaw tried to sleep too, but it was no good. His paws itched to be up and doing something. Careful not to disturb his littermates, he slid out of the nest and padded into the center of the cave.

He was beginning to learn his way around. He could distinguish the sleeping places of the cave-guards and prey-hunters and scent his own Clanmates who were sharing their space. Creeping across the cave floor with the waterfall behind him, he heard an echoing tinkle of water drops falling and discovered a trickle spilling into a pool. He crouched down to lap; the water was ice cold and tasted of the wind.

He found it hard to believe that the Clan cats would stay here in the mountains for much longer. They weren't welcome here, whatever Stoneteller said, and it didn't look as if forcing the Tribe to learn Clan skills would solve anything. But before they left he was determined to discover more about the Tribe of Endless Hunting. Rising to his paws again, he licked the last drops of water from his jaws and tasted the air.

Stoneteller's scent! Jaypaw picked up the faint trace on the cave floor and followed it toward the back of the cave, where a gap opened up. He slid through it and along a narrow tunnel until the movement of air and the faint echoes of his paw steps told him that he had emerged into another cave.

A wisp of chill wind told him that it was open to the sky, at least partly. Padding forward, his paw splashed in a puddle of water and he drew back sharply, shaking it in disgust. He brushed against stone and explored it with one paw; it jutted from the cave floor like a tree trunk. The air was filled with strange, whispering echoes, voices that were too faint to make out, like those he had heard in the waterfall.

Then a clearer voice spoke. "Jaypaw, welcome to the Cave of Pointed Stones."

Jaypaw froze. He had been too intent on his investigations to wonder what would happen if Stoneteller found him here. This was the Healer's private place, he could tell, like a Clan leader's den. But there was no point in pretending he wasn't there.

"Thank you, Stoneteller."

He heard the sound of paw steps and imagined the old tabby padding toward him. When Stoneteller's voice came again it was close to his ear.

"This is where I share tongues with the Tribe of Endless Hunting. They send me signs through the shimmer of stars and moon in the water, the dance of light and shadow on the stones that rise from the floor and jut down from the roof, the echoes of wind, water, and paw steps." His voice rose and fell, unlike normal speech, then dropped to a low murmur. "Yet now they send no signs that promise relief for my Tribe."

Jaypaw had lost respect for Stoneteller when the old cat had lied about the message from the Tribe of Endless Hunting. But he couldn't ignore the Healer's age and wisdom or the sharp sense of betrayal Stoneteller felt as he faced the destruction of his Tribe.

"Our ancestors have no help to offer," Stoneteller went on. "It is as though they don't care that we are dying."

Jaypaw wasn't sure if Stoneteller was really talking to him. He was speaking as if to a much older cat, one who might have wisdom to share with him.

"Clan cats look to StarClan," Jaypaw began hesitantly. "Yet not even StarClan is all-powerful. Perhaps the Tribe of Endless Hunting doesn't know how to help you."

"Then why did they bring us here?" Stoneteller rasped. "They promised us we would be safe."

Jaypaw's ears pricked. What did Stoneteller know about the beginnings of the Tribe?

"Where did you live before?" he asked. "Why did you have to leave and come here?"

Stoneteller sighed, his breath riffling Jaypaw's whiskers. "I do not know. It was many seasons, many lifetimes ago. The

Tribe of Endless Hunting has not told me this."

Every hair on Jaypaw's pelt prickled. So the Tribe hadn't always lived in the mountains! Perhaps the Tribe of Endless Hunting was so helpless because they were convinced they had been wrong, and the mountains were not the right place to bring these cats. He clawed the damp floor with his forepaws. If only he knew the whole truth, not just these tantalizing scraps!

"What do the signs say tonight?" he asked Stoneteller.

"Very little," the Healer replied. "The moon shines on the water, but—there!—a cloud drifts over it, as if all our hopes are blotted out. The echoes tell me nothing, but over there wind ruffles the surface of a puddle, and that means change." He sighed again, sounding unutterably weary. "What the change may be, I do not know. I will sleep now. Good night, Jaypaw."

"Good night." Jaypaw heard the old cat's paw steps retreating, and then a scuffling sound as if he was making himself comfortable in a mossy nest. He stood listening as the sounds died away, trying to make some sense of the echoes in the cave, but they told him nothing.

Padding to the side of the cave, he found a dip in the ground. It was bare stone, with no comfortable lining, but he curled up in it, knowing that only in dreams would he find the answers to his questions.

Jaypaw closed his eyes and woke once more on the jutting outcrop of rock with the wind flattening his fur along his sides. Rock sat on a boulder facing him. Moonlight glistened on his hairless body and his bulging sightless eyes seemed fixed on Jaypaw.

"These are not your ancestors," he mewed, before Jaypaw could speak. "Be careful."

"I *am* careful," Jaypaw retorted. "And I have to do something! The Tribe of Endless Hunting has given up on the Tribe. They're not doing anything to help."

"But your Clanmates are," Rock replied.

"But that's not right!" Jaypaw protested, twitching his tail-tip in confusion. "Isn't it the responsibility of warrior ancestors to look after their descendants? Otherwise what use are they?"

Rock said nothing, but Jaypaw sensed great sadness coming from him. Curiosity clawed at him again. Why should Rock feel so concerned about the Tribe cats? *And why will no cat tell me anything?*

He let out a yowl of frustration as he saw Rock's figure beginning to fade. For a heartbeat Jaypaw saw him as a shimmer against the rocks; then he was gone, dissolved into wind and starlight. He bounded forward and found himself scrabbling in the hollow in the Cave of Pointed Stones, where he had fallen asleep.

"Mouse dung!" he spat.

Scent told him that time had passed and Stoneteller had left the cave. Jaypaw rose to his paws and gave himself a quick grooming. His dreams still clung to his mind like stubborn cobwebs, and he felt that he might be able to find his own answers once he had time to think.

But the time was not now. He could hear faint caterwauling in the distance; his muscles tensing with the anticipation of disaster, he located the passage and pattered down it until he reached the main cave. The noise grew louder, wails and yowling that almost drowned out the noise of the waterfall. As Jaypaw stepped into the cavern, the stench of blood slapped him in the face like a damp wind.

"What's going on?" he meowed in alarm.

He tasted the air; the first familiar scent he encountered was Tawnypelt's. Bounding over to her, he asked, "What happened? Has there been a battle?"

"A fight." The ShadowClan cat's voice was terse. "The prey-hunters went out at dawn and brought down an eagle. Then the trespassers spotted them on their way home and fought them for it."

"And we lost!" an unfamiliar voice snarled. "Those mange-ridden fleapelts took our prey. It's all the fault of you Clan cats. You kept the cave-guards here, learning *battle techniques.*" The Tribe cat spat out the last words as if they were a curse.

"The techniques you use now wouldn't help you fight other cats." Brambleclaw's voice came from behind Jaypaw and his father's scent wreathed around him.

"They'd be better than nothing!" the Tribe cat yowled. "My mate was injured today." His voice shook suddenly. "I don't even know if she'll live."

"I'm sorry," Brambleclaw murmured. "Jaypaw, will you go and help Stoneteller? He could use another medicine cat."

"Sure." Thankful to have something to do at last, Jaypaw

located Stoneteller's scent among all the others and padded across to him, weaving his way among the bodies of injured cats screeching in pain.

"Honestly," he muttered to himself. "There can't be more than about six of them, but they're making enough racket for a whole Clan!"

"Jaypaw." Stoneteller's voice was calm and in control. He seemed a lifetime away from the weary, confused cat of the night before. "Chew up this tormentil root and put it on Gray's wound."

Jaypaw sniffed curiously at the root Stoneteller pushed against his paws. "I've never come across this before. What did you call it?"

"Tormentil," Stoneteller replied. "Good for all wounds and for poison."

"Hey, do you mind?" Gray's voice, tight with pain, came from just beside Jaypaw. "Talk about it afterward, okay?"

"Okay." Jaypaw sighed. "Have you given the wound a good lick?"

"No . . ." Gray sounded startled, as if the thought of licking his own wound had never occurred to him.

"Then do it," Jaypaw snapped. "What's the good of putting a poultice on a load of drying blood and messy fur?"

He crouched down to chew up the tormentil, hearing the steady rasp of Gray's tongue. The root had a strong aromatic scent and a sharp taste.

"We use wintergreen, too," Stoneteller meowed as he worked. "And tansy. Have you heard of those?"

Jaypaw spat out the last of the chewed-up root and scooped up a pawful to put on Gray's wound. "We have tansy, but mostly for coughs. Right, Gray, is that wound clean now?"

"Yes, it's okay," the prey-hunter replied.

"About time," Jaypaw muttered. "It's like dealing with kits!"

"Hey, calm down." Hollypaw pushed her muzzle into Jaypaw's neck fur. "Tell me what to do. I've come to help."

"The Tribe cats need to start helping themselves," Jaypaw snapped at her, then felt sorry for being sharp. Hollypaw didn't know that the Tribe's ancestors had given up on them, and he didn't want to tell her. But he knew that if the Tribe cats *didn't* start helping themselves, there was no hope left for them.

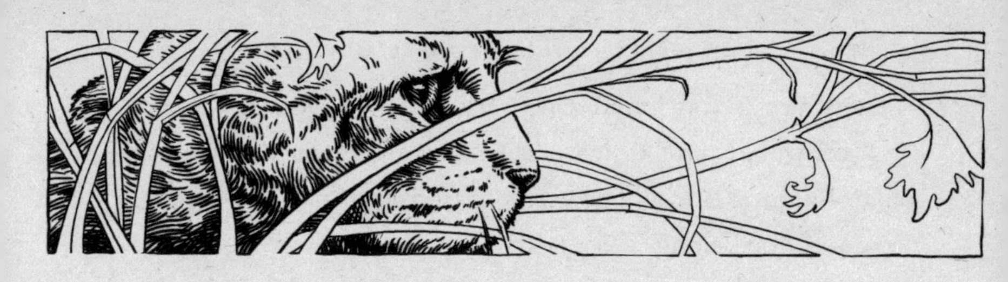

CHAPTER 26

Once the injured cats had been treated and were resting in their sleeping hollows, Stoneteller padded wearily toward the mouth of the cave. He beckoned with his tail for Brambleclaw to join him, and Lionpaw followed, eager to hear what their next move would be.

The light that came through the waterfall was dim and gray. Stoneteller sat down, a small, dark figure in the midst of the watery radiance, and tucked his paws underneath him.

"The Tribe cannot survive here," he sighed, his voice almost drowned out by the pounding of the water. "We must leave the mountains and find a home somewhere else."

Brambleclaw's eyes widened in dismay. "That's your decision to make, Stoneteller, but is it wise? It's dangerous for a large group of cats to move around together. The Clans lost cats on the Great Journey. Besides, where would you go?"

Stoneteller shook his head; he had no answer to that question.

Maybe they could come to the lake with us, Lionpaw thought. *But there are too many to join one Clan. They would have to split up, and they wouldn't like that. Anyway, the Clans would never accept them.*

"Even if you found a new home," Brambleclaw went on, "you would have to learn new ways of living, new hunting techniques. It would be better to find a way of surviving here, where you belong."

Stoneteller turned his head to look up at the dark tabby. "And how do you suggest we do that?"

"Give the border patrols a try," Brambleclaw meowed.

"Patrols?" Stoneteller's voice was disapproving. "Spend all our time scrambling over rocks?"

"Yes, it's hard," Brambleclaw admitted, an edge of annoyance in his voice. "But your cats are used to moving around in this terrain. That gives you a big advantage over the intruders."

The Healer blinked, his eyes on the eternally falling water. After several heartbeats, he asked, "Are you saying that the Tribe must restrict itself to one area?"

"It would be a big area," Brambleclaw promised. "Plenty of space for you to support yourselves. And isn't keeping part of your territory better than losing it all?" When Stoneteller didn't respond, he added, "Why don't you come and see for yourself, to make sure you'll have enough?"

"The Healer does not leave the cave, except for ceremonies above the waterfall," Stoneteller responded. "That is the will of the Tribe of Endless Hunting."

Brambleclaw looked frustrated, the tip of his tail twitching back and forth. Lionpaw was afraid he was going to give up the argument.

Then Stoneteller spoke again. "But perhaps the time is

right to break with some of our traditions, so that we can preserve the rest. I will come with you."

"Great!" Brambleclaw's tail went straight up. "I'll get a patrol together right away. Lionpaw, you can come." He flicked his tail at him as he raced back into the main part of the cave.

Lionpaw wasn't sure he wanted to clamber all the way around the territory again. His paws were still sore from the previous day. But he did want to help establish the border and to see what Stoneteller's reaction would be. He waited beside the Healer until Brambleclaw returned. Talon, Breezepaw, and Pebble were with him; Crowfeather followed a little way behind with Crag, Night, and a couple of the other Tribe to-bes.

"Crowfeather will take his patrol in one direction, and we'll take the other," Brambleclaw meowed to Stoneteller. "That way, we can get around the whole territory by nightfall. We won't try to explore every corner, just find landmarks along the way so that we all know where the border is."

Stoneteller nodded. "Very well."

He let Brambleclaw take the lead along the Path of Rushing Water and out into the open. Lionpaw paused briefly before leaping from the rocks to the flat ground around the pool. The sky was covered with gray clouds, so low that they rested on the mountain peaks. The air was heavy, with a taste of rain to come. The blue skies and warm sun of greenleaf could have been moons away.

Crowfeather's patrol climbed the path beside the waterfall and vanished, while Brambleclaw led his cats over the rocks opposite, the same route they had followed the day before. He set a brisk pace until they reached the twisted spike of rock that Lionpaw had picked out as the first border marker.

"We'll set a scent marker here," Brambleclaw announced. "Lionpaw, would you like to demonstrate?"

"Shouldn't it be Tribe scent?" Talon asked.

"Of course," mewed Brambleclaw. "You and Pebble can do the rest, once Lionpaw has shown you how."

The three Tribe cats glanced at one another. Lionpaw could see that they weren't sure that marking a border would make any difference to the aggressive intruders. He couldn't help agreeing; scent markers were useless unless they were reinforced with teeth and claws when it was needed.

"I don't know why we bother," Breezepaw muttered in his ear. "They just don't think like Clan cats. They have no idea how to make a border work."

When Lionpaw had set the marker the patrol continued along the ridge to the head of the valley with the stream, and then on across the plateau. Brambleclaw chose a stack of loose rocks as another vantage point for a marker. Water dripped over them from a narrow crack, leaving them slick and green with a thin covering of moss.

"What use is this in our territory?" Stoneteller objected, as Talon prepared to set the marker. "These rocks are always so wet that no prey can survive here."

"That's not the point," Brambleclaw explained. "Markers need to be seen and easily identified. It's great if they're useful as well, but they don't need to be."

Stoneteller gave a doubtful snort but didn't object anymore as Talon set the marker. He was silent as they continued around the pool where they had clashed with the three intruders and along the narrow valley where the young trespassers had ambushed them.

When they had climbed out of the valley, Pebble set a scent marker at the base of a huge boulder overlooking a craggy slope that led down to a clump of scrubby, windblown trees.

"What about those?" Stoneteller asked, pointing with his tail. "We need that place in our territory."

Brambleclaw surveyed the terrain with narrowed eyes. "It's not worth it," he decided. "They're too hard to reach from here."

"But Tribe cats have hunted there for seasons. The trees bear our claw marks."

Lionpaw saw the slight bristling of his father's neck fur that told him Brambleclaw was trying not to show his annoyance.

"Your border has to be manageable if you're to stand any chance of defending it," he explained. "Your main aim must be to enclose enough territory to support the Tribe. And you must leave the trespassers enough space for themselves; otherwise you're asking them to attack you."

Lionpaw saw Talon nodding as if he understood, but Stoneteller lashed his tail and hissed through bared teeth. "Suit yourself, Clan cat."

Brambleclaw just dipped his head and motioned to Talon to take the lead again.

Their route lay over the shoulder of a hill and down a

boulder-covered slope to a stream in the valley below. Before they reached the bottom, icy rain began to fall, stinging as the wind drove it into the cats' faces. Within a few heartbeats, Lionpaw's pelt was soaked. Shivering, he longed for the shelter of thick, leafy branches.

"How do you Tribe cats stand it?" he asked Pebble. "Even when the sun shines, it's so windy up here. And this rain is just—"

"I'll show you," Pebble interrupted.

She quickened her pace, bounding down among the boulders until she reached the side of the stream. Curious, Lionpaw followed her. He found her rolling in the mud on the bank until her pelt was thoroughly plastered with it.

"Try it," she invited, springing up. "It keeps the warmth in and the cold wind out. And prey-hunters do it when they're stalking prey so that they don't stand out against the rocks."

Lionpaw recalled seeing Tribe cats with mud-covered fur. He'd just assumed that they hadn't bothered to groom. Now he could see the advantages. Gingerly he lowered himself into a muddy hollow and rolled over and over until the brown mud covered his golden fur.

Hearing a snort of laughter, he looked up to see Breezepaw standing over him. "You'll have fun licking *that* off," the WindClan apprentice sniggered.

"So will you!" Before Breezepaw could react, Lionpaw leaped up and bowled him over, dragging him down into the mud with him. Breezepaw let out a startled yowl, scrambling to get out, but Lionpaw wrestled with him until his pelt was just as thoroughly mud-soaked.

"Stupid furball!" Breezepaw spat, hauling himself onto a nearby rock and surveying his filthy fur with a disgusted look.

Pebble was watching both of them, her tail curled up in amusement. "Fair's fair," she meowed. "You teach us Clan ways, and now you're learning Tribe ways."

Lionpaw clambered out of the hollow and shook himself. He hated the smell of the mud and the way it stuck his fur together, but he had to admit Pebble had been right. The muddy covering did keep the wind out.

"Okay," he muttered. "Let's keep going."

Talon jumped across the stream and led the way up the slope beyond. Lionpaw had only just begun to climb when he heard a yowl from somewhere above and looked up to see cat shapes outlined against the sky. Briefly he froze, expecting intruders. Then mingled Clan and Tribe scents reached him and he recognized Crowfeather's patrol.

"Great!" he exclaimed. "That's the whole border marked."

The two groups of cats met on top of the ridge. Crowfeather reported an encounter with a couple of intruders, who had slunk rapidly away when they realized they were outnumbered. Otherwise they had set their scent markers with no trouble.

"Then let's return to the cave," Stoneteller meowed.

To Lionpaw's relief, Talon led them back by a much quicker route. The rain eased off on the way, and when they reached the pool by the waterfall Hollypaw was in the middle of a training session with the to-bes who had stayed behind.

"Lionpaw!" She paused in the middle of demonstrating a fighting move, her green eyes wide with astonishment. "I hardly recognized you. You look just like a Tribe cat!"

Lionpaw shrugged uncomfortably, still hating the feeling of the mud on his fur. "I can't wait to get it off."

"Why? Doesn't it work?"

"Yes, it works fine," Lionpaw replied, "but it's yucky."

Hollypaw rolled her eyes. "Your golden fur really stands out against the rocks," she pointed out. "You'll catch much more prey the way you are now."

"I suppose so." Lionpaw sighed. He wished he was back in the forest, where his pelt blended with the dappled sunlight through the leaves.

The other cats had taken the path behind the waterfall, back into the cave. Only Brambleclaw was left, poised on the rocks above the pool. "Come on!" He beckoned the younger cats with his tail. "Stoneteller is going to call a meeting."

Lionpaw sprang up the rocks to follow him, with Hollypaw and the Tribe to-bes close behind. Wavering scarlet light from the setting sun outside shone into the cave like rivulets of blood. Lionpaw shivered, almost imagining that he could feel a sticky tide washing around his paws.

Stoneteller was seated on a boulder at the far end of the cave, near the passage that led to the Cave of Pointed Stones. The Tribe cats and the Clan cats mingled together, gathering around him; Lionpaw spotted Jaypaw with Squirrelflight. He and Hollypaw joined Breezepaw and the Tribe to-bes.

"Cats of Tribe and Clan," Stoneteller began. "Our borders have been marked. It remains to be seen whether the intruders will respect them."

Lionpaw could tell that Stoneteller didn't believe that the border would make any difference, and there were doubtful murmurs from the Tribe cats.

A skinny white she-cat spoke up. "Those mange-pelts don't respect anything."

"Cloud With Storm in Belly." Stoneteller dipped his head toward her. "I fear your seasons of wisdom speak true."

"Then what do we do now?" Night meowed, her forepaws working nervously on the cave floor. "Has all this been for nothing?"

"No." Brambleclaw rose to his paws and spoke commandingly, his head and tail held high. Lionpaw's pelt felt warm with pride that this noble cat was his father. "But the job's not finished yet. Now we must go to the intruders and tell them to stay on their own side of the border."

"And you think they'll listen?" Cloud asked scornfully.

"I don't know," Brambleclaw replied. "But they should be given the chance. We will seek out their camp under truce and ask to speak to their leader."

"Truce!" Screech, sitting between Lionpaw and Pebble, let out a snort of contempt. "He's beetle-brained if he thinks the trespassers will honor a truce."

"They might," Hollypaw mewed. "Back home, there's a truce every moon among the Clans."

When Screech didn't look convinced, Lionpaw added, "Yes, StarClan would be angry if any cat fought during the full moon."

Pebble blinked, more curious than disbelieving. "Do you

think these trespassers know about StarClan? Or the Tribe of Endless Hunting?"

Lionpaw exchanged a glance with his sister, seeing his own confusion reflected in her green eyes. *Did* the intruders share tongues with the spirits of their ancestors like the Tribe and the Clans?

"I don't know," Hollypaw replied. "But it's got to be worth a try."

While they were talking, the discussion had continued among the full-grown cats. Suddenly Stoneteller signaled with his tail for silence. "Enough! We will try Brambleclaw's plan. He and I will choose the cats to seek out the intruders tomorrow. But if the plan fails, then . . ." His voice trailed off, and he bowed his head. Lionpaw had to strain to hear his last few words. "If it fails, then the Tribe can no longer make its home in these mountains."

The milky light of dawn was in the sky as Lionpaw emerged from behind the waterfall. Dew misted the rocks and dripped from the leaves of bushes around the pool, but the heavy cloud cover of the day before was gone. He wondered if that was a good omen.

His paws tingled with a mixture of fear and excitement as the rest of the patrol left the cave and sprang down to cluster together by the pool. All the Clan cats were there except for Squirrelflight and Jaypaw; from the Tribe, Stoneteller had chosen Crag, Night, and Talon, and Pebble and Splash from the to-bes.

"I never thought *we'd* be chosen," Pebble mewed, bouncing on her paws. "Do you think we'll have to fight?"

"I hope not," Hollypaw replied. "If we do, remember those moves I taught you. You should be fine."

Brambleclaw called his cats together with a wave of his tail. "We'll head for the pool where we met the trespassers," he announced. "We should be able to pick up their trail from there."

"Good luck!" Squirrelflight's voice called.

Lionpaw turned. His mother had appeared from the cave and was crouching on a boulder beside the sheet of thundering water. Her flame-colored pelt glowed in the strengthening light.

"Thanks," Brambleclaw replied. "Keep an eye on things while we're away."

Squirrelflight's ears flicked up. "I will, don't worry."

So that's why she's staying, Lionpaw thought. *Just in case the intruders come visiting while all these cats are gone.*

The journey across the new territory to the pool didn't seem as far today. Lionpaw realized that his muscles were getting used to clambering up and down rocks, and even his pads were tougher.

"There's intruder scent," Tawnypelt meowed when they arrived. "But it's stale. I don't think they've been this way since the day we saw them."

"They went that way." Crowfeather angled his ears toward the boulders that led to the narrow cleft in the rock. "Maybe they were taking prey back to their camp."

"It's worth a try," Brambleclaw agreed, leading the way between the boulders and into the gap.

Lionpaw kept tasting the air as he followed, but the intruder scent was hard to follow, mingled with their own scent from the previous patrols. It grew stronger as they passed the place where they had fought the young cats, then seemed to fade away altogether by the time they reached the head of the valley.

"Mouse dung," Tawnypelt muttered. "Don't say we've lost them."

Every cat stood silent, tasting the air, then cast about over the rocks for any trace of the elusive scent. Lionpaw's belly growled as he detected the scent of mouse, and he had to remind himself sharply that they weren't hunting now. But there was no sign of the trespassers.

"Over here!" Lionpaw turned to see Hollypaw waving her tail urgently from beneath a huge, jutting boulder. "I think they went this way."

Brambleclaw padded up and drew in a long breath of air. "You're right." He touched his nose to his daughter's ear. "That was well scented. You'd better take the lead."

Hollypaw's eyes glowed with pride. She led the way beneath the overhang and up a slope so steep it was hard to find a paw hold. At the top she paused for a few heartbeats, then began to pick her way down the other side. Lionpaw's feet skidded as loose rock shifted beneath them. He hoped Hollypaw was right; he had lost all scent of the intruders.

"Your sister's great, isn't she?" Pebble murmured, catching

up to him. "I don't think even our prey-hunters could follow this scent."

"She's the best," Lionpaw meowed proudly. "Back home, she always brings back the most prey."

At the foot of the slope the scent grew stronger again. Lionpaw could detect traces of many cats, and his pelt prickled. They must be getting close to the trespassers' camp!

The trail crossed a dried-up watercourse, then led to a narrow cleft between two sheer rocks that tilted together so that they almost touched at the top. The gap led back into darkness; the intruders' scent was overpowering.

"I think this is it," Brambleclaw murmured.

"Do we go in?" Crag asked.

"No. We've got no idea how many cats we'd be facing. Besides, we'd just be asking them to attack us if we set paw in their camp uninvited. We'll wait."

The cats spread out into a loose semicircle. Lionpaw saw Tawnypelt staring at the cleft with as much concentration as if she were waiting for a mouse to come out of its hole. Crowfeather looked nervous, his ears flattened as he cast glances over his shoulder, keeping watch behind. Stormfur and Brook sat close together, quietly murmuring, while Crag paced restlessly back and forth.

Lionpaw padded over to Hollypaw until his pelt brushed hers. "Well done. You found it."

Hollypaw's whiskers twitched. "Let's hope they'll talk to us now that we're here."

Suddenly there was movement inside the cleft. A cat's head

poked out; Lionpaw recognized the young tortoiseshell he had encountered twice before. Her eyes stretched wide in horror when she saw the waiting cats, and she darted back at once into the shadow of the cleft. Lionpaw heard a panic-stricken yowling as she withdrew.

"It shouldn't be long now," Brambleclaw commented.

Every heartbeat felt like a season. Then Lionpaw spotted a pale pelt inside the cleft. Stripes, the silver-furred tom they had met when they first reached the mountains, stepped out of the cleft and faced Brambleclaw.

More of the trespassers crept out behind him. Lionpaw recognized Flora, the brown-and-white she-cat, and Flick, the skinny brown tom who had been with Stripes. The black tom was there, too, who had led the hunting patrol they met by the pool. They all looked thin, and some of them were limping. Lionpaw could tell that they weren't finding mountain life easy. But he couldn't ignore the glow of determination in their eyes.

"What do you want?" Stripes demanded.

Brambleclaw glanced at Crag, flicking his ears for the Tribe cat to speak.

"We need to talk to you," Crag meowed. "We want an end to this conflict. The mountains are big enough to support every cat, but we need to divide up the territory so that we all have an equal chance at prey."

He paused as if he expected Stripes to comment, but the silver tom just jerked his head and muttered, "Go on."

"The Tribe has marked borders closing in our territory,"

Crag explained. "Our scent will show you where they are. You are free to hunt in the rest of the mountains, but not to cross those borders. We—"

Outraged yowling drowned him out. The trespassers' fur was bristling and their eyes blazed with anger.

Stripes took a pace forward until he was barely a tail-length away from Crag. "You have no right to any part of the mountains," he growled. "You have no right to set borders. Any cat can take prey from where it likes."

"That's not fair!" Tawnypelt protested. "Can't you see, we're trying to—"

"This is about life or death," Stripes interrupted. His claws slid out. "If necessary, our life and your death."

Chapter 27

Horror slashed through Hollypaw like the claws of fighting cats. "They haven't any code at all!" she gasped, turning to her brother. "Even the Tribe understands about duty and being fair. These cats just don't care!"

Her muscles tensed, ready to leap into battle. The patrol had come in peace, wanting only to talk, but now it looked as if the truce would be shattered. *StarClan, help us,* she prayed, not even knowing if StarClan could hear her under these strange skies. *Show us what to do.*

Beckoning with her tail, she gathered the Tribe to-bes close to her. Lionpaw and Breezepaw flanked them on either side.

"Do we fight now?" Splash asked nervously.

"Let's hope not," Lionpaw replied. Hollypaw was grateful for the reassurance in his voice. "But Hollypaw will give you a signal if we have to."

She didn't have much hope that they could avoid a battle now. Stripes had made it clear that the trespassers had no intention of respecting the borders the Tribe had worked so hard to set in place. The Tribe were no better off than when they started.

At Stripes's challenge, Crag had stepped forward until the two cats stood nose to nose. His neck fur bristled and his eyes were narrowed menacingly. "If you're looking for a fight—"

Brambleclaw stopped him with a touch of his tail on his shoulder and motioned him back. "This isn't the right time," he murmured. "They outnumber us, for one thing. Best go back to the cave and see what happens."

"I *know* what's going to happen," Crag snarled.

For a couple of heartbeats Hollypaw thought that he would defy Brambleclaw and leap into battle. Then the rest of them would have to fight to back him up.

At last Crag let out a long sigh, bowing his head. "Have it your way," he mewed to Brambleclaw.

Brambleclaw touched his tail to the cave-guard's shoulder once again, a silent gesture of gratitude. Facing Stripes, he meowed, "We will defend our borders. It's your choice if you cross them."

"Fine." Stripes flicked his tail. "We'll bear that in mind. Not forgetting that some of you don't belong here."

"He means us," Lionpaw whispered. "He knows we'll go home sooner or later. Then the Tribe will be weaker. . . ."

He didn't need to go on. It was obvious to Hollypaw that Stripes meant to attack the Tribe as soon as the Clan cats left them defenseless. *But we can't stay here forever,* she thought, struggling against a pang of homesickness for the forest and the camp in the stone hollow.

Brambleclaw turned and led his cats away. Mocking

caterwauls followed them. "Don't bother coming back!" Flick yowled.

The sun was well above the mountains as the patrol made its way back to the cave. Golden rays warmed the rocks, but Hollypaw felt as cold as if she were padding through a bitter leaf-bare.

"Do you think that was okay?" Splash fretted. "They know about our borders now, so they should leave us alone."

"I hope I'll be on the first patrol!" Pebble added.

"Let's wait and see," Hollypaw mewed. She wasn't sure if the Tribe to-bes really hadn't understood what had just happened, or whether they were forcing themselves to be optimistic. She couldn't bring herself to tell them that borders didn't exist unless they were seen from both sides. The trespassers had shown that they had no honor, not a scrap of respect for their rivals, so it was only a matter of time before they crossed the boundaries and stole more prey from the Tribe.

The warrior code has failed, she thought. She had built her life on it, and now she felt as though she had stepped off a precipice and was plummeting down into darkness. *Even the Tribe doesn't really understand it.*

She gave herself a shake. The Tribe might not have the warrior code, but they had traditions just as ancient and important. Perhaps the Tribe of Endless Hunting would come to their aid at last.

The patrol had reached the boulder-covered slope that led down to the stream when Brambleclaw paused suddenly, raising his tail to bring the other cats to a halt behind him. "Intruder scent!" he hissed.

Hollypaw felt the fur on her shoulders begin to bristle. Tasting the air, she picked up a strong, fresh scent, carried on the breeze that swept across the bare rock. She couldn't see the intruders, but she realized that they must be very close.

"I don't believe this," Lionpaw muttered into her ear. His fur was fluffed up with anger and his tail-tip twitched back and forth. "We only just told them about the borders, and they're already trespassing."

"Look—down there!" Pebble angled her ears toward the stream.

Down below, the skinny brown intruder, Flick, emerged from behind a spur of rock, following the course of the stream. Four more of the intruders followed him; one of them, the black tom they had encountered before, had the body of a mouse hanging from his jaws. They padded along confidently, as if they had every right to be there.

I knew it, Hollypaw thought. *Everything we've done has been for nothing.*

"They're useless hunters," she commented, trying to push down the cold sense of failure that sat in her belly like a stone. "They can't even scent us. They have no idea that we're here."

"Or they don't care," Lionpaw added.

Brambleclaw, Crag, and Stormfur exchanged a few quick words, speaking too low for Hollypaw to catch what they said. Then Brambleclaw leaped up onto the nearest boulder so that his figure was outlined against the sky. "Trespassers!" he yowled.

The invaders halted. In the same heartbeat, Brambleclaw let out a fearsome screech and launched himself down from the boulder. The rest of the patrol poured down the slope after him; Hollypaw felt as if a rushing torrent were sweeping her on.

After one terrified glance, Flick's patrol spun around and fled downstream. Flick clawed his way up a steep rockslide until he reached a ledge. He glared down at the Clan and Tribe cats, his ears flattened and his lips drawn back in a snarl.

Brambleclaw bounded up to the foot of the rockslide. "You have crossed the Tribe's border," he meowed. Hollypaw could tell that he was trying to remain calm, though his voice vibrated with fury. "You are trespassing and stealing prey."

"Why shouldn't we?" Flick spat. "There's nothing to stop us."

"We explained the scent marks," Crag began, pacing forward to stand at Brambleclaw's shoulder.

"Oh, the *scent marks*!" Flick sneered. "I'm frightened out of my fur. So what are you going to do now, set stronger marks? We'll hunt where we please, and you can't stop us." Before any cat could reply he leaped upward and vanished over the top of the rock.

"We should follow him," Talon growled. "Maybe he'll listen if we rip his fur off."

"No point." Brambleclaw sounded despondent. "It's obvious that explaining the boundaries hasn't worked. The intruders crossed the border as soon as our backs were turned. No, we have to teach them a lesson, once and for all."

When Hollypaw entered the cave she was aware of a buzz of excitement. The Tribe cats who had stayed behind were clamoring to hear what had happened when the patrol met the intruders.

"So they know about the borders?" Bird asked, her eyes gleaming hopefully. "Does that mean they'll leave us alone?"

"Maybe we can hunt in peace now," Gray added.

Brambleclaw shouldered his way into the cluster of excited cats. "No," he meowed. "The battle is not over. There are no borders."

"But there are!" Screech slipped between two older cats to confront Brambleclaw, his neck fur bristling. "You helped set them yourself!"

"And the intruders have already crossed them," Stormfur meowed.

Gasps of astonishment and snarls of fury rose from the cats gathered around as the gray warrior quickly described their encounter with Flick's patrol. "They can't do that!" some cat exclaimed.

"They have," Talon replied flatly.

"There are no borders if the other side won't recognize them," Squirrelflight pointed out.

"That is true." Hollypaw whipped around to see that Stoneteller had taken his place on the boulder. The old cat's fur was fluffed up with anger and he glared at Brambleclaw.

"So all our efforts have been wasted. What do you suggest that we do now?"

"There's only one thing left to do," Brambleclaw meowed, dipping his head respectfully to the old cat. "We must take the battle to the trespassers and defeat them once and for all."

Stoneteller drew back his lips in the beginnings of a snarl. Every cat in the cave fell silent as his blue eyes searched out Stormfur. "No," he mewed. His voice was soft but charged with fury. "We tried that once, and too many lives were lost. Too many cats will never walk these mountains again."

"But this time will be different," Brambleclaw promised. "Your cats have been training to fight. And this time they will fight with a clear purpose—to defend their territory, instead of trying to drive out the intruders." He hesitated, drawing a deep breath, then added, "It's your choice. You can fight, or be driven from your home."

A babble of conflicting voices rose from the Tribe cats. Stoneteller silenced it with a single lash of his tail.

"Very well," he hissed. "The Tribe shall choose—and prove once and for all that we are not a Clan."

Hollypaw caught a startled glance from Lionpaw.

"What's he meowing about?" her brother asked. "Of *course* they're not a Clan."

"He doesn't want them to fight," Hollypaw mewed. "But perhaps he thinks it's fairer to let the Tribe decide. After all, they'll have to live with the decision."

The Tribe cats were looking at one another with bewilderment in their eyes. Confused murmurs came from them;

eventually Crag spoke up. "Stoneteller, we don't understand. What do you want us to do?"

"I should have thought that was clear enough." Stoneteller's voice was icy. "I want you to choose what we should do—find a new place to live, or stay and fight. The Tribe of Endless Hunting does not want me to influence your decision."

"I bet they don't." The furious mutter startled Hollypaw. She glanced over her shoulder to see that Jaypaw had joined them, sitting with his tail curled neatly over his paws.

"What do you mean?" she asked.

Her brother twitched his ears. "Don't you get it? Stoneteller can say what he likes about the Tribe of Endless Hunting. Who's to know any different?"

Hollypaw stared at him in alarm. How could Jaypaw say that? No Clan cat would dare tell lies about StarClan—how could it be so different for the Tribe?

Stoneteller began to speak again. "All cats who wish to fight should go to that side of the cave." He waved his tail. "Those who wish to flee, go to the other side. Remember that you choose the future of your Tribe."

"Let's hope they have a future," Lionpaw murmured.

For a few heartbeats no cat moved. Hollypaw thought that the Tribe cats were too bewildered by what Stoneteller was telling them to do. Then she spotted the skinny white elder, Cloud, muttering to another old cat, a speckled brown tom.

"What do you think, Rain?" Cloud asked him. "Fight or flee?"

The old tom let out a disgusted snort. "I never wanted to

fight, but I'm too old to flee far."

Just beyond the elders, two she-cats had their heads together, murmuring anxiously to each other.

"Swoop, what should we do? I can't fight while I'm suckling my kits. But they can't flee; their eyes are barely open! And I *won't* leave them."

"Don't worry, Flight," the other she-cat mewed soothingly. "No cat expects you to abandon your kits. I won't leave mine, either."

Talon loomed over them; both she-cats looked up at him uncertainly.

"Choose to fight," the huge cave-guard growled. "That way, the Tribe will protect you as it protects all kit-mothers and their litters." He encircled both she-cats with his tail and drew them over to the "fight" side of the cave, where he stood beside them as if he was already protecting them from danger.

By now Hollypaw could see that the Tribe was beginning to divide into two groups. Pebble and Splash bounded quickly over to choose fighting. Screech spat something after them that Hollypaw couldn't catch and withdrew to the far side with the other to-be prey-hunter. Night joined Talon, but to Hollypaw's surprise Gray chose to flee and Bird, after a brief hesitation, chose that too.

Hollypaw found that her heart was pounding and her muscles were tense. She didn't know why it should matter so much to her that the Tribe should keep its home in the mountains; she only knew that it *did* matter, desperately. If they left their home they would have to suffer the hardships and dangers of a long journey, and they would leave all their traditions, everything that was familiar, behind them. They would no longer be the Tribe.

Now very few cats remained to choose. Crag still stood in the center of the cave, his eyes troubled. Eventually, with a curt nod to Brambleclaw, he padded over to join the cats who had chosen to fight. Talon welcomed him with a tail-tip on his shoulder.

All this time Stormfur and Brook had stood silent, their pelts brushing. At last Brook glanced up at Stormfur, pleading in her eyes. He touched his nose to her ear, then laid his tail across her back and led her over to her brother, Talon.

"Do they get to choose?" Lionpaw asked in a whisper. "Are they Tribe or Clan?"

"I don't think even they know," Hollypaw replied.

The Clan cats remained in the middle of the cave, drawing closer together as the Tribe moved away. At last they were alone. Hollypaw's heart raced when she realized that there were more cats on the "fight" side of the cave.

"They've chosen to fight," she murmured to Jaypaw.

Her brother flicked his tail. "Good."

Brambleclaw glanced from side to side, then dipped his head to Stoneteller. "Healer, the choice seems clear," he announced. "Your Tribe wishes to fight."

Stoneteller's fur bristled. Hollypaw could see that he hadn't expected this. His eyes narrowed as he glared at Brambleclaw. "So be it," he hissed. "And may you sleep well at night, Clan cat. This battle will destroy my Tribe."

Brambleclaw waited until the Healer had leaped down from the boulder and vanished, with a final lash of his tail, into the passage that led to the Cave of Pointed Stones. Then he turned to face the rest of the cats in the cave. The Tribe, even those who had chosen to fight, looked nervous, as if they realized what a huge decision they had just made.

"Right, time to get ready." Brambleclaw's voice was brisk and confident. "We must strike at once, before the intruders have the chance to attack first. There's a full moon tonight, so that will help."

Hollypaw flinched, every hair on her pelt rising in protest. The full moon was a time of peace! Back beside the lake, the Clans would be Gathering on the island. Though she knew it was impossible, her paws wanted to carry her out of the cave and back down the mountain to be with them. *But the full moon's not special for the Tribe*, she reminded herself.

"Any cats who would like more battle training, go to Squirrelflight and Hollypaw," Brambleclaw continued. "Crag and Talon, I want you to help me plan our strategy. Jaypaw, see whether you can find some healing herbs for when we get back."

"Sure," Jaypaw muttered. "We'll get no help from Stoneteller."

"Remember," Brambleclaw meowed, glancing solemnly around the cave. "This isn't about the warrior code or the Tribe's code. It's about life or death, just like the trespassers said. And you—the Tribe—you will be the ones who live!"

He stood motionless, amber eyes glowing, as the Tribe cats yowled their approval.

* * *

Moonlight shimmered through the falling water, shedding silver light across the cave. The cats who were heading into battle gathered near the cave mouth, waiting for their turn to walk the Path of Rushing Water. Standing beside Lionpaw, Hollypaw sensed her brother's quivering excitement at the thought of fighting in a real battle. His tail was fluffed up to twice its size and his amber eyes glittered.

"Here." Hollypaw jumped as a tail touched her shoulder; she spun around to see Jaypaw. "Come over here," he repeated, beckoning with his tail. "There's something I want to say." There was a suppressed tension about him, too, as if he was facing a battle of his own.

"What is it?" Lionpaw asked, glancing back at where the cats were vanishing along the path. "We have to go."

"This won't take a heartbeat," Jaypaw promised, as he drew them into a quiet corner of the cave, sheltered by a boulder. "You have to take care," he went on, when both his littermates were crouched beside him. "Remember that you don't have StarClan to watch over you here."

"We have the Tribe of Endless Hunting," Hollypaw reminded him.

"Oh, no." Jaypaw flicked his ears. "The Tribe of Endless Hunting has given up. They won't lift a claw to help you."

How can he possibly know that? Hollypaw wondered. But there was no time to question him. In any case, she had learned not to ask how Jaypaw discovered the things he knew.

"Look, there's no need to worry about us—" Lionpaw began.

"I'm not *worried.*" Jaypaw's sightless blue eyes were oddly serious. "You *must* come back, whatever happens. It's more important than you realize."

"We're not going to run away, you know," Lionpaw meowed.

Jaypaw let out a furious hiss. "Will you *listen* . . ."

His intensity scared Hollypaw. She wanted to know whatever it was that he wasn't telling them. But just then she heard her name called from the direction of the waterfall.

"Hollypaw! Lionpaw!" Brambleclaw was waiting, his tail twitching.

"Coming!" she called.

She and Lionpaw scrambled to their paws and shot across the cave floor to head out along the path. As she padded underneath the arch of thundering water, she thought she heard Jaypaw's voice raised in one last yowl.

"You *must* come back!"

CHAPTER 28

Beneath the full moon the mountains were washed with silver, patched with the deep shadows of jutting rocks. Lionpaw padded at his father's shoulder.

"Remember," Brambleclaw mewed, glancing back at him and Hollypaw, "you're not trying to prove anything. Don't try to take on a cat you can't handle. Not if you can help it."

"We don't *want* to get our ears clawed off," Hollypaw pointed out, with a whisk of her tail.

"Be careful you don't, then." Brambleclaw's amber gaze was warm. "How would I face Firestar if I didn't bring you all home safe?"

Anticipation shivered through Lionpaw from ears to tail-tip. Every paw step was bringing him closer to his first real battle. He longed with every hair on his pelt to make his father and his Clan proud of him. Yet he wasn't just fighting for his Clan and the warrior code. He was fighting for the Tribe, too, alongside Tribe cats who had become his friends. Their enemies had become his enemies, because the intruders had shown that they had no code of honor; they couldn't admit the justice of dividing the mountains into separate territories.

A few tail-lengths away he spotted Breezepaw. The WindClan apprentice was ready for battle too, with bristling fur and his lips already drawn back in a fierce snarl. He was padding just behind Crowfeather, yet his father didn't offer him any encouragement. Lionpaw felt a pang of sympathy. Maybe Breezepaw wouldn't be such an annoying furball if he had Brambleclaw for a father instead of Crowfeather.

A shadow drifted over the rocks and Lionpaw looked up to see a cloud covering the moon. A chill crept through him, as though his pads had touched ice. Did that mean that StarClan was angry because they were breaking the full moon truce? *But StarClan doesn't walk these skies,* he remembered. Jaypaw had warned them that they would be alone. Besides, a moment later the cloud had drifted away and the moon shone brightly again. *Sometimes a cloud is just a cloud.*

The moon floated high in the sky by the time the battle-hungry cats reached the intruders' camp. Everything was quiet. Lionpaw gazed at the narrow cleft between the tilted rocks, but he could make out nothing in the darkness inside.

"I can't see any sign of guards," Hollypaw whispered.

"They probably don't think they need them," Lionpaw murmured. "After all, Tribe cats are too weak to give any trouble, right?"

Hollypaw's green eyes gleamed with amusement. "We'll see about that!"

Brambleclaw gathered the cats around him with a gesture of his tail and led them into the shadow of a rock. "Crag and I will divide you into attacking patrols," he mewed. "Tribe and

Clan, apprentices and to-bes, in each group. That way we'll have the best spread of skills. The plan is to lure the trespassers out here and then attack them, otherwise we'll be fighting in the dark on enemy ground."

Lionpaw glanced again at the dark cleft and then back at Brambleclaw. "That can't be right," he objected.

Brambleclaw cocked his head. "No?"

"No, because the cleft can't be totally dark. Their dens are in there—they can't be stumbling around blind, can they?"

Brambleclaw narrowed his eyes. "You're right. There must be a shaft that lets in light and air."

"We should go look for it!" Lionpaw's pads were tingling with excitement.

His father thought for a moment longer, then nodded. "Okay. We shouldn't attack without knowing exactly what we're up against. If there's another entrance, they might be able to get out that way and attack us from behind." He angled his ears toward the rocks. "Let's go. Hollypaw, Breezepaw, you come too."

"And me!" Pebble sprang up. "I know rocks," she added. "I might be able to help."

"Come on, then," Brambleclaw meowed. "Crag, you start dividing up the patrols. And every cat keep as quiet as if you were stalking prey. This attack will start when we're ready and not before."

Cautiously the five cats crept across the open ground in front of the cleft and onto a narrow trail that led upward beside one of the tilted rocks. Lionpaw was poised to spring into battle if there was any movement from the cleft, but it remained dark and silent.

The tilted rocks were set against a boulder-strewn slope leading to a ridge. The trail wound between the boulders until it emerged at the top, close to where the two rocks joined. Lionpaw crept toward them, his belly fur brushing the ground.

"Breezepaw, keep watch below," Brambleclaw whispered. "Tell me if there's any sign of the intruders."

Looking pleased to be singled out, Breezepaw wriggled forward on his belly until he could overlook the ground at the bottom of the slope. Brambleclaw and the apprentices spread out, examining the area around the tilted rocks.

Lionpaw sniffed around the boulders piled along the ridge. There was a strong scent of cat, the scent he was beginning to recognize as the intruders'. But he couldn't see where it was coming from. Then he spotted a gap between two rocks; the scent was especially strong there.

"I think I've found something!" he called softly.

Brambleclaw, Hollypaw, and Pebble joined him, brushing against his flanks. Thrusting his head into the gap, Lionpaw saw a shaft leading down through the rock. At the very bottom was a circle of sand, with the shadow of his own head outlined on it in moonlight. There was no sign of cats, but the scent was stronger still.

"Let me look," Pebble mewed impatiently.

Lionpaw stepped back to let the Tribe to-be into the gap. She stared down for a few heartbeats, then raised her head, her blue eyes glittering. "They'll never be able to get out this way. But I could climb down."

"Yes!" Lionpaw wanted to bounce up and down like an excited kit. "We could all go. We could chase the cats out into the open where our warriors are waiting."

Brambleclaw shook his head. "Not a chance. It's far too dangerous."

"No, it isn't." Hollypaw butted his shoulder with her head. "They won't be expecting us. They'll be too scared to do anything but run."

"Then I'll go," Brambleclaw countered.

Lionpaw let out a small *mrrow* of laughter. "Think you would get those shoulders through that hole? This is a job for small cats. Hey, Breezepaw!"

He beckoned the WindClan apprentice over and explained the plan. Breezepaw swallowed nervously. "I'm in."

"I haven't said you're going yet," Brambleclaw pointed out. "It's a good plan, but you could fall and break your necks. Not to mention what the intruders might do to you."

"I won't fall," Pebble meowed confidently. "And the others won't, either, if they're careful. There are plenty of cracks to dig your claws into," she explained, "and you need to make sure your paw hold is safe before you move. It's easy as eating prey."

For you, maybe, Lionpaw thought. But he wasn't going to back out now. "We've got to do it," he argued. "It could make all the difference to the battle and the Tribe."

Brambleclaw sighed. "You're right. And you're apprentices,

not kits to be protected in the nursery. Very well, you can do it."

Lionpaw gazed into Hollypaw's glowing eyes and hoped that he looked as certain.

"I'll go down and tell the others," Brambleclaw went on. "Wait until you see me down there. Then go; we'll be ready and waiting."

His amber gaze rested for a heartbeat on Lionpaw, then Hollypaw, before he turned and vanished down the trail.

Breezepaw took up his lookout post again while Pebble quickly repeated her instructions about climbing down. "And don't look down," she finished. "If you get dizzy, you'll fall."

Breezepaw crept back. "He's there."

"Then let's go," mewed Lionpaw.

"I'll go first." Pebble was already turning to lower her hindquarters into the hole. "Watch what I do."

There wasn't much room for all three remaining apprentices to gather around and watch Pebble. Despite Breezepaw's ear in the way, Lionpaw managed to spot how she crept cautiously down, testing each paw hold before she put her weight on it.

"I'm going next," he murmured. "She shouldn't be on her own down there."

Hollypaw and Breezepaw moved back to give him room. As he slid backward through the gap, Lionpaw had a moment's panic that he was too big to fit. His shoulders scraped the rocky sides of the hole, but then he was through, clinging with all four sets of claws to the inside of the shaft. Below him he heard Pebble mew softly, "That's fine. Take it slowly."

Remembering what she had said about not looking down, Lionpaw edged his way cautiously down the shaft, digging his claws deep into the cracks. Once the stone crumbled under his weight and he slipped, gasping with terror as he scrabbled against the rock face in a frantic search for another paw hold. When he found it, he had to rest for a few moments, his heart pounding at his rib cage so loudly that he thought it must wake every cat from here to the lake.

He heard Breezepaw's annoyed whisper just above him. "Are you going to hang there all night?"

Lionpaw gritted his teeth. He wasn't going to let the WindClan apprentice see that he was scared. He searched for the next paw hold to take him down safely. Sooner than he expected, Pebble's voice came softly from just below him.

"You can let go now."

Lionpaw tensed and pushed himself off the rock face to land on his paws on the sand a couple of tail-lengths below. Breezepaw thudded down beside him a moment later with Hollypaw just behind.

"Brilliant!" Pebble's eyes shone in the moonlight. "Now what?"

Lionpaw shook the grit out of his pelt and looked around. A passage led off from the sandy area where they stood, curving so he couldn't see what lay beyond the first few paw steps. The intruders' scent was overwhelming.

"Wait here," he whispered.

With paw steps as light as if he were stalking a mouse, Lionpaw crept up to the corner and peered around. Beyond the curve in the passage he saw a wider space, covered with sand, with moss piled along both walls. He could just make out the pricked ears of a cat lying in the moss and hear the squeaking of very young kits. Tasting the air, he detected the milky scent of a nursing queen. From farther down the passage came the sound of movement and murmuring voices, the noise of many cats settling down for the night.

Stealthily he drew back toward his companions. "There's a nursery just here," he reported in a low voice. "We don't touch the queens or the kits, okay? The other cats are farther down, nearer to the entrance. I don't think they know we're here."

"So what do we do?" Hollypaw asked.

"We don't want to fight in here, just scare them out, so we dash through, yowling like a whole bunch of badgers is after us."

Pebble looked confused. "What?"

Breezepaw rolled his eyes. "Big, scary animals with teeth."

"Try not to get trapped in here." Lionpaw crouched, tensing his muscles to spring. "Okay—*go*!"

He leaped forward, letting out an earsplitting screech. His companions sprang with him, yowling like a whole Clan of fighting cats. Wails of alarm answered them from the cats down the passage. Lionpaw caught a glimpse of a ginger-and-white queen cowering against the rock wall with her kits huddled against her belly. He swept past and into the middle of the intruders' den.

The trespassing cats were blundering about, caterwauling in shock and terror as they scrambled for the entrance.

Lionpaw was prepared to fight, but no cat tried to stop him as he bounded across the den. The narrow cleft that led outside was jammed with the writhing bodies of cats desperately trying to get through. Lionpaw spun around with the wall at his back, claws unsheathed, but the nearest cat, a rangy ginger tom, gave him a single horrified glance, then thrust himself into the cleft to escape. Within heartbeats the den was empty of all but the four apprentices.

Hollypaw let out a last fearsome screech and halted, panting. "It worked!"

The yowls of fighting cats came through the cleft; Brambleclaw was leading his warriors into battle outside. Lionpaw took a long breath and tasted blood on the air. "Come on!" he urged.

The way out of the den was clear now. Lionpaw hurled himself through the cleft and into the open. The wide space in front of the rocks seethed with knots of tussling cats as Tribe and Clan clashed with the intruders. Moonlight shone on mingled tabby, ginger, and white fur and glinted on sharp teeth and claws. Shrieks of pain and fury split the night.

Lionpaw's ears pricked as he thought he heard a whisper behind him. "Lionpaw—*now*!" His head whipped around. Had he really heard Tigerstar? There was no dark tabby shape in the shadows, no gleam of amber eyes, but the call to battle was compelling.

Just in front of him, the brown intruder Flick had Screech pinned to the ground while he raked his claws through the to-be's belly fur. Yowling in fury, Lionpaw leaped on top of him, biting down hard on his neck. Squalling in pain and shock, Flick reared up in an attempt to throw him off. Screech wriggled free and vanished into the darkness.

Lionpaw lost his balance but succeeded in pulling Flick down on top of him and battered at the intruder's belly with his hind paws. Brown fur flew out and he caught the hot reek of blood. He lunged for Flick's throat. Flick raked one paw across his ear and managed to stagger to his paws. Lionpaw let him go.

For a heartbeat he stood panting, looking for his next opponent, and he thought the whisper came again. "Lionpaw—look behind you!" He whipped around to confront a huge gray tom, whose pale pelt was already running with blood. Lionpaw just had time to dodge to one side, raking the intruder's pelt as he slipped past him.

Scrambling onto a boulder, he surveyed the moon-washed battle and caught a glimpse of Hollypaw and Pebble, fighting side by side, thrusting their way through the press of cats to where Brambleclaw and Stripes fought together, rolling over and over in a screeching tangle of fur and claws. He spotted Squirrelflight, too, leaping forward to chase a black tom around the curve of a boulder and out of sight. Her ginger tail streamed out behind her and her teeth were bared in a snarl of fury.

Just below Lionpaw, Gray was struggling with a black-and-white she-cat, his paws flailing as he tried to dislodge her teeth from his shoulder. He looked as if he was rapidly tiring.

Lionpaw let out an exultant yowl as he dropped onto the

trespasser's shoulders, digging in his claws in the move he had practiced with Ashfur back in the forest. The she-cat released Gray and instantly rolled over, crushing Lionpaw beneath her bulk. The breath driven out of him, his nose buried in her fur, he fought to breathe and convulsed with pain as he felt her teeth meet in his ear. *Think!* The whisper came again, and this time Lionpaw could picture Hawkfrost's ice-blue eyes.

He let every limb go limp. The she-cat relaxed her grip, and at once Lionpaw heaved upward, tearing his ear free and throwing her back onto the stony ground. She clambered to her paws and crouched to leap at him. He braced himself to meet her attack.

Suddenly Lionpaw spotted Hollypaw and Breezepaw dashing toward him. They split up, racing up on either side of the she-cat. The trespasser leaped, claws extended. Lionpaw dived beneath her belly and felt his fur ruffled as she overshot and landed just where Hollypaw and Breezepaw were waiting to slash her flanks with their claws. The she-cat wailed and fled.

"Great!" Lionpaw gasped, springing up again. "They must teach that move in WindClan, too!"

Battling cats were already separating him from the other two apprentices. He hurled himself into the fight again. He could hear the blood pounding inside him; he felt as if he had the strength of twenty cats. He felt *alive*, more than ever before. As one cat after another fled from his raking claws he knew this was what he had been born for.

There came a moment when no other cat leaped to

confront him. Lionpaw spun around like a kit chasing its tail. *Where are you? Come out and fight!*

"Lionpaw." No mysterious whisper now; the steady voice was his father's. "Lionpaw, stop. It's over."

Lionpaw halted, staring at Brambleclaw, his teeth bared. "It's not over," he hissed. "Not until every last intruder has been defeated."

"Calm down, Lionpaw," Brambleclaw meowed. "They *are* defeated. We've won."

Lionpaw's first reaction was disappointment. No more of that wonderful coordination of muscles, teeth, and claws? No more of the light of fear in his opponents' eyes as they fled? He took several deep breaths and looked around. Cats of Clan and Tribe were watching him, impressed—and maybe scared? *Why? What have I done?*

"You fought well, Lionpaw," Crag told him quietly. "Your skill and courage will be remembered as long as the Tribe exists."

Lionpaw looked down at himself and saw his fur clumped together with drying blood. He felt hot and sticky, and his stomach heaved at the stench of it. He staggered; then Hollypaw was at his side, her green eyes horrified.

"Where are you hurt?" she asked anxiously.

Lionpaw shook his head in confusion. The only pain he felt was from his bitten ear, and in his paws, which had been sore for days from scrambling over rock. "I'm okay," he mumbled.

Before Hollypaw could say any more, a few of the trespassers crept timidly out from among the rocks. Stripes was in the lead. He had lost most of the fur from one shoulder and his muzzle was bleeding. He limped up to Crag and Brambleclaw and dipped his head.

"You have won," he rasped. "We will respect your borders from now on, if only you leave our queens and kits alone."

Crag and Brambleclaw glanced at each other, as if they were considering what the silver tom had said. Part of Lionpaw wanted to yowl, *No! Drive them out!* But he kept silent.

"The Tribe has no quarrel with queens or kits," Crag meowed at last. "We will leave you in peace so long as you stay on your own side of the border."

Stripes dipped his head again and waved his tail to lead his battered companions back through the cleft into their camp.

Lionpaw watched them go. Had Tigerstar and Hawkfrost really fought beside him in the battle? Or did their shadows stalk the woods beside the lake, waiting for his return? There were no voices now, no praise for the way he had fought, nothing but Hollypaw trying to check him for wounds.

"Lie down and rest," she begged. "Do you want me to fetch Jaypaw? I'll get him here somehow."

"I'm okay," Lionpaw insisted. "I don't need help."

Brambleclaw was rounding up his warriors, Clan and Tribe, ready for the journey back to the cave. Lionpaw joined them, falling in beside Breezepaw and Pebble, trying to ignore Hollypaw's fussing as she padded along on his other side, clearly expecting him to collapse at any moment.

Pebble's eyes were gleaming. "Did you see them run?" she mewed.

"I always knew the Clans would sort out the Tribe's problems," Breezepaw told her loftily. "You'll be grateful to us *forever*!"

Catching Hollypaw's troubled green gaze, Lionpaw could see that she wasn't so sure. But the battle was won. *He* had won the battle. And he would fight it all over again in a heartbeat.

Chapter 29

Jaypaw lay in the sleeping hollow where the scents of his littermates still lingered. He did not try to sleep; his ears were pricked for the first sounds of the returning warriors. His belly churned with apprehension. What if Hollypaw or Lionpaw died in the battle? What would happen to the prophecy then, if three suddenly became two—or even one? How could he bear to be without them?

The endless thunder of the waterfall sounded different, hollow and echoing, with the cave almost empty. The two kit-mothers were with their litters in the nursery. The elders, Cloud With Storm in Belly and Rain That Rattles on Stones, had retreated to their sleeping places at the other side of the cave. Wing Shadow Over Water, the prey-hunter who had been badly injured in the fight over the eagle, was sleeping nearby. Every other cat had gone to fight, for there was no point in leaving guards to protect the cave when all the intruders would be caught up in the battle.

Eventually Jaypaw couldn't bear to keep still any longer. He rose to his paws and padded across the cave, pausing to lick up a few icy drops where they trickled from the rock into the pool of fresh water. Then he slipped down the passage that led to the Cave of Pointed Stones.

Inside, all was silent. Jaypaw felt the faint stir of wind against his face and drew in the scent of the Tribe's Healer, strong and fresh.

"Stoneteller?" he mewed.

"I am here, Jaypaw." The old cat's voice came from the far end of the cave; it sounded sad and defeated. "What do you want?"

"Is there any word from the Tribe of Endless Hunting?" Jaypaw asked.

"None. I stare into the puddle, and I see nothing but moonlight upon water."

A pang tore through Jaypaw's belly, sharp as thorns. He knew that Stoneteller had lied to his Tribe about the Tribe of Endless Hunting. He had tried to manipulate the Tribe into choosing to flee, to show Brambleclaw and the Clan cats how little influence they had. But his plan had failed. The Tribe had chosen to fight, and left him here to face the knowledge that if they survived it would be without the support of their ancestors. The Healer's pain flowed through the cave like a river; Jaypaw couldn't help pitying him.

"I'm sorry," he mewed.

"Perhaps they have lost faith in us," Stoneteller responded, his voice flat.

"I'm sure it's not that." Jaypaw pictured the pool among the sheer crags, where he had confronted the Tribe of Endless Hunting. He had revisited the dream over and over in his waking mind, and he thought he understood what it meant.

But what use the knowledge would be to him, he wasn't sure.

"Jaypaw." The rasping voice spoke behind him.

Jaypaw spun around. Every hair on his pelt rose as he saw the sagging, hairless body and sightless eyes of Rock. *But I'm not asleep!* The ancient cat glimmered as if he stood in moonlight, though all around him was dark; he seemed to float in shadow.

His heart beginning to race, Jaypaw reached out all his senses to Stoneteller, but there was no change in the old cat's scent or the dull pain that came from him. He made no sound.

"Stoneteller cannot hear or see me," Rock mewed. "Only you can."

"Why have you come?" Jaypaw's voice shook.

"The battle has been won. You can go home now—all of you."

Jaypaw forced down his delight. Hollypaw and Lionpaw were safe! But he was sure that Rock hadn't come just to tell him something that he would discover for himself before morning. There had to be another reason.

"The Tribe must have fought well," he meowed. "Perhaps now the Tribe of Endless Hunting will have more faith in them."

"Why should they?" Rock retorted. His voice was sour. "It was the Clans who saved the Tribe of Rushing Water."

"What's wrong with that?" Jaypaw demanded. Back at the lake, he had longed to speak with Rock again, but each time he encountered the ancient cat was more frustrating than the last.

"StarClan did not send you," Rock replied, "and the Tribe

of Endless Hunting did not summon you."

"But—"

"Silence!" Rock hissed with a sweep of his bare tendril of a tail. "You came and won—for this battle, at least. But do you think the borders will hold? The Tribe is not a Clan, with experience of defending its territory, and the trespassers have no code of honor that will make them keep their word."

"Then we came for nothing?" Jaypaw asked, dismayed.

Rock shook his head. "No. You have learned much. And the Tribe will eat well, for a while at least." His bulging eyes seemed to gaze into the shadows at something hidden from Jaypaw.

Jaypaw took a deep breath. "You knew the Tribe cats before they came here, didn't you? They came from the lake."

He had the satisfaction of seeing Rock's start of surprise. "Yes. How did you know?"

"It was the pool in the mountains that the Tribe spirit showed me," Jaypaw explained. "They found another Moonpool, just like the one near the lake."

"They turned their back on so many of their old ways." There was pain in the ancient cat's voice. "Yet they still sought for peace beside the water."

Jaypaw's heart thumped harder, but he had to continue. "The Tribe knew me, just as you did. The prophecy comes from when you all lived together, doesn't it?"

Rock bowed his head. "Yes. We have been expecting you for a long time. And now you have come." A shiver of mingled fear and delight passed through Jaypaw as he returned the stare of the old cat's sightless eyes. "The others deserve to know," Rock continued. "This is not just your destiny, and you cannot walk this path alone."

"Jaypaw! Jaypaw, where are you?" Hollypaw's voice echoed from the main cave. "Come quickly!"

As if a dark wing had folded over him, Rock was gone. Jaypaw was left alone in the Cave of Pointed Stones, except for the silent presence of Stoneteller. He found the entrance to the passage and raced out to meet his sister.

"It's Lionpaw!" she gasped, bounding up to meet him and giving his ear a hurried lick. "He's covered in blood. He says he's not hurt, but the blood must have come from somewhere. You've got to help him."

"Where is he?"

"Outside, by the pool," Hollypaw mewed. "I told him to rest."

Jaypaw followed her across the cave to the waterfall. Clan and Tribe cats poured past them, yowling the good news to those who had stayed behind. Jaypaw detected Crag's scent and heard the big cave-guard meow, "I'll go and tell Stoneteller."

Hollypaw dashed along the path beneath the tumbling water, for once not worrying about whether Jaypaw could manage it on his own. Jaypaw followed hard on her paw steps, his pelt pressed against the rock, feeling the cold spray on his exposed flank.

His heart had begun to pound again. After believing that both Hollypaw and Lionpaw had come back safe, was his brother's life to be snatched away from him after all?

Reaching the pool, he nosed at Lionpaw's fur. Shock clawed

at him as he realized how thickly it was clotted with drying blood. "We've got to get this off him," he mewed crossly, trying to hide his fear. "How can I tell what's underneath all that?"

"Come closer to the waterfall," Hollypaw suggested. "The spray will help us clean off the blood."

All three cats moved around the edge of the pool until Jaypaw could feel the spray soaking into his fur.

"I wish you wouldn't fuss," Lionpaw protested, raising his voice to make himself heard above the thunder of the falls. "I keep telling you, I'm perfectly all right."

His voice sent another shiver of fear through Jaypaw. His brother sounded distant, stunned, as if the battle had affected not only his body but his mind. "You're all right when I say you are," he snapped.

"I'm not hurt. . . ." Lionpaw sounded almost puzzled. "No cat could touch me."

"Shut up and let me lick," Hollypaw scolded him.

As he and Hollypaw cleaned the blood from Lionpaw's fur, Jaypaw began to realize that his brother was right. He *wasn't* hurt, except for a bitten ear and sore pads.

"I don't think you need any herbs," Jaypaw mewed, trying to hide that his paws were shaking with relief. "Just keep that ear clean. I'll give it a sniff every day until it heals."

"You're really okay!" Hollypaw's voice was unsteady. "All that blood came from other cats! Jaypaw, I wish you could have been there. Lionpaw fought like a whole Clan of cats!"

"We won the battle." Lionpaw was beginning to sound more like his usual self, as if the licking of his brother and sister had brought him back from some distant place.

"For what it's worth"—Hollypaw sounded troubled—"I don't trust the trespassers. And I don't know if the Tribe will be able to defend its new borders."

Jaypaw's belly lurched to hear his sister echoing the warning that Rock had given him in the Cave of Pointed Stones.

"I don't know why we came here if we weren't going to succeed," she continued, sounding a little desolate. "Did the Tribe of Endless Hunting get it wrong?"

Jaypaw reached out with his tail to touch her shoulder. "The Tribe's ancestors didn't want us here," he mewed. "And StarClan did not send us. We came so that we could win the battle, and because we needed answers to our questions." When neither Hollypaw nor Lionpaw responded, he added, "We all wanted to come to the mountains, didn't we?" There was a murmur of agreement from his brother and sister. "Then don't you understand? That's why things happened so that we came. This is all about *us*, the three of us. Without us the Tribe might survive, or it might not, but that doesn't matter now. They've all been waiting for us—StarClan, the Tribe of Endless Hunting, Rock—"

"Who?" Hollypaw asked.

"What are you talking about?" Lionpaw meowed. "Have you got bees in your brain?"

Jaypaw crouched on the edge of the pool and motioned with his tail for his brother and sister to draw closer. "Listen," he murmured. "There's something I have to tell you. . . ."

ERIN HUNTER

is inspired by a love of cats and a fascination with the ferocity of the natural world. As well as having great respect for nature in all its forms, Erin enjoys creating rich mythical explanations for animal behavior. She is also the author of the bestselling Seekers and Survivors series.

Download the free Warriors app and chat on the Warriors message boards at www.warriorcats.com!

DON'T MISS

POWER OF THREE

WARRIORS

BOOK FOUR: ECLIPSE

CHAPTER 1

Hollypaw crouched low, pressing her belly against the boulder. It was still warm from the sun, which was dipping behind the distant hills. A cold wind rolling from the mountains ruffled her fur. From here she could see green fields unfolding toward a swath of forest; somewhere beyond those trees lay the lake, and home.

Though the trees were still in full leaf, they were a shabby green, and the air had a new, musty taste that hadn't been there on the journey to the mountains. *Leaf-fall is coming,* she thought.

She couldn't wait to be home. It felt as though they had been with the Tribe for moons. At least they were safely out of the mountains. The ground would be softer underpaw from here on, the hunting easier, and the territory steadily more familiar than rock and water and stunted trees.

She glanced over her shoulder. Brambleclaw and Squirrelflight were talking in low voices with Stormfur and Brook. Tawnypelt and Crowfeather leaned in beside them. Were they saying good-bye?

Hollypaw was still shocked that Stormfur and Brook were

staying behind. Last night, at the farewell feast in the cave behind the waterfall, Stormfur had announced that he and Brook would accompany the Clan cats to the foothills, but no farther. Jaypaw, of course, had just shrugged and nodded, as though he'd known all along the two cats would not be returning to ThunderClan. But Hollypaw could only guess at why any cat would want to stay in the mountains when they could live by the lake. *Brook must feel the same way about the mountains as I do about my home. And Stormfur loves her enough to stay with her, wherever she is.*

Suddenly, a flash of brown feather caught her eye. An eagle was skimming over the rough slope below her. Ahead of it a hare pelted in terror, throwing up dirt and grass from its long back feet. Folding its wings deftly against its sides, the eagle attacked, tumbling the hare head over heels before pinning it to the ground with thorn-sharp talons.

Hollypaw envied the eagle's speed. To be able to fly like that! She closed her eyes and imagined skimming over the grass, paws hardly touching the ground, light as air, faster than the fastest prey. . . .

"I wish we could get moving again." Lionpaw's impatient mew broke into her thoughts. He padded onto the boulder and stood beside her, following her gaze toward the eagle feasting on its catch. "I wish I had something in *my* belly," he mewed.

"Do you suppose we'll ever be able to fly?" Hollypaw murmured.

Lionpaw turned and looked at her as though she'd gone crazy.

"I mean," she tried to explain hurriedly, "Jaypaw said we have the power of the stars in our paws." It still felt strange to say it out loud. "We don't really know what that means. I was just wondering if—"

"Flying cats!" Lionpaw scoffed. "What'd be the point of that?"

Hollypaw's ears were hot with embarrassment. "You've got no imagination," she snapped. "Here we are with more power than any other cat *ever*, and you act like it's nothing at all! Why shouldn't we be able to fly, or do *anything* we want to? And stop laughing at me!"

"I'm not laughing at you." Lionpaw flicked Hollypaw's flank with his tail. "I just think we'd look stupid with wings."

Frustration surged in Hollypaw's chest. She rounded on her brother, glaring. "You're not taking this seriously enough! We've got to figure out exactly what this prophecy means!"

Lionpaw blinked and took a step backward. "Keep your fur on. You know Jaypaw and his visions. They sound great, but we have to live in the real world."

"What does the real world mean, now that we have the power of the stars in our paws? We'll be able to do anything! Imagine how much we'll be able to help our Clan!"

Lionpaw frowned. "The prophecy didn't say anything about helping our Clan; it just mentioned the three of us."

Hollypaw stared at him. "But the warrior code says we must protect our Clan before anything else!"

Lionpaw's gaze drifted to the distant hills. "Are we bound by the warrior code if we're more powerful than StarClan?" he wondered out loud.

"How could you say such a thing?" Hollypaw scolded, but a shiver of foreboding ran along her spine. If the prophecy meant that they had to live outside the warrior code, how would she know what was right? How would she know what she was supposed to do if it came to a choice between her own safety and her Clan's?

Jaypaw's pelt brushed hers as he jumped up beside them. "Could you two speak a bit louder?" he hissed. "I think some of the others didn't hear you." His blue eyes were flashing with anger. Blindness had not robbed them of showing feeling.

Hollypaw spun around to see if any of the other cats had been listening, but the warriors were still deep in their own conversation. "No one's taking any notice of us," she reassured him.

"Not every cat has got such good hearing as you," Lionpaw added.

"I'm just warning you to be careful, okay?" Jaypaw mewed. "We have to keep this a secret."

"We know," Lionpaw assured him.

"Actually, I don't think you do," Jaypaw argued. "How do you think the other cats would react if they found out we've been born with more power than StarClan?"

Lionpaw glanced at Squirrelflight and Brambleclaw. "They'd never believe it."

"I hardly believe it myself," Hollypaw admitted.

"They'd believe it, all right." Jaypaw's voice was icy. "But I don't think they'd like it."

"Why not?" Hollypaw felt a jolt of alarm. She hadn't

thought about how her Clanmates would take the news. Surely they'd be glad? They must know she would only use her power to help them!

Lionpaw seemed to agree with her. "Won't they want us to be the best warriors we can be?"

"This prophecy isn't about being a good warrior!" Jaypaw warned. His claws scraped against the surface of the boulder in frustration. "It's about having more power than StarClan. Don't you think ordinary cats might find that a bit scary?"

"But we're not going to do anything bad," Hollypaw insisted. "This is a gift to our whole Clan, not just us." What did Jaypaw think they were going to do with their powers?

"Shh!" Jaypaw's hiss cut her off as Squirrelflight bounded toward them.

She halted at the edge of the boulder. "What are you bickering about?"

"Hollypaw and Lionpaw are just arguing about who's the best hunter," Jaypaw mewed smoothly.

Hollypaw opened her mouth to object, then stopped herself. She hated lying, but she couldn't give their secret away, not here.

"You shouldn't be standing around chatting," Squirrelflight told them. "Not when Brambleclaw has just told you to find fresh-kill. He wants to make sure Stormfur and Brook have something to take back to the Tribe."

They had been so busy arguing, they hadn't heard the order.

"You shouldn't *have* to be asked twice," Squirrelflight scolded.

Hollypaw hung her head. "Sorry."

Squirrelflight flicked her tail toward a cluster of trees at the side of the slope. "Try there, and hurry up!" The copse cast a long shadow that stretched up the hillside. The sun would be setting soon.

Lionpaw licked his lips. "There should be plenty of prey in there."

"Enough for everyone," Squirrelflight agreed. She turned to Jaypaw. "Will you come check Tawnypelt's pads? One of them is bruised where she trod on a sharp stone."

There had been enough sharp stones to bruise everyone's pads on the trek down from the mountain; Hollypaw guessed that Squirrelflight was finding Jaypaw something useful to do, since he couldn't hunt. She tensed, knowing how oversensitive Jaypaw could be. But her littermate just nodded and followed Squirrelflight back toward the warriors. He didn't even bristle when his mother bent down to lick a grubby patch of fur behind his ear.

The gesture pricked at Hollypaw's heart. Squirrelflight still saw them as kits. It would be easier if they still were; kits didn't have to worry about having more power than their warrior ancestors. *But things change,* she told herself. She turned away, suddenly anxious. Would there come a time when Squirrelflight would be afraid of her own kits?

"What's ruffling your pelt?" Lionpaw asked.

Hollypaw licked the fur prickling on her shoulder. "It doesn't matter." She nodded toward the copse. "Let's hunt."

She padded to the front of the boulder and let her paws

slide over the edge. It was a short, steep drop, but the grass below looked like it would make a soft landing. She leaped. As she landed, a flurry of fur and paws knocked the breath from her body and sent her flying. *Who's attacking me?* Gasping, she scrambled to her paws and prepared to defend herself.

"Why did you get in the way?"

Breezepaw!

The black WindClan apprentice was shaking out his fur beside her. "I almost had that mouse!"

"Sorr—" she began to apologize, then bristled. Why didn't the dumb furball look where he was going? "I thought we were supposed to be hunting over *there*!" She flicked her tail toward the copse.

"*I* decide where I hunt!" Breezepaw snapped. He glanced up at Lionpaw, who was peering over the edge of the boulder. "At least I *was* hunting and not sitting around chatting with my denmates."

"Your denmates wouldn't want to sit around and chat with you even if they were here!" Hollypaw retorted. She felt instantly guilty. Even though he was as bad-tempered as his father and twice as smug, she had begun to feel sorry for Breezepaw. Crowfeather treated his son with such scorn that Breezepaw sometimes seemed a loner among his own Clanmates.

Lionpaw jumped down beside her. "Are you okay?"

"Of course she is!" Breezepaw snorted. "She'd be even better if she were hunting like she's supposed to, instead of getting in my way. The sooner we get this fresh-kill, the better. Then we can go home."

It had been obvious from the start that Breezepaw hadn't wanted to come to the mountains. And Crowfeather hadn't acted like he was glad to have him along. He didn't seem proud of anything Breezepaw did, unlike Brambleclaw, who made Hollypaw feel like the best warrior in ThunderClan when he praised her. Compassion welled in her chest as she looked at the miserable WindClan apprentice. "We'll be back at the lake before long," she mewed gently.

Breezepaw glared at her. "Why do we have to find fresh-kill for the Tribe, anyway? Why can't they hunt for themselves?"

The compassion evaporated. Hollypaw wondered if she should remind Breezepaw that the Tribe cats were exhausted by their recent battle, and that prey was scarcer than ever in the mountains because of the gang of rogues who had invaded their land and forced them to set borders around their hunting grounds. But if he didn't know that already, she wasn't going to waste her breath. Let him figure it out. All she wanted now was to be back home, warm in her nest with a full belly and her denmates sleeping peacefully around her. She glanced at her brother. Would he set Breezepaw straight?

But Lionpaw just rolled his eyes at the WindClan apprentice. "Go catch a rabbit." He snorted and stomped away across the grass.

Breezepaw curled his lip. "ThunderClan cats think they're so special," he sneered before stalking down the slope.

Hollypaw hurried after her brother. He was muttering under his breath as she caught up to him.

"I wish I had the power to shut that furball up once and for all!"

Is he joking? Hollypaw looked sideways to see if Lionpaw's eyes were shining with their usual good humor, but they were half closed in a frown. She skipped in front of him and blocked his path. "You don't mean that, do you?"

Lionpaw flicked his tail. "Of course not," he grumped. "I'm just tired."

"But do you think that's what 'the power of the stars' means?" Hollypaw persisted. "The power to make any cat do what we want?"

Lionpaw shrugged but didn't meet her gaze. "I suppose," he answered. "I haven't really thought about it."

"You must have!"

Lionpaw padded around her and kept going for a few moments before he spoke again. "I hope it will make me stronger than any other cat, so that I can always win battles." He paused. "What about you?"

"I hope it means I'll know things other cats don't."

"Like what?" Mischief lit his gaze. "How to speak to Twolegs?"

"Don't be stupid!" Hollypaw's claws itched with impatience. "I mean the power to understand"—she groped for the words to explain—"*everything*," she mewed at last.

Lionpaw nudged her shoulder affectionately. "Is that all?"

Hollypaw flicked him away. "You know what I mean."

They had almost reached the trees before Lionpaw spoke again. "Perhaps each of us will feel the power differently," he ventured. "Jaypaw can already tell what cats are thinking, can't he?" He caught Hollypaw's eye. "He does it to you, right?"

Hollypaw nodded.

"Leafpool can't do that," Lionpaw went on. "None of the medicine cats can. Jaypaw is already making predictions about trouble in other Clans, too. That must be his power—to see things other cats can't."

"He's the least blind of us all," Hollypaw murmured, feeling her pelt prickle the way it did when Jaypaw said exactly what was running through her mind.

Thick foliage grew at the edge of the wood, and she halted to let Lionpaw take the lead. "Have you felt anything yet?" she ventured as he began to nose his way into the bushes.

To her surprise, Lionpaw spun around to face her. His eyes glittered with a strange intensity. "At the start of our journey, we stopped on the ridge to look down on the lake, remember? Then you went off to catch prey and rest, but I wasn't hungry." He blinked. "As I was looking at the territories, I started to feel . . . well, kind of strange."

Hollypaw leaned forward. "Strange? How?"

"I felt like I could do anything!" Her brother's eyes flashed. "Run to the farthest horizon without getting tired, fight any enemy and win, face any battle without being afraid."

Hollypaw shifted on her paws and realized that she was backing away from him. Something about him suddenly made her feel uncomfortable: the way he had tensed his shoulders so that he looked more powerful than before, the faraway look in his eyes, as though he could see beyond her, beyond the woods, to some distant place where he could take on enemies single-pawed. She thought back to how he had fought for the Tribe; how he had come staggering out of the battle covered in blood—none of it his own—still ready to fight until there were no cats left standing.

The fire in his eyes sent a shiver through her pelt.

How could she be scared of her own brother?

THE TIME HAS COME
FOR DOGS TO RULE THE WILD

SURVIVORS

BOOK ONE:
THE EMPTY CITY

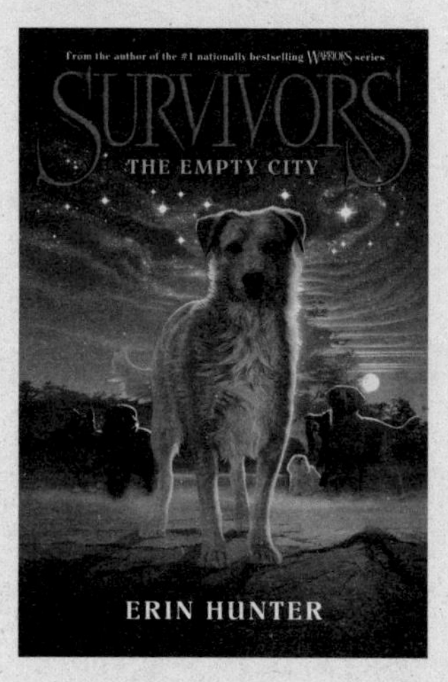

Lucky is a golden-haired mutt with a nose for survival. Other dogs have Packs, but Lucky stands on his own . . . until the Big Growl strikes. Suddenly the ground splits wide open. The longpaws disappear. And enemies threaten Lucky at every turn. For the first time in his life, Lucky needs to rely on other dogs to survive. But can he ever be a true Pack dog?

DON'T MISS

RETURN TO THE WILD

SEEKERS

BOOK ONE: ISLAND OF SHADOWS

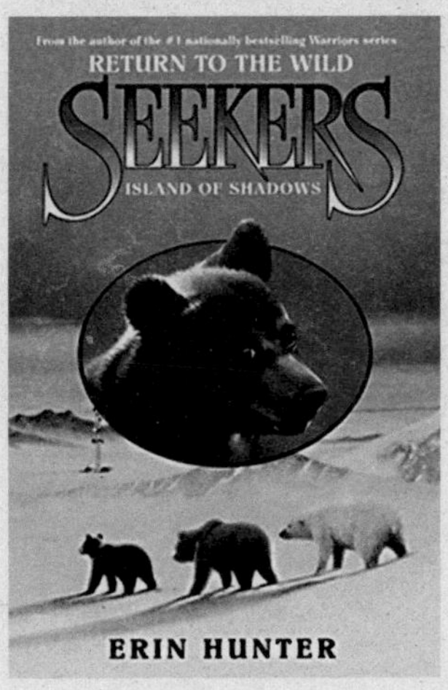

Toklo, Kallik, and Lusa survived the perilous mission that brought them together, and now it's time for them to find their way home. When the group reaches a shadowy island covered in mountains and ice, Kallik is sure they're almost back to the Frozen Sea. But a terrifying accident leads them into a maze of abandoned tunnels, unlike anything they've ever seen before—making them question their path once again.

WARRIORS: THE NEW PROPHECY

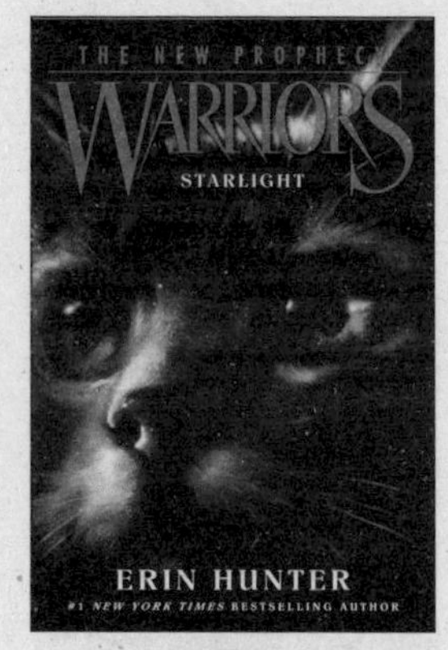

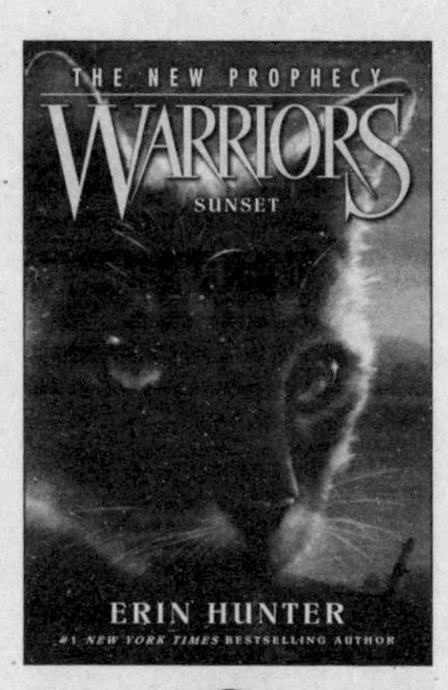

In the second series, follow the next generation of heroic cats as they set off on a quest to save the Clans from destruction.

HARPER
An Imprint of HarperCollins*Publishers*

www.warriorcats.com

POWER OF THREE
WARRIORS
THE SIGHT
ERIN HUNTER
#1 NEW YORK TIMES BESTSELLING AUTHOR

1

POWER OF THREE
WARRIORS
DARK RIVER
ERIN HUNTER
#1 NEW YORK TIMES BESTSELLING AUTHOR

2

POWER OF THREE
WARRIORS
OUTCAST
ERIN HUNTER
#1 NEW YORK TIMES BESTSELLING AUTHOR

3

POWER OF THREE
WARRIORS
ECLIPSE
ERIN HUNTER
#1 NEW YORK TIMES BESTSELLING AUTHOR

4

POWER OF THREE
WARRIORS
LONG SHADOWS
ERIN HUNTER
#1 NEW YORK TIMES BESTSELLING AUTHOR

5

POWER OF THREE
WARRIORS
SUNRISE
ERIN HUNTER
#1 NEW YORK TIMES BESTSELLING AUTHOR

6

WARRIORS: OMEN OF THE STARS

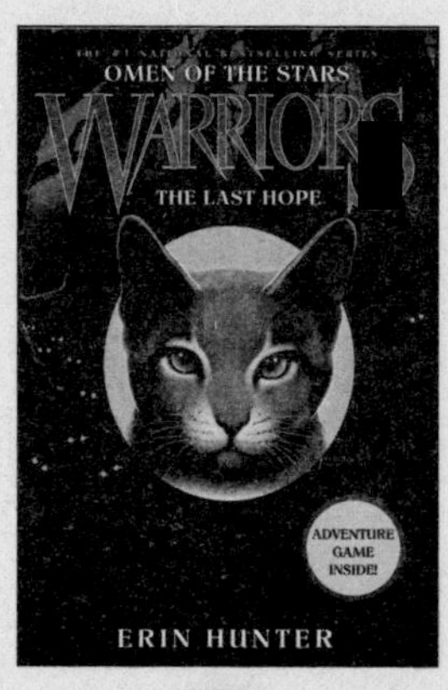

In the fourth series, find out which ThunderClan apprentice will complete the prophecy.

NEW LOOK COMING SOON!

HARPER
An Imprint of HarperCollinsPublishers

www.warriorca om

WARRIORS: DAWN OF THE CLANS

1 2

3 4 5

In this prequel series,
discover how the warrior Clans came to be.

WARRIORS: SUPER EDITIONS

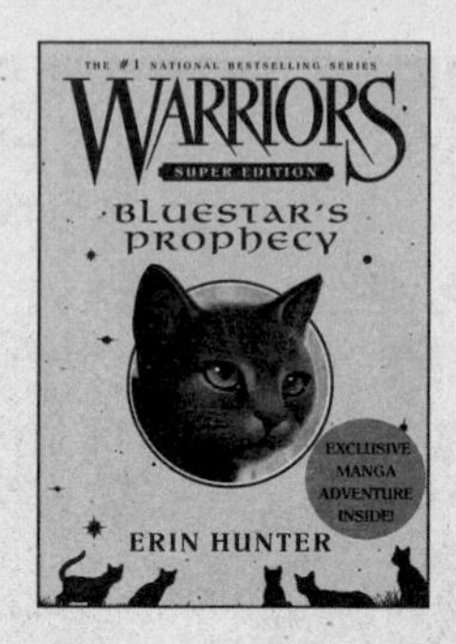

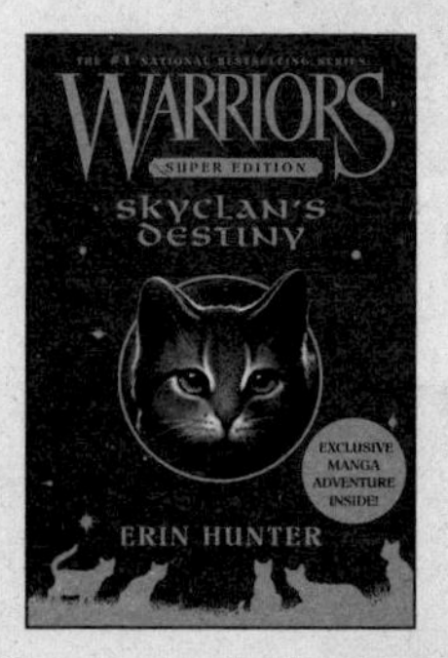

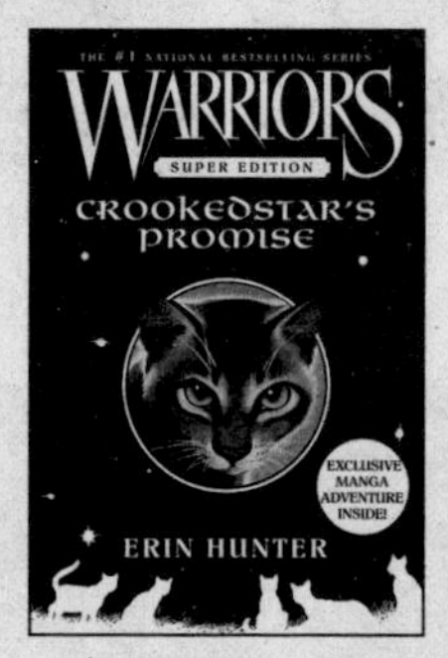

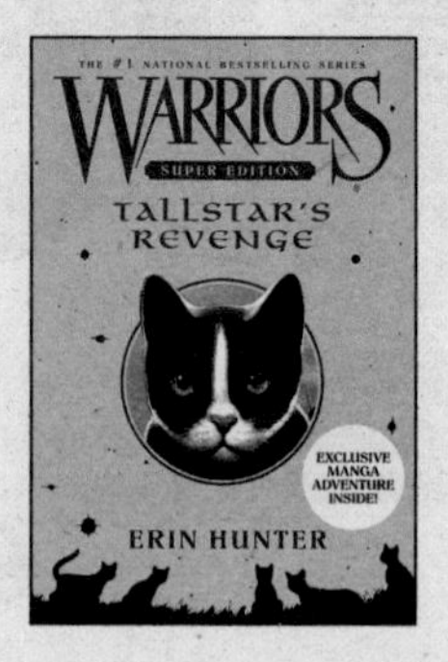

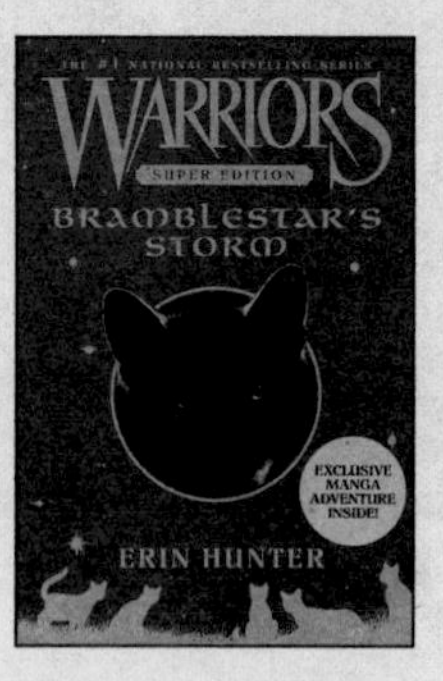

These extra-long, stand-alone adventures will take you deep inside each of the Clans with thrilling adventures featuring the most legendary warrior cats.

HARPER
An Imprint of HarperCollinsPublishers

www.warriorcats.com

WARRIORS: BONUS STORIES

Discover the untold stories of the warrior cats and Clans when you download the separate ebook novellas—or read them in two paperback bind-ups!

WARRIORS: FIELD GUIDES

Delve deeper into the Clans with these Warriors field guides.

HARPER
An Imprint of HarperCollinsPublishers

www.warriorcats.com

ALSO BY ERIN HUNTER: SURVIVORS

SURVIVORS: THE ORIGINAL SERIES

The time has come for dogs to rule the wild.

SURVIVORS: BONUS STORIES

Download the three separate ebook novellas or read them in one paperback bind-up!

HARPER
An Imprint of HarperCollinsPublishers

www.survivorsdogs.com